WOLF CAGED

HUNTERS OF THE FOREST, BOOK TWO

M.P. STARKWEATHER

PHOENIX ECLIPSE PUBLISHING

I want to dedicate this book to my two biggest fans, my husband Josh and my son Thom, who will probably never read any of my books. Thanks for pushing me to chase my dream. I love you both to the moon and back.

CONTENTS

ONE
FERAL WITCH

ORYM

"Grab her, Orym!" The shout pulls me from my thoughts.

I tackle her just as she gets to the edge of the forest.

Since Luca's kidnapping, Garnet has been a little psycho. And that's putting it mildly. I brace for her attack, knowing that it's coming.

"Garnet, love, you can't just rush in there. You gave Eli your word." It's a struggle to hold her, because she electrifies her skin and it burns. I wince at the pain, but don't dare let go of her. I know I'm crushing her with my weight, but I don't lift myself either. She'll just run again. Like last time.

"I can't leave him in there alone. He'll think we've forgotten about him," she cries. Tears stream down her face, and I pull her close. When she breaks down, the electricity drops. I'll still have to talk to Grammy about burn cream, but at least Garnet isn't actively trying to hurt me. She's just upset about Luca. We all are.

"It won't be much longer now. We have to give Eli time to get someone from his team in the camp."

"But you've seen what they're doing to him. I can't take it. I have to save him." Her stubbornness is frustrating and amazing. I've never known anyone so completely committed to something in my life. My heart swells at her determination. We will get him back. It's just going to take longer than she wants.

"I understand. We all want him back." I turn her face to make her look at me. "Do you trust us?" It's a cruel question, but it's necessary. I know that her answer has a chance of destroying me. And with our bond in place, she knows that. I watch as she realizes exactly what this could mean for us.

Garnet stares at me, her eyes going wide. "Of course, I trust you guys. I just," she pauses for a split second and I don't let her finish.

"Okay, then trust us to help you. Trust me to get this all situated. Please. We can't keep you from chasing after him. There are other things we need to do to get the plan ready." I feel like I'm lecturing a toddler, but she seems to understand.

When her head drops sheepishly, I know that I've made my point. I pick her up and carry her back to Ryland's cabin, where we've all basically moved in. James and Ryland have been working on plans to expand it, but Garnet is still on the fence if she wants to stay in the wolves' territory. She's not keen on letting Gunnar control her life anymore.

It's completely reasonable, but also a source of frustration. As wolves, Ryland and I—and Luca, when we get him back—are still tied to the territory's alpha, no matter who that is. Right now, it happens to be Gunnar. Unless someone challenges him, it will remain that way until his death.

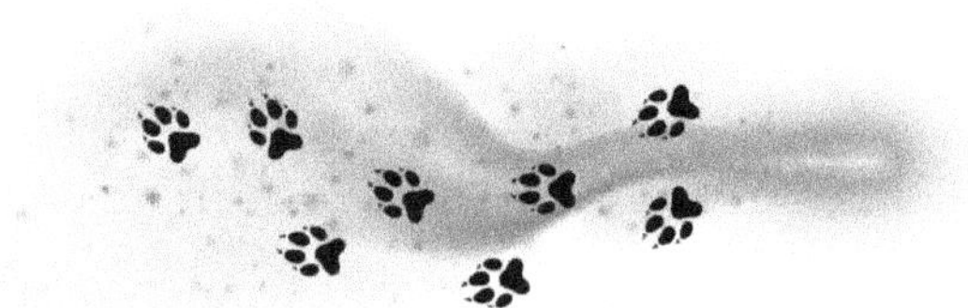

JAMES

Watching Orym tackle Garnet makes me shudder. He doesn't pull his punches or treat her like she's fragile. But she is. She's not a wolf like Orym, Luca, and Ryland. She's a witch. I guess that makes her a little sturdier than me, but not by much.

We've been working on healing spells and potions lately, because we know they'll be needed when we go after Luca.

I see how much it hurts her that he's gone. It's worse since she has no connection to him. Eli won't let her in Midnight after her reaction to Luca's torture. She nearly took the building down with all of us in it. I don't blame him for that decision. They have to have a place to live. And it's almost impossible to command a vampire army if you're decapitated.

So, here we are, trying to train in the forest while avoiding Gunnar. At least, Garnet and I are. Orym and Ryland still have to answer summons and get permission to train with us. It's ridiculous and childish how Gunnar is lording his power over them. This is bigger than just wolves or just vampires. Vik learned that some humans have also gone missing. This situation is like a virus that keeps spreading, taking out more and more people in its wake.

Ryland and I are making plans to expand the cabin, but I'm not sure Garnet will ever agree. If she actually looked at them, she'd see that it would be perfect for the five of us. Each of us will have our own space, and the biggest master suite I've ever seen. It's even bigger than my brother's.

Honestly, that project is more to distract us from the holding pattern we're in right now than anything. Gunnar is threatening to keep all the wolves from helping with the rescue. He wants Eli's men to handle it all. It's as if he wants to pretend that the wolves who were captured are dead already. But we don't know that.

I think he's scared that Vincent has flipped sides on him. Easier to think your son dead than a traitor. I have no idea if Vincent has joined Amber's cult or if he's just being controlled. But Eli's surveillance showed that he is working with the witch. There's no way to tell if it's by choice or force, though. The cameras are good, but can't get that close.

And since Garnet's little tantrum, we don't even get to see the videos anymore. Eli is afraid that she'll go nuclear and take out everyone near her. He's probably not wrong. So, I've been getting updates from my brother, Declan, when he has time.

It's been weeks at this point, and I know that Garnet is going crazy with worry. But after Dec's explanation of what they've been doing to Luca, I'm glad she can't see it. I think she would go completely nuclear and we'd all be dead. But I think she'd take Amber and her camp out too.

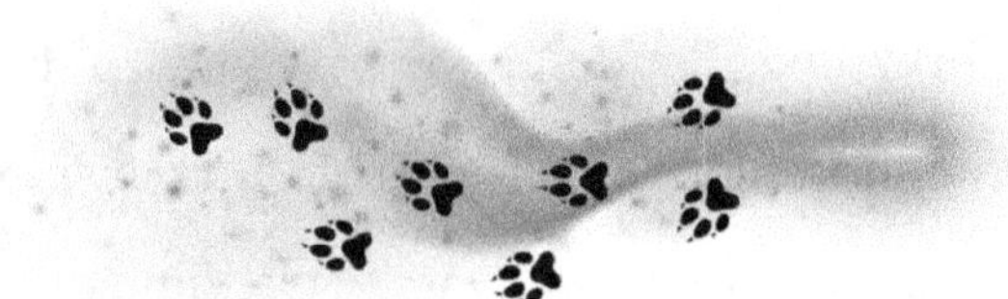

GARNET

Every day that Luca is gone feels like I'm being torn in half. Having four fated mates is not as easy as one might assume. Sure, I can focus on the three who are here with me, and I do, but then guilt tears at my heart because Luca is not with us.

Ry, Orym, and James all claim to understand, but I don't think they can. I already love the four of them so much it hurts.

But missing Luca is the worst pain I've ever felt. It's like a part of me has been ripped away and I struggle to function without it.

I'm having added challenges lately, too. Some days it feels like my powers are burning me up from the inside out. I can sense changes in my magic, and I'm not sure if that means it's growing or fading. I'm doing my best to keep that from my mates. They don't need to be worried about my powers giving out or being inconsistent while we're planning to rescue Luca. I'll work through it.

After Orym stops me from running into the forest after Amber, I sit on the couch and pout. I'm not proud of it, but I have no idea what else to do. Eli won't let me in Midnight, and I can't view the surveillance footage anywhere else. He has it completely locked down. I can't train with Delilah, because Kayden vetoed that. He's worried that I'll hurt her, since my magic is wonky.

I know it's ridiculous, but I feel isolated and alone. I'm constantly surrounded by three of the men who love me, yet all I can focus on is Luca's absence. It's unfair and not at all helpful. But I can't stop myself from feeling these things. I miss my best friend. I hate that I didn't take the opportunity to bond with him when I had it. Kicking myself over my regrets won't help the situation, but that doesn't stop me either.

Ry seems to be pulling away from me a little, and I worry that he's growing tired of my obsession with Luca. I should put more effort into spending time with the guys who are here, but I can't stop the guilt that eats at me because Luca isn't here.

I don't know how long I sit on the couch, staring out the window, before James comes to see what's wrong. "I know what's wrong, but how can I make it better?" It's obvious that he's tapped into our bond so he can be aware of what I need. They all seem to do that now, making sure I eat when I'm hungry and sleep when I'm tired. But no one can help me with the frustration I feel at not being able to defeat Amber and save Luca.

I glance at him before turning back to the window. Talking about it won't help. "Garnet, you can't keep ignoring us and freezing us out. We're trying to take care of you. Please let us."

I shrug in response. Even if the three of them abandoned me, I know that I would deserve it. I'm not strong enough to be their mate anyway. And, yeah, I know that having a pity party won't help. I'm feeling stuck, and can't figure out what else to do.

James walks away, and I feel a little sad that he's gone. I expect them to try harder to get through to me when I'm like this. It seems like I'm pushing them further away every day. I don't like it, but until I get Luca back, I can't force myself to do anything different.

"You wanna be a bitch to me, fine. You wanna be hateful, okay. But you will not treat James or Orym that way. Do you understand me?" Ry appears in my face, growling. I can tell that he's barely holding back his shift. The wolf inside of him wants to rip me apart for the way I've been acting. And I deserve it. Part of me wishes that he would lose control and put me out of my misery.

"That thought. Right there. That's exactly what I'm talking about. Stop it, Red. You're better than this. Or have you completely given up? You wanna go after Luca, go ahead. I won't stop you. But you'll be on your own." His words stab me in the heart.

"You won't go with me?" I hear myself ask.

Ry shakes his head. "No, and no one else will either. You're being a brat, and we're not going to support that."

"Fine, I'll go by myself." I stand, forcing him to take a step backward. If that's how it needs to be, that's what I'll do. I'm not scared to go alone. The lie tastes foul, even in my brain.

"Then go," he says, stepping out of the way so I can get to the door. "But be sure that's what you want. If you do this alone, we won't be here when you return."

I don't expect the ultimatum from Ry. It stops me halfway to the door. "What?" I turn to face him.

"You heard me. If you go into the forest alone, we won't be here when you return. If you survive, that is." I think he's baiting me now, but I'm not sure.

"So, if I go save Luca, I lose my other mates? That hardly sounds fair," I snarl.

"No one is asking you to choose between us. We're asking you to let us help you. But if you don't need us or want us, you're free to make that choice for yourself." Now I know he's baiting me. He wants to get a reaction, and I'm not sure what exactly he's trying to do.

"I won't choose between you four, so I'm glad that's not what you're asking. But telling me that you won't help me or be here when I get back is hateful."

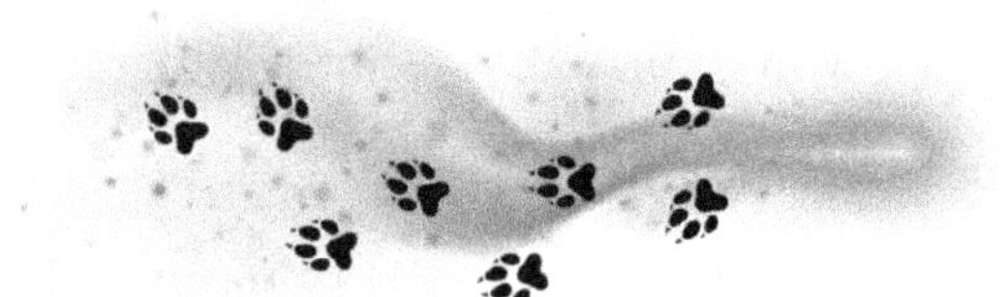

LUCA

I've lost track of the days. I have no idea how long I've been a prisoner here. Amber has me working alongside the other prisoners. We grow food for the camp, build furniture and shelter for the other victims, and basically do whatever we're told.

If anyone resists, they're beaten. I've lost track of how many times I've stepped in and taken a beating for someone else. I don't know if Red and the others made it out of the witches' territory, but I'm hopeful that they're somewhere coming up with a plan to free us.

Every day, someone else goes missing. New people come into the camp, and others disappear. I have no idea where they go or why they don't come back. But it seems like Amber is taking people for a specific purpose, even if I can't figure out what it is.

It's hard to stay positive. I know that Red won't give up on me, no matter what Amber says. She's only talked to me twice since I've been here. One of those times, I'm sure that she was trying to control me with her powers. I fought it off, and she hasn't tried since. There's no reason to, anyway. I don't know my way out of here, and I won't leave these prisoners to fend for themselves.

When I was first taken, I spent a couple of days thinking that Red and the guys would be coming after me as soon as they realized I was gone. That didn't happen, and I realized that it means one of two things. Either they're formulating a plan and gathering help, or they got captured themselves.

After my talk with Amber yesterday, I'm sure that they weren't captured. She asked me strangely specific questions about how the wolves protect their territory. I wonder if she's planning to attack them in their homes. I wish I could get a message to Red, but I don't know how.

The guards seem worked up today, and I've been listening a little closer to see if I can figure out what's going on. "I'm telling you, it's the wrong time of year for there to be this many bugs around. Some of them have to be listening devices," one of them says quietly.

The guy he's talking to shakes his head and laughs. "Where would the wolves get that kind of tech?" Except I know where they would get it. If there are listening devices around, it's because Eli has been recruited to help save us. Just like that, my hope is restored.

I have to hold out a little longer and do what I can to keep these guys ignorant of what's happening. I may regret this decision, but here goes nothing. "You really think someone has listening devices like that? I'm from the wolf territory and I know we don't have anything like that."

The first guard glares at me, annoyed that I've interrupted.

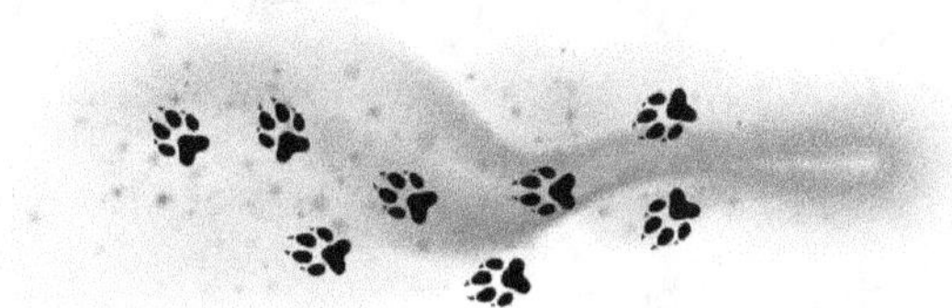

RYLAND

I know that pissing Red off isn't the best idea, but I need her to focus. I don't know how to break her out of this funk other than pissing her off. When she calls me hateful, I almost cave. I hate that she sees me that way. I don't care if other people do, but not her.

She's the one person I want to see the good in me. And here we are fighting. I don't even know why I threaten that we'll leave her if she goes into the woods alone. I already know that we won't. Orym, James, and I would follow her and keep her safe. But I don't need her to know that.

"Look, you can make your own choices. I won't stop you. But there are always consequences to those choices. You have to be prepared to face those," I warn as she glares at me. I realize what she's thinking before she moves.

I'm not fast enough to stop her fist from slamming into my jaw, but I do grab her and pin her against me. "Red, you don't want to do this. I'm not the enemy here." She fights against my hold, then relaxes. I know it's a ploy, so I don't let go.

"Why won't you guys just help me save him?" I can hear the tears in her voice and my heart breaks for her. There's a certain pain that only comes with an uncompleted bond, and that's what she's dealing with right now.

"We are helping you. You're being impatient. That won't help him. We need to stick to the plan. Eli is still watching the drone footage and formulating the best plan. They'll move camp in the next few days because of the moon, then we'll have a few days to move on them." She hasn't forgotten the plan; she's just never been on board with it.

I turn and walk out the door before she can. I meant it when I said I won't stop her, but I won't just let her walk away either. As expected, she follows me, still pissed that I've given her an ultimatum. She really doesn't trust that we're hers, so she doesn't see that it's never going to happen. There is nothing she could do to push me away.

"Don't walk away from me," she insists, rushing up behind me and grabbing my arm.

"Why not? You want to walk away from us." I know it's harsh, but that's what I'm good at. I have to be the big bad wolf so that she'll see that she needs us.

Red growls and swings at me again. I jump out of the way and get hit with a burst of electricity for it. Damn, that smarts. I snarl at her, letting my wolf slip a little. Fear crosses her features, and I reign myself back in. I can't lose control here. It won't do any good to attack her. Not now.

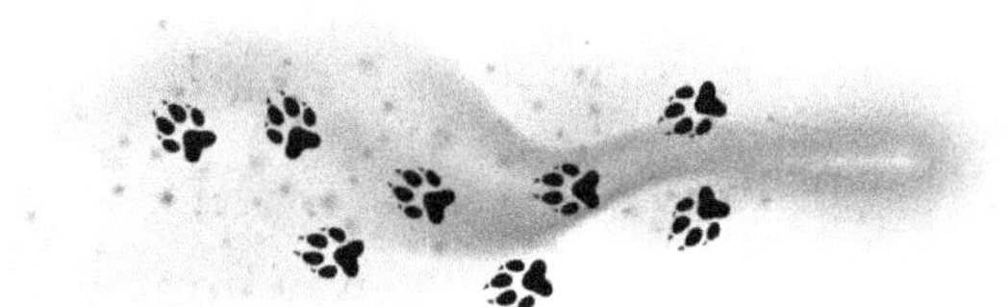

GARNET

Baiting me or not, Ry has crossed the line. I punch at him and miss, then smack him with a jolt of electricity. Now he's as pissed as I am. We're pretty evenly matched in temper, so I'm not really scared of him. Until he growls low in his chest and shifts unexpectedly.

I've never been terrified of Ry before, but when he's standing in front of me in his wolf form, my knees start to shake. He's almost as tall as I am, with jet black fur, and rippling muscles. That's not mentioning the mouth full of sharp teeth that are currently bared at me.

Another low growl rattles my insides as he steps closer. At this point, I don't know if Ry is still in control or if his animal instincts have taken over. I shouldn't have pushed him, even though he was pushing me. I hope I can defend myself if he attacks.

I was never scared of any of the wolves before, because I believed that somewhere inside of me, I was one of them. Now that I know I'm not, it's extremely intimidating to be stared down by a snarling beast that could tear me in half without thinking about it.

I know that I could submit, and that might settle him down. But it could set him off worse, too, since I'm not one of his kind. It should be enough that we're mates. There's no way to know, though. I stand perfectly still as Ry steps closer, sniffing me.

A shiver runs up my spine and I fight to remain still. He's too close for me to run from, and there's no way for me to fight against him without using my magic. I'm not sure I can do that and avoid hurting him. I send electricity dancing along my skin. It won't be my fault if he gets shocked because he attacked me. I'm not going to attack him. I take a step backward and he growls again. I freeze.

Fuck. This is going to be harder than I thought. Ry moves forward again, sniffing at me. I force myself to hold still, even though his breath tickles me and his sharp teeth graze my skin. I could call for James or Orym through the bond, but I'm not sure either of them would help me right now. As if I somehow did call them, both men appear behind Ry. Concern lights their features and I hold up a hand cautiously to stop them from coming closer.

Please, just wait. I beg them through the bond. James nods and takes a step backward. Orym glares at Ry and doesn't move. I don't know if he'll intervene or not. Before I can stop him, Ry turns on Orym and jumps. Orym shifts and meets him bite for bite. I have no idea what just happened, or how to stop it.

Did Orym say something to him to provoke an attack? I didn't hear anything, so if he did, he purposefully blocked me from it. That idea doesn't make me happy, but I guess they're more evenly matched than I would be against either of them. But I can't let them kill each other.

I wave my hands in a figure eight motion in front of me, pulling water from the humid air. Then I blast it at the wolves who are wrestling around in the dust. Too late, I realize that I didn't drop the electricity. I've just shot my mates with electrified water. Both wolves drop to the ground and shift back to men. Oh, no. What have I done?

James rushes over and checks each one for a pulse. "They're knocked out. Both have strong pulses, and both are breathing. It's okay. You did what you had to." His words don't make me feel much better about using my powers against my mates.

I'm sure he sees my thoughts in my expression. "Do you want to tell me what happened with you and Ryland?" he asks.

"Not really," I respond, knowing that I'll have to tell him at some point. "But I will. He yelled at me, and I got upset. He goaded me into attacking him—not with my magic. Although I think that's what he was going for."

"Why?" The simplicity of the question had me wondering the same thing.

"I'm not sure. It was like he was determined to pick a fight with me today. Maybe to get me out of my funk. Maybe to hurt me because I've hurt all of you. It doesn't matter now." I can't defend myself against what I've done. I know I've hurt them because of my obsession with rescuing Luca.

"I see. That would be a very Ryland thing to do, wouldn't it?" he laughs. How can he laugh at this situation? I stare at him until he realizes what my issue is. "I know this isn't funny, but it kinda is, right? Ryland picking a fight, so you'd knock him on his ass."

To be fair, I can see why he's amused. That doesn't mean I have to be. "You're sure they're gonna be okay?" I'm worried about the effects of using my magic on my mates, and being forced into it doesn't help that.

"They seem fine. Let them sleep it off, then we'll see when they wake up. We can practice your healing magic if they aren't okay," he offers. It makes sense, but I don't want to use my magic on them again. That's what got us into this mess in the first place.

James takes my arm and leads me away from the cabin, toward the clearing where we have a picnic table set up. I should have known that he was getting study materials ready when he disappeared earlier. He has my spell books laid out along with Amber's journal. "We won't go far. Just enough space to study for a bit while they rest."

Two

GUNNAR'S APOLOGY

JAMES

WATCHING GARNET KNOCK RYLAND and Orym out was amusing and terrifying. She's stronger than she knows. It seems like her powers have been growing or changing lately. I don't know much about magic, but I've seen her do things that she couldn't before or that other people say aren't possible.

She hasn't seriously injured anyone, but she's come close. I have to distract her so she'll calm down. If she stays this upset, she may hurt one of us without realizing it. I watch her closely as she steps away from where the wolf shifters lay on the ground. Her breathing is a bit erratic, and I need that to slow down a bit.

I've been reading the journals and trying to learn as much about magic as I can. So, I know that a centering meditation is a good place to start. It'll work even better if I can get her into it before her panic attack fully starts.

"What did you have in mind?" she pants the words, trying to get her breathing under control. I rub my hand up and down her back.

"How about we start with that meditation you were teaching me? I could use a little refocus. Then we can pick up where we left off yesterday if you want," I suggest. Garnet nods, and I bite back my sigh of relief. I can see her starting to relax.

I move the books out of the way, and we both sit cross-legged on the top of the picnic table. I follow her instructions to close my eyes and count my breath as I inhale slowly and exhale just as slowly. Once I'm sure that she's doing it too, I open my eyes and glance over at the two figures lying on the ground.

Garnet mutters to herself as she breathes. I turn my attention back to her for a moment, then look at Orym and Ryland again. They are starting to stir. I make sure that my breathing matches Garnet's, so that she doesn't know that I've stepped away.

As the last visible tendrils of panic fade from her face, I stroll over to where the guys are waking up. "What the fuck?" Orym says, shaking his head.

Shh, she's still pretty upset. I'm blocking her so she can't hear this. I need you two to figure your shit out. You know that she could go nuclear if we put her under stress. I tell him what I need to, then check him for injuries. Satisfied that Orym is okay, I turn my attention to Ryland.

I'm fine. I just need a break. Maybe a run will help. I glare at him, and he continues. *I'll take Orym with me, okay? We'll work through it.* I shouldn't be so pleased that the wolves do as I ask. But there aren't many humans who have this kind of success at giving orders to shifters.

With them settled, I return to Garnet.

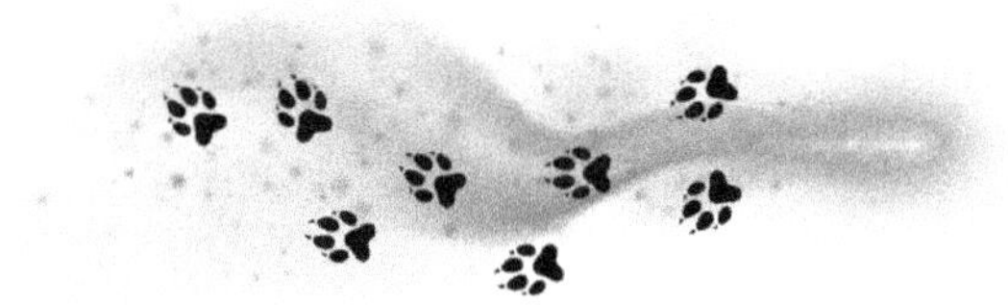

LUCA

Amber graces the camp with her presence today. Everyone is so excited, because her being here is a distraction for the guards. It means fewer beatings and less work. I don't slack off, because I don't want to see her or deal with her at all. The guards focus on getting her attention, and the captives try to lay low and avoid it.

I just keep hauling buckets of water until each tent in the camp has one that's full. Then I move to gathering our food supplies for dinner. We don't get cooked food here, only vegetables that we've grown in the small garden. If we're lucky, the guards will have someone bake bread, and we'll get some of that.

A group of wolves race past me, and I hear them talking excitedly about something. I follow them so I can figure out what they're talking about. "I heard she brought pizza!" one of them says.

Interesting. Did Amber show up to bring takeout and try to win over the starving captives? That wouldn't surprise me. She seems like the type to try bribery to get what she wants. But what is that exactly?

I shiver at the feeling that I'm being watched. Maybe those guards were right and there is some sort of surveillance going on. But is it Amber watching everything, or someone else? I look around nervously but don't see anything.

I'm careful to hide my thoughts, since I don't know who's watching. I know from being here a while that it's almost time to move the camp again. Amber doesn't like to keep us in the same place for very long. That just means we'll have to walk further to care for the small garden of crops she allows us to grow so we can eat.

I stop just short of the tents, watching as Amber steps in front of everyone as if she's making an announcement. "As you know, we're getting closer to our goal." That might matter if I knew what the goal was, but okay. "In light of that, we'll be splitting the camp into three groups. Each group will be moving to a cabin, where you'll be staying until we reach our goal."

That feeling of being watched is on me again, and I hope that it's someone who's here to help. And that they caught all that. Three groups, moving to cabins. I miss part of what she's saying because I let myself get distracted. "That means we'll be packing up camp tomorrow and splitting up. Each cabin is fully stocked with food and whatever you'll need, so you won't be coming back here."

It seems strange for a witch who claims to care for the land would just abandon crops, but Amber is strange. I don't understand what's happening, but true to the rumor, she's brought pizza. It appears as if there's enough pizza for everyone. Once it's passed out, each person gets half a large for themselves.

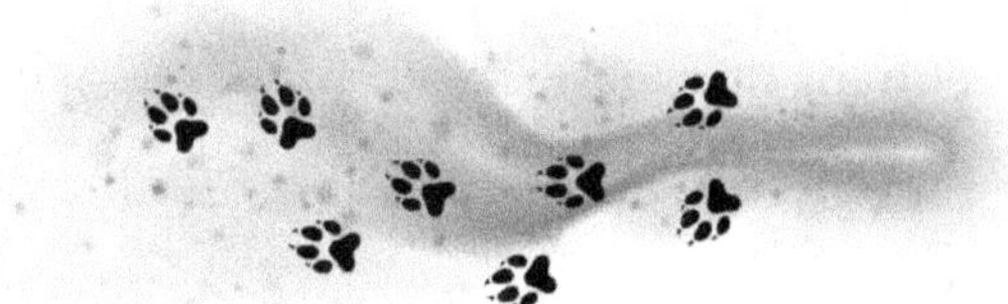

GARNET

I know that James is trying to distract me, and I love him for it. I focus on my breathing but notice when he steps away. I'm sure it's to deal with Orym and Ry. Those two need to find a way to get along. I know that Ry was baiting me to get me to do something besides stare out the window. It doesn't help that I let him do it. Then Orym tried to defend me. I'm sure that's what happened.

But even knowing doesn't stop me from reacting. And I know that attacking them with my magic is dangerous. I can't control it, and one of them could get seriously hurt. That's the last thing I want, so I have to get this figured out.

I refocus on the meditation, letting my body relax and concentrating on my breathing. Inhale to the count of ten; exhale to the count of ten. Suddenly, bright lights fill my vision, even though my eyes are closed. How is this possible?

The brightness fades, and I can see that I'm somewhere else. The picnic table is gone; I'm sitting on a large rock next to a pink stream. Wait, water isn't pink. I shake my head to try and refocus. This has to be a dream. A noise catches my attention and I look toward the forest.

The trees look strange. They're shimmering and purple. What is wrong with me? Purple trees and pink water. Am I having a stroke? I try to scream for my guys, but no sound comes out. I turn in a circle, panic gripping my heart.

James, Orym, and Ry are gone. Or I'm gone. I don't know what's happening right now, and I'm terrified. *All will become clear in time, young one.*

I spin in a circle, looking for the source of the voice, even though I know it was in my head. The forest floor is covered with tiny green and orange flowers. There's something completely otherworldly about this place. It's as if I'm in a different dimension or something.

Oh, no. Did Amber find a way to kidnap me? I have to get back to my guys. Luca needs me. I can't stay here. When I start walking toward the cabin, I realize that it's not there. I scream, hoping that one of my guys will hear me and help me get back home. I know that I'm screaming, but no sound comes out.

My heart races, pounding so hard that I'm certain it's going to burst through my chest at any moment. I feel like I can't breathe; the air is thick and moist. I can't stop the tears that stream from my eyes. I drop to the ground, surrendering to the panic. There's nothing I can do.

This isn't a prison, child. It's your home. It's that voice again.

"Who are you?" I ask, even though my voice makes no sound.

All will become clear in time. That's a bullshit answer, and I won't stand for it.

"Send me home. I don't want to be here. I don't even know where here is." I'm hysterical, and I don't care. I want to lash out at the disembodied voice, but there's no way to tell where it's coming from.

The voice doesn't speak to me again, but I feel myself being forced to sleep. My eyelids are heavy and I can't stop them from closing. I know it's not safe, but I collapse onto the ground near the pink stream and drift off.

"Garnet!" I hear my name shouted over and over. Why are they yelling at me? Wait, they're not yelling *at* me, they're yelling *for* me. I sit up and open my eyes. I'm on the bank of the river, near the waterfall.

Everything is the same as it was before. The leaves are green, tree trunks are brown. The lilies and honeysuckle look like they should. I'm back home. It seems odd that I'm not on the picnic table, and that it sounds like my mates are searching for me.

Guys? I'm by the waterfall. What's going on? I ask through the bond. I don't get a response, but in just a moment, James, Orym, and Ry rush to my side.

"Where have you been?" Ry asks, checking me for injuries.

"We've been looking for you for hours," Orym adds.

"Are you okay?" James joins Ry in searching my body for injuries.

"I'm not hurt. But something strange happened. I don't know how I got here," I insist. The three of them help me to my feet. Orym brushes his hand across my cheek.

"You've been crying," he says softly.

I nod. "I was terrified that I'd lost you all. I don't know where I was, but it wasn't like here at all. The river was pink, the trees were purple, and the flowers were green with orange specks. And there was a voice."

He scoops me into his arms. "It's okay, love. We're going to take you home now. Just relax and let us take care of you." Clearly, he thinks I'm crazy. Hell, I think I'm crazy.

"I believe you," James whispers. I lock eyes with him and he nods. "I've been reading about portals and other realms. I think you might have somehow been pulled through one."

"What? That's ridiculous," Ry scoffs.

"No more ridiculous than you changing from a man to a wolf and back again," James counters. I know that he's not just defending me, but also making his point. It's still sweet.

"Let's get Garnet home and talk about this inside. It's safer there," Orym suggests. With Amber on the loose, he's right. I shouldn't have been so far from my mates without protection. He carries me back to the cabin, and I see that someone has already cleaned up the table where I left all my books. I'm sure it was James, because he's the one who's been helping me train.

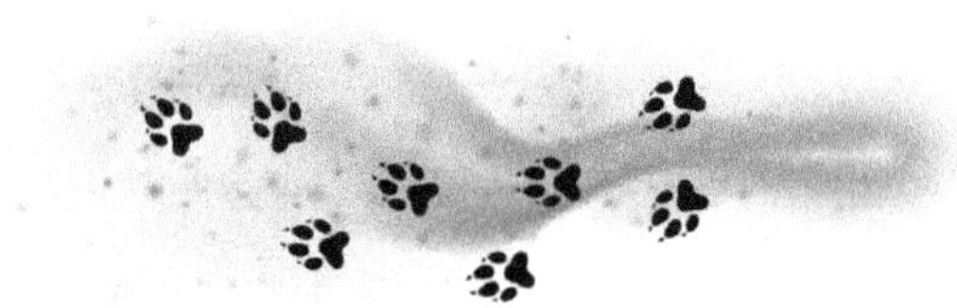

RYLAND

"It's just not possible," I declare. There's no way that Red got pulled through a portal into another realm. The idea is ridiculous; it's the stuff of fairy tales. I will admit it's strange that she disappeared and reappeared somewhere else

"I'm telling you; it is. You'll see. I'll show you the books when we get home," he responds. I can't keep going back and forth with him because it's starting to upset Red. She's shaking as if she's cold, and I know that she's not. Her anxiety is coming through the bond clearly.

Getting her home and settled in has to be our priority. I hear a noise behind us and shift as I turn to see what it is. *Keep moving. Get her home, no matter what.* I tell the others through the bond. I stand perfectly still, waiting to see what's following us. A small, silver-gray wolf steps into the clearing. A larger, dark brown wolf follows. I glance over my shoulder and see that Orym and James are still moving, just as I asked. I shift back and greet my alpha and his mother.

"Gunnar. Grammy." They shift as well, and Gunnar starts to walk toward Red. I step in front of him. "Could I ask why you were following us?"

"I need to talk to Red. It's not your business. Get out of my way," he growls. When he walks forward again, I step in front of him once more.

"She's my mate, and that makes it my business. Red isn't a wolf, so she doesn't fall under your rule," I spit, knowing that

I do fall under his rule and he could choose to punish me for speaking to him this way. I will protect my mate, though, no matter the personal cost.

He steps closer, ramming his chest against mine in a show of authority. "You can't keep me from talking to her. I'm your alpha. I can make you submit," he insists.

I don't get a chance to find out if he's right or not, because Grammy clears her throat, then positions herself between us, pushing Gunnar away from me. "We can follow them back home. You don't have to stop them in the middle of the forest for this. If she doesn't want to talk to you, you'll have to accept that."

Gunnar growls, but doesn't argue with his mother. I can't help feeling that she's taken him down more than once for him to back down like that. All I can think is that I would pay to see this tiny woman knock my alpha down a peg or two. Unfortunately, he just looks at me and nods in acceptance. I know it won't be that easy. If Red doesn't want to talk to Gunnar, I'll have to fight him to keep him away. Unless Grammy does step in and proves that she can take him out.

I barely keep my smirk hidden as Grammy admonishes her son. "Let's go."

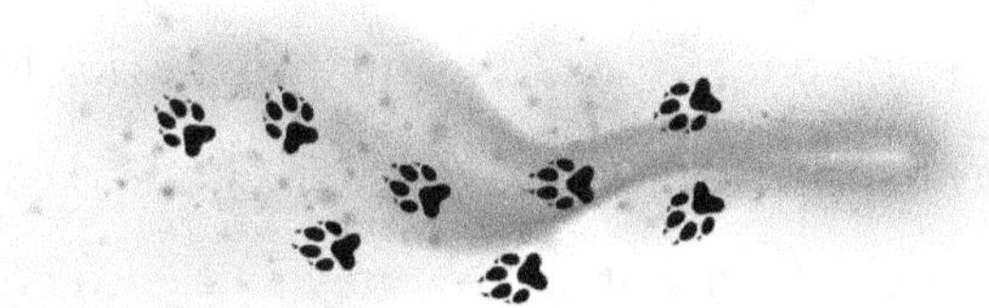

ORYM

I sense that we're being followed just before Ryland tells us to keep going. I know that he can tell that it's wolves tailing us, but for some reason, he doesn't trust them. I suppose they could be some of the wolves that are working with Amber. I hesitate for a moment when he turns and shifts, then decide that I'll trust his instincts. James and I pick up our pace, rushing to get Garnet back to the safety of the cabin.

Once we're inside, I leave James to protect Garnet. "I'll be right outside. I just want to check on Ryland." I don't give either of them a chance to object, heading out the door. I stand on the porch for a moment, searching the tree line, before I see Ryland stomp out of the forest and into the clearing.

"What happened?" I ask. He snarls and gestures behind him. That's when I notice Grammy and Gunnar following him. Fuck. This can't be good.

"He wants to talk to Red. But if she isn't interested, he'll be leaving," Ryland explains, loud enough that I know Gunnar hears him. So, we're getting into a pissing match with our alpha over the girl who, until a few weeks ago, we all thought was his daughter. Great.

Ryland pushes past me, grabbing my arm and dragging me with him into the cabin and slamming the door in our guests' faces. "Ryland, that was extremely rude. You know he's not going to go easy on you for that," I warn him.

"I don't give a fuck. He's not going to come to our home and bully our mate." He turns to Garnet. "Gunnar wants to talk to you. It's okay to say no. We'll make him leave if you don't want to deal with him. He's not your alpha, and you don't have to put up with his abuse anymore."

It's sweet that he wants to protect her from the man we thought was her father, but he's still our alpha, and can make our lives miserable. I'm guessing that Garnet sees my thoughts as they cross my face, because while she grimaces, she shakes her head.

"It's okay. Let him in. I'll hear what he has to say." Our mate is the most selfless person I've ever known. I'm certain she's doing this to protect us from Gunnar's wrath, and I love her for it.

"If he gets out of line, I'll throw him out," Ryland insists. Garnet reaches for him and he goes to her. She pulls Ryland down onto her lap and kisses him. When she releases him, he scrambles off her lap as I open the door. It's already been long enough that Gunnar probably feels disrespected.

"Alpha, please come in," I say, hoping that he doesn't throw a fit once he's inside.

Grammy walks in first, heading straight for Garnet, and pulling her into a big hug. They settle on the couch together as Gunnar slowly enters the cabin.

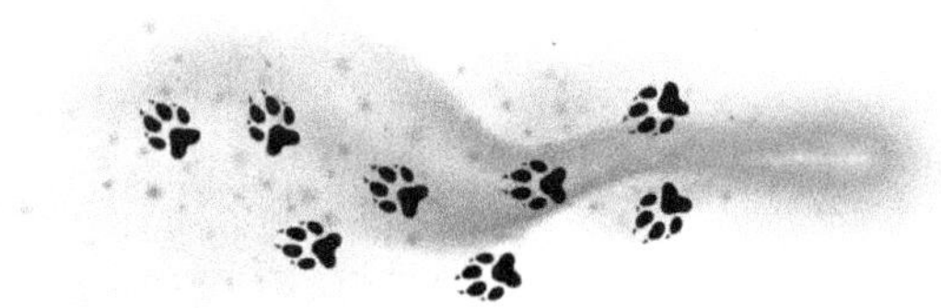

GARNET

I'm thankful that Grammy came with Gunnar. It's hard to remind myself that he's not actually my father. I don't have to be scared of him anymore. He can't hurt me. But the scars are still there from every harsh word and action he had for me when I was growing up. This man doesn't deserve my respect, but I give it to him, because I know he will hurt my mates if

I don't. It's the only reason I agree to talk to him. I can't call him Father, and using his name feels wrong.

"Alpha," I say instead. I will not ask him why he's here. If he wants to talk to me, he can start. It's childish, but I don't care. This is my home, and he will not bully me in it. At one point, I trusted him. Then he broke me.

When he doesn't speak right away, I look at Grammy. She glares at him and nods her head toward me as if she's telling him to get on with it. I'm confused, but don't want him to see that.

"Yes, well. Thank you for inviting me into your home. I won't take up a lot of your time. It's been brought to my attention that I owe you an apology, Red." Gunnar's cheeks turn red, and I'm not sure if he's embarrassed or pissed. I don't think I care either way.

"I see. Then you should get on with it. Not to be rude, but we have things we need to take care of tonight." I cannot believe I just spoke to him this way. For a moment, I worry that he's going to punish Ry and Orym for my disrespect.

"Of course. Red, I am sorry. I wasn't as kind to you as I should have been. And it was rude of me to refuse your help with the current situation. I've come here today to ask if you would consider letting some of the wolves assist you with the rescue operation when you're ready."

Holy shit. Did Gunnar Trion just apologize to me? The man who made my childhood miserable with every word, every strike, every punishment, is standing in front of me now, asking for my help.

Are you okay? The question comes from James. I know that all three of my mates can sense my roller coaster of emotions right now.

I'm not, but I will be. He has no power over me anymore. I don't know if the last statement is true, but I desperately want it to be. At this point, I just want him to leave us alone.

"I believe that would be acceptable. Thank you, for the apology and the manpower." I know I sound cold and uncaring, but I can't let my emotions show right now. If I do, then he'll realize that he does still have power over me, as much as I don't want him to.

He nods and walks out the door. Grammy hugs me again. "Just let me know when you need to meet with the wolves. You know him; this wasn't an easy thing for him to do." She kisses my cheek and follows her son out.

When the door closes, I let out a huge sigh. "That was more stressful that I wanted, but at least it's over for now. Do you think he'll retaliate against you guys for the way I spoke to him?"

Ry looks at me and grins. "I don't think Grammy will let him. She seemed to have him under control, didn't she?"

I can't help laughing. "She really did. I wonder why she never did that when I was growing up." The thought makes me sad, because she could have saved me a lot of pain if she'd just done what she did tonight. I guess I don't need to understand.

"Let's leave the past in the past. Wondering how things would have been different won't help anyone," Orym says.

James nods in agreement. "Besides, everything you went through made you the person you are today, and I like her."

I roll my eyes at him and laugh. But they're both right. I can't change the past, and spending time wondering about it is a waste. "You said you'd seen something about what might have caused me to disappear and reappear somewhere else?" I remind James of what we'd been discussing before the interruption.

"Yes! Give me a minute to find the book." He starts flipping through the journals I've been studying. "Here it is." He hands me a book, open to a specific page. I take it and start to read.

Then I realize that this particular book is Ruby's journal. She detailed visits to another realm, and described it exactly like what I saw. My jaw drops, and I hand the book to Ry. He can't argue now.

He takes the book and reads. "This just proves that you read this book before you ran off. None of us saw what you claim to have seen. Look, I'm not saying you're lying, I'm just not sure that you traveled to another realm."

"It hurts that you don't believe me. But I get it. Sometimes it's hard to believe things we can't see. And you're right. You didn't see it. I did. I was there. In the same place that my mother claims to have visited on multiple occasions." I know it's pointless to argue with him, because once Ry has his mind made up, he doesn't back down.

"If it helps, I believe you," Orym says quietly. And it does help. I feel a lot less crazy knowing that two of my three mates that are here with me believe what I'm telling them. I wish Luca were here with us. I'm certain that he'd believe me too, then it would be four against one and Ry would have to concede that I did somehow travel to another realm.

THREE
AMBER COMES TO VISIT

LUCA

I START TO HEAR the rumors as we pack up the camp. People are saying that Amber is going to the wolf territory in an attempt to take over. I should have played nice and pretended to be on her side so I could have gone with her. Now I have no way to get Red a message.

The guards are paying less attention to us, since some of them are getting ready to escort Amber. This may be my only chance to escape. I keep packing supplies into the boxes we were given, watching the guards' movements and waiting for my moment. My heart starts racing so fast that I'm sure everyone around me can hear it.

One of the other wolves pauses for a moment. "Are you okay? You look sick," he says. I nod, brushing his comment away. He makes a face as if he's not convinced but walks away. None of us have been too friendly with each other since we've been here. Anyone who's tried has been punished to discourage us from trying to rise up against our captors.

The bracelet I wear keeps me from shifting. My wrist is raw and scabbed over from where I've tried to remove it. It's better than the shock collars they have on some of the wolves and vamps, though. At least the bracelet won't prevent me from running. A few more minutes, that's all I need. I watch the guards closely without making it obvious what I'm planning.

When the moment arrives that they're distracted, I run into the forest. I have to be careful to stay away from the paths, but near enough that I can figure out where I'm going. I race back toward the cabin Amber kept us in. I have to know if Red made it out, or if she's still a prisoner there. Then I can decide what I need to do.

After I've been gone for a few minutes, I hear shouts. I had hoped to have more time before being discovered. I'll just have to make this work. I arrive at the cabin, and find it deserted. With the layer of dust on everything, it looks like Red's been gone as long as I have.

Has she given up on me? Or is she back home, planning my rescue? I have no way to know. I need to find her. Panic grips my chest, making it hard to breathe. What if something's happened to her? I wouldn't be able to go on without her. She's my everything.

I slip back into the forest, following the trail that leads from the cabin in the direction I just came from. I can't smell any of them, so their trails are definitely not fresh. All I can do is stay on the path and hope I make it home.

I stay low and move as fast as I can. I hear something behind me and duck behind a tree.

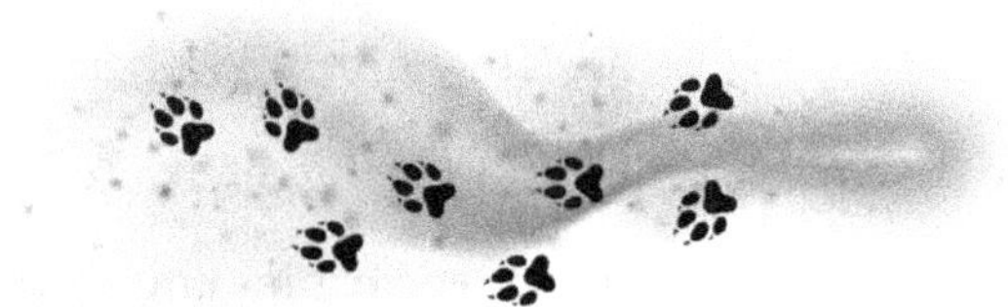

RYLAND

I'm still not sold on this 'other realm' shit James and Red are spouting. It doesn't matter that Orym believes them. If that were possible, we would know about it already. This wouldn't be something that randomly happened. I don't know if I'm struggling to believe it's possible or just trying to convince myself that it's not. The whole idea is terrifying.

If there are other realms, someone could come and take Red from us without having to fight us first. My mind can't handle that idea, so I'm fighting it. But I'm not fighting her. "I can't pretend to understand, but I won't fight about it either."

She smiles at me. "I'll accept that compromise." Red grabs me by the neck and pulls me down for a kiss. I could drown in this woman and die a happy man.

I growl and deepen the kiss, thrusting my tongue in her mouth to taste her. Red wraps her legs around my waist and grinds against my hardening cock. I know this isn't the ideal time to fuck my mate, but it seems to be what she needs, and I won't refuse her.

I know that standing up to Gunnar the way she did was rough. It was worse because she didn't even tell him how she feels or what she thinks of him. And I know she held back to protect us. I will show her my appreciation for that. We've been together long enough that we know what our woman likes. Because of that, James and Orym are already completing the circle around her.

I have her lips, so one of them starts undressing her. The other slips a hand between us, and strokes against her core through her pants. She starts to writhe, so I ease her down to her feet again, not breaking the kiss. With her clothes out of the way, she jumps at me again. I catch her easily, giving one of the guys easy access to her sweet pussy.

I can't tear myself away from her lips; her kisses become more and more intense. It's as if she's trying to devour me from the inside out, and I'm happy to let her do it. Hands work my shirt up, and we part long enough for James to help ease it over my head. As I capture her lips again, I see Orym sliding his hand between us to stroke her.

My pants fall to my ankles, and I can feel Orym's hand between us as he strokes along Red's slit and circles her clit. His hand brushes against my erect dick, and I moan into her mouth. The hum she responds with tells me she likes what he's doing. I can't say I mind it either, though I won't tell him that.

I keep my hands cupped on her ass. My body tenses for a moment when another hand snakes between us. Then I realize that James is pinching Red's nipples, making her squirm.

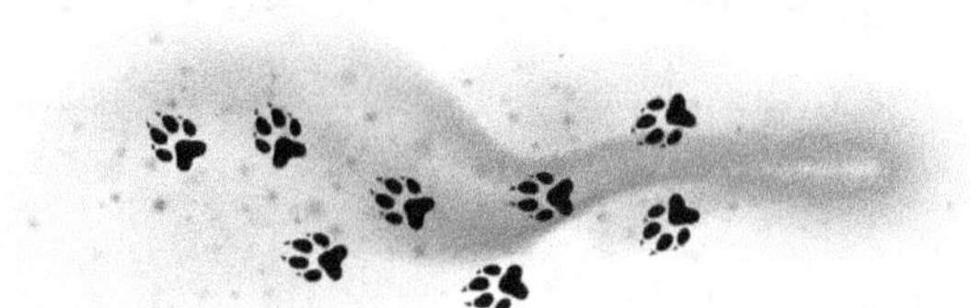

GARNET

Even with my guilt over Luca being gone, I need the attention of my mates. I need to be with them. I'm desperate for the comfort they can give me.

When Ry starts kissing me, Orym and James strip me down. Before I know it, the four of us are naked and I have three sets of hands on me. The sensations are too much and not enough at the same time.

Ry carries me to the bedroom and drops me onto the bed. The three of them look at me as if I'm the sexiest thing they've ever seen. My mouth waters at the sight of their bodies. I'm wet and ready for them. Each of them crawls onto the bed and moves toward me. I hold my breath in anticipation of being touched again.

Pounding on the door interrupts us. "What is that?" I ask, hearing voices shouting. Ry pulls on a pair of pants and rushes toward the door. James drags on his pants, then finds me a shirt and leggings. Orym follows Ry to the door, putting his pants on as he walks. I dress quickly, so I can find out what's happening. I'm not thrilled about being interrupted. Whoever this is pounding on the door had better have a good reason.

"Give us a minute," Ry says to the person at the door. He and Orym exchange a look, then turn toward me.

"What is it?" I ask, getting impatient. James wraps an arm around my shoulders. Neither of them answers me at first. I growl in frustration.

"Amber is in the clearing by Gunnar's place. She's demanding to talk to you," Orym finally tells me.

Fuck. The last person I want to deal with is practically on my doorstep. But maybe I can use this to my advantage and get Luca back. I have to stay positive. "Let's go." The words are out of my mouth before I decide what I want to do.

The three of them look at me as if I've gone crazy. "You can't seriously want to meet with her, can you?" James asks quietly.

"Of course, I do. I want Luca back and the only way to manage that is to confront her. Besides, we may be able to capture her," I reason.

"Fine, but you're not going alone. We do this together or not at all. There will be none of this sacrificing yourself to protect us crap. Understood?" Ry growls the words at me. I nod and grin at him. I hadn't planned to go alone, but I'll let him think he's won this time.

We walk quickly to Gunnar's cabin, following the wolf he sent for us. I'm not sure how I feel about his willingness to give us up like this, but maybe he finally realizes that I'm capable of handling this situation. Who am I kidding? Gunnar doesn't trust anyone to do anything. I bet she threatened him and he decided giving me up was less hassle.

As soon as we get close, the wolf leading us runs off. We step into the clearing and come face to face with Amber, standing in the center. She's alone, which seems odd to me. Where are her followers? Does she really think that she can just stroll into the wolves' territory and not get attacked?

The moment Amber sees me, she starts to walk toward us. "Stop. Do not come closer. I will not hesitate to defend myself," I declare, covering my arms with electricity. I mean what I say. Part of me wants her to keep moving so I can prove it.

Another part of me wants to beg her to give me Luca back. But I won't beg. "I mean you no harm, dear niece," she purrs. I want to rip her face off and feed it to her.

"Then you won't have a problem returning my mate," I suggest. I know she won't do it, but I can't stop myself from trying.

She shakes her head with a sad smile. "I'm sorry, dear girl, I just can't do that yet. You could join me and then you would be able to be with him."

I glare at her, refusing to acknowledge her suggestion. I will not join her cult, even if it means I get to see Luca again. We'll continue with the original plan and rescue him ourselves.

"What do you want?" Ry asks, stepping forward to stand at my side. I feel James and Orym do the same, one on the other side of me, and the other behind me. I feel safe and protected, even though the biggest threat I've ever faced is standing in front of us.

"I just wanted to have a conversation with my niece. Is that a crime?" Amber's voice is like butter; smooth and inviting.

"It is when you've been known to kidnap people," James snarls. Amber laughs at his response. She appears to find the whole situation amusing. And that pisses me off.

"Well, then, I guess I'll just come right out with it. I'm taking over this territory, and everyone here is going to follow me." Her announcement makes my skin crawl. She's still wearing the magic blocking cuffs, so I have no idea how she plans to keep everyone here in line. I don't wait to find out, instead, I attack her.

I zap her with the electricity that's been building along my arms. When she falls down, I wave my hand, pulling vines from the trees down to tie her up with. I have no idea what I'm doing or how I'm doing it, but that doesn't stop me. I have to restrain her.

This magic feels different than any I've used before. I wonder if it has something to do with that strange realm I was in earlier, but I don't say anything. I can talk to the guys about it later. When the vines are tied securely around her, I walk over and tap her forehead, putting her to sleep.

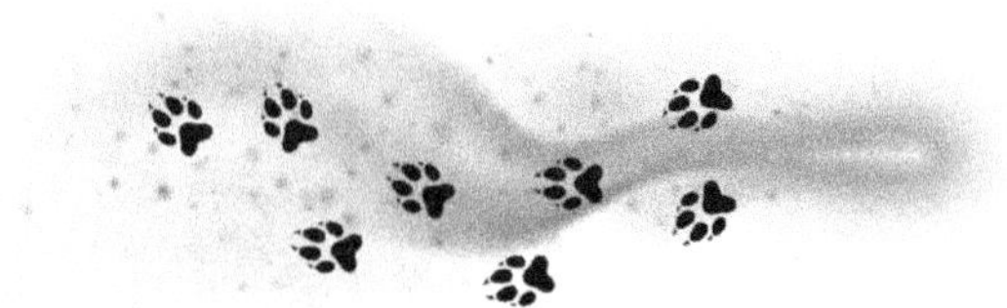

ORYM

"Get me some rope," I order one of the wolves who are hiding in the tree line. "We need to secure her before she wakes up."

Gunnar brings me a length of rope and helps me tie Amber up so she doesn't escape. Garnet looks as if she's going to collapse. I glance at Ryland and he scoops her up before she can fall down. Apparently, we're getting better at communicating without words. I breathe a sigh of relief when I know Amber is secure.

"Where can we lock her up?" I ask Gunnar.

"You can use the cages in the training center. She shouldn't be able to get out of there, and I can station some wolves to keep an eye on her." I nod at his offer and gesture for a couple of wolves to take her. I have to check on my mate before I follow.

Gunnar heads back to his cabin, obviously satisfied that we have the situation under control. I hope he's right.

"Is she okay?" I turn my attention to Garnet and her needs. I know that using her magic like that is taxing.

Ryland adjusts her in his arms, and I hear a soft snore. "She's out cold," he says with a chuckle. "We should get her home. She can interrogate Amber in the morning."

"That's a good idea. I'm going to make sure they get our guest settled in, then I'll catch up to you."

James and Ryland both nod, then head toward Ryland's cabin. It's not that I don't trust the wolves to lock Amber up, it's just that we've spent some time with her and I know how manipulative she can be. I'll feel better knowing that she's secured in a cage.

I watch as my family disappears into the trees, then make my way toward the training center. Gunnar's description is generous at best. It's more of a barn than a center, but I won't be the one to tell him that. I'm just relieved that he finally listened to those of us who wanted a more sheltered area to train in during the winter months.

It amuses me that he waited until it came out that Garnet isn't a wolf before he finally caved and let some of the wolves build it, though. The things that alpha did to make her life harder piss me off. But that's in the past. He can't hurt her now, and she no longer has to follow his rules. Mostly.

I carefully open the door to the training center and look around. It's a cozy barn, with cages in the back. My best guess is that they're here for wolves who disobey Gunnar. He won't hesitate to lock them up until they decide to cooperate.

The rest of the building is pretty sparse, making it apparent that it's a new structure. I walk to the cage that holds Amber.

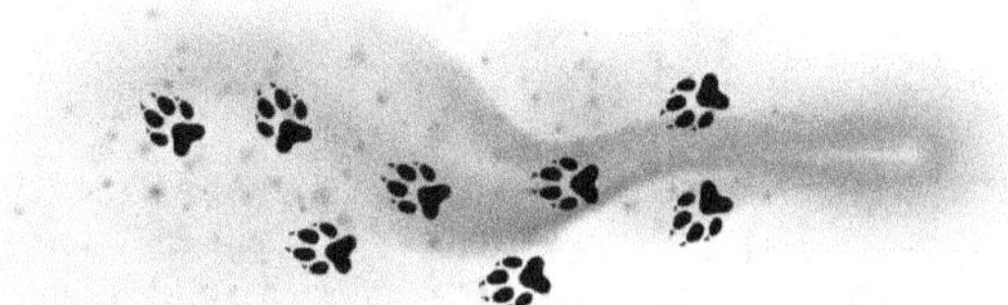

JAMES

"Do you have her?" I ask, feeling as if there's more I could be doing right now.

"Yeah. I'm going to run over and check on Amber after we get her settled. As long as you can handle protecting Red," Ryland answers. I have no problem taking care of our mate, so I nod. When we get to the cabin, I jog ahead and open the door, making sure no one else is inside.

Ryland carries her in and eases her down on the couch. I grab a blanket and a bottle of water. Anything else can wait until Orym and Ryland get back. "I've got her. You go make sure they've got our 'friend' settled."

He doesn't respond, shifting as soon as he's out the door. I get comfortable on the couch next to Garnet, wrapping the blanket around her and pulling her close to me. I won't let anything happen to her. I take this opportunity to grab Ruby's journal and read through it. This time, I'm looking for clues as to what's going on with Garnet's powers and how to help her control them.

Ruby never said who Garnet's father is, but she does talk about the differences in their powers and how that may affect their child. She wrote of plans to test the child and see if the father's powers were more apparent than hers, but sadly Ruby never got to complete those tests on her child.

With no information about Garnet's father, it's nearly impossible to know what kind of supernatural he is or was. We don't even know if he's still alive. Maybe Amber will answer that question for us, though I can't be sure she'll be honest about anything.

Finding nothing useful for our current situation in the journal, I turn to one of Amber's next. These are much darker than Ruby's. Amber kept track of every experiment she did on animals and people. Reading her thoughts turns my stomach. The way she talks about killing makes it seem as if she enjoys it. Her words paint a picture of a jealous psychopath who didn't know right from wrong.

I wonder where their parents were, but there's no mention of them in either woman's writing. Only spells and experiences that happened after they were teenagers and leading up to Ruby's death. I hate that Amber cataloged that experience as well. I know that Garnet has read it several times, and it hurts her every time.

I want to kill Amber myself, but I know it isn't my place to do it. Garnet would never forgive me, even if it would free her from the strange hold Amber seems to have on her. No, if anyone is going to take Amber's life, it will have to be Garnet herself. The rest of us don't have that right.

Garnet whimpers and shivers next to me. I pull her onto my lap and hold her close until she relaxes against me.

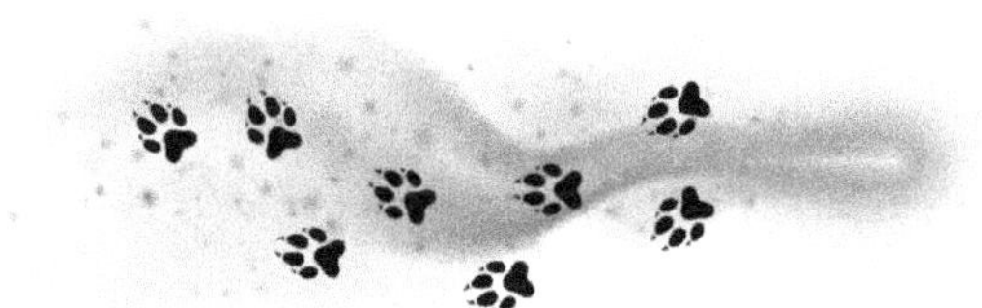

GARNET

Using that much magic to subdue Amber was foolish. I know that. I could have simply knocked her out in the first place, then had someone fetch rope. That would have been the smart thing to do. Part of me wants her to know that my powers are growing. I want her to be afraid of what I'm becoming.

I need her to fear me. I know that she'll never respect me, so I'll take her fear. I want her to grovel before me; to beg for her life the way she made my mother beg. She took my family from me. It's her fault I was miserable. Amber is the catalyst for all my suffering.

But I won't kill her, only if I have to. I don't want her dead. I want her scared and controlled. I can sense that the cuffs are still working. She can't get to her powers unless I let her. And I won't let her.

I let myself collapse against Ry's chest as he carries me home. When he leaves me with James, I succumb to the sleep that's trying to take me. I know that the dreams aren't real, but that doesn't stop me from whimpering and having cold chills. The instant James pulls me onto his lap, I relax, finally feeling safe.

I wake a little while later, not remembering what I dreamed that had scared me. It doesn't matter now, I'm with James, and I'm safe.

"Where is everyone?" I ask, interrupting his reading. I notice that it's one of Amber's journals that has his attention.

"Checking on Amber to make sure she can't escape. They should be back soon," he answers with a smile. "Are you feeling better?"

I nod. "Yeah. Do you think we could go see where they took her? I don't want to just make sure she's secure. I want to talk to her."

"I think Ryland was planning to take you to her tomorrow. You need to rest and recover today." I know that James is just trying to help, but I'm not going to wait. I will go talk to Amber tonight, even if I have to go alone.

"I don't want to wait until tomorrow. I want to talk to her now. You can come with me or you can wait here. I'm good either way," I snap.

He holds up his hands in surrender. "I'll go with you. I'm not about to let you walk around alone after what happened earlier. I can't keep you from realm jumping if I'm not with you."

"Did you figure out how to keep it from happening?" I think he's trying to distract me, but I honestly want to know.

James shrugs. "I'm not sure. I have some ideas after reading Ruby's journal and Amber's. Ruby talks about doing it purposefully, and Amber talks about blocking her from it. So, there are maybe some things we can try."

I climb off his lap and grab his hand, dragging him to his feet. We rush to the building where the wolves were supposed to take Amber, watching to be sure we don't pass Orym or Ry on the way. I feel like I'm doing something bad, but I refuse to apologize.

I need answers, and she's the only one who can give them to me. The moment I touch the door, I pause for a moment. A sense of dread courses through me and I want to run away. I'm not scared of Amber; not when she doesn't have her magic. There's nothing she can do to me. I've taken that ability away from her.

I shake the feeling off and head inside with James behind me. We find Ry standing across the room from Amber's cage, and Orym crouched in front of it. He's speaking in low tones, so I can't make out what he's saying.

James and I exchange a glance, then head toward the cage. It's clear that Amber is awake and at least listening to Orym, even if she's not responding. As we get closer, I can hear Orym's words. "I will not ask her to take the cuffs off. You don't need your magic here. You can't control her, and you should realize that now."

Ry sees us coming and tries to stop me from going to the cage. I shake my head and James steps in front of him. "She has to do this. We have to let her."

I think that I've finally convinced James that I have to talk to Amber. It's not that I want to; I need to. She's the only one left who knows who my father is and can give me answers about my magic. I'm not above lying to her to get answers if I have to. I can promise to remove the cuffs and let her have her powers back if she tells me what I want to know.

Or we can just keep her locked up until she decides to cooperate. I really don't care anymore. I just need to know what I'm dealing with here.

"Amber. I see you're awake now," I say, standing just out of reach outside the cage.

"My darling niece. How lovely of you to come visit. I was just telling your wolf boy here that I need these cuffs off. Be a dear and remove them," she purrs. I laugh at the request.

"No." The word falls from my lips easily and with no malice.

"What do you mean, no?" Amber's shock amuses me, and I laugh harder.

"I mean—No, I will not remove the cuffs. You will not have access to your magic until I decide to let you. You will not manipulate or guilt me into doing your bidding." I lean a little closer and lower my voice to ensure that only she and my mates hear me. "My powers are growing, auntie, so don't fuck with me." The thinly veiled threat makes her eyes go wide.

FOUR
NEGOTIATIONS

RYLAND

WATCHING RED THREATEN AMBER has me pushing James out of the way and moving closer. It's hot the way she's taking control of the situation. Amber is doing her best to hide her fear, but I can smell it. She's terrified of Red. I wonder if Red can sense it as well.

"If you take the cuffs off, we can call a truce. Then I'll train you how to use your powers," Amber offers. If Red falls for that one, then she's more naïve than I ever thought.

I watch her face, unsure of what she's thinking. Is she going to agree? I hold up a hand when Red starts to speak, but she brushes it aside.

"Absolutely. Give me just a moment and I'll take care of that for you." As soon as the words are out of her mouth, Red doubles over laughing. "Seriously? Do you think I'll ever trust you after everything you've done? No. I won't be taking the cuffs off. We aren't having a truce. The only chance you have to get out of here alive is to answer my questions honestly."

I have to admit, I like the dark side of my mate. It also helps to know that she sees through Amber's manipulations. "I can't believe you'd speak to me this way," Amber laments.

Red wipes the tears from her eyes and the humor drops from them as well. "Oh, auntie. You are hilarious. I'm not some weak child that you can control. Are you going to answer my questions or not?"

Amber grabs the bars of the cage and snarls at Red, who touches a finger to the metal cage, shocking Amber. The older witch drops to her knees. With any luck, Red will accidentally fry her and we won't have to worry about keeping her locked up anymore.

"First question. Who is my father?" Red's face is neutral, but anger burns in her eyes.

Amber stares at her. "What makes you think that I know?"

"Your journal entries indicate that you do. But you're not going to tell me, are you? Of course, even if you did, I can't trust anything you say, so I guess there's no point in this little talk, is there?" Electricity sparks along Red's skin. For a moment, I think I'll get my wish for her to end Amber.

Then she lets the magic drop and walks away. I can't tell if she's upset or angry. I turn to the wolves who helped us lock Amber up. "Keep watch. Make sure she stays here."

Orym and James are already following Red out of the center. I jog to catch up. "Is she okay?" I ask them.

"Not sure. She's upset, but I think she's more angry at herself for thinking that Amber would tell her anything useful," James explains.

That makes sense. Amber should have answered them instead of being hateful. We have to find a way to break her.

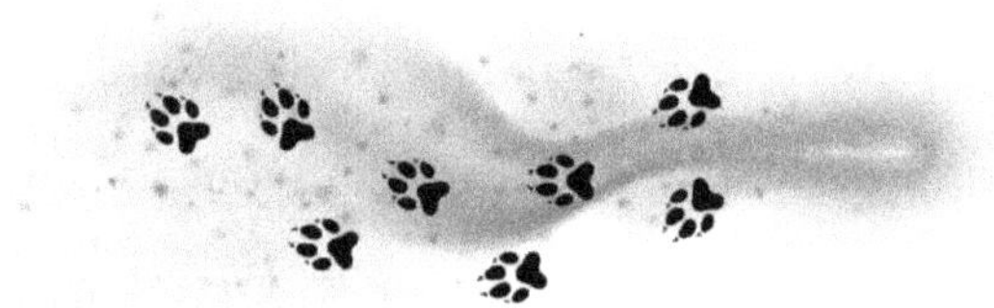

ORYM

The moment Garnet turns away from Amber, I follow her. I won't let her leave by herself. James catches up to me, then Ryland meets us. He's concerned about Garnet's feelings. I ignore the conversation, focusing on her storming out ahead of us.

I leave the guys behind to catch up to our mate. I grab her hand and thread my fingers through hers. My reward is a sad smile. She'd been hoping to get answers from Amber. It was disappointing that her aunt refused to cooperate, but not surprising.

"We'll get through this," I tell her. Garnet nods, but doesn't respond. I know that she's fighting back tears. "Let's go home and rest. You can try again tomorrow."

"That sounds good," she whispers. I want to scoop her into my arms and carry her, but I know she'll refuse. My mate is trying to hold herself together and if I show her that tenderness, she'll break down. That won't help her show strength in front of the lingering wolves. She's still recovering from the changes that her life has gone through lately.

It's been too much at once, but there's nothing we can do about it. Gunnar isn't her father, and no longer has control over her. Because of this, the wolves aren't sure how to treat her. As our mate, they should be showing her respect. But as a witch, not a wolf, they aren't required to even speak to her. Since she's trying to save their people, they should be bowing at her feet.

The whole situation has put her in a hard position. I understand her desire to remain visibly strong in front of them as much as she can. Adding to that, she collapsed earlier and they all saw it, which will make her more determined to be strong now.

By the time we're back at the cabin, Garnet looks exhausted. James and Ryland seem to be working out some sort of plan. They're probably trying to find a way to make Amber talk. I wonder if they're considering torture. I know that Ryland wouldn't be above that, but I would expect better from James.

I shift my focus back to my mate. I need to make her comfortable and take care of her. I'm desperate to get Luca back so that her spark returns. Garnet hasn't been the same since he was taken. She's trying, which is good, but she won't be herself until he's back with us. We have to find a way to make that happen as soon as possible.

"How about a shower?" I ask Garnet as I lead her inside.

"That sounds nice. I could use a few minutes alone with my thoughts," she answers. Hopefully she'll be okay with one of us outside the door, then. Because we're not leaving her alone at all. "I know that someone will sit outside the door." She rolls her eyes. At least she's not mad about us taking care of her.

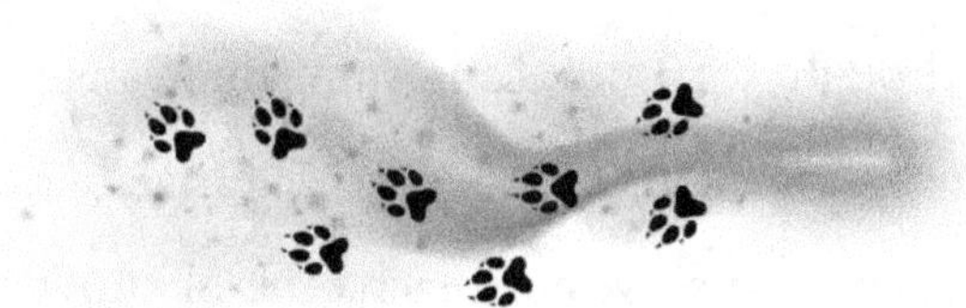

GARNET

I know that my mates are trying to protect me, and it's sweet. But never having a moment to myself is getting annoying, and it's only been one day. So, I'm taking a shower. Alone. They can sit outside the door if they want, but I'm going in this bathroom alone. Or I'm zapping their asses.

I just need a few minutes to figure out how to approach Amber to get answers. I lock the door to ensure that they don't sneak in. Then I strip down and step into the shower. Ry has been upgrading things all over the cabin since the four of us are living here now, and I'm sure he'll make more changes once we get Luca back.

That thought, of Luca, causes my emotions to spiral. I've been trying so hard to keep everything together. Fighting to get him back because we need each other. I know exactly what has me so out of sorts now. I feel like I'm failing him. I can't get Amber to talk to me, and we haven't managed to work out the best time and place to rescue Luca.

On top of that, Kayden won't let me back in Midnight, so I can't train with Delilah anymore. But I can train on my own. I need to keep working on the spell that almost blew up the nightclub. I know that I can get it if I just figure out how to control it.

I feel overwhelmed and out of control. My emotions are too much. I can't hold back the tears anymore, so I let them fall as I stand under the hot spray of the shower. There's something comforting about the way the water cascades along my skin. It's almost as if the water is trying to make me feel better. The thought is ridiculous, but it's there. My tears slow, then finally stop.

Now that I'm cried out, I feel numb inside. Luca being taken has hit me harder than I realized. It's like having a part of my soul ripped out and being expected to go on without it. I'm not sure that I can for much longer. There has to be a way to convince Amber to cooperate. Or to force her to return the people she's kidnapped.

I try to convince myself that I'm spiraling because I can't see how Luca is doing. I know that's a lie, though. I was more upset when I could see the beatings he took. I know that those videos were making me more out of control than I am now. I need to refocus on my training and get ready for our attack.

I barely register the change in temperature of the water before I use my magic to heat it back up. I consider my options while I wash and condition my hair. By the time I'm finished in the shower, I have the beginnings of a plan forming in my head.

After I'm dried off and dressed in jeans and a sweatshirt, I open the bathroom door to find James half asleep against it. He jerks awake as his support is removed. "Hi," he says cautiously. I know he's the most in tune with my emotions, so he knows I was crying.

"Why are you on the floor?" I know the answer, and don't expect him to tell me anyway. I hold a hand out to help him to his feet.

"I felt your emotions and needed to be close. Sorry." He blushes and gives me a sheepish grin. I can't be mad at him. He didn't pick the lock and camp out in the bathroom. James gave me the space I needed, and I appreciate that.

"No apology needed. Where are the other two?" I'm kind of surprised that all three of them weren't right here when I exited the bathroom.

I follow James to the kitchen, grabbing a mug and filling it with coffee. He takes the mug from me and adds just the right amount of sugar and creamer to make my taste buds happy, then hands it back to me. I think my caffeine addiction is getting worse, but I'm not complaining. I could get used to being waited on like this.

I take my coffee and head to the couch. James joins me with his own steaming mug, but doesn't answer my question. I glance at him beside me, then decide to take matters into my own hands.

Where are you two? I send the thought along our bond, focusing on Ry and Orym. Then I settle in and wait for a response. When there isn't one after five minutes or so, I try again. *If you don't answer me or get in here, I'm going to be tempted to restrain James and make my way back to talk to Amber alone. Do you really want that?*

I hate making threats, but part of me wants to do it. This time, I get a response pretty quickly.

I'd hold off on that, Garnet. Gunnar called us to his cabin while you were in the shower. Orym's sweet voice floats through my head.

The witches have taken more wolves, Red. They know we have their bitch leader, and they want her back. Ry's voice is less sweet, but just as welcome. Now that I know where they are, I can relax a little.

We're going to have to deal with Amber's followers soon. If only we can come up with a way to get the wolves released in exchange for her. I can't imagine that idea working, though, so I push it aside. We need something better.

I sip my coffee while my mind wanders. James picks up one of the journals and starts reading again. This man has been my rock when it comes to studying magic. He probably knows more about it than I do at this point. I wonder if I'll catch up.

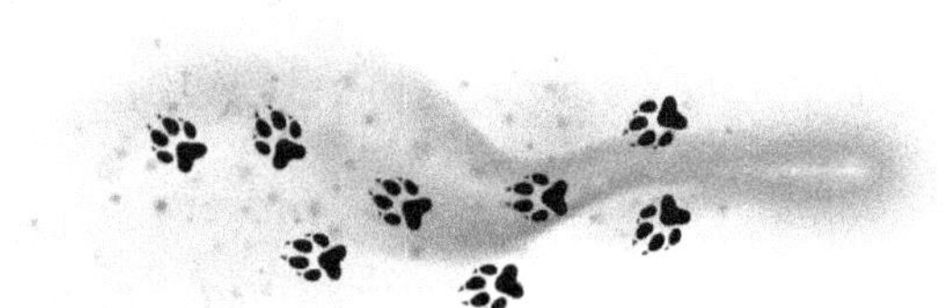

JAMES

I've been reading these journals and studying magic as much as Garnet has. I know that she's communicating with Orym and Ryland, and I let her have that moment in privacy. I can't tell her where they went, because I'm not sure. And I know that she won't believe that, so I'll let them answer for themselves.

I continue reading Amber's journal and something catches my eye. I hold my place with a finger while I grab Ruby's journal. I'm sure I saw a passage in Ruby's journal that was nearly identical to this one in Amber's. If I'm right, I may have stumbled upon part of Amber's motivation. I just need to find the passage and make sure.

I flip through Ruby's journal, searching each page for the words that will tell me if I'm right. There! I stop and stare at the page, then open Amber's journal and compare them. The handwriting is different in each book, so I know the passages weren't written by the same person. But the wording of the interaction is exactly the same.

I know why Amber killed Ruby, and why she wants Garnet's power. The realm travel makes perfect sense now as well. I may have even figured out what Garnet's father was, although I still don't know who. I sense her staring at me and I know that I've got her full attention.

A grin spreads across my face, and I can't stifle the laugh that bubbles up. "What are you so excited about?" she asks.

"I think I know how we can make Amber talk," I say. Garnet gives me a confused look, and I start to explain what I've found. "Look at this page. Read it carefully, paying attention to the exact wording used and the date at the top." I wait while she reads Amber's journal entry.

"Okay, so she met a guy. How is that going to get her to talk?"

"Now read this passage and pay attention to the same things—the exact wording and the date," I instruct as I hand her Ruby's journal.

Garnet reads for a minute, then scrunches her face and reads it again. Then she switches back to Amber's journal and reads it again. "Fuck."

"I think that all of this is about a guy. Everything Amber has done is for revenge. She's in love with him but hates him for what he did. It explains everything," I declare.

"You're absolutely right. But if that's all true, then..." she pauses.

"Yeah, if it's all true, then we know why your powers are different. And we have a clue about your father. It doesn't tell us who he is, or if he's still alive, but it does give us an idea of what to expect from your powers."

Garnet's jaw drops and she stares out the window, trying to process the bomb I just dropped on her. We won't know if any of this is true until we talk to Amber.

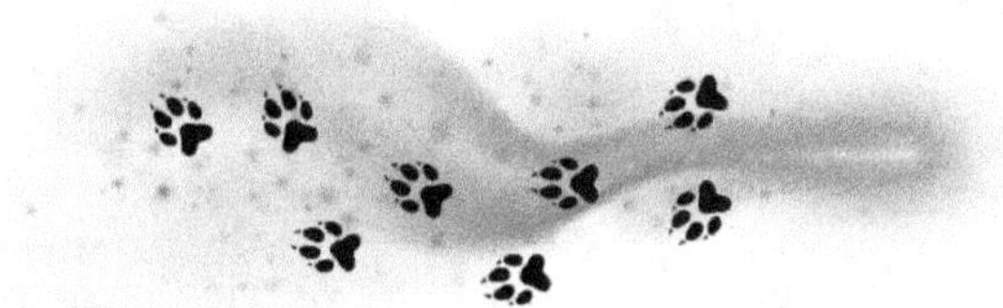

LUCA

Hiding isn't my favorite option, but I don't have much choice at this point. I press my back against the tree and pray to the Goddess that these witches don't find me. At this point, I'm relieved that they didn't send any of the wolves they're controlling after me. A wolf would have been able to track me and capture me faster than any of these witches can even move.

My pursuers pass by, and I hold my breath. I can't relax yet, because I'm not out of this part of the forest yet. Now that I know Red and the other guys aren't still trapped here, I have to get home. When I'm certain that the witches following me have gone, I silently move away from the tree.

I'll have to stay close to the path, because I know how difficult these woods are to navigate. I'm smaller in my human form, so I'm glad that I can't shift. I need to find a way to remove this bracelet, but nothing I've tried has worked. Since I can't shift, I'm going to move as quietly and quickly as I can. I stick to the trees and brush along the sides of the worn dirt path, heading away from the cabin.

Every time I hear a noise, I drop to the ground or flatten myself against a tree. I feel paranoid, but I refuse to discount how dangerous these witches are. Each time, I freeze and hide, and each time, there's nothing. No one attacks me. I'm not captured. I remain vigilant, though, listening for each noise and paying attention to my surroundings.

A twig breaks somewhere behind me, and I drop onto my stomach, scurrying under a bush. "I was sure he went this way," a voice says. I hold my breath as the response comes.

"I told you, he's closer to camp. Think about it. There's no way this guy is going to leave all those wolves. Not after all the beatings he's taken for them. We need to look closer to the camp. He's going to try to rescue the others," the second voice reasons with the first.

Relief washes over me as they turn and head back the way they came. I might actually make it back home. Hope swells in my heart. I wait a few more minutes before getting to my feet and trekking along the path again.

The further I go along the path, the more I feel something pulling me in that direction. I can't say what it is, because I don't know. It feels like I'm being called home. Red. That has to be it. Somehow, she knows that I'm free, and she's leading me to her. I rush forward, following the feeling and letting myself get lost in the draw.

A strange but familiar feeling washes over me. I've felt this before, but I don't remember when. The colors of the forest change somehow. It's as if I'm no longer there.

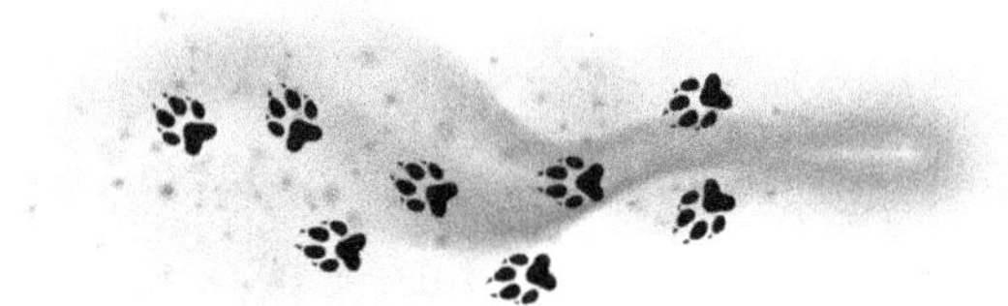

GARNET

When I read the pages that James points out, my heart starts to race. This can't be right. There's no way. Is there? If he's right, then my father is a total player. Or at least, he was. My aunt wrote of meeting a handsome man, then the next day, my mother's journal entry was identical. They both started whirlwind romances a day apart, with a man who was described exactly the same in both women's books. So, it stands to reason that he's the cause of the rift between them.

I think that James has inferred more than I have with the selections. "Wait, what? I see that they both fell for the same man. That's why Amber killed Ruby. What are you seeing that I'm not?"

He looks at me for a moment, then gestures to the books. "You don't see the connection?" James is a very patient man, but I can see the frustration starting to surface.

"I'm not sure what you're talking about. I'm sorry, James, can you just explain it to me? How does any of this explain my powers?" I'm not playing dumb, but I think he suspects that.

"This part," he points to a sentence as he speaks, "is a description of where they each met this man. Doesn't that place sound familiar?"

I blink a few times and read the passages again. Oh, shit, he's right. "That's the place I went to earlier today. But how? How did I miss that when I read these before?"

"You weren't looking for it. I wasn't either at first. Then while you were talking to Orym and Ryland, I started reading again and it hit me."

I tilt my head to the side and narrow my eyes at him. "You knew I was talking to them?"

"Yeah, but since I didn't know where they were, I figured you'd have better luck asking them anyway," he answers.

"Oh." I'm not sure how to feel about that. James seems more in tune to me than anyone else lately, and it makes me miss Luca a lot. But it is nice to have someone who knows me so well already.

"They got called to a meeting with Gunnar. I don't know how long they'll be gone." I pause and stare at the pages again. "What are we going to do about this?"

James takes my hand, giving it a comforting squeeze. "I don't know what we can do about it, other than continue your training and research how your powers could develop. I'm not sure who would know, but I can ask around." I nod, trying to process what I've just learned. Going from being a wolf who believes she's cursed, to learning I'm a witch, to finding out I'm actually a half-breed is a lot to process.

Especially when the other half of me has always been thought to be a myth. Where am I going to find information about a species of supernatural that's believed to be fiction? Before I can even think of a way to find answers, the door opens and Ry follows Orym inside.

"Tell us about the meeting, then we have news," I insist. I don't give James a chance to explain. I want to know what Gunnar has planned to retaliate against Amber's people.

"I offered to negotiate with them, but he refused. Gunnar wants to attack the witches and dive head first into war with them," Ry states.

Orym drops onto the couch beside me. "Amber's second in command or whatever told Gunnar that there would be no negotiating. We release her or they'll keep kidnapping wolves and start killing them. We have until tomorrow at noon to set her free."

This is bad. But we'll figure it out. We have to. Luca and the others are depending on us. My heart is racing, and my chest feels tight. I'm struggling to breathe, and James senses it. He squeezes my hand again, and I take his cue to breathe deeply a few times to settle myself.

"You said something about news?" Ry asks, easing himself into the chair next to the couch. "What's up?"

"James made a breakthrough." He starts to protest at me giving him credit, but I hold up a hand. "You figured it out. The question is, do we explain it to them, or see if they can figure it out too?"

He laughs at my question, but both Ry and Orym look confused. "It's okay, we'll just tell you. I've been reading Amber's journals, and something hit me. There's a passage in hers that's identical to a passage in Ruby's."

"Yeah, so?" Ry doesn't sound impressed.

"So, both women were in love with the same man. And they met him a day apart. They were dating the same guy. They didn't find out until Ruby discovered she was pregnant. That's when Amber started to hate her. But that's not the most important part of what we discovered." James stops talking and looks at me. This is my news to share. I wonder how they'll take it. I'm not sure how I'm taking it.

"Okay, so what's the most important part?" Orym asks.

"We know what my father was, but not who. And we don't know if he's still alive or not," I explain.

"What was he?" Ry asks, suddenly interested.

"It sounds crazy, but he was Fae," I finally voice the words that have been dancing around in my head. "I'm half Fae. Which is why my powers are weird and don't do what Amber said they would. It's also why she wants my powers."

Silence fills the room. James squeezes my hand again as I stare between Orym and Ry, waiting for a reaction. I have no idea what to expect from either of them. The stories we've grown up with about the fae are not flattering. I wouldn't blame either of them if they didn't want to be with me anymore.

Five
FORCED RELEASE

ORYM

GARNET'S ANNOUNCEMENT HITS ME hard. The Fae people are a myth. They aren't real. One certainly can't be her father.

Of course, Amber and Ruby being in love with the same man would explain all of Amber's hostility toward everyone. But that doesn't mean the man they were in love with is Fae.

"That's not possible," I insist. "Fae are fictional creatures created to keep the rest of us in line." I know from childhood stories that my parents used to tell us. There is no basis in fact for them to be real.

"I understand why you feel that way, but I'm pretty sure we're right. I mean, until my brother was turned, I thought vampires were fictional. Then I met Kayden and discovered that wolf shifters are real too," James admits. It makes sense, but I'm struggling to wrap my head around it.

If Fae are real, then every story we were told as children has a basis in fact. Which means all the horrible things the Fae did to trick people and hurt them could be true. I don't want to think about my mate being one of them. Garnet is the kindest person I've ever met. She can't be Fae.

"Orym, I know this is a lot to process. I don't fully understand it either. If you need some time, I get it," she says. And it proves my point. She can't be Fae. They would never react that way to someone getting unbelievable news.

"I don't know. I can't believe it," I repeat. James just looks at me. I watch as tears fill Garnet's eyes. I want to comfort her, but I don't know how. It's all too much. I glance at Ryland, who's been uncharacteristically silent during this conversation. "What do you think?"

He scrunches his face for a moment, then smiles wide. "I think it's fantastic. That's just the edge we need to defeat Amber and her stupid cult."

"So, you believe it? No doubts at all?" I ask, amazed at how easily Ryland accepted this new development.

"Yeah, I mean, why not? It's like James said, he didn't know that vamps and shifters were real, but we are. Why would Fae be any different? I bet there are a lot of things out there that we don't know about," he says.

"But all those stories; they can't be true," I insist again. There has to be a way to prove that I'm right.

"Of course, they're not all true. But parts of them have to be. Any legend or myth is that way. Pieces of it are based in truth, and the rest is made up," Ry argues.

I don't want to fight with them, but I still can't accept that our fated mate is part Fae. The stories I've heard about them are awful. The Fae kill without reason, trick people into making insane deals, and steal anything they can. I refuse to believe Garnet is that.

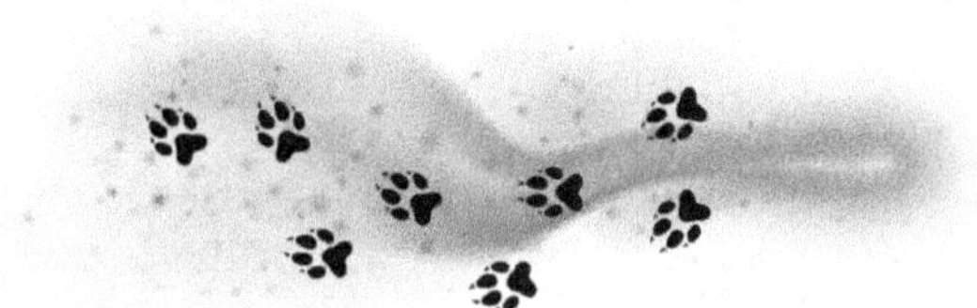

JAMES

I understand Orym's hesitance at believing what we're telling him. I wish there was a way I could prove it to him and make this easier to accept. Sadly, I can't figure out a way to make him believe. I know some of the stories he's trying to wrap his head around, and I get why this is hard for him. The Fae are a cruel people, who cause mischief for fun.

If even half the stories are true, then we're all in for more than we bargained for. Without any concrete proof, all I have are my suspicions. "What if we play this safe? We'll start training Garnet as if she is half Fae, then if it turns out that I'm wrong, it won't hurt anything."

I see Orym relax a little at my suggestion. "I can go along with that. I can't believe it until I see proof, but I'm all for preparing for the worst." With that settled, we start to plan Garnet's new training.

"We need everything written about Fae and their powers. That way we know what to test her on," Ryland suggests. It's a great idea.

"Where are the written records and stories for the wolves?" I ask, already suspecting I know the answer.

"Gunnar's place. Grammy has it all in her study. I don't know if they'll help us, especially if they didn't already know about this new development," Garnet says with a hint of sadness.

"I'll ask her. I don't have to tell her what we've discovered, just that I'm doing some research on how to defeat Amber. That might be enough," I offer. Garnet nods, but doesn't speak. She's less excited now and more serious.

Orym knows that he fucked up with his reaction. He'd better fix this. But he can't, because he's still struggling to process his feelings. Ryland and I will have to handle her, then. "Maybe Orym can go check on Amber and make sure that she's still locked up while we figure out the best way to interrogate her." I feel bad for essentially sending him away, but Garnet needs support right now, and he's not in the right head space to give it.

"I can do that." He turns to Garnet. "I'm sorry that I'm having trouble with this." He kisses her cheek, then leaves.

Ryland pulls her into his arms as the tears start to fall. I'm glad to know I wasn't the only one who expected her reaction. It has to be difficult when your fated mate seems to reject part of you. But we'll figure it out and get through it.

"I'll go talk to Grammy and see if I can get those books. You two can start with what we already know from the oral stories. There are certain things Garnet should only be able to do if she really is Fae."

Ryland nods. "Like shapeshifting or creating that otherworldly fog from that one story. That kind of thing."

"Exactly," I agree.

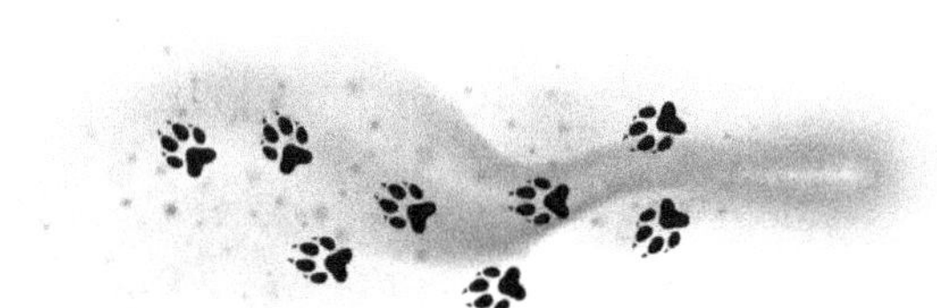

GARNET

With Orym checking on Amber, and James on a mission to retrieve books about the Fae, that leaves Ry and I to start training. Or testing, if that's how they want to see it. I don't mind, but Orym's words stick with me. He believes that the Fae are heartless creatures. Which means if I'm one of them, I am too.

Ry distracts me with his first test. "I know you don't have wings, so flying is out of the question, but what about levitating? Let's see if you can do that."

It sounds ridiculous, but I guess if I believe what James and I found, it shouldn't. Maybe I'm having just as much trouble processing as Orym is. What the hell? It can't hurt to try.

"Okay, let's do it," I agree. We step outside into the clearing in front of the cabin. I don't really know how to attempt this, but I figure that clearing my head is a good place to start. I sit on the ground and cross my legs under me. Focusing on my breathing, I do the exercise James taught me. Once I feel centered and grounded, I focus on the idea of levitating. What would it feel like for my body to lift off the ground?

When I feel like I have that figured out, I push myself to visualize it. Then I reach out and pull my powers close, pushing them at the ground. It takes a lot of focus, but I feel my body start to shake before I hear Ry's gasp. I get a little distracted and almost fall, but take another deep breath and stop myself.

I carefully open one eye, then the other. I glance around, and the forest looks the same as always. Ry's cabin is in front of us. But for some reason, Ry is a lot shorter than he was earlier. I look down and realize that I'm floating about six feet off the ground. It worked!

Of course, that thought distracts me and I fall. Ry races to catch me, keeping me from hitting the ground. "That was awesome, Red!" he gushes and hugs me close.

I'm trying to catch my breath and laughing because I did it. I know it's not definitive proof, but it's close. I know there's more to do, but I'm giddy with the small success. Now I just have to figure out how to do it on command.

"It was a rush, for sure!" I exclaim.

"What's next?" he asks me. I'm surprised that he wants to let me take the lead. What should we try next? There are so many stories of things the Fae could do, it's hard to choose something.

"What about glamouring? I should be able to make myself look like someone else, right?" I suggest. He nods and sets me on my feet. I feel like this will be harder than levitating was.

Taking a moment to refocus, I do my breathing exercise again. Then I imagine how glamouring would work. Then I choose someone to become. I wave my hand in front of my face slowly with my eyes closed. When I drop my hand, Ry gasps again. I wonder if that means it worked or it didn't.

"So?" I ask, raising my eyebrows.

"You look just like Grammy. How did you do that?" His shock is apparent. I reverse the process, making myself look like me again.

"I'm not really sure how I did it. I thought about changing my face, then who I wanted to look like. After that, I just moved my hand and told my magic to do it. Was it really that good?" I'm convinced that I'll have to practice all of this for hours before I get good at it.

"It was like, one second, you're standing in front of me, then the next, Grammy was there. You even changed height to match her. You did amazing. And it looked really easy," he praises me.

"I wonder if that's something I could use against Amber," I think out loud. She killed my mother, but if I could appear in front of her as my mother, it might be enough to rattle her. It's an interesting thought, and I'm not sure how I feel about it right now.

"Maybe. Do you want to try anything else? Or do you need a break?" I love that Ry is concerned about me, but I don't have time for a break right now.

"I'm okay. I need to keep working. How about we try that fog thing? I have an idea of how that could come in handy when we go to rescue Luca." I turn away from him, taking less time to do my breathing exercise and refocus before I start to pull at my powers.

I keep my eyes open this time, watching as the fog starts to form along the ground. I make it move toward us, getting thicker and reaching into the air higher as it moves.

"That's awesome. Can you change it? Like the color and density?" Ry asks, standing next to me in awe.

I smile and do as he asks, turning the fog from a dark gray to a cotton candy pink. Then I make it dissipate a bit so it can easily be seen through. After a minute, I change it to deep purple and make it so thick you can't see through it at all. Then I change it back to the dark gray color and play around with the thickness of it.

I bring it closer until it surrounds us, then push it away, before I dissolve it completely. I can tell that I'm starting to get tired, but I don't want to give up. I have an idea and decide to try it without telling Ry.

A moment later, without even refocusing, a light rain starts to fall on us. "Are you doing that?" he asks.

I smirk and nod.

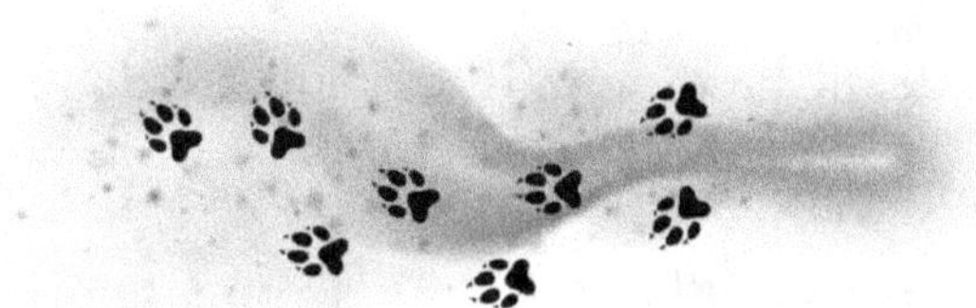

LUCA

I look around cautiously, searching for anything familiar to tell me that I'm home. Nothing looks right. The trees are purple, and the stream is pink. Wait, there wasn't a stream there a minute ago. Where am I?

You're close, boy, but you have a way to go yet. I hear the voice in my head, but still turn in a circle trying to pinpoint where it's coming from.

"Is someone there?" I ask quietly, worried that I'll draw attention and be captured again.

I'm always here, my boy. Don't you remember me? The voice, even inside my head, sounds so familiar. I do remember but can't place who it is.

"Who are you? Where are you?" I look around again, trying to figure out not only who I'm talking to, but where we are. This isn't the same forest I was in a moment ago. It can't be.

But it is the same, just in a different plane of existence, my boy. Wait, what? This being can speak in my head and hear my thoughts. That's freaky. Even more than that, I'm in a different plane? How is that possible?

"I don't understand. Please tell me who you are and where we are. I need to get home. Red needs me." I don't know if pleading with this disembodied voice will help, but I'm not above begging if it gets me home to my girl.

You'll get there soon, my boy. I can tell it's a man's voice, and somehow, I recognize it. Where have I heard this voice?

I'm hit with a flash of memory. Red and I were kids, playing near the stream. Suddenly we were here, in this strangely colored place. There was a man with kind eyes and red hair. He'd played hide and seek with us, then told us stories of the Fae folk.

"Am I in the Fae Realm right now? Is that where I know you from?" As soon as the question leaves my lips a blue fog descends on me. I'm surrounded, and my heart starts to race. My body wants to shift, but the bracelet keeps me from it.

"I knew you'd remember," the voice says. But this time, there's a body attached to it. A man appears from the fog. It's the same man I remember from my childhood. How could I have forgotten him? We spent hours with him, playing and listening to stories. "I'm glad to see you again, my boy. A lot has changed, but not your love for Garnet."

"Red and I are fated mates. I have to get back to her. She's in danger and I have to help protect her," I explain, unsure why I'm telling him all of this. I have no way to know if I can trust him, other than the fact that Red and I played here when we were kids.

"That's why I brought you here, my boy. I want to help. But I need your help too."

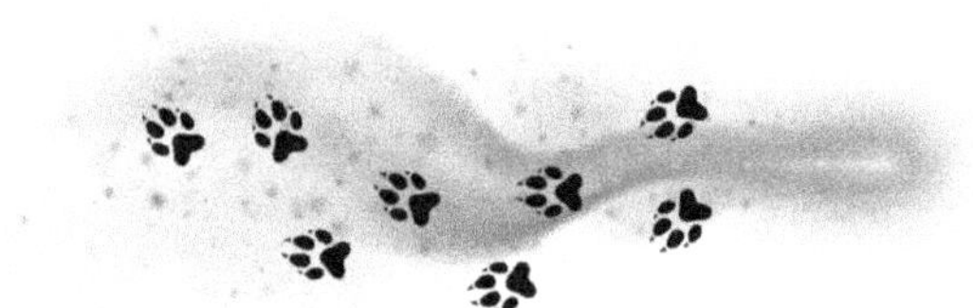

RYLAND

When the soft rain starts, I realize that Red is the one doing it. Her smirk warms my heart. It's the first time she's seemed to be herself since Luca was taken. I worry that if we don't get him back soon, she'll never recover.

I can tell that she's getting tired. We have to figure out how to boost her energy levels while she's using her magic. Hopefully

James will have some thoughts on the subject when he gets back with the books from Grammy. As if I called out to him, he responds in my head.

I think you two should head this way. Amber's minions are back and making threats. Gunnar and Orym are having a discussion with them right now.

"Red? We have to go now. Did you hear James?" I ask, unsure if he sent the message just to me or included her. She shakes her head.

We're on our way. I tell James before turning to Red. "They need us to help with negotiations. Amber's followers are at Gunnar's," I explain to her as I pull her in that direction.

"Is everything okay?" she asks as she jogs beside me.

"I don't think so. We have to hurry. Do you want a ride?" When she nods, I shift and she climbs onto my back. I race through the forest with her holding onto my fur. I see what has James so worried when we enter the clearing by Gunnar's cabin.

Amber's followers have brought two wolves with them. The wolves are in chains, being held between witches. This doesn't look good. Red slides off my back and I shift before we walk into the center of the clearing.

"You will release Amber, or we will start delivering wolves to your camp," the dark-haired girl says.

"We want our wolves back, so how is that an incentive to let her go?" Gunnar growls. His temper is going to ruin any chance of negotiations.

"Do it," the girl says to one of the witches. A blade flashes out and slices across the throat of one of the wolves. We watch in horror as the wolf bleeds out in front of us before the witches toss the body toward Gunnar. "We didn't say they would be returned alive."

Orym holds Gunnar back so he can't attack the witch. There's no point in more death. I step forward to offer a compromise. "We'll release her if you give us all the wolves—alive."

Red is shaking beside me, and I know that she wants to use her magic but is concerned about making things worse.

"Silly wolf. That isn't how this is going to go. You do not have the upper hand here. Release Amber, or we will kill every wolf we've taken. You have until noon tomorrow to comply."

"And if we don't?" Gunnar snarls. The girl nods, and another blade slices the throat of the second wolf captive, causing more unnecessary death.

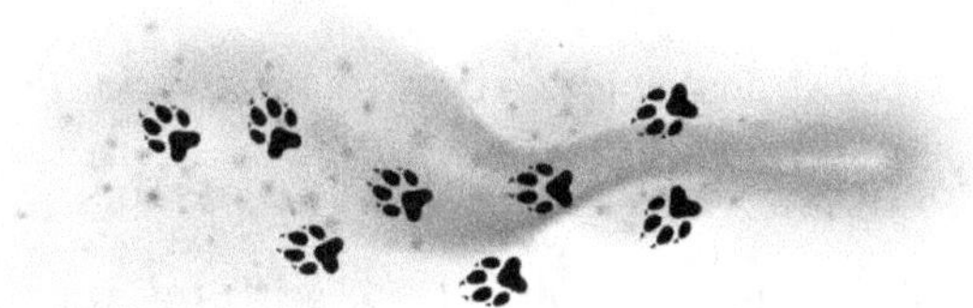

GARNET

I can't hold my magic back anymore, but I don't use it to attack the witches. Instead, I create a force bubble around Gunnar, letting Orym release his hold on the man. *I have him, Orym, you can let go now.* With Gunnar contained, I step toward the witches.

"There was no reason for killing those wolves. This could all be settled peacefully, without bloodshed. We will release Amber, at noon tomorrow. And that is conditional. If I find out that you've harmed another wolf, I will kill her, then come after you." I feel my eyes glow and watch as the girl shivers. She doesn't know what I am, but she does know who I am. Good.

They rush to leave, expecting to be attacked on their way back into the forest. Part of me wants to let it happen, but I find myself holding all the wolves back with my magic. My heart races, and I can feel the strain on my powers. I don't release any of them until the witches are far enough away. Then I send a small tornado after them to disburse their scent so the wolves can't follow.

It would be a trap, designed to capture more of the wolves. Of course, they can't see that. But I can. And I refuse to hand over any more of the people I grew up with. I don't care if they're pissed at me right now and want to attack. I can hold them off.

I face Gunnar as I release the bubble from around him. "I understand that you're angry, but you were making it worse. They have a camp full of your people. You need to remain calm and hold your tongue, so that your people don't pay for your actions."

I turn my back on him without waiting for a response. I feel more powerful than I ever have before. It's like knowing my heritage has given me a new hold on the magic that courses through me. I walk to the training center without looking back. One of the wolves makes a move to jump me, but they're stopped by an invisible forcefield a few feet away.

Ry laughs and I hear Orym snarl at the wolf. I'm not concerned, leaving them to deal with that issue. I need to talk to my aunt. It's about time she gave me some answers. I glance over my shoulder to see James following Grammy back into the cabin. I'm glad they're getting along. I'm sure that she's on our side.

I storm into the barn that serves as a holding cell for our prisoner. I see her face light up when she sees me, then watch the fear creep into her eyes. "Amber," I say quietly.

"What do you want?" she spits.

"I want answers, and you're finally going to give them to me." I stare at her, waiting for her snarky reply.

"Why would I tell you anything?" she asks, her voice trembling a little.

I take a step closer to the cage and send electricity across my skin. "Because I know what I am now." I watch the fear spread from her eyes to her face. "And you should be afraid."

"I don't know what you're talking about," she whimpers.

I laugh at her, then move my hands slowly across my face. My features morph into her dead sister, my mother, Ruby. "You don't know what I'm talking about? Don't lie to me, Amber." Her eyes go wide at being face-to-face with the woman she killed.

"What do you want to know?" she whines. "I'll tell you anything. Please don't hurt me." I thought that her fear would make me happy, but it doesn't. It just makes me sad.

"Who is my father?" I ask forcefully.

"I don't know. I told you before that I have no idea who my slut sister was fucking." Her voice is sharp, but I know what she's hiding.

I wave my hands in front of my body and we're standing in the exact spot where she met my father, near the pink stream. "You're a horrible liar, Amber." I let the glamour of my mother drop, so that my aunt is looking at me now.

"I'm not lying," she insists.

"Amber, I've read your journal, and Ruby's. I know you were both dating my father. I can't help that he was a colossal dick who played you both. But I will not let you lie to me." I zap her with electricity, and she drops to her knees. I wave my hands again and we're back in the barn where she's locked in a cage.

"Fine," she winces. "His name is Briar Novus. He was the Fae prince when you were born. And he loved me, not Ruby. She seduced him and trapped him with you."

Well, I have a name now. Maybe I'll be able to find something about Fae royalty in the books Grammy has. I can't even consider what her words mean for me. If my father is a Fae prince, what does that make me?

"I'm not worried about what you think happened. I want the facts. He was dating you both, then Ruby got pregnant. He dropped you, didn't he?" I can tell from her flinch that I'm right. "Don't worry, you don't have to answer that."

"Let me go. Take these cuffs off and set me free, otherwise my people will kill your precious wolves," she threatens.

"Oh, they've already told me that. And I believe them. But I'm not done with you yet." I pause and step closer, causing her to step back. "What do you want with the wolves?"

She shakes her head. "You have no idea what you're dealing with here."

"Tell me, now." She shakes her head again.

I zap her with more electricity and she doubles over on the ground, holding her stomach. I know that she's not going to tell me anything useful.

Six
MISTAKES

JAMES

After Garnet's conversation with Amber, we have confirmation that Garnet is half Fae, but little else. We pour over the books Grammy lent me, searching for Briar Novus in them. While there is mention of the family being Fae rulers, there is no specific mention of Briar. I'm not certain he even exists. Amber could have been lying.

Since negotiating with the cult is useless, we continue our search while Gunnar and his wolves prepare for Amber's release. The last thing I want is to let her go, but we have no choice. I've already called my brother and tried to push our operation ahead. The vamps refuse to move any sooner. Eli will hold them off until he's sure it's the exact right time.

Dec tells me that they've been working on getting a mole into Amber's camp. He won't confirm if they've been successful, but I know from experience that they won't give up until they are. I'm also certain they won't just use one mole. If Kayden has any influence, they'll have a vampire operative and a wolf one.

At this point, all we can do is wait and study. I hate it, because I can see how hard this situation is on Garnet. She's holding up better today. I think the discovery of who and what her father is has given her something else to focus on for the moment. But I know that Luca is not far from her mind. He never is. I would be upset or jealous, but I understand their connection. They loved each other before they ever knew that they were fated to be together.

Being that close to someone for that long then having them ripped away is enough to make a person crazy with grief. At least he's alive. I hope. We know that with Amber, there are no guarantees. But she has to suspect that Garnet would kill her if she harmed Luca. It didn't stop her followers from beating him, but he was never the actual target. He just stepped in to take the abuse for those who couldn't survive it.

I'm shocked when Orym and Ryland join us as we study the books about Fae. I can tell that Ryland is forcing Orym to be here, but I'm not sure that Garnet sees it. His reaction to her heritage was offensive to say the least. She deserves better, and I hope that he makes up for it. If not, her heart will be even more broken than it is over Luca.

The four of us sift through the books, noting anything interesting that Garnet needs to be tested or trained on. There isn't enough information on the royal family to know for sure if Amber lied, but there isn't anything to prove she did, either. So, we're back at square one with Garnet's father. I'm not too worried about it, since we've proven that she has Fae powers and is learning to use them.

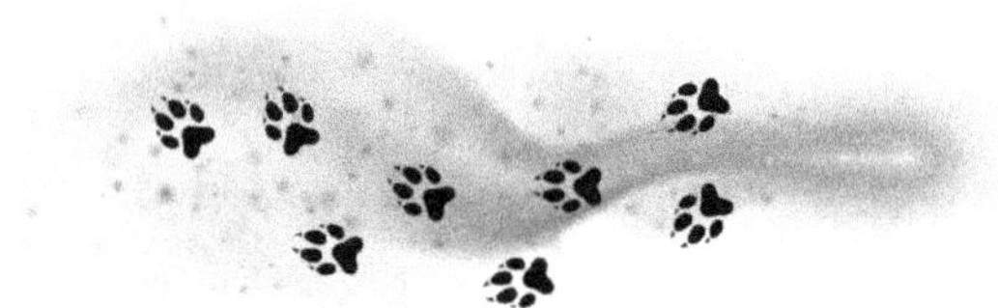

LUCA

This strange man makes me nervous. I don't know why, but I feel like I should definitely not make a deal with him of any kind.

"And you're absolutely right again, my boy. No deals. An exchange, yes, but no requirements or expectations. Just two friends helping each other out."

"Stop reading my mind, would ya? It's unnerving," I growl.

"Here, as a gesture of good will, and to prove I'm not trying to trick you," he says, waving his hand over the bracelet on my wrist. It heats up and turns red, burning my arm, then it falls o ff.

"Ow! What the fuck?"

"I'm sorry, that was the only way to break through the magic and remove it, since I wasn't the person who put it on you," he offers.

I shake all over, allowing my body to shift into my wolf form. It feels amazing, like being myself again, since my wolf has been kept from me for the past few weeks. I'm not even really sure how long I've been away from Red. I just know that I have to get back to her. And this guy is going to help me.

I stalk forward, backing him up against a tree. I bare my teeth at him and growl. "Wait, please. Let me explain. Then you can choose to help me or not, and I'll send you home."

I shift back and grab his shirt, pulling him to my face. "What the fuck are you playing at? Now you just want to talk to me, then you'll send me home? No strings attached?" I can't just believe him. He could be lying to me the way Amber lied to Red.

He nods his head and swallows hard. "Please." I let go of him and take a step backward.

"Talk," I order, dropping onto the ground and sitting. He sits across from me and starts to explain what he wants.

"I really should be telling her this, but there's no time. You see, I am Garnet's father. My name is Trevan, and I need your help to protect her from the witch who wants her powers."

"Amber," I add.

"Yes, you know her? Then you know how twisted and crazy she is. We have to keep Garnet away from her at all costs." I can see the panic on his face, and almost don't want to tell him what's already happened.

"It's too late for that. The only option now is to take Amber out, permanently."

He looks at me for a moment, confusion passing across his sharp features. In any other situation, I would have called him beautiful. There's a hint of Red's features in his, but she's softer and more rounded. I'm guessing like her mother.

"Oh, dear, I'm too late. What can we do?" he asks, wringing his hands.

"You can come back with me and help us fight against Amber and her cult of followers." I can tell he doesn't like that idea.

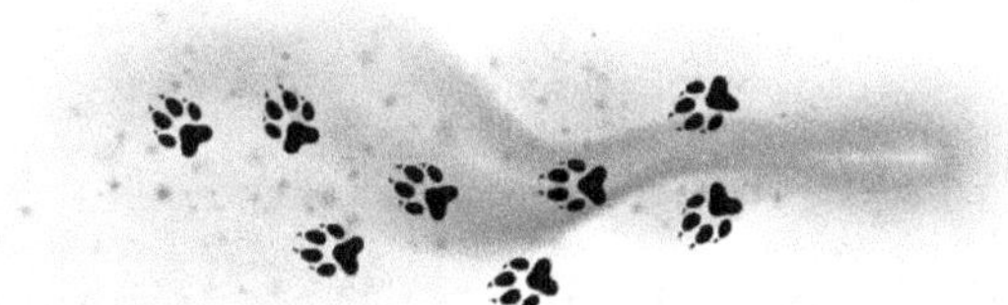

GARNET

I decide to let Gunnar handle returning Amber to her people. I'm not taking a chance that they will attack one of my mates while trying to get the upper hand. I know it's cowardly of me, but I have to save my strength so I can fight her when it's time. I feel like there's a battle coming, but I don't know when or where. I'm not even sure why. But that's not important right now. What is important, at this moment, is getting Luca back.

We have to rescue all of the wolves, vampires, and humans who have been taken. And we need to do it as quickly as possible. I know that Eli wants the timing to be perfect, but I can't stand waiting. It's worse since I know they're abusing my mate. Who knows what else they're doing to him. This situation is impossible, and I have to prepare.

"I'm going to figure out the bomb spell," I announce, putting the Fae book down that I've been reading.

"What?" James asks.

"No, it's too dangerous," Orym insists.

"Okay, what do you need from me?" Ry answers. I did not expect him to be the supportive one here, but I'm relieved. My big bad wolf has always been the one I've butted heads with. It's nice to have a different reaction to my plan.

"I need a large area to practice it, where I'm not going to destroy homes or set things on fire. Can you figure out a good place?" I turn to the other two. "I know this isn't what you want to happen, but it's the only way that I can face Amber and get Luca back, along with the other victims. I've tried everything else, and I'm certain that this is the one thing that will work."

I watch their faces as they process my explanation. "I don't know," Orym says.

"Do you trust me?" I pause, seeing the expression on his face. He doesn't trust me. Because I'm Fae. Great. "Don't answer that. Just give my idea a chance. If I practice it for a few days, and can't do it, I'll give it up in favor of something else. Okay?"

He seems satisfied with that compromise, and James no longer looks shocked at the idea. This is good. I need all three of them on board for what's going to happen next. I will figure this spell out, even if it kills me. I don't have a death wish, but I do have a desperate need to save my missing mate and the others who have been taken from their families.

This is my purpose, and I will not give up. I don't want to die, but if that's what it takes to get these people home, I will gladly sacrifice myself. I refuse to tell them that, because that will be the fastest way to get them all turned against me. And I don't need that.

A knock at the door interrupts our conversation, and I'm happy for it. I'd rather not have my mates asking too many questions about what I'm planning to do. James answers the door, letting Gunnar inside.

"Amber is back with her people. They didn't exchange any wolves or information for her. I can't believe you just let her go like that. Now we'll never get Vincent back," he says with a growl.

Ry steps up to him, but I jump to my feet. "She's my problem, and I'm handling it. Unless you want more trouble, you'll stay out of my way and let me take care of it." I know this is the worst possible thing I can say to him, but I'm tired of walking on eggshells where this man is concerned. If his fragile ego can't take my attitude, he can leave my home.

"What did you just say to me?" he snarls.

I can't help but smirk, because there is literally nothing that he can do to me for anything I say to him. "You heard me."

"I see. Ryland, I'm going to need you to clean up the training course tonight after everyone is finished. Orym, you'll be cleaning the training center. Report to my cabin at dusk." Gunnar's barked orders make me jump, then he turns and walks away.

Well, that backfired. It could have been worse, though. At least it was just a little cleaning. That won't be so bad for either of them.

"Thanks for that," Orym says before walking outside.

"What's the big deal? I mean, it's not like I wanted him to give you extra work. I'm just tired of him talking to me that way," I argue.

Ry takes my hand and pulls me to him. "It's okay. Orym will forgive you. But you have to understand that the two of us are taking the punishments that Gunnar used to give to you. So, when he says clean the training course, he means,"

I break in, "With a scrub brush and a bucket. Fuck. I wasn't thinking."

The one time in my life that I wasn't worried about how my actions would affect someone else, and I've made things worse for my mates. I feel awful, but there's nothing I can do about it now. Except go with them and help with their punishments. But I can't be in two places at once.

James must be tuned in to me today. "I'll go with Orym. You can go with Ryland. It's okay, I'll talk to him. He can't stay mad forever. We'll get through it."

"Yeah, maybe you can use your magic to get things done faster," Ry suggests.

I roll my eyes at him, then consider his words. Maybe I could use my magic to clean both areas faster than if my mates have to do it themselves. It's not a bad idea, especially since this is my fault. I wonder if it'll work, or if I'll just make a bigger mess.

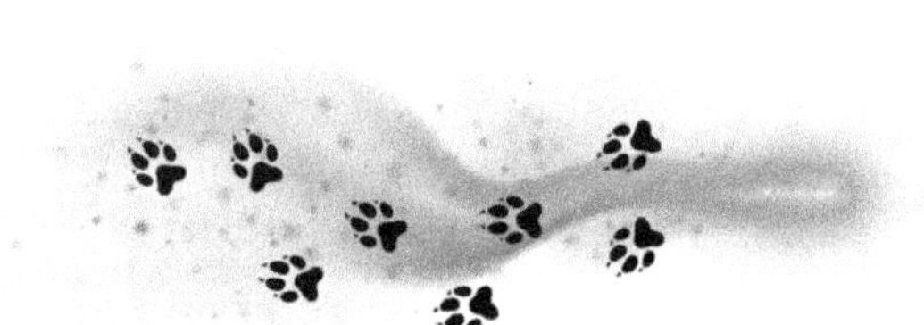

RYLAND

While I'm not thrilled about the extra work my alpha just gave me, I am excited for the opportunity to get Red a different type of practice for her powers. Maybe if she can use them to clean, she'll be able to figure out how to make other things work the way she wants.

Red's determination to learn the spell that got us kicked out of Midnight is invigorating. She seems to be more herself than she has been since Luca was taken. I have to find a way to get him back. Since I believe she's still the best option for that, I'm going to be as supportive as possible. In this case, that means finding an abandoned warehouse where Red can practice her explosion spell without burning down the forest.

As soon as Gunnar leaves, I step outside and pull out my phone. I wish there were other options, but Kayden is really my only friend outside of the pack.

"I need a favor," I say as soon as he answers.

"Ryland, it's nice to hear from you. We're doing well, thanks for asking," he responds.

"Sorry, you know I don't do small talk. I'm trying to get Garnet ready to take on Amber. I can't do that without a place for her to practice magic where she can't hurt anyone. Can you help me with that?"

There's a pause, then he answers. "I can see why you're calling. I can't override Eli's decision to keep her out of our home. But I may have an alternative. I own a warehouse on the other side of the river, away from the city. I used it for storage for a while, but it's been cleared out recently. I'll text you the address and the security code. You can take her there to practice. It should be safe enough."

"I can't thank you enough for this. I'll take care of any damages, I promise." I mean the words, although we both know that I don't have any money, since I live on pack land and work for the alpha.

"Just make sure she's ready. We don't have much more time. Eli and Vik have almost pin pointed the day we need to move on them. We'll talk soon." He disconnects the call and I stare at my phone, watching the text he mentioned come through.

Now that we have a location to practice, I can breathe a little easier. With our training issue solved, we have to get ready for tonight's work. It's a relief that James offered to help, and it will give him a chance to talk to Orym about Red being part Fae. Orym is still struggling to accept that, and it's putting a strain on his relationship with all of us.

I don't know what we can do to fix the issue, but something has to happen. He couldn't even tell her that he trusts her earlier. That was like a slap in the face.

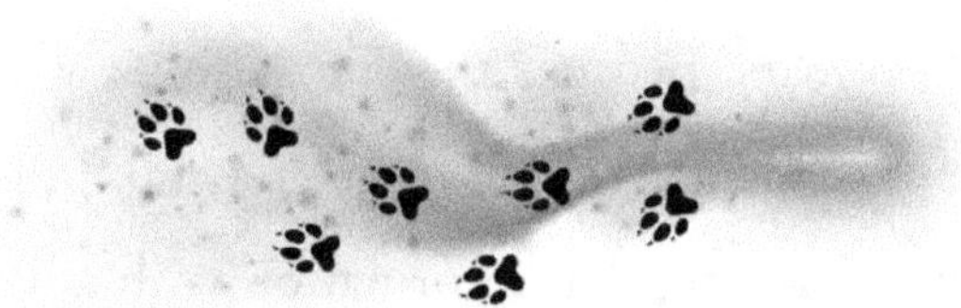

ORYM

I know I'm being unreasonable. I'm an ass. Understood and agreed. However, I can't stop myself from storming out after Gunnar drops his punishment bomb on us. All because Garnet couldn't keep her mouth shut. It's not her fault, really. I know that, but still. It's hard to accept that I'm being punished because of something someone else did.

Of course, now I know how she's felt her entire life. That thought pushes me out the door and down the path before anyone can chase after me. I don't want to be an ass toward her, but I'm not sure how to wrap my head around her being part Fae. The stories my family used to tell about them are horrible.

I'm not surprised that Fae are real. I knew they were. I've known for years. Because they're the ones who killed my grandparents and almost killed me as a cub. I just didn't see the point in sharing that information with anyone. I don't understand why they're reappearing now, though. That was nearly thirty years ago.

Right around the time when Garnet was born. I stop walking and stare into space. That's why the Fae were in our forest. They were searching for her after Ruby had left her with Grammy. My grandparents and I were in the wrong place at the worst possible time. It's the only thing that makes sense.

I know I shouldn't blame her for what happened to my family, but it was her people who did it. I can't just let that go, can I? I've held on to this hatred my entire life. I struggled with the scars on my arms and legs. Yes, they've faded now, but I know exactly where they are. Logically, I know this isn't Garnet's fault.

But my heart refuses to accept that she's one of those monsters. She can't be. There has to be another explanation. I pace back and forth on the path as I try to work out something that makes sense. There is nothing else that makes sense. She's not only part Fae, but she's one of their princesses. That is the one thing that does make sense. They were searching for her because Amber killed her mother, and maybe her father too.

How am I going to get past this? I have no idea, but I'm going to have to. For Garnet's sake and my own. We're bonded, and that's permanent. It's not like I can turn it off and walk away. That's not an option for fated mates. At least not after completing the bond.

If I'm being honest, I don't want to walk away from her. I want to run to her and beg her to forgive me for being an idiot. But I'm scared of her, too. What if that Fae power corrupts her and she's not my Garnet anymore?

I can't let the what ifs control me. I have to make a decision and stick with it.

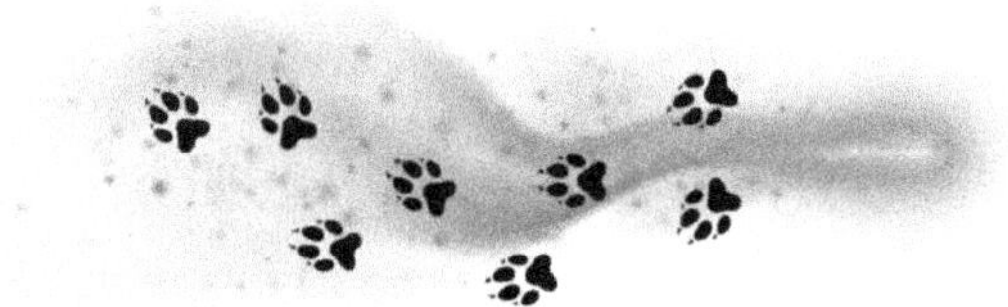

GARNET

I'm relieved that Ry isn't mad at me for getting him assigned extra work. I wish I could find a way to get Orym to accept my new discoveries, too. He's just so against the Fae, and I don't know why. But maybe he'll talk to James tonight and they'll work something out.

I follow Ry to the wolves' obstacle course, knowing that Gunnar won't be there. He never oversees punishments himself. The worst that will happen is one of his loyal subjects will tell him that I came with Ry and that James went with Orym. Hopefully that doesn't make things worse for them.

This situation is hard enough to maneuver without Gunnar pushing my buttons and causing problems. Although, I know that this one is my fault. I shouldn't have said anything to him. I've let so much go over my life. Why couldn't I do that this time?

I'm starting to care less and less about his opinion, though. I just have to make sure that my mates don't suffer for it. I wish there was a way for us to be free of him, but that's not possible. He's the territory's alpha, and all the wolves have to follow him. Unless one of them challenges him. I wonder what that would look like.

When we get to the course, there's a bucket and a rag waiting for Ry. If he uses those to clean the course, it will take all night. But that's the point. Gunnar is flexing his power, and proving that he's the alpha. Well, I'm going to use my magic to do the cleaning for us, and we'll be done in no time.

"I'm not sure how to do this," I admit, looking from my hands to Ry and back. I thought I would just know what to do, but I don't.

"Think about what you want to do, then about how you need to do it. You've got this. Take a breath and figure out a plan," he offers. I'm really liking this supportive side of Ry. I hope I get to keep it after we're done dealing with Amber. I would hate for him to go back to being a total ass when this is all over.

I take a deep breath, then really consider what he's asking me to do. I need to scrub every surface of the metal and wooden structure that serves as a training course for the wolves. There are platforms, ropes, and obstacles. I consider each section, realizing that I'll have to do it in phases to get it right.

For the first section, I focus on the metal bar that has wooden steps attached to it. This ladder leads to the first platform. I need to pull the dirt from the steps and scrub the mud from the metal bar. I take a deep breath, then concentrate on forming a small cannon of water that will spray off the structure from the top to the bottom without creating a giant puddle of mud underneath.

As I work, Ry stands back and watches. He's trying not to get in my way or distract me. I work quickly, cleaning each section before pulling the water from the ground and drying up the mud. Walking slowly around the course, I tackle each section in turn, until I'm back at the beginning.

"Wow, you figured that out pretty quickly," Ry states. "That barely took two hours."

"Your advice helped. Now let's go help Orym get done." I lead the way to the training center. When we open the door, I hear Orym and James stop talking. I wonder if this was a bad idea. I turn to Ry, "Maybe we should leave."

"No, love. You made this mess, now you're gonna clean it up. And the two of you are going to do it together. James and I will wait outside." He nods at James, who follows him outside, leaving me alone with Orym.

It feels awkward and I hate it. I want to pull him into my arms and kiss him, but I know that's not what he wants right now. Instead, I start at the ceiling and work my way through the training center, using my magic to clean it the same way I did the training course outside. I can feel the strain on my power, but I refuse to slow down.

I will do this so that he doesn't have to. It's the only way to prove that I wasn't trying to get them in trouble with Gunnar.

"I know you weren't trying to get us in trouble. And I don't even care about the punishment. I'm struggling with what your father is. I don't know how to handle it. I'm sorry." The quiet words hit me like a hammer.

I freeze, dropping the magic. "What?" I ask, feeling stupefied.

"It's not you. I'm the problem, and I don't know how to fix it. I've had bad experiences with Fae. I know that you're not them, but it's hard to separate in my head."

I blink slowly, trying to process what he's said. "You've had bad experiences with Fae? I didn't think anyone knew they were real."

"I was a kid, and didn't want anyone to know, so I kept it to myself. Then as time passed, I pushed the memory away. I remembered a little while after you discovered what you are. They killed my grandparents, Garnet. They almost killed me."

I understand now why he's so adamant that I can't be one of those people. He can't equate the difference between me being half Fae and the full Fae that killed people he loved.

"I don't know why that happened, Orym, but I am sorry for it. If I could change it, I would. I care about you, and I hate seeing you upset. If this is too much for you, I completely understand." My heart breaks when I say the words, but I mean them.

"I don't think you do. It's not as easy as that. Even if this was too much, there's no way out for me. We're already bonded. That's forever," he insists.

"It doesn't have to be."

LEARNING NEW TRICKS

LUCA

My friend isn't keen on going home with me. "I'm afraid I can't do that," he insists. "But I can send you home, if you'd like."

"Why can't you come with me?" I ask, feeling suspicious. With everything I've been through, I thought I'd finally found an ally. Besides, what if Red has accepted that I'm gone and is moving on with her life?

"The time isn't right for me, yet. Soon, I will join your fight. But not until the time is right. Fae cannot simply walk through portals the way others can." His explanation sounds legit, so I let it go.

"Can you send me home now?" A spark of home ignites in me, even with my doubts.

My friend nods and waves his hands. A shimmering circle appears, and I can see the forest on the other side of it. "Is that the witches' or the wolves' territory? I can't go back to being a prisoner." Panic shoots up my spine. My heart is racing and I'm struggling to catch my breath.

Instead of responding, Trevan moves the portal a few feet to the left, and I can see my cabin. It's the wolves' territory for sure. "Do I just walk through?"

He's looking at me with a pained expression. "Yes, hurry. I can't hold it open much longer." I take his encouragement and run through the portal, collapsing as soon as I'm through it. I turn my head, but the shimmering window to another realm is gone. I'm alone here, and it's quiet. Almost too quiet.

Dragging myself to my feet, I debate my next move. Amber won't know that I'm gone yet, or so I hope. Her followers can't track me here, can they? I have no idea. I know that they aren't allowed on pack lands, but I'm not sure that they care about the rules. It seems as if they're trying to start a war.

Maybe I should head to Ryland's cabin. I'm pretty sure that's where everyone else will be if they made it home. I find myself stalking into my own cabin, showering, and changing into clean clothes. I'm nervous about seeing everyone again. It's almost like going on a first date, but with people you've known all your life.

I know that I can't tell anyone how I got here, or about my Fae friend. But I wonder if Red remembers him. We spent so much time with him that I'm shocked that I could forget. I push the thoughts away as I walk down the path to Ryland's cabin. I'm exhausted and not looking forward to dodging all the questions I know I'm going to get.

The lights are on in the living room when I arrive. The sun set while I was showering, but I'm not afraid of the dark. I walk up to the door, feeling awkward again. No, this is my home now too, until they tell me differently.

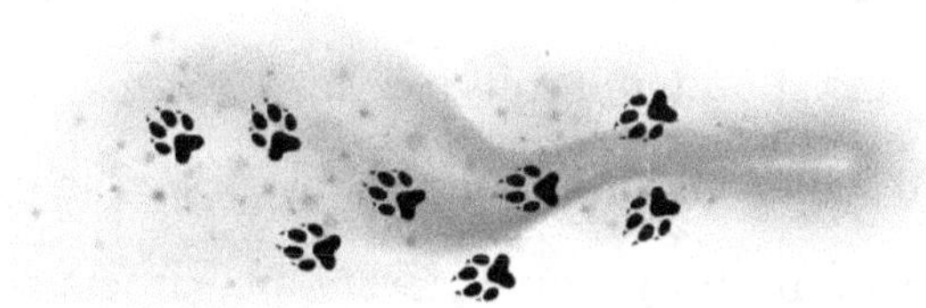

RYLAND

We finish cleaning up and walk back to the cabin in silence. Orym and Red still aren't really talking. I can tell that James didn't make much progress with him. But our extra jobs are done, and Red feels a little better since she helped. It was good practice for her magic, too.

Once we're inside and settling in to watch a movie before we go to sleep, there's a noise outside. The four of us look at each other and wait, anxious that Amber may have sent one of her followers to watch us, or worse, to attack while we were sleeping.

The door opens slowly, and it takes me a minute to register Luca standing there. He looks as awkward as I feel right now. "Luca!" Red shouts and runs to him.

Before she reaches him, he collapses. We carry him inside and settle him on the couch. Everyone gathers around him, checking to make sure he's not injured. James is the only one of us with medical experience, so we turn to look at him.

"It looks like he's just exhausted and weak. Probably from the lack of nutrients while he was being held by Amber." James' explanation makes sense.

"Is there anything we can do to help him?" Red asks.

James shakes his head. "We just have to wait it out and be ready with food and water when he comes to."

When he starts to stir, everyone springs into action. "Where am I? What happened?" Luca asks, looking up at us.

"You're finally home. We've been preparing a rescue mission for weeks. Eli refuses to let anyone move until he knows exactly when the best time is. It's been so frustrating," Red admits.

"I want to help with the rescue. Maybe I can talk to Eli and tell him what little I know. It could help," he offers.

Red stays by his side, constantly touching him, even though he looks uncomfortable. I don't think she notices.

"That can wait until morning. For now, you need rest and nourishment." Orym delivers a plate of pasta that we'd had for dinner, warmed up, along with a glass of water.

Luca happily accepts the plate and starts eating. I wonder how long it's been since he had a full meal, or an actual bed to sleep in. I don't want to push, but I know we're all dying to know.

"If you feel like talking, we'd be happy to listen," I offer. I'm glad that I got to it first, because Red looks annoyed, as if she was planning to grill him until he answered all of her questions. I have a list of questions for him, too, but he needs to recover first. Something tells me he went through more than we know abou t.

"Of course, he's going to tell us all about it, aren't you, Luca?" she insists. He winces at her question, and I step in again.

"Red, we have to let him rest and recover first. His health is more important than answers."

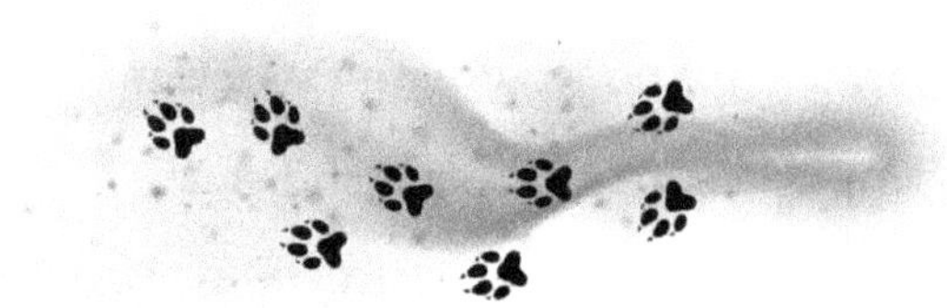

GARNET

Ry's admonishment hits me hard. Why wouldn't Luca want to tell us everything? And why does it seem like Luca is shrinking away from my touch? Luca is home. I'm thrilled and terrified by what that means. We can finally be a family, the way the Goddess meant.

Granted, we still have to rescue the other wolves, along with the vamps and humans who have been kidnapped. "I just wanted to know how you managed to escape. That's not unreasonable, is it?"

Luca stares at the floor but doesn't say anything. Ry touches my shoulder and I turn to face him. "We have to give him time. He got away and he's home now. That's all that matters."

I can tell that my other three mates are having a debate through the bond, but they've all blocked me from hearing it. I guess that leaves me more time to focus on Luca and making sure that he's okay. "Fine, I'll let it go." I return my attention to Luca. "Are you injured? Is there anything I can do for you?"

He finally looks at me with a sad smile. "I'm okay. Just tired."

"We know what they did to you. Eli managed to get drones into the camp and we saw a lot of what went on," James tells him quietly. Luca's cheeks turn red, but he doesn't say anything.

"None of that matters now. You're home and safe. That's what's important. If you need medical attention, all you have to do is tell us. James can take care of it," I offer. "Otherwise, we'll let it go."

"Like I said, I'm just tired," Luca insists. "Is it okay if I sleep out here on the couch?"

"What? Why?" I ask, before Ry interrupts.

"Whatever you need to make you more comfortable," Ry tells him. Orym leaves, returning with a pillow and blanket. He sets them on the couch next to Luca.

Tears fill my eyes at this obvious rejection. But this shouldn't be about me. It should be about Luca. So, I push them down, blinking the moisture away and smiling at Luca. "Anything you need."

Orym is strangely silent throughout this interaction, which tells me that they're still having their conversation. I'm dying to know what it is, but I refuse to let Luca know that they're blocking me out. All I want is to be happy with my mates. Is that too much to ask for?

Luca stands and drapes a blanket over the couch. He wants us to leave him alone, but I can't. he just got back. I can't risk losing him again. Ry gives me a look and jerks his head toward the bedroom. I sigh, but follow him to the doorway.

James is right behind us, but Orym hangs back for a minute, and I hear Luca say something to him. "Of course, just give me a moment."

Ry drags me into the bedroom. James stops to talk to Orym, and I lean closer to hear. "He asked me to stay with him. I don't know if he'll talk or not, but I don't think he wants to be alone. I'll sleep out here with him tonight."

I turn away, not waiting for James to respond. My heart is breaking as the tears I thought I'd avoided stream down my face. I turn away from both of them and walk to the window. I don't want to be alone, either, but I want all of my mates with me. I can't have that right now, and while I understand why, I don't have to like it.

"Red? Talk to me. What's wrong?" Ry's warm hand presses against the small of my back as he turns me around and wraps his arms around me.

"I'm so happy he's home and devastated that he doesn't want to be around me," I sob into his chest.

James presses against my back and I feel his hands rubbing up and down my arms. "It's not like that. He's just overwhelmed and tired. Probably in shock too. I think we just need to give him some time to recover. Then he'll be back to himself."

I want to believe James, but something bothers me about his words. "What were the three of you talking about out there?"

I glance up as they exchange a glance. "Nothing. What do you mean?" Ry defends. But I know better, and they both see it.

"I know you were having a conversation of some kind along the bond while we were out there with Luca. Tell me," I insist.

"It's not important right now," James offers. I shake my head and cross my arms, stepping away from them both.

"It's important to me. So, you can tell me, or I can find somewhere else to sleep tonight." I'm not great at empty threats, but hopefully he'll believe this one. I have no intention of sleeping alone tonight.

They exchange another glance, no doubt discussing if they want to tell me or not. "I can see you two. You're talking along the bond right now. Don't hide it. Just tell me. We're not supposed to keep things from each other," I whine.

James sighs and Ry rolls his eyes. "Fine. Orym is concerned that maybe Amber was able to turn Luca to her side."

Ry holds up a hand. "He's not accusing Luca of anything. Orym just pointed out that it was a little odd how Luca got free the same day we let Amber go. And he thinks we should keep an eye on Luca, that's all."

"That makes sense. Especially with how he doesn't want to talk about anything with us. He's definitely hiding something, but I don't think it's an alliance with Amber," I declare.

"We don't either," James admits.

"But if Luca wants Orym to hang out with him, there's no reason to prevent that. It might help Orym process things faster, too," Ry suggests.

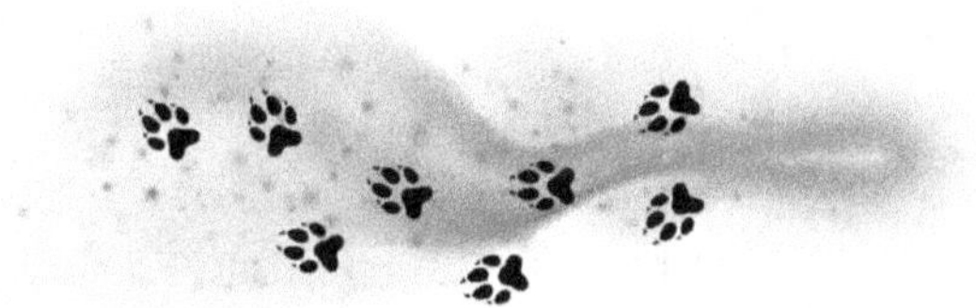

ORYM

I'm suspicious the moment Luca walks into the cabin. I don't want to believe the worst about him, but when he can't even tell us how he got back here, I can't help it. James, Ryland, and I discuss it without Garnet and decide to watch him for now. I hope that I'm wrong about what he's hiding.

I hate feeling so torn about Garnet's heritage. I know that she's not the person responsible for my grandparents' death, even if the Fae who killed them were looking for her. I can't bring myself to tell her my theory. That's too much guilt to put on her. I'm certain that no matter how I explain it, she'll feel guilty.

Right now, I'm focusing on keeping Luca calm and maybe getting him to talk to me. "Is she mad?" he asks when I walk back from the bedroom.

"Nah, just worried about you," I offer.

"I guess you've bonded with her," he says. It's not a question. I wonder how he knows, but don't ask. Instead, I just nod. "Good. She needs you guys."

It's a weird statement and I don't like the connotations of it. "She needs you too," I insist. He shrugs. I can tell this is going to be an argument if I don't let it go. Deciding to let him push for further conversation, I lay out a blanket on the floor and settle in. If Luca tries to leave in the night, he'll have to step over me to do it.

After laying here in the dark for a while, Luca speaks. "You don't trust me, do you?" I lean up and prop my head on my hand, with my elbow on the floor.

"What makes you ask that?"

"Because I can't explain how I got back here. It's okay, I understand. It's just," he pauses, then continues, "the story is so crazy, I'm not sure that I believe it myself."

I stare at him. The hazy glow of the moon is the only light in the room, and it casts an eerie glow on everything it touches. "I'm willing to listen if you want to tell me. I won't push or force you to talk, though."

He closes his eyes and I think he's gone to sleep, but then his voice cuts through the silence. "Do you believe in the Fae?"

I feel like he's somehow read my mind and knows exactly what's been happening here since he's been gone. "What do you mean?"

"I know they're supposed to be myth, but they're real."

"Yeah, they are. How do you know that?" I ask, terrified of his answer.

"One helped me escape. I'm not sure why, but he wants to help Red. He knows about Amber and how dangerous she is."

I ignore the tremble in his voice. I won't call him out for tears; not after what he's been through.

"Do you know who he is?" I fear I already know the answer.

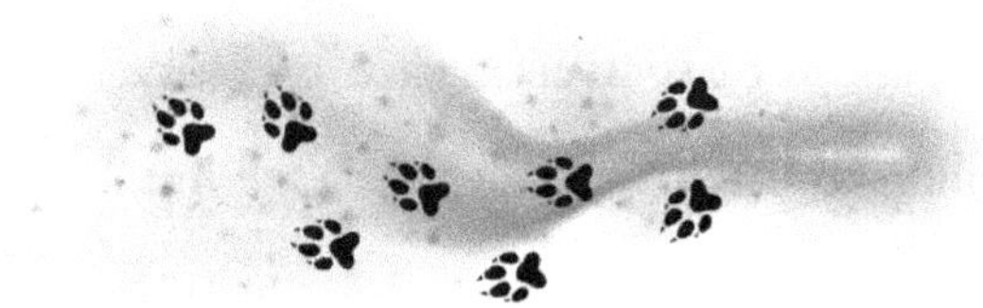

JAMES

It's hard to watch Garnet's heart break again at Luca's apparent rejection. I hope that telling her about Orym's suspicions will help her. I know she feels like he's rejecting her too. I'm sure he's not, but I can't convince her of that.

"I just feel like we should be doing something," she pouts, crossing her arms over her chest and flopping onto the bed.

"I have a few suggestions," Ryland says, making her laugh and roll her eyes.

"I really don't think this is the right time for those suggestions," I laugh. He shrugs and lays back on the bed.

I don't think Garnet is going to get much sleep tonight anyway, because she's worried about Luca. But that doesn't mean I shouldn't try to get her to rest.

"Don't say it, James. I know you're thinking it, and that's enough."

My eyes snap to her and I grin. I love that she's getting to know me so well already. "Then you also know that I'm going to say it, even if you don't want me to. You need to rest. You can't take care of Luca if you don't take care of yourself."

Garnet narrows her eyes at me and sticks out her tongue. "I told you not to say it."

"I can't help myself. Besides, we have a lot to get done before we rescue the captives. Especially if we have to get Luca up to speed on the plan." It's a good point, and I know she can't argue.

That doesn't stop her from trying, though. "I understand that, but what if Luca isn't ready to be pulled into the plan?"

Ryland raises up on his elbow, turning toward Garnet. "Then we don't force it. He can help when he's ready and however he can."

"Do you think that he can't tell us what happened because he's scared? Or do you think that he's decided he doesn't want me because we didn't rescue him?" Her words are quiet, accented by the quiver in her voice.

"Oh, love. I think he's overwhelmed tonight. If he's in shock, he may not know how he got here. As for deciding he doesn't want you—there's no way. I saw the way he looked at you when he came into the cabin. He's scared, sure, but it's more that he thinks you won't want him," I explain. I can't say how, but I'm certain that's what Luca's problem is.

"You really think he's worried I won't want him? That's not possible."

"We know that. But he may not. So, take James' advice and get some rest. You can spend tomorrow convincing Luca that you love him and you're not going anywhere. Deal?" Ryland kisses her forehead, then turns to face the wall. He's snoring softly within a minute or two.

"He's right, you know," I tell her, walking over to the bed as she scoots to the center.

"I know. But that doesn't mean I like it." Me neither.

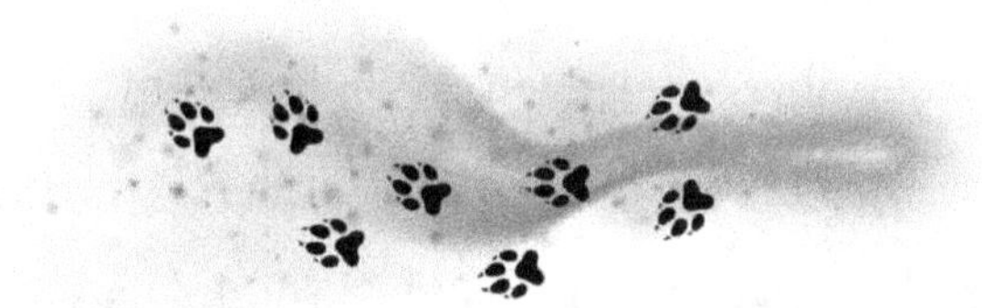

GARNET

My sleep is fitful and not nearly enough. I wake before James and Ry, somehow managing to slip out of the bed without disturbing either of them. I shower and get dressed quietly before heading to the kitchen for coffee.

I'm greeted by the earthy scent of the freshly ground beans Orym prefers. After pouring myself a cup, I take a chair at the table and stare out the window. I'm not sure if Luca is awake yet, and I don't want to disturb him. Orym isn't in the kitchen, but I know he's the one awake, because Luca doesn't like coffee. I can't argue at the quality—this is a delicious cup.

I sit with my back to the room, wondering if I've made a mistake by bonding with these men. If I was unbonded, I could face Amber on my own. Then I wouldn't be terrified of losing the men I'm growing to love. Guilt rips through me over Luca's suffering at Amber's hands. I should have been able to protect him.

Everything has been too much lately. I haven't taken any time to process, and I need to. I have four mates that were selected for me by the Moon Goddess herself. I'm a witch, not a wolf. And I'm half Fae, even though I thought they were just a myth.

I know all of that is true, but I'm not sure that I've really processed any of it. I have to come to terms with my past so I can save my future. I just don't know how to do it. Or how to feel like I'm not doing it alone. You'd think with four mates, a girl wouldn't feel lonely, but I do.

Ry and James try their best, but I need all four of my men to make me feel complete. With Luca hesitating and Orym pulling away, I feel rejected. The pain in my chest is getting worse, and I think it's because I haven't bonded with Luca yet. I won't push him, though. I can't force him to love me. If this pain is what I have to suffer because of what Amber did to him, I will do it silently.

I finish my coffee and still don't hear anything from the living room. I decide to tiptoe in and see if Luca is asleep. The room is empty, and for a moment, my heart starts to race. But the room is empty. The blankets are folded. The room has been cleaned up.

I step out onto the porch and look around. The rustling in the bushes near the cabin tells me exactly where they are. I won't interrupt their run. I know that wolves need that time in their animal form. I sit on the porch steps and listen to the sounds of the forest. It feels strange to be sitting here, not freaking out about what's coming. It's like the calm before the storm.

Garnet? Are you okay? James' soft voice enters my head.

I'm outside. Luca and Orym went for a run, I guess. I'm just listening to the forest.

A moment later, James is sitting on the porch beside me. He drops a sweatshirt over my shoulders, and I wonder how he knew I didn't have one. I smile, remembering that he's always in tune with my needs, even when I'm not sure what they are.

"Thanks," I say quietly.

"I know this isn't easy. We'll get some training in later, and that will help. Unless you want to do a little now?"

"What did you have in mind?" I smirk at him, pulling my powers to me and circling the wind around us for a moment.

"That's a good start. What about something a little bigger?" He's hinting at something, but I'm not exactly sure what it is. I'll just have to try to figure it out.

I wrap my power around me like a blanket, standing and walking into the clear space in front of the cabin. It crawls along my skin, tickling me like a thousand spider legs tapping along my arms and legs. I let the electricity crackle as I raise my arms to the sky and shoot a bolt above my head. "Better?" I smirk.

"Eh, I've seen better," he teases. The fact that he's trying to mask his expression into one of disinterest.

I laugh before sending a low power bolt at him. He jumps and makes a yip sound. "You've seen better? Fine, I'll do something else."

I press my hands together in front of me, trying to decide what I can do to get the reaction I want from him. I don't realize at first that I have an additional audience behind me. By the time I sense Orym, I have a ball of fire between my hands that's almost as big as my head.

"Woah, that's new," Luca says. I turn, dropping the fire on the ground in front of me. I'm not sure if he's impressed or scared, and I don't know how to feel about that.

"She's been practicing every day. The plan was to get stronger so she could take Amber out and save your ass," Ry calls from the door as he exits onto the porch.

"I guess I should have waited for her, then. That's pretty impressive," Luca calls back. I refocus my attention to creating another, even larger ball of fire. If Luca is impressed, I can keep working.

If he'd been scared, I would have insisted on practicing my magic somewhere else away from him. I don't ever want my mates to be scared of me. Which hurts, because I'm convinced that Orym already is. He won't tell me, and that's hard too, but I understand. Alpha males have a real problem with telling someone their fears.

I thought things were getting better between us after I did his cleaning at the training center. We talked and I believed we were working it out.

EIGHT

WAITING GAME

RYLAND

RED GETS SPOOKED BY Luca's praise. Tears fill her eyes, and her hands start to shake. I think she expected him to be scared

of her. With her concentration shattered, Orym walks over to the porch. "We need to talk in private. All of us." His quiet statement sends a shiver down my spine, but I nod.

"Are we ready to check out the training space? We can pick up breakfast sandwiches on the way." I hope there are no objections, because if this is big enough that Orym doesn't want to use the bond to discuss it, we need to get moving.

Once everyone is in the SUV, we get breakfast and head to the warehouse Kayden is allowing us to use. Armed with the security code and a few extra weapons, we march inside. I flip a switch and the entire place lights up. My jaw drops at what I see.

There's a hallway directly in front of us with two rooms on either side. The path opens into a large room that has to be where Kayden trained after he left the forest. There are obstacles set up and what look like mazes. This is not at all what I was expecting.

"Okay, we're here. What's got you so on edge?" Red asks. It doesn't surprise me that she notices the way my hands shake or how jumpy I am.

"Orym said we need to have a family meeting. This is the most secure location for that." My explanation gets nods of approval. We go into one of the conference rooms and sit around a large table while we eat.

"I guess there's no better time than now." Orym turns to Luca. "I hope this doesn't upset you, but I'm going to tell them what you told me last night. Then I'll explain why, because I don't take breaking a confidence so lightly."

Luca's face contorts in pain for a moment, then clears. "I had help escaping," he admits. "I was taken to the Fae realm by a man who claims he wants to help defeat Amber." He locks eyes with Red. "We know him. He used to take us there to play when we were kids."

Shock fills Red's eyes. I know this is a memory she's forgotten and wonder if it's coming back to her now. I'm a little taken by Luca's statement. I'd suspected that Fae were real before, but I had never known anyone to have directly dealt with them.

"What? I don't understand," Red says quietly.

"Now that everyone knows," Orym begins, "I think this Fae man could possibly be Garnet's father." Silence fills the room as we all try to process what he says.

"Wow, that's insane," James says, breaking the quiet. "But I can see how you'd get there."

I stare between Luca and Red, wondering if they knew all this time, or if he'd kept the truth from them. Garnet shakes her head.

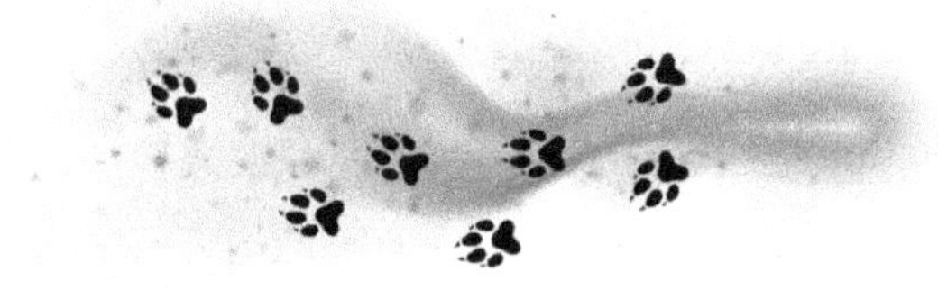

ORYM

"That can't be. There's no way. Wouldn't I have known?" Garnet works her way through her objections and questions all at once. "How could I have forgotten this?"

"I'm guessing Grammy had something to do with that," Ryland offers. He's probably right. That old woman is good at manipulating things and keeping secrets.

"We have no proof that Grammy knows about Garnet's heritage, though. It's easier to believe that the Fae was the one who did it," James insists. I can see that too. It's hard to know who's right here. We may never get the answers we want.

"There has to be a way to find out," Luca says quietly. He's more reserved, and I hate that I basically forced him to tell the others how he got home. He wasn't ready to talk about it, and still isn't. But he doesn't have a choice now, because I made a connection. Guilt eats at me, digging into my heart and making it ache.

I'm not the kind of guy who ever tells someone else's secrets. And I know that while I wasn't the one who did this time, I forced Luca to do it. They all need to know what I'm thinking and how I got to that conclusion, though.

"We could summon him," I suggest. "I have no idea how that works, but I know it's possible. I did a lot of research after my grandparents were killed. If I could have figured out exactly which Fae were responsible, I would have found a witch and summoned them."

"So, it has to be a spell, right?" Garnet's face lights up. "Wait, does that mean that I could just summon my father? If it's the guy who helped Luca, that's fine, but if it's not, we'll finally know." She's rambling, but no one stops her. As she speaks, she starts digging through her backpack and pulls out a book and pencil.

"You're going to write a spell for it?" I ask, surprised that she's so excited to try this. I would have expected her to search for an existing spell in her other books first.

"Maybe. I'm going to jot down some notes and look at some other spells. If I have to write one, I will. I think I can do it, especially if I'm using my blood to call him forth." She looks at the four of us and laughs. "You guys should see your faces right now. I'm not going to bleed myself out. It would only take a few drops to do a blood-to-blood spell. Right, James?"

I forgot for a moment that he's the one who's been helping her go through the books and train while Ryland and I dealt with Gunnar and his ridiculous demands.

James nods, grinning from ear to ear. "Definitely. From what we've studied, it should be as simple as pricking your finger and figuring out what to say. That's the hard part. You don't want to call him to you if he's dead."

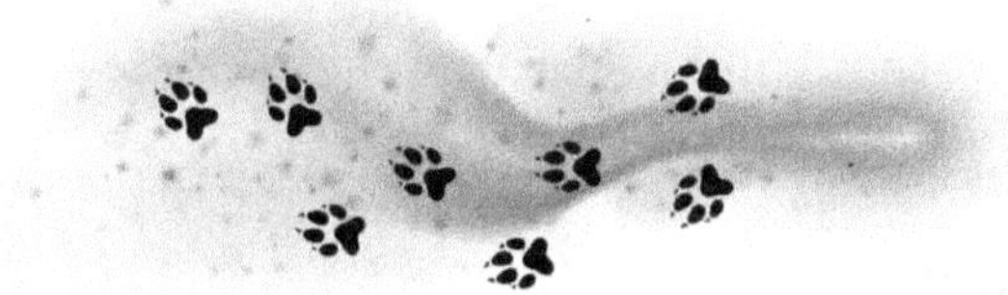

GARNET

I freeze at James' words. What would happen if I called my father to me and he's already dead? Would he come back as a zombie? Are those even real? Shit, I don't want to find out.

"So, it becomes a little more complicated. No problem. I'll just make some notes, and we can revisit that in a while," I say. "Was there anything else we needed to talk about?"

I'm not in a rush to get to training, but I don't want to discuss the possibility that my father is dead and summoning him could be a disaster. James and I need to do more research, and the only way that will happen is if we get training out of the way.

"Luca, are you okay? Can you tell us more about the Fae realm? We thought that Garnet went there a few days ago, but there was no way to be sure." James jumps in, peppering Luca with questions.

"I think I'm in shock. I didn't know that Red was part Fae, and you guys are just tossing it around like you've known forever. I'm gonna need a few minutes to process all of this." Luca pauses, then continues. "I guess, after we found out that Red was a witch, I thought that she was half wolf, and that was why she couldn't shift. This is something else entirely."

My heart drops, and I'm not sure if he's unsure about us, or just needs a minute to adjust. I want to ask, but I'm terrified of the answer. Instead, I let them discuss me as if I'm not sitting right here.

I try to focus on my notes about the summoning spell. There has to be a way to find out if my father is alive before I call him to me. I can't stop thinking about what would happen if he was dead. I don't know how I would react to facing an undead version of my father. My brain keeps picturing Gunnar and that's terrifying.

I shudder, then remind myself that Gunnar isn't actually my father. Closing my eyes, I force the images of a Gunnar zombie away.

I wish I could remember the man Luca told us about. We used to play in the Fae realm. That thought feels strange to me, but I know Luca is telling the truth. Now if I could just remember. Oh! What about a memory spell? I jot down more notes, completely ignoring the conversation happening around me. I write furiously, making notes about how to r-efine the blood-to-blood and make it only call living people. Then I turn a page and write down my thoughts on a memory spell that would return my memories that have been lost or taken.

I have some ideas of how to make that spell work, but need to research ingredients that will help push the intent of the spell further. I note which books I'll have to check, then realize that everyone is staring at me.

"What?" I ask, finally looking up from my book.

"You were muttering a little," James says.

"And you're glowing," Orym points out. What? Glowing? That's ridiculous. I look down at my arm, and he's right. My skin is glowing a faint pinkish hue.

"What the fuck is happening here?" I stand up and back away from the table. I didn't realize that I was muttering when I was writing. And I had no idea I was glowing. Terror grips me, making my heart race as they stare at me.

"Just breathe. It's okay." Luca jumps over the table, landing by my side. "There you go. In, good. And out, there. Again." He does the motions to regulate my breathing, and my eyes follow his hands. After a few breaths, he touches my arm and I collapse into him. I want nothing more than to be in his arms. It's the one place I've always felt protected and safe.

"Okay, the glow is gone. You can open your eyes." Ry's voice breaks through the panic, and I realize that I'm squeezing my eyes shut tightly. When did that happen? I was just watching Luca as he guided my breathing.

"What was that?" I ask as Luca eases me back into my chair.

"The last twenty minutes was a panic attack, but before that, we don't know," Luca tells me. Twenty minutes? What is he talking about?

"What?" I'm so confused and feel lost. It's like they're speaking a different language.

"I told you she wasn't really here," Orym insists.

"She was literally standing right next to me, though," Luca argues.

"Her body was, but her mind or spirit was somewhere else," James agrees. What are they talking about?

"I've been right here the whole time. I haven't gone anywhere," I say defensively. I feel as if I've lost time somewhere, and I don't like it.

Ry holds up a hand and everyone stops talking. "Look, we can argue about this all day, but we're never going to agree. Red, do you know what time it is?" I shake my head and he hands me his phone.

Fuck, we've been here for an hour. I didn't think it had been that long. "What is going on here? It hasn't been that long, has it?" I don't understand how I lost almost an hour.

"You were writing in your book and mumbling something about zombies and memories. We all stopped talking and watched you for about thirty minutes. Then your panic attack took another twenty. So, yeah, it's been about an hour. I understand that it didn't feel like that to you, but I promise, we're not messing with you." Ry's quiet voice bolsters my resolve. I have to figure out how to work these spells.

"We have a lot of work to do today. We should get started," I announce, pushing myself from my chair and walking out into the main room of the warehouse.

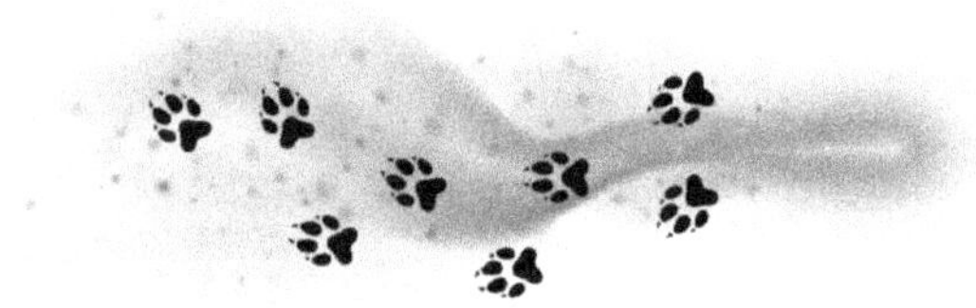

JAMES

Garnet leaves her books and bag in the conference room. With all the security, I think it'll be safe there. I grab my notebook and pen, following her. It's my job to note what works and what doesn't, so I have to stay close. Since she's trying to find a way to blow herself up, I hope the others stay back far enough.

Ryland, Orym, and Luca discuss the obstacles and decide to move a few of them from the center of the room to give Garnet more space. As they work, I speak softly to Garnet, preparing her for what she's trying to do. "You have to clear your mind. You can do this. Focus on what you're trying to do, and let everything else go."

She nods, but I can tell that she's not there yet. I can't let her try this spell if she's not focused properly. Someone could get hurt. "Garnet, listen to me." She locks eyes with me, and I can see how badly she's hurting. The distance with Luca and Orym is hitting her hard. I want to fix it, but I can't make them accept her.

I pull her to me, capturing her lips with mine. I kiss her as if she's the only thing I need to live, because she is. I'm determined to kiss all her worries away. I need her clear headed for this spell to work. I know she won't put off practicing it, so I use my lips to distract her. When she melts into me, I break the kiss. "I think you're ready now," I say.

The dreamy look in her eyes makes me want to take her into a conference room and worship her. But that's not why we're here. Today is about training, not sex. We can take care of that later. What she needs right now is to figure out this spell.

"Okay," she giggles. Good, she's relaxed. I step back as she walks to the newly cleared center of the room. Ryland takes a seat next to me on one of the obstacles. We're close enough to watch without being in her way. I'm not sure where Orym and Luca are, but when Garnet looks around the room, she gives a thumbs up and starts to chant.

As we watch her, a small round flame forms between her hands. The flame grows and expands until it's bigger than her head. I'm starting to worry, because this wasn't how she did this spell before. We didn't discuss changes before, so I'm not exactly sure what I'm trying to judge.

I'm forced to look away as the flaming ball grows larger and brighter. When it explodes, Ryland and I are on our feet and rushing toward Garnet. It must be instinct, because we meet Orym and Luca in the center of the room. Our girl is doubled over with her palms on the ground. Her panted breaths tell me she's alive.

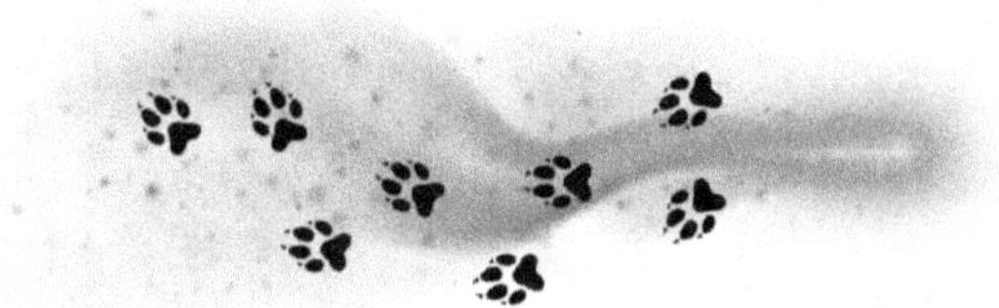

LUCA

Watching Red blow herself up is insane. The ball of flames grows larger and brighter, until I can barely stand to look at it. Then it explodes, and I run toward her. I don't even think. My body just needs to know she's okay. I meet the others as we circle around her. She's collapsed on the ground, panting.

As much as I want to go to her and pull her into my arms, I can't. So much has happened since I was taken, and I don't really know where I stand with her. She's already bonded with the other three, so I'm sure that she needs them more than she needs me right now. I step back and observe as James checks her over for injuries.

I don't know how she can be untouched by the flames. Smoke wafts from her hair and body. But when she stands up, there isn't a mark on her. It's as if the fire didn't touch her at all. I struggle to wrap my head around this as much as I'm struggling with her Fae heritage. My entire life, I'd been convinced that she was like me, but special.

I was half right. She is special. But she's not like me. Red is not a wolf at all. She's a witch-Fae hybrid. It's a strange combination, but I guess if Delilah can be a wolf-vampire hybrid, anything is possible.

My heart aches with need. I want nothing more than to claim Red as my own. But I can't do that, because I wasn't strong enough to protect her from Amber. I couldn't even protect myself. I'm broken now and don't know if I can be repaired.

Knowing that she's safe has to be enough for now. I can't ask for more. I won't ask for more. She deserves to be with men who are more capable than me. I have nowhere else to go, and can't leave her if I try, so I'll stay close and make sure she's okay. But I can't allow myself more than that.

She shakes herself, as if trying to get rid of stiffness. I'm fascinated at how the magic works. I have so many questions that I'll never get to ask. "I'm going again. Back up." Her words push me toward the wall. I can't be the reason she gets hurt here. James said we have to give her space to work on this spell, so I'll keep my distance.

Honestly, I'll keep my distance anyway. There's no point in getting my hopes up for anything to happen between us. I'll just have to be satisfied with having my best friend back. It's not like this is a new situation. I've been pining for her since I turned ten. This is my usual. I'm just so drawn to her, that I can't take myself out of her life. And I know that she wouldn't want that anyway.

We need each other, just not the way I want.

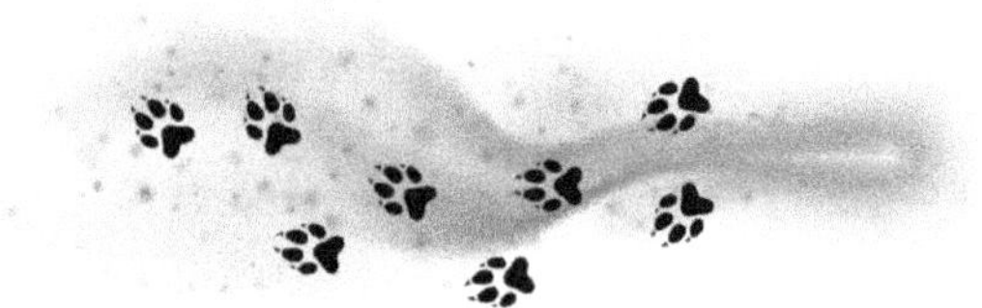

GARNET

I reset myself to do the bomb spell again. As I create the fireball, a phone rings and breaks my concentration. The fire I'm holding shoots out at the wall, barely missing Orym. Fuck. I know he's going to hold that against me now. He'll think I did it on purpose because he's struggling with accepting my Fae parentage.

"Damn. I'm sorry, Orym," I call to him anyway. "Who's calling?"

Ry holds up a hand and points to James walking into the conference room with his phone at his ear. It must be Dec. I wonder if it's about the spy they managed to get into Amber's camp. It feels like we've been waiting forever to figure out the right time and place to attack.

Knowing it's a bad idea, I walk over to Orym, determined to apologize again. As soon as I get close, he grabs my arm and pulls my sweatshirt up. "Garnet, you're burnt. Does it hurt?"

I shake my head. I didn't even know that the fire had touched me. "I'm okay, really." But he doesn't believe me. Instead, he tears the sleeve of my sweatshirt before ripping it off me completely. Fuck, that's hot. Except that now, without the fabric touching it, my arm does burn. "Maybe I'm not as okay as I thought."

Admitting that has him pulling me into his arms. I get exactly what I wanted, just not in the way I wanted it. "I'm sorry for throwing that at you," I say into his chest. He holds me tightly, making sure not to touch my arm.

I feel someone grab my arm and pull it out to the side. Ry is checking the burn to see how bad it is. I can't make myself look. I don't want to know. It hurts worse now than it did when

Orym noticed it. I won't tell them that, because I can see how worried they already are. I won't make that worse.

"Luca, get the med kit. We need burn cream." Ry shouts the order and I catch Luca's movement out of the corner of my eye. Pain lances through me, and I'm not sure if it's my arm or my heart at the fact that Luca was so far away when Ry shouted at him.

I have to give him time. Just like Orym. They both need time to accept or reject me. I can't push the issue. Hot tears stream down my face, and again, I'm torn between the reason for them. Am I crying because my arm burns like a hot poker has been shoved into it? Or is it because I feel like two of my fated mates are rejecting me?

Either way, the tears get me more attention than I want. Orym turns my face to his, wiping my tears away with his thumb. "Does it hurt a lot?"

His question breaks me. Tears fall harder, and I can't answer him. At this point, my heart and arm are competing to see which will kill me first. The burning sensation is intensifying, and I'm sure that I'm being burned alive. My heart is breaking in half, crumbling inside my chest. I can't tell if the tears are making it hard to inhale, or if it's the pain.

"Here's the burn cream." Luca's voice is like a balm for my soul. I know that he loves me, even if he decides to reject our bond. I can't think about that right now. I have to push my heartache away and focus on the physical pain.

Ry gently rubs the ointment onto my arm, and I sigh in relief. Then I scream as everywhere the cream touches lights up the nerves in my forearm. It's like he added gasoline to the flame, and I can't stop it.

"Grab the cooler. Maybe ice will help," Ry suggests, still holding onto my arm.

"Water," Orym says calmly. "It's a magical burn. She caused it, so she'll have to fix it. We need to get her water, and she can freeze it around the burn."

I'm touched that he's been paying attention, but annoyed with myself for not thinking of that. Of course, in my defense, my arm feels like it's being stabbed with red-hot pokers. There's no trace of the emotional pain I was feeling a few minutes ago. All that's left is the searing misery of my arm burning off.

I wonder if I'll be able to save it. James and I have been working on healing spells and potions, but I don't know if they'll be enough. Maybe we should have worried about protection, too. That's something to think about later, when my brain is less occupied by this pain.

Luca returns with the cooler, and Orym eases me to the ground. "What can I do?" he asks, clearly feeling similar panic to mine.

"Hold her other hand. Ryland, keep that hand in yours. I'm going to support her back and pour the water on her arm. Garnet, I need you to freeze this when it covers the wound. Can you do that?" Orym's calm voice eases my panic. I nod, trying to focus on what I'm agreeing to.

"Okay, everyone ready?" He pours the cold water over my arm, and it stabs through my arm. I suck in a breath and grit my teeth. "Okay, Garnet, now."

I know what I need to do, but I have to fight through the pain to get there. I take a deep breath, squeezing Luca and Ry's hands tightly as I try to focus on freezing the water that's covering my arm. I need to make the burning stop.

The water evaporates quickly because of how hot my arm is. The sensation creeps down my arm toward my hand. I have to stop it before I burn Ry. I know he won't let go, even if I set him on fire.

That's enough to kickstart my magic. Orym pours more water on my arm and a thin coat of ice appears.

NINE
TENSION RELIEF

ORYM

WITH GARNET'S INJURY, I'M less concerned with my feelings about her being Fae or even rescuing the missing groups of people. What I care about right now is helping her. And in that moment, I realize that I don't care if she's full Fae. She's my mate, and I've fallen in love with her.

"Good girl, keep the water frozen. Let's do another layer just to be sure."

Sweat pops up on her brow, and I wish there was another witch here to do this for her. I'm worried that if she passes out, her arm will continue to burn until it kills her. We've kept her arm turned so she can't see the worst of it. The flesh is black and split open. The injury is deep and looks a lot like she's been stabbed with a fireplace poker.

I have no idea how to treat magical wounds. "Is James still on the phone?"

Before any of us can move to find out, James comes back into the large, open room we're in. "What happened? Is she okay?" He rushes to us and takes her hand from Ryland. "Oh, love, this looks awful. How bad is the pain?"

She whimpers, struggling to hold the ice magic. "I need to see the wound. Just relax and let the ice fall away."

I don't blame her for shaking her head. Her screams were unbearable. There's no way I can ask her to go through that again. "She's in too much pain to drop it. The ice is the only thing that's helped."

"Okay," he relents. "Hold the ice spell a bit longer. Let me see if I can whip up a potion that will help. I've read the books and know what to do. I may need a boost from you, but I can do the work." She nods at his suggestion, gritting her teeth as she struggles to keep the water frozen.

"Do you need more water?" I ask, not expecting her to answer.

"Please," she pants. I'm not sure how much longer she can hold out. I carefully drip water over her arm and marvel at how quickly she freezes it into the ice that encases her forearm. A slight sigh escapes her lips and she closes her eyes.

I relax a little until I realize that her body just went limp in my arms. "Hurry, James, she's passed out. The ice is melting, and the burn is spreading."

"I should have asked him for a way to call if we needed help. I'm sure he could stop this," Luca whispers. None of us have to ask who he's talking about. I agree with him that his Fae friend could probably be more useful in this situation than we are. But we're the ones Garnet has right now, so we will have to make it work.

James brings his bag over and starts working.

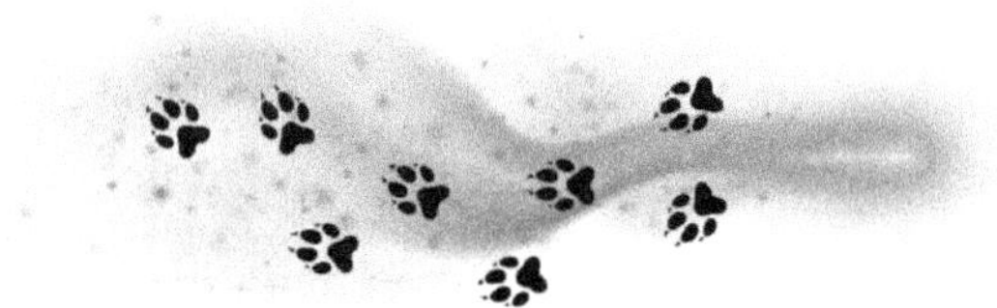

JAMES

I grab my bag and the spell book, rushing back to Garnet's side. The phone call I just got is nearly forgotten with the urgency of this. I have to create a healing potion that will combat fire.

The book tells me which herbs and ingredients to mix. I don't have everything I need, but I'm not afraid to improvise if it means saving Garnet's life. I use my medical knowledge to substitute, and hope for the best. With her unconscious, that means I can't use her magic to help with the potion.

Or can I? A thought occurs, and I grab my pocketknife. When I reach for her hand, Luca stops me. "What are you doing?"

"I just need a couple of drops of her blood to make the potion work. I promise, it'll just be a little prick and then I'll bandage it up." I silently beg the universe to make them let me do this. I can't win a fight against three wolf shifters, no matter how hard I try.

Luca exchanges a glance with Ryland and Orym before nodding to me. He holds her hand over the bowl I'm mixing the potion in. I poke her finger with the tip of the blade, then let a few drops fall into the mixture. I pull out a bandage and cover the injury. Luca continues to hold her hand as I mix the potion together.

Right now, I'm begging the Gods to let this work. I hope there is enough magic in her blood to give it the boost it needs to work with my substitutions. By the time I'm finished mixing the potion, the ice is completely melted from her arm.

Steam rises from the charred area on her forearm, evaporating water escaping into the atmosphere. The flesh under the charred skin glows like charcoal in a grill. Her arm is heating up, and we can see the damage getting worse. I have to use this potion now, before it's too late.

With one last mental call to the Gods, I drip the potion onto the raw, burning tissue. When she continues to burn, I worry that I've messed up and made it worse. "Fuck," I lament.

I close my eyes and think about what I should do next. There has to be a way to stop this and heal her. "I guess we'll have to go to the hospital and see if they can do anything for her."

Luca and Orym object at the same time, "No!"

Then Ryland holds up a hand to get our attention. "Look," he gestures to Garnet's arm. A faint blue glow has started around her arm. The fiery red glow inside her has stopped. It seems to be cooling slowly. "It's working. We just have to give it a few minutes."

As we sit there, staring at Garnet's injury, the blackened skin starts to fall away, leaving fresh, new skin underneath. The angry red blisters fade to pink scars.

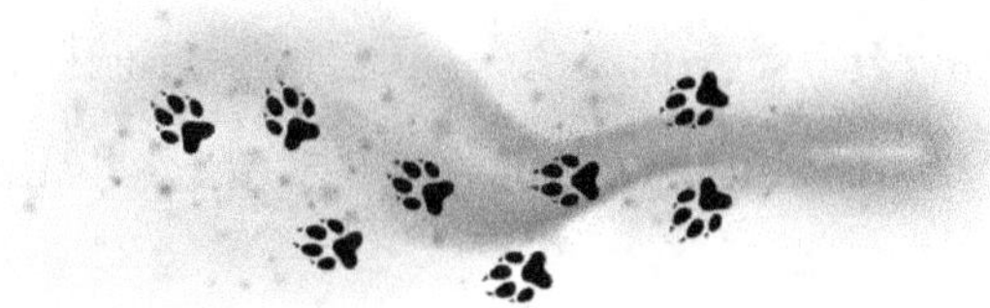

GARNET

I hold onto the magic that's freezing my arm as long as I can before the pain takes me under. In the darkness, I'm convinced that I won't come back. I regret not telling my mates exactly how I feel about them. I want to fight, but I don't know how.

Something pokes my finger. Then a cooling sensation spreads across my arm. The burning stops, and the darkness recedes. My eyes flutter open, and my four mates crowd around me so closely that I should feel claustrophobic, but I don't. I feel loved.

"What happened?" My voice cracks when I try to speak. I'm not sure if I actually say the words or not.

"The phone rang and it broke your concentration. The spell went wrong and set your arm on fire. James made a potion and fixed it, though." Luca's quiet explanation tells me that I did speak.

"What was the call about?" I know how close I just came to losing my life, but I don't want to focus on that right now.

"It was Dec. The spy in Amber's camp gave us the coordinates for our attack. We can move on them tomorrow," he explains. "But you're going to take the rest of the day off. No more training. We saw that you can do the spell. That's what you were working on. Now you're going to rest."

I should argue. There are so many other spells and potions I need to work on, but I'm exhausted and just can't fight all four of them. "Okay. I'll take the day off. But only if the four of you do too." It's not a fair request, but I don't care. If they want me to cooperate and relax, they will too.

"Done." Ry's strong alpha influence washes over the group, and no one argues. They gather our supplies and load the SUV.

Then Luca picks me up and carries me to the car. I wish that it made me feel more connected to him, but I can still feel his hesitation. I want to bond with him, but I can't even make myself suggest it.

I don't want him to commit to me unless it's his choice. I won't force him into a bond that he doesn't want, no matter how badly the rejection hurts me. I sit in the back seat, alone, until James climbs in beside me. He pulls me to the center spot, and Orym gets in on my other side.

I sense that something has changed there, but I can't even begin to hope for that. When he threads his fingers through mine, a few of the cracks in my heart start to mend back together. I don't want to say anything and ruin our progress, so I just steal a glance at him before turning my attention to the front seat where Ry and Luca are whispering quietly.

I want to know what they're saying, but I can't find out without making it obvious that I'm listening. Luca growls and flops back against the seat, then Ry pulls out of the lot and onto the highway. The ride back home is silent. No one makes a sound, even through our bond. Which means that either they're being quiet, or they're talking around Luca and me along the bond.

I push that thought away. Surely, they wouldn't do that.

We get home and Orym carries me inside. I'm beginning to wonder if I'll be allowed to walk at all for the rest of the day. I'm not arguing, I like being carried by my men. "Do you want to watch a movie to relax?" James asks.

"That sounds nice. Is everyone going to watch?" I glance around the room to find that my other three mates are not here. Where did they disappear to?

"Yes. They're getting snacks, drinks, and blankets for us. Which movie do you want?" I feel like he's trying to distract me while the others argue about something, but I can't prove it.

"Hmm. How about the rom-com where the woman is about to be deported and she makes a deal with her assistant to marry her? It's my favorite movie ever." I'll never admit it to my mates, but that leading man gets me hot every time.

"That's a good one," he agrees, pulling the DVD from the shelf and getting it ready to play. The one drawback to living in the middle of the forest is that we can't have satellite TV or even cable. We barely have the internet. I wonder if Eli has some kind of adapter that would help us have better signal. Maybe after this is all over with, I'll ask him.

Ry comes in with an arm full of blankets and pillows. Behind him, Orym carries a tray of snacks. He has chips, candy, and queso, along with my favorite cookies. A moment later, Luca brings drinks. When these guys decide to pamper a girl, they go all out. Luca has six different drinks, and it's clear that the extra one is for me.

I decide that I don't mind being spoiled a little. My heart drops a bit when Luca takes the seat farthest away from me. I've been hoping that we'll have some time to talk. The ache gets marginally better when Orym snuggles close on one side and Ry takes the other. Poor James has to sit on the floor to be close to me.

My brain fixates on the fact that James is sitting in the spot Luca usually takes. It hurts that he's pulling away from me. But at least he's here. And I know that he's safe. If I had to worry about him, I wouldn't be able to relax at all.

Given his reaction to my injury, I'm pretty sure he still cares about me. I'll just have to give him space to make his own decision.

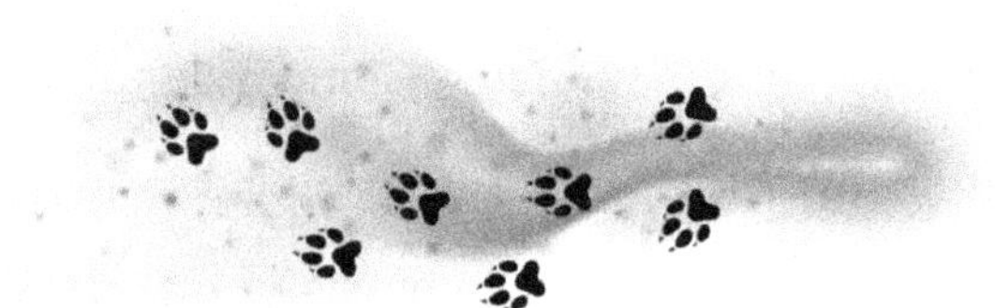

LUCA

I know that at some point, I'm going to have to talk to Red about everything. She deserves that. But I can't do it tonight. I should just leave, but I can't bring myself to get that far away from her. It's killing me to not sit on the floor by her feet.

Feelings of dread take hold inside of me. I'm not what she deserves. I can't be what she needs. I don't know where these thoughts came from, but I can't get away from them now. I sit alone as the movie plays. I'm an observer, an outsider, watching as the woman I love enjoys time with her fated mates. Technically, I'm one of them. But we're not bonded, and she hasn't said anything about changing that. My heart is crushed by that revelation.

She doesn't want me, but can't bring herself to tell me. Or worse, she just wants to be friends. Yeah, that's definitely worse. Because then I have to be here and watch as she gets her happily ever after. I don't know if I'm strong enough to do that for her. I may have to be selfish and leave. Soon, but not today.

My mind wanders as the evening stretches on. If the man in the Fae realm is Red's father, why wouldn't he come back with me? He said that he wants to help protect Red from Amber. If that's true, he should be here. I have to figure out a way to contact him.

There has to be a spell or something in Red's books that will help me figure it out. The question is, how will I get my hands on her books long enough to find it? I know that she and James have spent a lot of time studying them. Maybe I should just ask James. But then he'd tell Red that I asked.

I can sense the bond between the four of them, and I definitely feel like the odd man out. I could say something, and I'm sure they would deny it. I push the negative thoughts away, but they come back with a vengeance. I'm convinced that the four of them would be happier if I wasn't here at all.

I should leave, but I'm too scared. I'm terrified that if I'm alone, Amber will find me and I'll be her prisoner again. And since I escaped, I'm sure that she would follow through with all of her threats. I can't deal with that. The thought of her touching me makes my skin crawl. Knowing that there's a spell she can use to control my body while my mind knows that I'm doing things I don't want—I can't take that chance.

Even if that means being the fifth wheel and watching as Red spends time with her mates. I can't think of myself as one of them, because I don't deserve that. I don't deserve her, I know it. I just can't remember why.

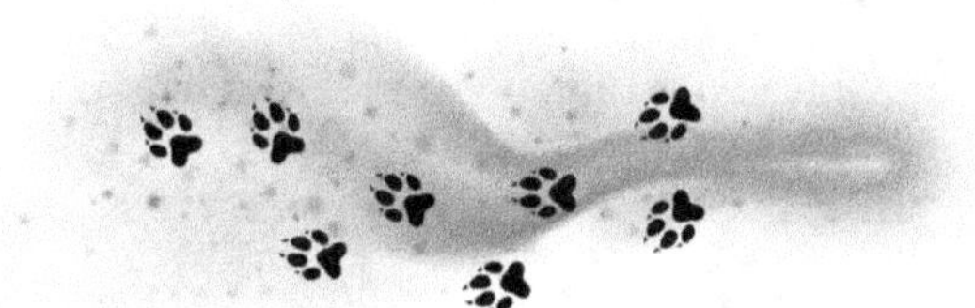

RYLAND

Something is off with Luca, but I don't know what it is. I would swear that he's sitting over there, having a conversation with himself. Or someone else. I don't know who he would be talking to. Amber. It has to be. And if he's talking to Amber, that means we can't trust him.

Do you think Luca is acting strange? I pose the question to Red, James, and Orym along the bond. I don't want to interrupt the movie, but this is important.

He's being a little distant, but not strange. Red replies.

I wait for Orym and James to weigh in. *Maybe, but he's been through a lot. It'll probably take a while for him to feel like he belongs here.* James' explanation makes sense, but I'm still not convinced.

I don't think he's a spy, if that's what you're getting at. I think he's feeling left out because he's the only one of us who hasn't completed the bond with Garnet. But he's hesitant because he's not sure he fits in here anymore. Orym may be onto something here.

You don't think he's a spy? I hate to accuse him, but I just can't get past his behavior today.

No, I don't. I think he's upset and scared. He needs us, but someone or something has made him feel like he doesn't belong here. That's just my impression, though. I don't want to admit that Orym is better at reading people than I am, but I know he is. So, if he doesn't think Luca is working with Amber, I have to give Luca the benefit of the doubt.

We have to talk to him. He needs to know that he's part of this family. I know it's not my place to make that call, but I'm doing it anyway. If Red can't see that he needs to know how she feels, then she's blind. I know that we've all been trying not to push, but I think we need to.

I'll talk to him tomorrow before we leave. I don't want to pressure him. Can we just watch the movie and relax? Red sounds annoyed, and I understand why. We're supposed to be resting up for a big battle tomorrow, and I'm starting shit.

It wasn't my intention. I just feel like Luca needs us; like he's in danger somehow. I can't explain why. I just have this unshakeable feeling that something is wrong here and if we don't fix it, it's gonna be bad. Instead of pushing, I simply agree with Red. *That's probably a good idea. I know he's been through enough already. I'm just worried about him.*

Since I've said my piece, I go back to watching the movie. I can feel Luca's eyes on me. It's as if he knows that we were just talking about him. He locks eyes with me and for a moment, I see him relax. Then the fear comes back, and I wonder what's up with him.

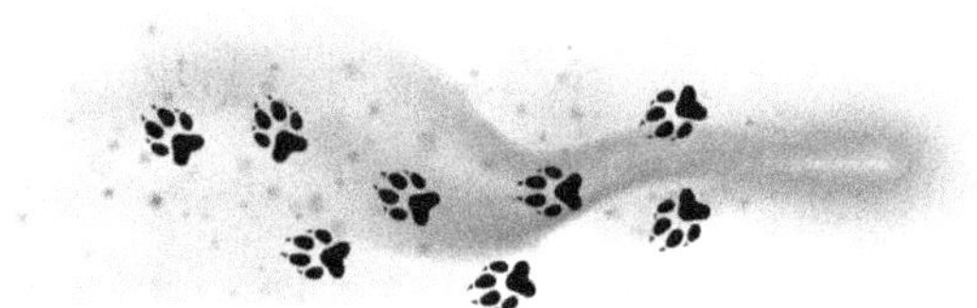

GARNET

I want to completely dismiss Ry's concerns about Luca, but the more I think about it, the less sure I am. I don't think he's working for Amber, but I'm not convinced that he wants to be here. Something is off, and I really should talk to him about it now. But I'm scared that he will openly reject me if I try.

So, I'll wait. I can come up with dozens of reasons to put off that conversation. It's not the right time. I almost died today, and really should be resting. We're about to go into battle—I should be focused on that instead of whether or not Luca wants to be with me.

After all the excuses, I decide that my heart just can't take the chance. If he officially rejects me, I won't be able to fight tomorrow. Everyone is counting on me and my magic. I can't let them down.

It doesn't take much to convince myself that I'm doing the right thing. I settle back in to watch the movie, letting my stress melt away as much as I can. I get lost in the love story that's unfolding on the screen. It always amuses me how the leading man's character has no idea that he's in love with his grumpy boss. She realizes her feelings before he does.

In the end, they have an honest conversation about their feelings. That brings me back to Luca, and my heart hurts again. Maybe I should risk it and talk to him tonight after all. When I sneak a glance at him, he's curled up in the chair, sleeping peacefully. I can't wake him just to ask if he wants to be my mate or not.

That wouldn't be fair to him. Now that I've waited too long to take care of it tonight, I'm going to freak myself out with 'what ifs' until we actually get to talk about it. Moments like this make me sad that I'm not a wolf. I need to run. I need that physical exertion to wear my brain out so that I can sleep.

The credits roll on the movie that I only half paid attention to, and I realize that everyone will be going to sleep soon. I can't ask them to stay up because I'm questioning my decisions. But I know I won't be able to sleep.

I go through the motions getting ready for bed, but instead of pajamas, I put on a pair of shorts and a sports bra. "I'm sorry, but I need to run. I can't ask any of you to come with me. I promise I'll stay on the paths and in our territory. But I won't sleep if I don't do this."

James climbs out of bed to get dressed, but Orym stops him. "I'll go with her. I'm not quite ready to sleep yet either." He pulls on a pair of shorts and tugs me from the room.

"You don't have to," I start, but he pulls me to his chest and kisses me. It's the first real kiss he's given me since we discovered what my father is. I'm caught off guard. I hadn't expected this to happen.

"Let me come with you, please. I have so much to make up for, and this will barely get me started," he insists. My cheeks are flushed from the kiss, and my heart flutters at his words.

"Okay, if you want to go." My response is lame, and I know it. But who am I to stop him from coming along?

Luca is still asleep when we go through the living room. I cover him with a blanket and kiss the top of his head. He barely stirs at my touch. I can't stay here another moment.

Once we're outside, I start to stretch, preparing to run. Orym does the same, mimicking my movements. "I know that you could have gone running on your own. You don't need someone to protect you. Thank you for letting me come with you."

I smile at him. "I figured maybe you wanted to talk, and this will be a chance at privacy." He grins at my words, and I know that he has more in mind than talking. Well, if that's what he wants, he'll have to catch me first.

"Which way do you want to go? Toward the waterfall or toward the main camp?" he asks. I'm sure he wants to go to the waterfall, so I have to decide if that's what I want or not. Part of me wants to, because that's my favorite place. The rest of me wants to run the opposite direction because sex isn't what I need tonight.

But if it's what Orym needs, then maybe I should cooperate. We don't have to have sex. We can just make out a bit and see what happens. I could use some alone time with him, too. We've been at odds for a little while and I hate that feeling.

"Waterfall. It's my favorite place," I admit.

"I thought so. It's my favorite place too." I'm not sure if he's saying that to gain favor with me or if it really is his favorite place. Why would he lie about that? We're already bonded, so it's not like this is a first date or anything. I shake that thought away and take off down the path toward the waterfall. It's dark, and I can barely see where I'm going.

Luckily, I know these woods like the back of my hand. As long as no random portals to another realm open up, I can make it to the waterfall and back blindfolded. I can hear Orym keeping pace behind me. He's letting me lead, knowing that he can catch me at any time if he wants.

The thought is thrilling to me. It's like he's chasing me, but he's really not. I'm in no danger, except of losing more of my heart.

TEN
RESCUE

JAMES

I DON'T KNOW HOW long Garnet and Orym were gone, but when I wake up, they're curled up on the couch. I guess they didn't want to wake us. Sleeping alone with Ryland should have been awkward, but it wasn't. I'll never admit it, but he even snuggled me for a while.

I know that wolf packs are affectionate with all their members, so it wasn't really an odd thing to have happen. I'm not sure he'd be thrilled about me telling the others, though, so I won't.

We have a couple of hours before we have to meet Eli and his army at Gunnar's so that we can head into the woods. This rescue mission has to go off without a hitch. We can't handle anymore bloodshed. Even as I think the words, I know there's no way out of this without sacrifices.

I don't want any of us to be those sacrifices, though. I will fight alongside the wolves and vamps, but I'll be doing it to protect my mate, my family.

I may not have super strength or the ability to shift, but I do know about spells and magic. I plan to help Garnet with her spells and attacks. I'll have the books and her supplies ready. And I'll tend to injuries, because we know there will be some.

We're expecting this to be a 'final battle' between us and Amber, but the more we learn about her, the less sure I am of that. I think she'll find a way to escape capture and continue whatever her plan is. I'm annoyed that we haven't learned more about what she's been trying to do with all these captives. There has to be more to it than we're aware of.

Instead of focusing on that idea, I double check the spell books and ingredients in my bag. Ryland is making breakfast, and the others are finally up and moving. This isn't the time to get stuck on an abstract thought.

We eat together in near silence. No one voices their concerns or fears. I'm guessing they don't want to somehow manifest them. I may not hold the exact same beliefs as the wolf packs, but I understand that hesitation. I would feel guilty if I mentioned something bad happening and then it did.

"We should get going soon," Garnet says aloud. "Eli's team will be preparing, and we have to get Gunnar's crew organized." Everyone nods solemnly before we clear the table and grab our bags. Each of us will have a supply bag with us. The bags are filled with medical supplies and extra weapons. With any luck, Amber's people will see us coming and surrender.

Yeah, right. Like Amber is going to let her cult surrender to us. I almost laugh at the thought as we walk out the door. I feel like everything I've done the past few days has been wishful thinking. It's time for action.

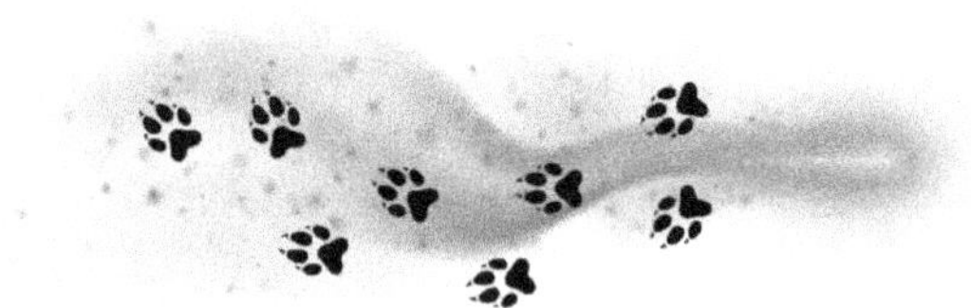

LUCA

The eerie quiet of the morning has me in my head about everything. Red wants me to stay behind, because she can't bear the thought of something happening to me. I feel like a complete coward, because I actually consider her request. In the end, I shake my head and refuse. "I'll be okay."

"I can't make you stay behind. It's your decision. Just be careful. We should talk after," she insists. I nod, convinced that I know what she'll say when this is done. Maybe I won't survive, so that she doesn't have to reject me.

I'm already broken, so it won't matter if I don't come back. Right?

Something feels off about that thought, but I can't figure out where it came from. I don't have a death wish, and I didn't think I was broken, did I? I've been having strange thoughts since I came back from Amber's camp. I'm not sure what caused them, though.

Maybe I should tell someone. But if I do, they'll definitely make me stay back. And I can't miss this fight. I have to help save those people I was locked up with. I promised to protect them, then ran away. I can't let that happen again.

My thoughts continue to war with each other as we make our way to Gunnar's cabin to meet up with the waiting armies. That's what we are. Armies. And we're about to go to war. The only question is, will we survive? Not if I don't push my internal conflict aside and focus on the external one that's about to start.

The crowd at Gunnar's is insane. There are wolves and vampires everywhere. I guess I'd expected them to be separated and lined up or something, but this is nearly chaos. I see Eli standing next to Gunnar as they prepare to address the troops. As soon as they see us, we're ushered to the front. Eli pulls Red to stand between him and Gunnar. It's almost amusing how both Red and Gunnar bristle at being near each other now.

It's as if he finally understands how uncomfortable she's been around him for years. He doesn't seem to know what to do about her since he can't yell and boss her around anymore. I try not to be too amused at the sight as they prepare to speak. I hope that Red is okay. I know she doesn't like to be the center of attention.

Eli holds up a hand and the crowd stops moving. Everything goes silent. Power radiates off the vampire as he steps forward. "We are here today to rescue those who have been captured by someone we thought was an ally. Please stay focused on the objective and keep your eyes open."

He gestures to Gunnar to speak next. "Do what you have to in order to save the prisoners. Don't take unnecessary risks, and watch each other's backs." He steps back, and then Eli practically shoves Garnet forward.

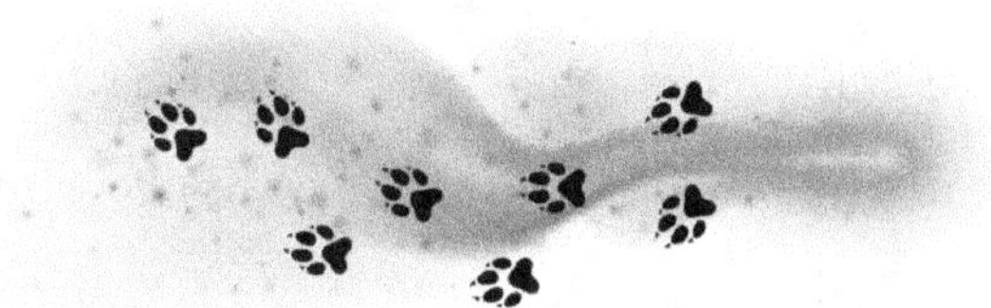

GARNET

Eli's hand is rough on my back as he gives me a not-so-subtle nudge to address the crowd. I'd rather not, but it doesn't look like I have a choice here. Okay, what am I supposed to say? Shit. What if I fuck this up?

"Thank you all for volunteering to help with this rescue. Some of you don't know me, but I'm Garnet." I start to introduce myself as Gunnar's daughter, then stop. I'm not, and I never was. "I'm a witch, but I'm on your side. I will use my powers to fight against Amber and her followers and rescue those who have been taken. We have to work together for this to be successful."

I have no idea what else to say to this crowd, so I step back and let Eli finish getting them ready. When he announces that it's time to go, everyone picks up their supplies and heads into the forest. We're all moving as quietly as possible, hoping to sneak up on Amber and her cult.

I'm worried about Luca more than the others. He's been so distant and quiet since he came back. With the exception of when Orym made him tell us about his escape. It's crazy that he might have been helped by my father. If that Fae man is my father. I'd hoped to be able to talk to Luca before this battle, but I'll have to hold out hope that we'll have time after. And maybe I'll get that spell figured out to talk to my father too. But finding my father isn't a priority.

Defeating Amber and saving the people she's kidnapped is the only thing that matters right now. I focus on keeping my magic at the surface, ready to strike. Electricity crackles along my arms, and I catch a few wolves and vamps staring at me. I'm not sure if they're impressed or scared. Probably a combination of the two, if I have to guess. None of them get close to me.

I shouldn't be surprised at how few people speak to me as we move through the forest. I would think it's just because they are focused on what we're heading toward. But I catch snippets of conversation, so I know it's just me.

That's okay, I have what I need. Mostly. All of my mates stay near me, even Luca. I wish that he had agreed to stay behind, but I understand that he needs to face Amber with me. I hate my aunt for what she did to him. I'm sure that I don't know everything that happened, either. There's a reason why Eli refused to let me watch more of the surveillance videos. I don't buy the excuse that I couldn't get the bomb spell right.

Yeah, I did some damage to Midnight. But from what Delilah told me, it was nothing compared to what that poor building had been through the first two times it was attacked. That's beside the point, though. What was my point? Oh, yeah. Luca has been through some shit, and I want him to feel like he can talk to me about it. But that won't happen unless we make it out of here today.

Since I can't do what I need to if I'm thinking about how my bitch aunt tortured my unclaimed mate, I have to push those thoughts away. I need to be singularly focused on taking her out. I know that everyone wants us to take her alive, but if I have the chance to kill her, I know that I will.

I want revenge for her taking Luca from me. If it wasn't for her, we'd already be bonded and he wouldn't be doubting me. I'm not even sure that's what's going on with him, but Orym is pretty perceptive, so I'm trusting his opinions.

And we had a nice long talk about it at the waterfall last night. I know that Luca was hesitant to even talk to Orym, and that he got upset when Orym made him tell us about the Fae man who helped him escape.

What I don't understand is why. Luca and I have been best friends for as long as I can remember. There's never been a time when we couldn't share everything. Until now. A branch breaks in front of me, and I freeze. I let myself get distracted by my thoughts and someone snuck up on me.

The woods are silent besides the crackle of electricity along my skin. I turn in a circle, and realize that I'm alone. How did this happen? Fuck, I'd been so careful to keep an eye on everyone so we could stay together. Did they get captured?

I reach out with the bond. *Ry? Orym? James? Where are you?*

There's no answer, and for a moment, my breath hitches. My heart is racing, and my hands are moist. Then I realize that something is off here. The shadows are wrong. We've been in the forest for two hours, and the sun was barely up when we left. It shouldn't be so low now.

This is a trick. One of Amber's witches is casting a glamor spell on me. Which means that I'm probably standing next to one of my guys. I just have to get their attention so they can snap me out of it.

Without the bond, I have to rely on something else. I flail my arms around, trying to hit one of them. Nothing. Okay, I'll have to try something else. I have an idea, but it's a long shot. Will this work? I don't know, but it might be enough.

I focus on the connection the witch has with me and send a jolt of electricity along it. If I'm wrong, and there is no witch, I might hit one of my guys. That's why I don't send a full-strength blast, just enough of a shock to let them know I'm aware.

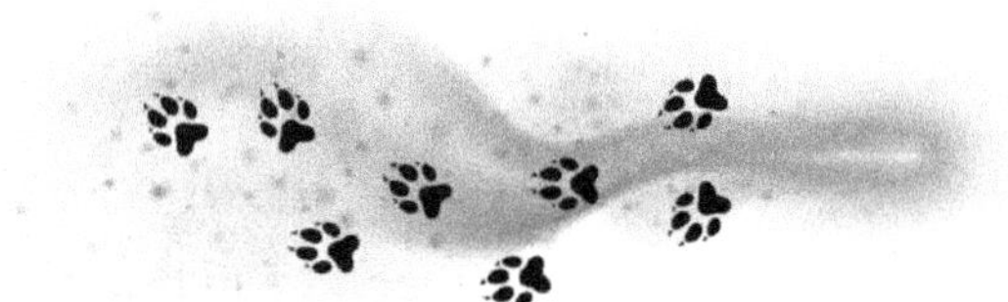

RYLAND

We get to the center of the clearing where the mole said the camp is when Red stops short. I watch her to see if she's okay. Her eyes are glossed over and she shakes her head a lot. Something is wrong, but I have no idea if I should try to wake her or not.

"James!" I shout over the noise of our allies attacking the witches. "Something has her, what do we do?"

He turns toward us. "Shit. I've got her. Keep the enemy away. Have Orym and Luca see if they can find the witch responsible."

I nod and leave him to snap her out of the trance. Luca and Orym hear his command and waste no time finding the witch who is casting the spell to incapacitate Red. Once that enemy is taken care of, I see her collapse as she comes back to us.

"*I've got her.* Keep us covered for another minute or two. She's coming back now." James' voice cuts through the chaos around us. I do my part and punch anything that comes too close. When Orym and Luca come back, we form a triangle around James and Red, fighting anyone who tries to get to her.

I see the blue flash seconds before the magic hits me. I'm thrown back five or so feet, landing on my back. My breath comes in short pants as I pause long enough for the world to stop spinning. I sit up to see another blast coming my way. This is it; my life ends here. The blue energy hits something invisible and dissipates.

I turn my head to see Red standing in the center of the triangle where I left her, but James has taken my spot protecting her. She must have tossed a shield at me somehow. I grin at her and get to my feet. Once I'm back at her side, we expand the triangle to a square, keeping her in the center. The four of us continue to battle, while Red tosses magic out at random, taking out threats that we don't see.

The five of us work pretty well together, even though we didn't practice this at all. I can't help feeling like we have no idea what we're walking into. If only Luca could have explained about the camp and how things were run. Eli's surveillance and mole are effective, but I think Luca would have caught things they didn't have time to.

It doesn't matter now, because we're in the middle of this fight. We have to protect Red so she can fight Amber. Part of me hopes that Red kills the bitch, but I don't expect that from my girl. She's too kind and caring. I think she could kill someone, but only if she had to protect one of us. She's not malicious enough to do it in cold blood.

We continue toward the building where Amber is supposed to be, staying in formation.

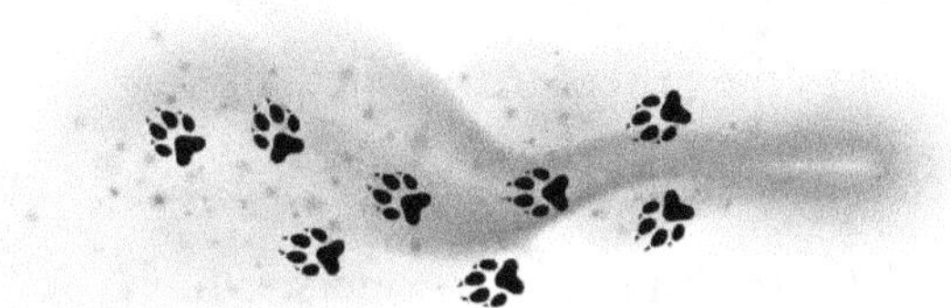

ORYM

My entire focus is on protecting Garnet. And James, since he's human. These witches aren't fighting fair, but we expected that. It's unfortunate that we don't have any way to block them from getting into our heads.

We all watched a few minutes ago as one of the witches got into Garnet's head. She was all but catatonic in the middle of a battle. If they can do that to a fellow witch, then they'll be able to do so much worse to the rest of us.

I can't let those dark thoughts take over. I have to stay aware of our surroundings and make sure we get Garnet where she needs to be. Each group of vampires and wolves has a section of forest to evacuate. Our job is to find Amber and keep her occupied until the others are finished.

Between attacks, I can see the other groups getting into position. We aren't taking prisoners, which means that any witches who are stupid enough to get close are going to die. That's probably why most of them have used distance spells so far.

The one who took over Garnet slipped up by getting too close. It was easy for Luca and I to sneak up on her. I don't want to think about what we did, because I'm not a monster. But we had to protect Garnet. Our mate's life is more important than anyone else's.

The noises of the forest have stopped. It's nearly silent now. I barely hear our footsteps as we gingerly stalk through the trees. Something has changed, but I can't tell what. Paranoia starts to take hold, and I'm convinced that we're trapped again.

"We have to get out of here," I say to Luca.

"We will, as soon as we finish our mission," he replies. A moment later, he's being tossed backward and hits the ground hard. When he doesn't move, I hear Garnet's scream and it snaps me out of the trance I was falling into.

James rushes to Luca's side, and I take his place next to our mate. Ryland and I will have to protect her now. Guilt eats at me, making me feel like Luca's injury is my fault. If I hadn't gotten distracted, I would have seen the attack coming. But I didn't. Because they didn't want me to.

I shake the thoughts away and watch as Garnet's scream sends out a blast of magic similar to the bomb she's been working on. Waves of purple and blue energy fly through the air, not harming Luca, James, Ryland or myself, but destroying the trees and witches who were hiding in them.

We're standing in a new clearing, in the middle of the densest part of the forest, when Amber steps out of the trees. She's still wearing the magic blocking cuffs that Garnet put on her, but somehow that makes her more terrifying. How does she expect to fight someone more powerful than herself when she has no magic?

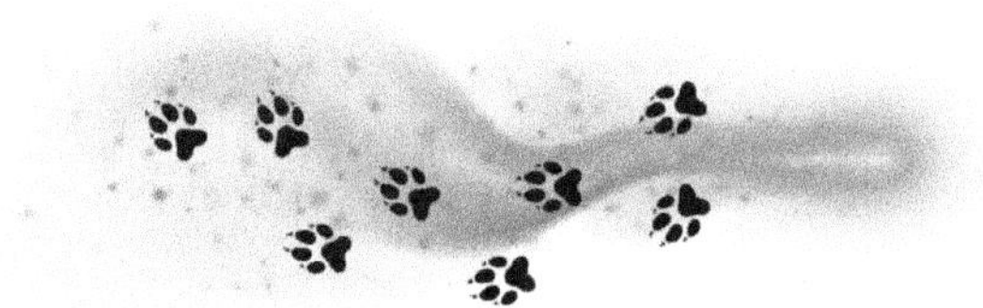

GARNET

Luca hits the ground, and my world cracks. I scream as James runs to him. Power builds inside of me, begging to be set free. I know that if I turn this blast loose, there's a chance that my men will be destroyed. I can't let that happen.

But somehow, I can feel Luca's pain as if it's my own. I scream again, letting the energy inside of me take over. It blasts from me in waves of blue and purple. Trees disintegrate, and fear grips my heart. The minute that power touches Orym, I'm certain he's going to disappear. Instead, it seems to go around him, as if my magic knows that he's not a target. My jaw drops as it does the same for each of my mates.

I finally figured out how to blow shit up without hurting my guys, and I have no idea how I did it. I would be amazed, but there's no time. As soon as the area we're standing in is cleared, there's nothing left but us. Then Amber steps out of the shadows. The smirk on her face can only be described as evil.

I know that I have to push everything else out of my mind now and face her. I can't be worried about my mates or anyone else. I have to focus on defeating Amber.

"It's cute how you think you have a chance," she laughs.

"It's annoying how you just won't give up," I reply. I have to keep her attention on me, so that James, Orym, and Ry can get Luca out of here.

Take him home. I'll be right behind you. I just have to handle her, first. I tell them through the bond.

I'm not leaving you, Red. James and Orym can take him home and get him settled. Ry's growl in my head warms my heart. I should have known my big bad wolf wouldn't leave me.

Okay, but stay back. I've got Amber. I know that he won't listen if he thinks she's winning, but I want to do this on my own. Even if that means becoming the thing I never wanted to. A monster like my aunt.

"You should just leave me to my work, child." Her voice is cold and sends a shiver down my spine.

"What work would that be?" If I can get her to tell me, then maybe, just maybe, we can find a way to defeat her. I don't think she'll actually fall for it, though.

"Don't worry, you'll find out soon enough," she says with a chuckle. Well, shit. That didn't get me anywhere. I look around and don't see Ry, but I also don't see James, Orym, or Luca. Good. That means they got him out of here. I have to trust Ry to stay out of the way and keep himself safe.

She takes a step forward and I send a shot of electricity slamming into the ground in front of her. Amber stops and holds up her hands as if she's surrendering. I know better, but I pause my attack. I'm waiting for her to do something. I know she isn't here to talk to me.

"What do you want, Amber?" I ask, keeping her focused on me.

"I came to see why you're killing my followers. Would you care to explain that?" she counters. I smile, pleased that she's giving me something to distract her with. The teams need time to get the prisoners out of the witches' territory.

"We're here to take you down. You have to be stopped." I glare at her as I speak. I want her to call me out on it.

"But you don't even know what I'm doing? How do you know that I need to be stopped?" she asks with a smirk.

"If you'd tell us, then maybe, just maybe, we could come to a compromise," I offer. I know that she's not going to go full on villain and lay her plan at my feet.

"I'm afraid that I just can't do that. If you'd like to volunteer, however, I could show you."

It's tempting to pretend that I'm willing to do that, but I doubt she'll believe me at this point. I've made it pretty clear that I'm going to stop her no matter what. If only we could find out what she's hiding, though.

"I think I'll pass," I reply, shooting another blast of electricity at her feet. As it hits, she backs up a few feet, returning to the safety of the trees. I stare at her, waiting for her to retaliate in some manner.

Nothing happens. She simply stands there and stares back at me. It's as if we're both daring each other to do something. I'm not sure how long we stay like that.

At some point, Ry calls to me through our bond. *The groups are retreating. They've rescued as many as they could. James and Orym got Luca out. We need to go.* I jump at his voice in my head. I'd gotten used to the silence.

I start to walk backward slowly, watching Amber the whole time. She still doesn't move. When I get to the trees on the opposite side of the clearing that I made, Ry is there in his wolf form, waiting for me. I climb onto his back and we race through the trees as quickly as he can run.

I know that Amber won't just watch us leave. She proves me right when bolts of magic start whipping past us. Ry has to dodge and run in a random pattern until I can get focused enough to make a shield for us. I fumble with it a few times before I get it in place around us.

A blast of blue energy hits the shield and reverberates through me, but it doesn't hurt. I know that it would have without the shield. He doesn't stop running until we get home.

ELEVEN
RECOVERY

LUCA

I STEP IN FRONT of Red just in time for a blast of magic to knock me backward. I can still hear and see everything that's going on, I just can't move or speak. Then the darkness starts to creep in, and I'm worried that this is the end for me.

How can I still be aware of what's happening if I'm dying? I feel arms lift me, and we're moving. I silently pray that it's Red or the guys who have me, and not Amber. I don't think I can go through that again.

All is under control, child. Do not fear. Your mates will care for you. That voice. It's him. The Fae man who might be Red's father. I call out to him with my mind, since I can't actually speak.

Where are you? Can you help us? We're still moving through the trees. Now that the darkness has taken over, I can't see anything, but I can feel the branches and leaves against my skin. There's a cool breeze blowing, and goosebumps raise along my arms.

I can't hear the others now. All I can do is wait and see what happens. I hate feeling helpless. I'm so lost in my self-pity that I nearly miss the voice speaking to me again.

I cannot cross into your realm without invitation, my boy. And you aren't the one who can invite me. I will do what I can to help from here. His reassurance does little to ease my fears.

Silence surrounds me and it seems as if everything gets darker and colder. *Open your eyes, my boy. You're safe now.* I hear the voice in my head, echoed in my ears. "Come on, boy, open your eyes."

I flutter my eyes open, not realizing that they've been closed. One glance around and I know that I'm not in the forest anymore. At least, I'm not in *my* forest anymore. "What did you do?"

My eyes meet his. For a moment I'm distracted by how blue his eyes are today. They're almost glowing. Then I realize that he's not answering my question. I sit up and look at my hands in front of me. They're translucent and it's really disturbing. "What happened? Why can I see through myself?"

"Take a breath. Everything is fine. I just intercepted your spirit before it could move on. You're safe here until your mates can repair your body," he answers.

"Am I in the Fae Realm again?" I shift my gaze to meet his, and he grins suspiciously.

"Not exactly. You're in what I call the 'in between,' which is a place between life and death. The reapers were taking your spirit to the 'after,' but I tricked them, and brought you here."

I don't like his explanation. It's less disturbing than realizing that I nearly died, though, so I'll just be thankful that he brought me here. "So now what do we do?"

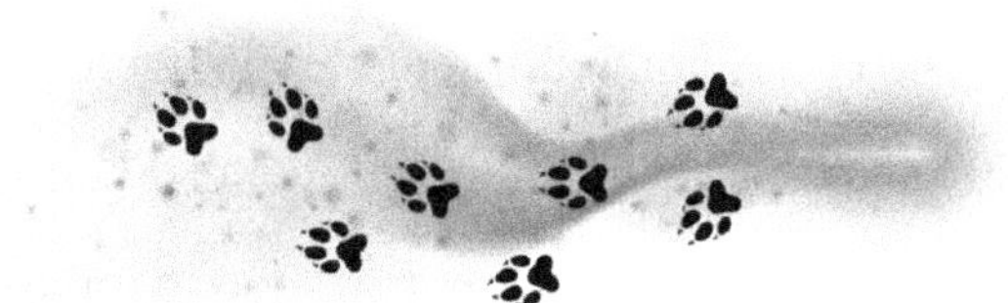

RYLAND

Red orders me to go with the others, but I can't leave her alone. I'm prepared for her anger when I refuse, but I'm met with gratitude and relief instead. I step back into the shadows to watch her as she faces off with Amber. I don't trust the bitch to be alone with my mate, but I want her to forget that I'm here.

The more they talk, the more anxious I get. I shift into my wolf form and wait for Red just inside the tree line of the clearing. I check in with the guys and find out what's going on, then send Red a message along our bond. *The groups are retreating. They've rescued as many as they could. James and Orym got Luca out. We need to go.*

She backs away from Amber, heading toward me without turning her back on the witch. As soon as she's close enough, I step forward and she jumps onto my back. We race through the forest, dodging magic attacks as we fight to get home.

I know that there are still more missing wolves, vamps, and humans. As annoyed as I am that we weren't able to rescue them all, I'm happy we got as many out as we did. There has to be a way to stop Amber from coming into our territory, but I'm not sure what that would be.

Maybe Eli will know of something that would repel witches. Hopefully, it wouldn't affect Red, since she's half Fae. But there's no way to know until we can have that conversation. I should focus more on where I'm going instead of how to stop these assholes from following us. After I almost slam into a tree, I shake my head and pay more attention to what I'm doing.

I get Red back to Gunnar's place before letting her climb off my back. Then I shift and follow her as she walks to the training center. It's the only place large enough to house the wounded and rescued, so it makes sense that they would have been taken there.

She heads inside, looking for Luca, I'm sure. I walk around the perimeter, making sure there are wolves at every entrance. Once I'm satisfied, I go inside and find my girl. "I don't understand. He's really not here? Where did they take him?"

"We're not sure, but they didn't come here with the rest of us." I overhear the conversation, and rush to Red's side.

"Let's head home and see if they took him there. James has medical training. He'll be able to take care of Luca. If they aren't at home, we'll start searching." I wrap my arm around her shoulder and guide her to the exit.

"Do you really think James and Orym would have taken him home instead of here?" Concern laces with her words and tugs at my heart. I know that she's hurting because Luca is injured. I have to ease her worries.

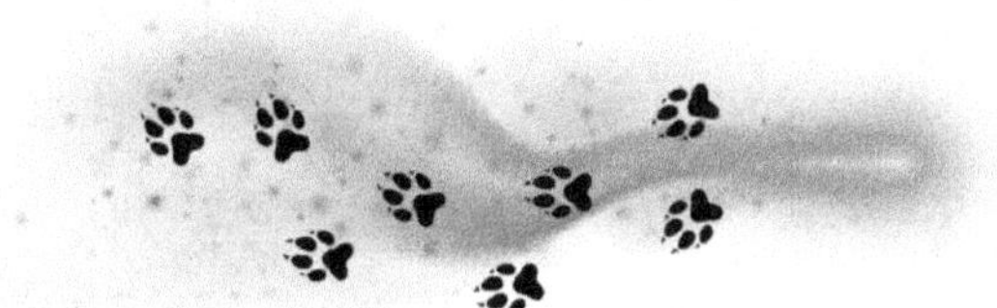

GARNET

I let Ry lead me out of the makeshift hospital. I don't want to think about how badly Luca is injured. I can't bear the thought of losing him. I just got him back, and we haven't even sealed our bond yet.

"I'm sure that they took him home because it's quieter there," Ry tries to reassure me, and I love him for the effort.

I hope he's right, but I'm just not convinced. The closer we get to the cabin, the more my heart tries to pound out of my chest.

I trust James to take care of Luca, but I'm not sure what he can do to combat injuries caused by magic. I don't know what I could do about it either. The whole thing terrifies me. I don't want to voice my concerns, although I know that Ry can feel everything I'm going through with our bond.

That thought makes me sad, too. Luca can't feel me through the bond, because it's not there. Not fully, anyway. He has to survive this. There's no other option. I will do whatever it takes to heal him and bring him back to me. I have to claim him and be claimed by him.

Ry pulls me up to the door, and I freeze. "I can't. What if?" I can't bring myself to complete the thought. I won't say it out loud.

"It's okay, Red. Please, just come on." When my feet don't move, he picks me up, tosses me over his shoulder, and carries me inside.

Luca is on the couch, unconscious. James wipes his forehead with a damp cloth. I don't see Orym anywhere. "How is he?"

"As far as I can tell, he's stable. I know that's not much, but it's hard to figure out how to fix him when I'm not sure what's wrong," James offers.

"He's been muttering something off and on for a while, but we can't tell what he's saying," Orym says as he steps into the room carrying a tray of food. "I figured everyone needs to eat."

I don't think I'll be able to eat, but the moment my nose senses food, my stomach starts to growl. We sit on the floor in front of the couch and eat while keeping an eye on Luca. As if triggered by Orym's words, my unconscious mate starts to murmur under his breath. I can't tell what he's saying either.

When we're finished eating, the three of them stare at me. I have no idea what they want, and I'm getting paranoid about it. "What? Do I have food on me?"

"No, but your worry over Luca is palpable," James tells me.

"Oh. I don't know how to block strong emotions yet. You guys know that." I shouldn't be defending myself, but here I am. I need to figure out a way to stop sharing everything with them. So far, I've managed to block them all for short periods of time. But that doesn't seem to work when I'm upset.

"I was thinking," Orym starts, then pauses to look each of us over. "What if you try to heal him?" Fuck. I don't want to think about that. I haven't practiced enough with healing magic yet, and I'm not confident that I won't make things worse. There has to be another way.

"I understand that you're scared, but he's right. It might be the only way to fix whatever is wrong with him," James agrees. I want to throttle them both for ganging up on me. I turn to Ry, hoping to see some sympathy or reassurance in his eyes. Instead, I meet an expression that tells me he agrees with my other mates.

"You can do it, Red. I know you can. You and James told me that magic is all about intention. As long as you intend for him to get better, he will."

I groan in frustration. I can't argue with his logic, and I hate him for it. He's using my own words against me. It's unfair, but completely warranted. They're right. If I want Luca healed, I'm going to have to do it myself. I just wish I knew how to heal him.

"I don't know how to do it," I argue. At this point, I know that I'm only arguing because I'm scared. I won't admit that to them, though. It doesn't matter, because they can sense my emotions. They already know that I'm scared, or Ry wouldn't have pulled out the logic card.

"But you do. Look in your heart, and you'll find the answer," James says. Since when has my human mate become a philosopher? It's annoying and heartwarming how supportive they all are. I want to punch them and hug them at the same time.

"Why are you all ganging up on me? It's not fair." I'm whining, and I don't care. They can't be putting so much pressure on me. What if I fuck this up and make it worse? Then what? It's not like we have anyone else we can call on to help me heal Luca.

Which means, it's up to me. I have to do it, and I have to get it right. Fuck, I hate when these assholes are right. "Fine, I'll do it. But I really don't know how. So, you're all going to help me," I announce.

Ry's eyes go wide, James smiles, and Orym looks over my shoulder at Luca. I know they'll do whatever they have to in order to heal him. And they won't just do it for me. Each of them cares for him too. We all felt the pain of loss while he was gone. We've just started healing our relationships, and this puts a damper on that.

James goes to the bookshelf and grabs one of the journals. He and Ry go out in search of ingredients for the spell he chooses. I trust him, so I wait with Orym.

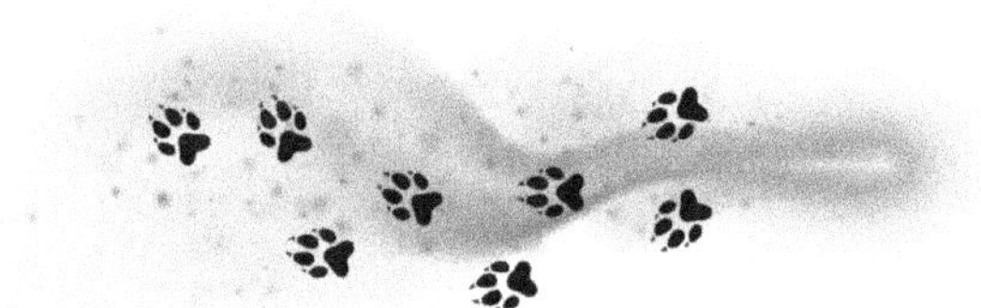

ORYM

I stay back with Garnet when Ryland and James go out to gather ingredients. She needs all of us right now. I know she's scared of messing this spell up, but I'm confident that she'll heal Luca. Once he's better, we'll be able to work on fixing our relationship with Garnet. He and I have some work to do in that department.

Between my issues with the Fae and his jealousy about not bonding with her, the two of us have spent too much time pushing her away. Maybe I can use this as an opportunity to pull us back together, then help Luca afterwards.

"What can I do?" I ask, suddenly feeling useless. I should have gone to help the others gather ingredients.

"Just being here is enough," she responds. Garnet still sits on the floor in front of the couch, but she's turned to face Luca now. This position has her back to me, and I can't quite tell what she's thinking. I can feel her emotions as if they are my own, though. So, I know she's not okay.

"Can I hold you?" I want to do so much more to comfort and reassure her, but I just don't know how right now. She looks at me over her shoulder and my heart studders.

"That would be nice," she admits. I drop to the floor next to her and pull her onto my lap. I know that she won't let me take her away from Luca, and I wouldn't ask her for that. He needs her now more than any of us do.

"We'll figure all of this out," I tell her, running my hand up and down her back. I wish I knew exactly how, because I'm sure that she would love to hear that. But I don't know, and I won't lie to her.

"I'm just so scared. I can't lose him. I can't lose any of you. My heart won't survive," she whispers, burying her head in my chest. I hold her tighter because it's the only thing I can do.

"I know, love. But you won't lose us. We're all right here with you. Luca needs healing, sure, but he's still here." My words are lame, but they're all I have right now.

James and Ryland come back with the herbs she'll need for her spell. Ryland picks Garnet up and cradles her so I can help James set things up. We lay out the herbs in the order they're listed, along with a small cauldron and a wooden spoon. James pours water into the cauldron.

"What's that for?" I ask quietly.

"She has to mix the herbs into the spring water, then recite the incantation. If it works, there should be a puff of smoke as the herbs disintegrate, and the smoke should surround Luca. When that happens, the spell will heal him," James answers.

Once we have everything set up, Ryland brings Garnet over to us. "Let's get started."

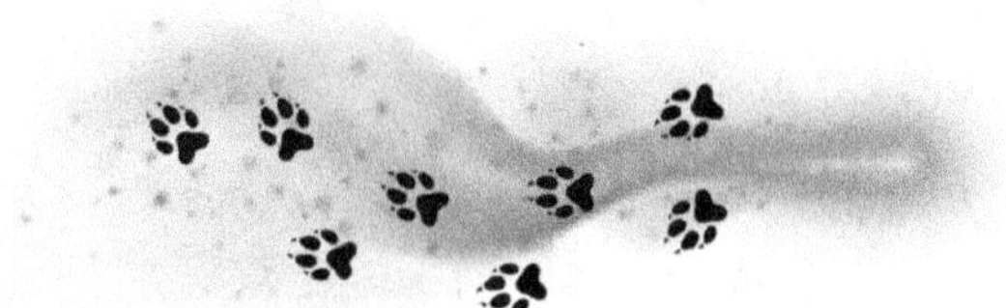

JAMES

I sense her hesitation and I understand her fear. Magic is new to me; really to all of us. We each have a different reaction to it. But there's always a healthy respect for the power that courses through our girl. She's more powerful than she realizes, and there's no way to know how her Fae powers will factor into this healing spell.

If I had more time, I would encourage her to write her own spell. It would be better in this situation, but time is of the essence. We'll have to make do with the one I found, and hope that her Fae half doesn't change how it works.

I walk her through the steps of the spell, including the incantation she needs to say. When she's ready, I motion for Ryland and Orym to step back. If this goes sideways, I don't want anyone else to be injured. I won't let her know I have doubts, though. She needs our strength right now, so that's what she's going to get.

The moment she starts the spell, I fear the worst. The smoke isn't the right color, and I worry that it's not going to work. The book says the smoke should be blue, but this is clearly pink. Garnet's brow furrows, and I know that she's noticed the difference too.

I take a calming breath and step forward to place my hand on her shoulder. She needs my support, and I'll risk myself to give it to her. A moment later, Orym and Ryland do the same. With each of us touching her, she seems to relax.

Even with the smoke being the wrong color, the moment she relaxes, I feel more confident in the spell's success. We all hold our breath as she repeats the incantation after all the herbs are in the cauldron. The pink smoke swirls before moving to circle around Luca.

It lifts him from the couch and encases his entire body before turning purple and easing him back to the couch. We wait as each second drags out into a minute. The spell didn't work. Fuck. This will break her heart. And she won't be easy to convince to try again. This may very well ruin things for us.

"It didn't work. What did I do wrong?" She turns to me with tears in her eyes. I pull her to me and hold her against my chest. Her tears soak my shirt, but I don't care about that.

Orym taps my arm and points. "Look." I lift my head and my jaw drops. Luca is glowing. It starts faint, just barely no-ticeable, then brightens to an almost painful intensity. I turn Garnet to see what's happening, and we all just stare.

When the glow fades, Luca begins to stir. "What the fuck just happened?" he asks as he sits up. Garnet races over to him and hugs him tightly.

"Red healed you," Ryland tells him, looking amazed and proud of our girl.

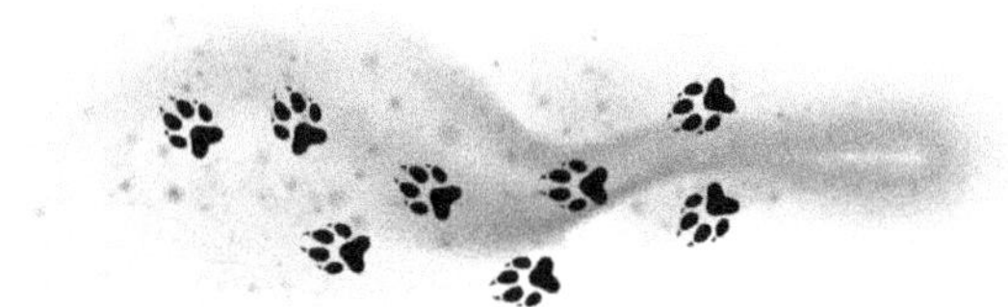

GARNET

I'm exhausted and elated that Luca is awake. He seems fine, but I'm not convinced. I have no idea what Amber hit him with, so I can't know that I've healed him fully. And that bothers me.

"How do you feel?" I ask him tentatively. I don't want to admit my fears to him or the others.

"Like I got hit by a truck," he says. "But better than before. My spirit went to the Fae Realm for a bit. Our mutual friend said that he saved me from dying. I was so worried that I'd never see you again." For a minute, everything feels right. Except that the moment I step closer to wrap my arms around him, he flinches.

"I'm sorry," I whisper and walk into the kitchen. I can't force things with him, and I won't try. Instead, I busy myself by making a cup of hot tea with honey. I sense Orym before I turn around. It's funny how I can tell which one of my mates walks into a room simply by their scent.

"I'm okay. I know he needs time. I'm just relieved that he's alive, and I don't want to push him for something he's not ready for," I say before Orym can speak.

Strong arms wrap around me, and I find my back pressed against his chest. "I understand that. But I'm not here to ask why you left. I'm here to make sure you know that he's not rejecting you. Luca almost died. He's probably going to be a little sensitive for a bit, physically and emotionally."

I nod, holding back a sigh. With all the time we lost while he was Amber's prisoner, I feel like I've lost Luca altogether. I know it's not true, but I can't stop the nagging feeling in the back of my brain.

"Garnet?" The way Orym says my name, I'm certain that this isn't the first time he's tried to get my attention.

"Sorry, I was just thinking about everything Luca has been through lately. It's not about me, but this is hard. I want to comfort him and show him how I feel, but he doesn't want that. I'm trying really hard not to be selfish." The justification sounds silly, but Orym doesn't judge me for it.

"It's hard not to be selfish in this situation. One of your mates was kidnapped, then escaped but has been distant, and now he almost died. I understand the desire to hold him close. Hell, Ryland and I want to do that to him too."

"You do?" I haven't stopped to consider how being mated to me would change their relationships with each other. I wonder if they'll all develop feelings for each other the way they have for me. I expect to feel jealous, but I don't. I'm intrigued by the thought.

"Yeah, we do. We all care about each other, Garnet. We're family now. It doesn't matter that Ryland and I hated each other for the longest time. We're your mates, and that makes us family. We'll figure it out." Orym's statement coupled with the way I can feel his dick hardening against my ass gives me wicked ideas.

"If you need help figuring it out, I'd be happy to supervise your *discussion*." I make sure to emphasize the word discussion to see if he understands what I'm thinking. From the growl in my ear, I'm pretty sure he does.

"You are a naughty girl. Everything is sex with you lately. I know we haven't been taking care of you in that department lately. We'll make up for it," he promises.

"We've all been a little preoccupied with other things, Orym. I'm not going to hold that against any of you. Training and preparing for today was top priority. Now, making sure Luca gets what he needs will be." I hate feeling like I'm turning him down, but I don't want him to stress over our lack of sex since Luca came back.

Orym nuzzles my neck and gives me a little squeeze before he releases me. I turn around to face him, but he's already gone. Luca stands in the doorway, and I understand his sudden retreat.

"Hi," he says as he steps closer. I back up against the counter and let him come to me. I want to kiss him so badly that I think I'll die if I can't. But I already know it's not going to happen. I won't push him for things he's not ready for.

"Hi. Tea?" I offer him my cup, and he takes it from me. After a small sip, he sets the cup down on the counter and moves closer. "Are you okay? Really?"

He nods. "I think so. It's a weird experience, almost dying." Luca steps closer and puts his hands on the counter on either side of me. He's careful not to touch me, and it stings. I understand that this is difficult for him, but the sting is still there. "I can't explain how it feels to come back to this after being gone."

"You don't have to. We won't push you for anything. You decide when you're ready," I reply, licking my lips and watching his gaze as he stares at my mouth.

"I want you, Red, so bad that it hurts. But I can't. Not yet. I'm sorry." My eyes meet his and I see the tears I'm holding back mirrored in his golden ones.

My hand raises to touch his cheek, but I pause. "There's nothing to apologize for, Luca. You're here, and that's all that matters. I missed you so much." He leans his head to press my hand to his cheek. A sigh escapes me at the contact.

"Fuck," he whispers as his eyes close. I start to pull my hand away, but he moves before I can. Luca captures my lips with his and kisses me fiercely. His kiss is soft but passionate. It makes me want more.

TWELVE
TRUST ISSUES

RYLAND

I FEEL RED'S PAIN through our bond at Luca's words. I don't
know what his issues are, but I'm sure they have to do with

him being kidnapped and held against his will. Or that he was beaten while he was trapped there. It's a lot to work through, especially when your captor is your fated mate's aunt who wants to kill your mate and take her powers.

I know that eavesdropping isn't a good idea, but I can't force myself to step away from the wall that attaches to the kitchen. Both James and Orym seem content to leave Red and Luca alone to have their moment, but I can't do it. I need to protect her from pain, even if it's caused by another of her mates. I can't seem to do that either. There's no way to step in here and stop Luca from being honest with her any more than there's a way to keep his words from hurting her.

So, I'm eavesdropping while trying to work out what I can do to help them get back on equal ground. There has to be something that can heal Luca's trauma and allow him to be what Red needs. I just have to figure out how to do that. Easy, right?

I don't have time to disguise what I've been doing when Luca walks out of the kitchen and looks right at me. Fuck. He doesn't look happy. Instead of yelling at me, he turns and walks outside. We've been keeping an eye on him since he got back. I'm not worried since Orym and James had just gone out before I decided to be nosey.

No point in pretending I don't know what's going on. I walk into the kitchen, where Red has silent tears falling. I drag her into my arms and hold her close, pressing a kiss to her forehead. "It's okay, love. He'll come around. We just have to give him some time."

I don't know how to comfort her more than that, so I let my body do it for me. She clings to my waist as the tears continue to fall. I can't remember when I've seen her cry before all of this fated mates stuff happened. No matter what Gunnar did to her when we were growing up, she never shed tears over any of it. She's always been so incredibly strong.

That's probably why it's so hard to see her like this and not be able to fix it. "Do you want me to beat him up? Because I will."

She offers me a small smile and shakes her head. I'd hoped that she would laugh, or agree to my offer. Either one would have been better than seeing that defeated look in her eyes. Orym seems to have the best connection with Luca lately, so maybe he'll have more luck talking to him. I know if I try, my fists will take over.

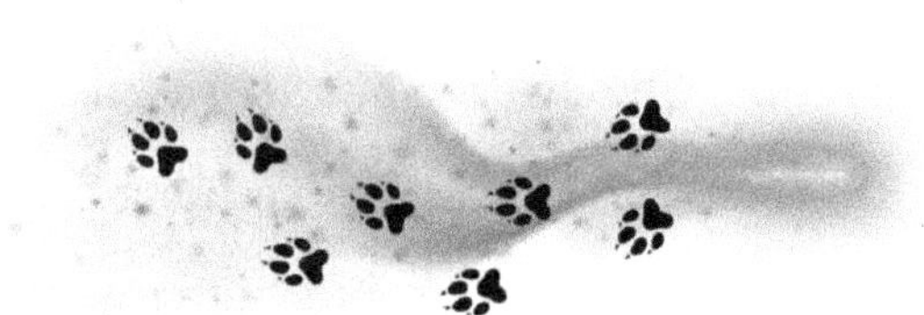

ORYM

I can't bear to listen to Garnet and Luca's conversation. Ryland seems to be a glutton for punishment, leaning against the wall to hear every word. I nod at James and he follows me outside.

"I want to help them, but I don't know how. He's different now, but I can't explain it," James says once we're alone.

"I know. I don't know how to help either. I just don't think listening to their conversation is the best idea. If they want our help, or even for us to know what they're talking about, they'll tell us," I respond.

This whole situation is crazy. Amber has turned everything upside down with her conquest for power. I know that this didn't start with Garnet, or us. But it has to end here. We have to stop her. And I can't help feeling that to defeat her, we need Luca on board. Garnet will need the four of us by her side.

I can't explain why or how I know; I just do. However this ends, it's with the five of us. We will be the ones who take Amber out, or we'll die trying. I just wish I knew how to beat her without risking our lives. She's proven that she's dangerous and not afraid to kill anyone to get what she wants.

I don't want my family to be her next victims. Maybe it's time we call Luca and Garnet's Fae friend and ask for help. I hate to admit that we need a Fae to help us, but I'm learning to accept that Garnet is one of them.

It's not easy, and I don't like it. But I've fallen in love with her, and that's enough to make me admit that not all Fae are bad. At least, *she's not*. And that has to be enough for now. Reminding myself of that helps, but sometimes, the pain takes over and I know that I need a little space.

I don't want to keep mistreating Garnet because of something that was done before she even knew what she is. It's not her fault that Fae people came to our village and killed my family. I push the thought away and start to pace.

The door swings open and Luca strolls out. His expression is a mixture of pissed and confused. "Are you okay?" I ask as he passes.

He doesn't answer, storming past me into the woods. James and I exchange a glance before he turns and follows Luca. I guess it's his turn to attempt a connection. Luca doesn't seem to be open to talking with me. I wonder for a moment if I should go inside and check on Garnet, then decide to follow James and Luca just to be on the safe side.

I plan to stay far enough back that neither will know that I'm watching them. My intent is to make sure they're not being followed or trapped by Amber's goons.

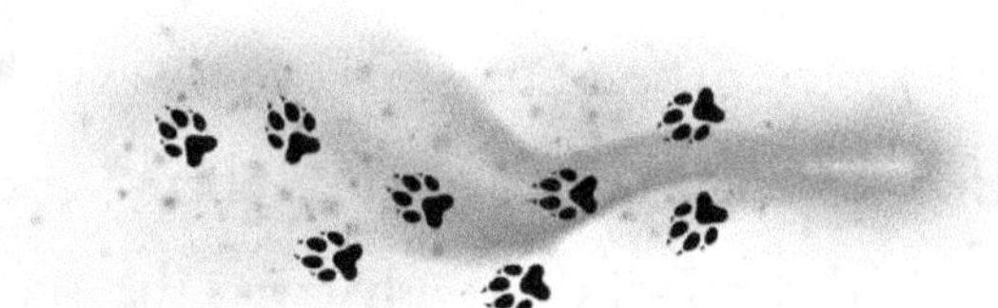

GARNET

I let myself sink into Ry's arms after Luca walks away from me. I should chase him down and make him talk to me. I want to force him to explain how he can say those things to me then walk away as if he hadn't just ripped out my heart and stomped on it. No matter how many times he tells me that he loves me and wants to be with me, it's devastating that he always follows it with "just not yet."

How many times can my heart take being rejected before I finally give up on him? I take comfort in Ry's embrace. He may not know what to say to make it better, but the fact that he's holding me while I cry it out means that he wants to help.

When Ry offers to beat Luca up, I know he's trying to make me laugh. I just can't quite make it happen. I give him a sad smile, and he deflates a little. I wish it were that simple. If only Luca could be beaten into submission. But then he wouldn't be the man I fell in love with.

Why does this have to be so hard? All I want is to settle down with my mates and have a normal life. Is that too much to ask? It must be, because every time I think we're getting close, something else happens and we're thrown back into the fray. I'm already so tired of fighting, and we're nowhere near finished with this battle.

I know that I have to let my frustration with Luca go. It's not his fault that he's nervous about bonding with me. No doubt, Amber fucked his brain up while she held him captive. Since he won't talk about it yet, I can't figure out how to help him get over it. So, I'll have to be patient.

I snuggle closer to Ry for a minute, then pull away to wipe my face. "I'm okay. Sorry about that." He gives me a sweet smile and kisses my forehead.

"Any time you need me, I'll be here." It's the sweetest thing he's ever said to me, and nearly makes me cry again.

"Thank you. I know how difficult this situation is on everyone. Luca and I will figure it out. I just have to be strong until then. Besides, we have a ton of more important stuff to worry about without me stressing over this." I don't mean for it to sound so flippant, but Ry gives me a censuring look.

"Nothing is more important to me than you. If it upsets you, then it's important enough for us to focus on fixing it. Do you understand?" I feel like a child being scolded. I tense up the way I used to when Gunnar would tear into me.

Ry takes my hands in his. "I'm not him, Red. I didn't mean to sound like I was getting on you about it."

"I know that. I'm sorry. It's an automatic reaction." I feel stupid for apologizing, but can't stop myself.

He nods and pulls me closer. "I get that. I don't ever want you to think of him when you're with me. I will do everything in my ability to protect you from feeling that way again."

I know he means it, but it's hard to reconcile him being so sweet when I'm used to him being cranky to everyone. "I can't push him, but I want to. I want to scream and fight with him the way I could before he was taken." I look up at Ry and see the sympathy in his eyes. "I miss my best friend. It's like he's here, but he's not. I don't know how to adjust to that."

"It's harder with the added stress of the mate bond between you and the three of us always hanging around. I mean, with the exception of James, we all knew that we'd be sharing a mate. We just didn't know who we'd be sharing with. I think that's a lot of the problem. It's not like any of us were really friends before. We're all going to need time to adjust to everything. But we will adjust." Ry says the words like a declaration of his intent. He's going to do what he can to shove the others into cooperation.

I would laugh, but I'm not sure how he's going to manage it. Will they fight him or will they cooperate? I honestly don't know what to expect anymore. "Okay. I'll try to let it go, then. It's hard to do nothing when it feels like I'm losing someone I love."

"It is. But you're not. I won't let him leave you unless that's what you want. He loves you, the same as the rest of us do. I don't have to be bonded with him to know that. I've known it for years. Everyone has. We don't know how you didn't know about Luca's feelings, especially given your own."

I stare at Ry, too shocked to answer. Everyone knew before the mate announcement that I was in love with Luca? How? I did the best I could to keep those feelings to myself. There's no way people knew. And for him to say that Luca felt the same all that time? I can't believe that. It's not possible, is it?

"It's okay, Red. I've got you. You don't have to do this alone anymore. The four of us will stay by your side and protect you. We will fight against Amber and anything else that tries to come between us. Luca will come around. He's only been back a few days, and he's already nearly been killed fighting beside you. This will all work out. You'll see." Ry's words are comforting, but I still want to chase after Luca and make him talk to me.

There are so many things I want to ask him about.

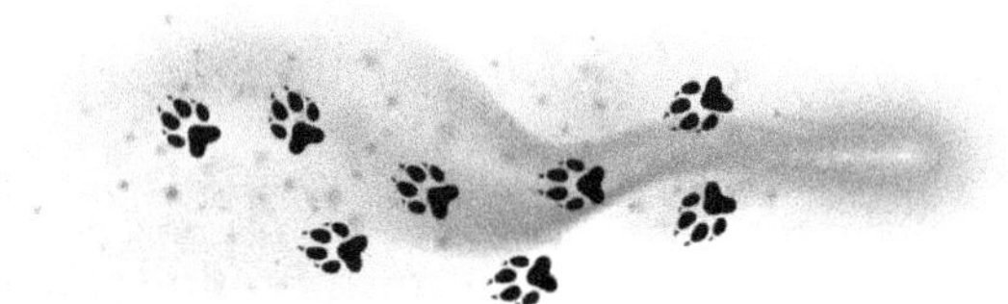

JAMES

Chasing after Luca isn't the high point of my day. I'm growing to care for these men, but that doesn't mean I want to sneak through the woods and follow them around. It's not safe out here. Which is exactly why I'm following him. I don't want any of us to be out here alone. Especially after what he's been through.

"Luca, wait," I call quietly to him as he races off ahead of me. I wonder if Orym stayed behind or is following us. I'm not a tracker, so I probably wouldn't know if he was in the woods right now. Leaves rustle in front of me, and I slow my steps as I investigate.

I've lost sight of Luca, and I'm not sure if it's because he shifted or if he just realized that I'm following him and is hiding. Before I can call out to him again, a hand clamps over my mouth and an arm pulls me back against a firm chest. Orym.

Shh, don't make a noise. Something feels off here. I should be upset that he grabbed me out of nowhere, but I'm relieved that I won't have to face whatever this is alone.

I don't see him anymore. Not sure where he disappeared to. I feel Orym nod behind me, then he releases his hold. We need to find Luca before something or someone else does. He motions for me to follow him, and I happily fall in step behind him as he moves silently through the trees.

When we get to the clearing, I hear something ahead of us that stops me in my tracks. Luca is talking to someone. His voice echoes around me. I can't hear the responses, though, and that scares me. Is he talking to himself? Or is there some-one else in the woods with us?

Orym moves faster instead of stopping. I jog to catch up with him. As we step into the clearing near the waterfall, Luca is pacing and jabbering. No one else is visible. *Who is he talking to?* I ask along our bond.

I don't get an answer to my question. Orym just shakes his head and continues to creep slowly toward Luca. "No, I haven't bonded with her." Luca pauses, as if listening to someone speak. "Yes, I want to. But I can't right now. It feels like they're all against me."

I exchange a glance with Orym as we watch Luca have a full-blown conversation with himself in the middle of the clearing.

"Of course, I don't want to reject her. I just don't know if I can trust them, that's all." It sounds as if he's speaking with a friend who's trying to convince him to bond with Garnet. "Yes, I love Red. I've always loved her. But I can't drag her down with me. I don't deserve her, not until I help take out Amber."

I don't want to interrupt, but Orym obviously has other ideas. "Luca?"

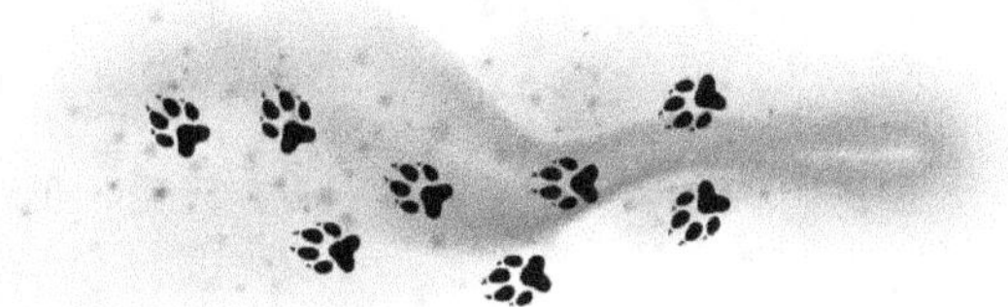

LUCA

I can't handle being this close to Red anymore. I shouldn't have kissed her. It was a mistake. I can't bond with her until I'm sure Amber has been dealt with. I won't risk her getting Red's full powers. I race past Orym and James into the woods. I don't know where I'm heading, but I have to get away. Logically, I know it's not safe to be out here alone, but I don't expect them to just let me run off.

If I cared, I would know I'm being followed. Since I know it's Red's other mates, I don't care. They aren't out to hurt me. Or are they? I should understand that the voice I'm hearing in my head isn't my own. I should realize that it's left over from when Amber held me hostage and tried to break me. Instead, I let her words dig into my brain until I'm not sure if they're hers or mine.

So, when a familiar voice joins the others in my head, I don't hesitate to respond out loud. *Boy, you know that they're just trying to help you.*

"You can't know that. It could all be a set up," I insist.

Have you bonded with the girl yet? That could help to ease your fears. I don't understand why everyone is so worried about if Red and I are bonded. First Amber, now this guy.

"No, I haven't bonded with her." I can't keep the defensiveness from my tone.

Don't you want to? Anger seeps through the question in my head. Of course, I want her. But I can't have her. Not yet.

"Yes, I want to. But I can't right now. It feels like they're all against me." It's hard to admit how I'm feeling, but somehow, I trust this man more than anyone else right now.

Are you planning to reject her? Another question that pisses me off. This guy is on a roll today. I don't understand why he doesn't just show himself.

"Of course, I don't want to reject her. I just don't know if I can trust them, that's all."

Don't you love her, boy? How can he question my love for Red? It's ridiculous and I don't even want to give him an answer. But I know that if I don't, it will sound like admitting that I don't love her.

"Yes, I love Red. I've always loved her. But I can't drag her down with me. I don't deserve her, not until I help take out Amber."

I hear James and Orym sneak up behind me, but pay no attention until Orym says my name. "Luca?"

I turn to face them. That's when I realize that my half of the conversation with my Fae friend was out loud, and they couldn't hear his part. Fuck. Now they probably think I'm crazy.

"Hi, guys. I was just," I gesture around, searching for an explanation.

"Talking to the Fae guy again?" Orym asks. I nod.

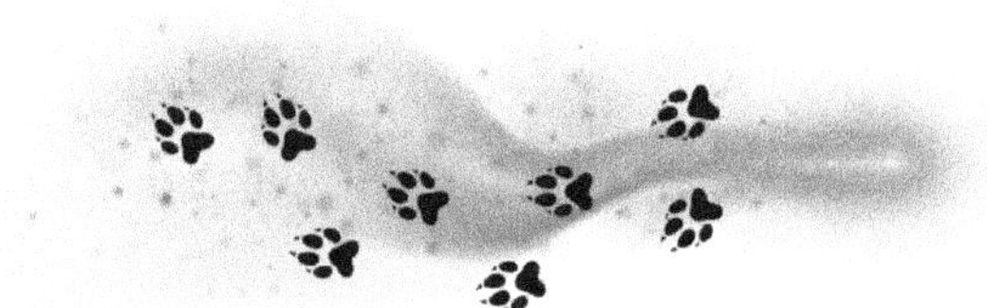

GARNET

"I know we can't push him, but I have to make sure Luca is okay. He kind of freaked out after he kissed me," I tell Ry before pushing away and heading for the door.

"You should let Orym and James handle him. They won't let anything bad happen." Ry's words are meant to comfort, but instead, they annoy me. I can't just sit here and wait for someone else to handle things for me.

I roll my eyes at him and step out onto the porch. "Are you going to help me track them, or not?"

With a sigh, he meets me outside and grabs my hand. I know he's irritated with me, but he doesn't argue. Ry leads me through the woods until we're almost to the waterfall. I should have expected Luca to head here. It's always been our favorite place.

He squeezes my hand to slow me down as we get closer. Words bounce along the trees, and I'm certain the others are nearby. "Yes, I was talking with the Fae man. I don't know how he's able to communicate without coming into our realm." That's Luca.

"Did you ask him about helping us with Amber?" And James. Orym can't be far from them. Ry pulls me along again after hearing the conversation.

"You know he can't just ask the guy to come over and help us defeat her. Realm jumping doesn't work that way. He can't come here unless he's invited by the territory holder. And I'm pretty sure they banished all Fae when we were kids," Orym explains.

Ry and I step out into the clearing and the three men turn toward us. Guilt washes over Luca's features. I don't know how to make this easier for him. But he has to know that teasing me isn't going to work. At least not without ground rules and a safe word.

"You don't have to run away every time you get frustrated," I say, locking eyes with Luca. He ducks his head and turns toward the water. I feel like I've said the wrong thing again and he's pulling away from me. I don't know how to fix this.

"Red," Ry warns. I shake my head at him. I can't stop myself from trying to talk to Luca. Maybe it'll be easier with the other three here. I don't know.

"Luca, please. I just want to talk. I can't take the way you've been pushing me away and avoiding me. Especially after that kiss." I don't normally talk about what I do with one of my guys in front of the others, but I'm making an exception here.

"I know, and I'm sorry. I just can't be what you need right now. I'm working on it." His quiet admission has me stepping closer to hear him. I stand beside him, as close as I can be without touching him. Electricity zings through me when he reaches over and takes my hand.

"I just want to be enough for you. I don't want these thoughts in my head. But I can't make them go away," he whispers, staring at the water.

"Let us help you," I beg. This distance between us is killing me. I can't take it, and I don't know what I'll do if he doesn't let me back in. I need this man more than I need to breathe, but I'm not sure he understands.

He brings my hand to his lips and presses a gentle kiss to my palm. "I love you, Red. More than I'll ever be able to show you. I can't put you at risk. Amber is still in my head somehow. I can't bond with you and give her access to your head like that. I won't."

Wait, what? He never told us that Amber had gotten in his head. "What do you mean? How is she in your head?"

Luca shakes his head and I look at my other mates. They're standing behind us, close enough to hear what we're saying, but far enough to give us a small semblance of privacy. "I don't know how to explain it. I can hear her voice sometimes inside my head. She's telling me that you're all out to get me and that I can't trust you. I know it's ridiculous, but I can't make it stop. And sometimes, I believe it."

"Oh, Luca." I turn and wrap my arms around him, pulling him close for a hug. I don't know how long I stand there holding him before he finally gives in and lets his arms wrap around me too. "Thank you for telling us. We'll find a way to get her out of your head. There has to be a spell or talisman. Something that will block her access."

"You think you can fix this?" The hope in his voice is tiny, but it's there. I nod against his shoulder and he hugs me tighter. I feel the tears streaming down my face. I don't care that I'm crying again. I realize that I've spent more time crying since I found out about my mates than I did my entire life. This situation with Amber is almost too much. The stress of what's coming has to be hard on my guys as well.

"I think if anyone can, it's our girl," James responds. Luca tenses for a moment, then relaxes against me.

"Especially if she has James to help her. He's the one who figured out the healing spell," Orym offers.

A pair of arms appear around Luca and me, and I know without looking up that it's Ry. "We'll figure it out together, Luca. That's what a pack does."

Before Luca can respond, two more sets of arms work their way around us, and it's a group hug. I can't help laughing at the absurdity of the situation. My mates and I are standing in the middle of the woods, hugging while preparing to take out my aunt.

Thirteen
SEARCHING

ORYM

WHILE I'M SURPRISED THAT Garnet chose to confront Luca with all of us as witnesses, I'm not really shocked at his response. I suspected that Amber was messing with his head somehow when he started to withdraw and refused to talk about it. Knowing allows us to help, though. The five of us stand there, next to the waterfall, in a group hug. It should feel awkward, but it doesn't. It feels right.

My doubts about Garnet fall away. In this moment, I know that the five of us are supposed to be together. We're meant to be a family. I won't fight it anymore. Instead, I will put more effort into helping Luca overcome Amber's hold on him. Once we do that, he'll be ready to bond with Garnet and our family—our pack—will be complete.

After our confrontation at the waterfall, the days pass quickly. James and Garnet focus on finding or writing a spell to block Amber's access to Luca. Ryland and I focus on training and preparing to fight against the witches. Luca bounces between the two groups. He's still skittish and unsure of us all. I don't know how to help him, other than just being here and supporting his feelings.

That means I'm somewhat of a go-between, though, and I hate that. Whenever he starts to feel overwhelmed, Luca comes to me and I step in, handling the work or conversation he was having when it happened. It's put a lot more stress on me, but

I'll deal with that if it means my family is working toward being whole.

I know that he's not trying to put me in the middle. Garnet knows that I'm just helping to keep him calm. That doesn't stop her from yelling at me when she's irritated at him. Everyone is on edge, and tempers flare.

"If you're not going to be helpful, then why are you here?" she asks in a huff.

"I certainly don't have to be," I reply, storming from the kitchen and slamming the door.

"I'm sorry for putting you in the middle there, Orym," Luca says as he strolls over to me.

I shake my head. "It's okay. You can't be expected to act like yourself after everything you've been through. She just needs to remember that."

He gives me a sad look. "I wish I could be myself again. I miss it. I hate feeling like an outsider in my own home." I hate that he feels that way, but I understand. It's why I'm willing to step in when he needs a break.

"Eh, she'll get over being mad at me by dinner. And if not, I'll just grab my food and eat out here. Don't worry about it." I want to encourage Luca to relax and take small steps toward being himself again.

"You know our girl. She holds a grudge better than anyone I know," he offers.

"True, but she's not really mad."

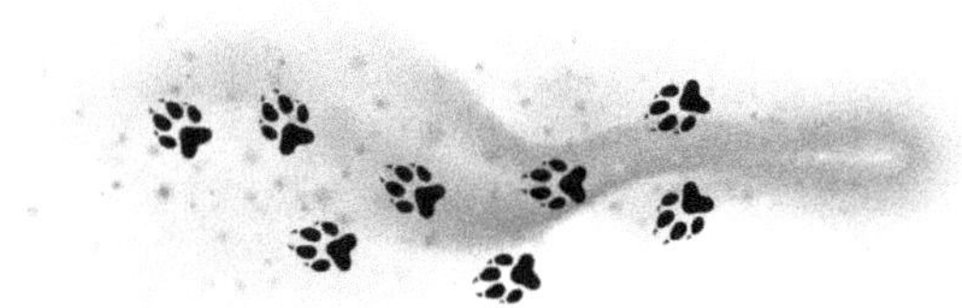

JAMES

"Maybe we should take a break," I suggest, taking the book out of Garnet's hands.

"Why? We were just starting to make progress," she protests.

"That was before you basically kicked Orym out, and after you yelled at Luca about being heartless. You need a break, love," I insist.

Garnet growls at me, but doesn't resist when I pull her into my arms. "When is Ry coming back?" she asks against my chest. He seems to be the only one who can ground her lately. I hate Gunnar for putting him on patrols, but I understand that he needs to maintain a semblance of control here. Especially since he's letting Garnet and me stay on pack lands.

"As soon as he's done with his patrols. You know that. Basically, whenever Gunnar decides to send him home. It's a small price to pay for him letting us stay here."

She grumbles against my chest, but makes no move to pull away. I know that my scent calms her too. It's just not as effective as Ryland's stern tone. Orym and I both have tried to mimic that tone, and nearly got beaten up by Garnet because it didn't work. Each of us has our strengths, and being bossy just isn't our way.

"Ryland will be here all day tomorrow. It'll be Orym's turn to go on patrols. I just need you to take a break, then we'll get back to it." I know that she hates being away from any of us, especially when Gunnar is the reason. But she understands the need for them to remain part of the pack and contribute to the community. I even offered to take patrol shifts as well, but Gunnar shot that down. Apparently, a measly human can't possibly protect wolf territory.

I laughed at his words, because this measly human has protected wolf territory on more than one occasion, and I will continue to do so. This has become my home, and these people are my family. I will protect both as fiercely as possible.

"Fine. I'll take a break. I'm wiped anyway." Her admission has me moving her toward the couch. If I can convince her to take a nap, then I can check on Luca and Orym. I'm sure neither of them is really upset by her outburst, but it never hurts to check in.

"Here, love, let me make you some tea. Just lay down and relax for a bit." I ease her down on the sofa and head into the kitchen to make her a cup of Jasmine tea. It seems to be the most calming thing we have on hand. I'll have to talk to Grammy about getting some other blends to relax Garnet.

By the time I carry the steaming cup of tea into the living room, she's out cold. I knew she was exhausted, but didn't expect her to fall asleep so quickly. I set the cup down and head outside to talk to the others.

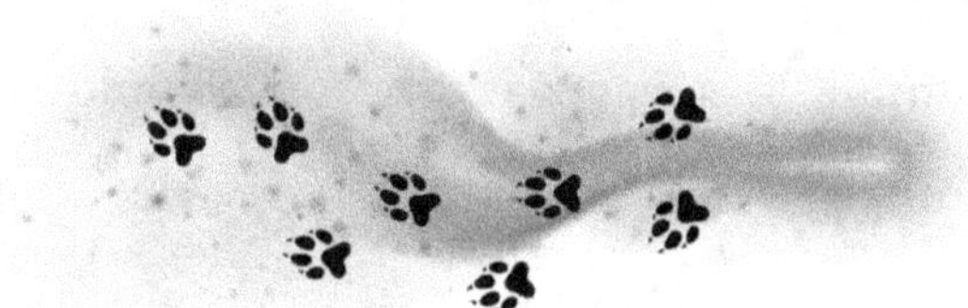

GARNET

I've spent the last few days alternating between working on a spell to protect Luca and being annoyed at everyone. I have to give them credit, they're trying so hard to keep me calm and focused. What I want is to find Amber and destroy her.

"We should go searching for the ones who are still missing," I suggest at breakfast. My four men all turn and stare at me.

"No," Ry says easily. He's been my moral compass since Luca was taken, but I can't agree with him now.

"It's not safe for Luca," James insists. I've already prepared for this argument.

"That's why he's not going. Luca will stay here and help with the patrols. Before you object, I've spoken with Gunnar and Grammy. They agree that no one should be patrolling alone. From now on, everyone will be teamed up in groups of three or more." I give my men a satisfied smirk.

Luca hangs his head in defeat. Or is that relief? I can't be sure. Either way, he doesn't fight me on this. That's good. I need him to cooperate.

"Well, I'm game," Orym responds. I turn to face Ry, knowing that he'll be the biggest challenge. I'm confident I can talk James into anything.

Ry meets my gaze, and for a moment, I think he's going to give in. "Why do you constantly try to overrule me?" Annoyance is written all over his face, and I feel my cheeks go red.

"I'm not trying to overrule you. I just can't sit here anymore and wait for Amber to attack us. I need to do something productive. We're stuck on the spell for Luca, so it just makes sense to take care of another important mission while we try to figure it out." I don't want to beg him, but I will if I have to.

"I can see her point," James backs me up. Three against one means I should be getting my way any time now.

"I guess I have no choice then, since you've turned everyone against me." Ry's growl makes me cringe for a moment. I know that he's not really mad, but it scares me all the same.

"That's not fair and you know it." Luca's voice breaks the silence. My eyes go wide as he lays into Ry. "Red is just trying to do something proactive and you're over here treating her like she's done something wrong. Just because you don't want to go searching for the missing people and the rest of us agree with her doesn't mean she's turned us against you. You owe her an apology. Now." He stares at Ry, and for a second, I think they're going to tear each other apart.

Orym and James shift in their seats as if preparing to grab Ry and Luca to keep them apart. Ry growls low and glares at me. I'm scared, but I won't back down. I can't stop them from fighting, no matter how badly I want to.

"I'm sorry, Red. It wasn't fair of me to accuse you of turning them against me just because they agree with you instead of me." Ry spits the words at me, and I'm certain that he doesn't mean them. Luca seems satisfied with it, though, so I'll let it go

.

"Thank you." I expect him to growl at me again, but he doesn't. Instead, he stands up and walks outside. "I really wasn't trying to piss him off."

"It's okay, Red. He'll get over it. You know how he is," Luca says quietly. "So, Gunnar is expecting me?" I nod and he presses a kiss to my cheek before he walks out the door after Ry. I hope they don't fight about this.

"You know it's less about you getting us to agree with you than the fact that you went to the territory leader without him, right?" Orym explains. I hadn't considered how Ry would react when I'd gone to talk to Grammy and Gunnar. It had been a hard enough conversation because things are still strained between me and the old man.

I don't know if I'll ever really forgive him for the way he treated me when I was growing up. I thought he was my father, and that he hated me. I don't even know if he really knew my mother, or if he just hates me because I'm not actually a wolf.

"Oh."

"That's what I figured. Just apologize to him after Luca leaves and you'll be okay. It's not like you were really trying to undermine his authority. You just tried to arrange things."

Orym pulls me into his arms and kisses my forehead. Then he walks outside too.

I exchange a look with James. He shrugs. "I don't know much about wolf politics, but I can see how that would upset him. All you can do is talk to him about it."

"Yeah. I feel pretty stupid right now. I should have talked to him about it before. I just didn't expect him to freak out about it because it was my idea." That's not fair, either, but it's how I feel.

"Orym and Luca say he'll get over it. They know him better than I do. It'll all work out. We should get ready to go if we're going to search today." I give James a hug and kiss him before I turn and head into the bedroom. I need to get dressed so we can get moving.

It's hard enough to search those woods in the daylight, but it's nearly impossible to do it in the dark. We're going to have to get going if we want to get back tonight. My heart constricts and I worry that I'm making a mistake trusting Gunnar to keep Luca safe. Part of me expects him to hand Luca over to Amber just to spite me. Surely, Grammy wouldn't let that happen, would she? I hope not.

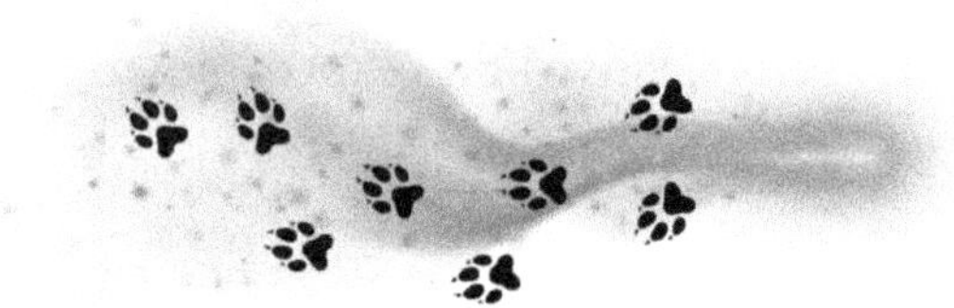

LUCA

By the time I get to Gunnar's, the meeting is almost over.

"You're late, Luca," he growls at me. "I'll talk to you when I'm finished here."

Fuck. I don't want to fight with him, but given that I just found out I'm supposed to be here, I can't just take his abuse. I've wanted to beat the shit out of the old man for years over the way he treats his daughter. No, not his daughter. Red. The girl he was charged with protecting. Somehow, that makes it even worse.

I know that I can't attack him here, in front of everyone. That would be officially challenging him for his role. I don't want it. I just want to defend Red for everything he put her through. I wait, listening to him tell the wolves who will patrol about sticking together in groups of three. He wants them to stay close to each other because the threat from the witches is getting worse.

I wonder how much of that is true and how much is what Red convinced him to say. How did she even get him to agree? There is no way he would just take her word for anything. I'll have to ask him—not that he'll answer.

"Okay, get into your groups and get moving. Jack and Paul, go help Grammy while I fill Luca in on the plan," Gunnar orders. At least I know who I'll be with this morning. Jack and Paul are good guys, and I can trust them to keep me safe.

The old man gestures for me to walk with him. I fall into step easily, wondering how bad this is going to be. "Look, Luca, I'm sorry for everything Amber did to you. We're going to keep you safe and make sure it doesn't happen again. But you have to be on time, otherwise, I'll have to punish you just like I do everyone else. Do you understand?"

"Yes, sir. I'm sorry. There's no excuse for my tardiness, sir." I can't exactly tell him that Red just told me about this plan five minutes before I got here. That would undermine what she did to get this arranged. "What exactly did I miss?"

"Your girl is something. She convinced Grammy to side with her and they blackmailed me into this plan of theirs. We're doing our usual patrols while the rest of your little family searches for the rest of the missing. If they find anything, we'll get called in for back up." His words are hateful, but there's no bite in his tone. If anything, he sounds impressed that Red found a way to force his hand. "Don't do anything stupid. You're watching their backs just the same as they are watching yours."

"Yes, sir. I won't let you down." After giving him my promise, I run off to find the others. Grammy usually harvests in her garden at this time of day, so I know that's where they are.

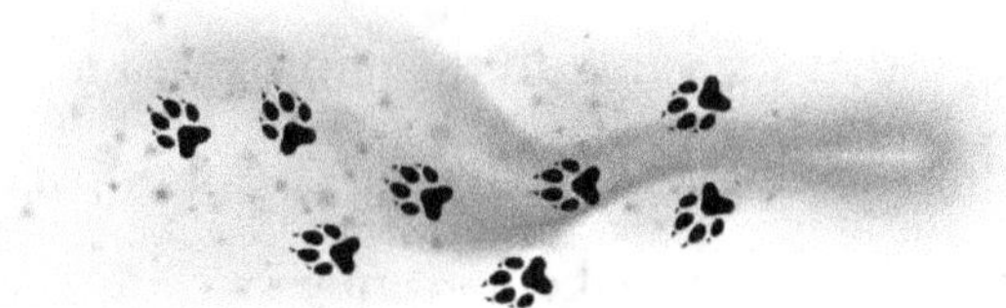

RYLAND

As pissed as I am that Red planned all of this out without even bothering to tell me, I'm impressed too. I can't believe that she talked to Gunnar and found a way to convince him to cooperate. I wonder how she did it. I'll ask her later, because right now, I'm not done being mad at her.

When Luca races out the door, I turn and watch him run. With Gunnar's patrol times, he's going to be late. I hope that doesn't end poorly for him.

A minute or so later, Orym joins me. "She didn't do it on purpose. Give her a break, would ya?"

"I know. I'm more proud than angry. But I have to make her understand that she can't do that stuff anymore. I can't have her putting herself at risk by chasing after Gunnar and arguing with him. How do I make her understand?" I'm frustrated with her and myself. I need to figure out a way to fix this. But first, I need to allow myself to be angry or annoyed.

"I think talking about it is the best option. We should get together as a family and discuss the situation. If you lay out specific expectations, there won't be any way for miscommunication to happen," he suggests. Why did I hate him? I can't even remember now.

"Thanks, Orym. I think that's probably a good idea." I'm about to head back into the cabin when James walks out the door.

"She's getting ready. And she understands why you're upset. Go easy on her, okay? She's pretty upset with herself right now, too." James' words are like daggers in my heart. I don't want to punish Red anymore. I want to comfort her. We'll definitely have to have a conversation about this later.

"We'll be okay. Don't worry about it. Everyone needs to focus on the search. We have to stay together. None of that splitting up to cover more ground stuff, no matter how hard she argues for it. Understood?" I can't be an effective leader if everyone is going off in different directions. Orym is right, clear expectations are the best way to handle this.

Both men nod. The door creaks open and we all turn to watch Red come outside. Even in jeans and a sweatshirt, she's gorgeous. Her flame-colored curls are pulled back into a messy bun today, and she looks tired. Am I to blame for that sad look on her face? Fuck.

"Red, we're okay. We'll talk about it as a family when we're done with the search. Don't be sad, please?" I can't help myself. I should be stoic and angry, but the sadness in her eyes is my undoing. I won't be able to focus on anything until I know that she's okay.

"I'm sorry, Ry. I didn't think about how it would look. I just wanted to help. I've been feeling so useless lately since we can't figure out that spell."

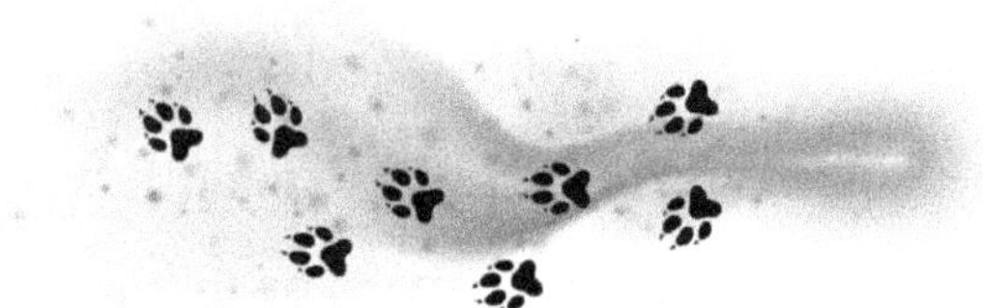

GARNET

I hate admitting that I feel useless, but it seems like honesty is the only choice here. Ry's reaction is not what I expect. I know I made him angry, but he seems more disappointed now.

"I don't want you to feel that way. I just need you to understand that pack rules still apply, even though you're not a wolf. James has to follow them too, so it's not like you're being singled out here. Gunnar is being nice enough to let me keep my family together, but it's *my* responsibility to deal with him, not yours." Ry's words hold no anger, though I can still see hints of it in his eyes.

"I was just trying to help. I had to have Grammy convince him to make the patrols work in groups. I should have talked to you about it instead of going around you. I'm sorry." I mean the apology, although Ry doesn't look convinced.

"Let's just focus on the task at hand. We can talk everything through when we get back and Luca is with us. It does no good to discuss pack hierarchy without the whole pack here," Ry says, dismissing the conversation. He pulls me close for a hug before releasing me and grabbing his backpack from the cabinet on the porch. Each of us has a pack in it, and it's kept locked at night.

We check our supplies then head into the woods. "We're staying together. No exceptions," Ry insists as we enter the witches' territory. I won't object to that, even though it grates my nerves for him to boss me around. I prefer to be subservient in the bedroom, not outside of it. And that only happens on occasion.

"How many are still missing?" James asks. We haven't exactly been briefed on the numbers, so I'm not sure either. He and I look to Ry for the answer.

Orym responds before Ry can. "At least thirty. There are still ten wolves unaccounted for. We think there are five humans who've been taken, and about fifteen vamps. The rest were either slaughtered by Amber, or rescued the day Luca got hurt."

"That's a lot of people to keep hidden. Where should we start?" I realize that it probably would have been better to discuss this before we entered the other territory, but I'd been so set on going that I didn't stop to think.

"I think the cabin near where she kept us is a good place to start. That place had holding cells and chains to keep the wolves and vamps in line," Ry suggests.

I can't argue with his logic, so we follow him toward that cabin. Once we get there, a cold chill washes over me. "Wait," I whisper, stopping in the same spot where I'd had a vision the last time we were here.

"What's wrong?" James asks, wrapping an arm around my waist. Orym steps up to my other side and puts a hand on my shoulder.

"Are you okay?"

Even Ry turns to look at me. "Something just feels off here. I want to try to do the thing I did before. Looking inside the cabin before we get there."

The three of them exchange a look and Ry nods. "That sounds like a good idea." They surround me, both holding me up and protecting me.

James gets me to breathe deeply a few times before I try to push my consciousness out. I close my eyes and focus on the cabin. I've never done this on purpose before, and it feels strange. When I open my eyes, I'm inside the cabin. There are six people inside, chained to the wall in the kitchen. I recognize four wolves from Gunnar's camp and two vamps I'd seen at Midnight the first time Kayden took me there.

I carefully search the rest of the cabin, going down to the dirt cellar. There are bodies down here. More than we expected. They're tossed in a pile as if they were trash to be discarded. We have to save the people upstairs.

I try to force myself back into my body, but it doesn't work. I walk back up the stairs and look at the prisoners again. I blink against the bright light, and the kitchen is empty. What the fuck is going on here? There were six people I knew tied up here a few moments ago, and now there's nothing. Am I going crazy?

I close my eyes and call to James along our bond. *Help me. I can't get back.* I feel his presence urging me to follow it. I chase that feeling until I open my eyes and I'm surrounded by my men. Everyone but Luca.

"That was strange. When I went into the cabin, there were four wolves and two vamps chained in the kitchen. I went downstairs to investigate, and there's a pile of bodies. When I came back up, the chained prisoners were gone. I don't know if they are there or not."

I'm shaking, so James pulls me closer. I lay my head on his chest, then feel Orym wrap himself around us. With the two of them holding me, I feel more centered. I take a few deep breaths before I life my head and lock eyes with Ry.

"We should go in and check it out. You didn't see any guards, right?"

I hadn't considered that. There were no guards. It seems strange to me, but if there aren't any guards, we can check it out without issue. "I didn't see any."

"Okay, let's go. Stick together. This could still be dangerous. Keep her between you," Ry gives the order, and for once, I don't want to fight him on it. I would prefer to stay sandwiched between Orym and James because it's where I feel safe.

We quietly follow Ry into the cabin, and find it empty. I would have sworn those people were in the kitchen.

TRAINING EXERCISES

JAMES

WE INSPECT THE ENTIRE cabin. The scent of death hits me as I walk down the steps to the dirt carved basement below the wooden structure. I know what I'll find before my feet hit the bottom. Just as Garnet described, a pile of dead bodies occupies a corner of the room. I wonder why her vision showed her live captives when there aren't any. Maybe it was one of Amber's tricks.

The disappointment of not finding any of the missing people hits us all hard. I don't know why we'd expected to just walk into the forest and locate them when an entire army of vampires and wolves couldn't find them before. It seems ridiculous, really. Yet, here we are.

We make it all the way to the cabin where Amber held us hostage, but there are no prisoners there, either. With heavy hearts, we creep through the woods until we're back in the wolves' territory. I don't know how we're going to find the people Amber has taken, and I'm not looking forward to telling Gunnar and Dec about finding the dead bodies.

I know my brother will take it better than the old wolf, but it's not something I would ever *want* to do. The more time we spend searching for these people, the less certain I am that any of them are still alive. I hate feeling hopeless, but I'm getting to that point.

Ryland doesn't even stop at our cabin when we exit the woods. He passes it, dropping his backpack on the porch. Orym, Garnet, and I do the same, following him to the clearing in front of Gunnar's place.

I steal a glance at Garnet to see how she's doing with this. Her hands shake and her body starts to tremble the closer we get to Gunnar. She looks like she's about to freak out and run away. I reach over and grab her hand to center her. If she goes into a panic attack right now, I don't know how her magic would react. She could blow us all up. I have to calm her down or get her out of here.

"Are you okay?" I whisper in her ear when I pull her against my side.

"I'm just worried about Gunnar punishing Ry because I overstepped," she admits.

"It'll be okay. You'll see. Ryland will handle it. Just focus on breathing. I've got you," I insist. I hope I'm right. I know how badly it will hurt her for Ryland to take another punishment because of something she said or did.

It would help if Gunnar wasn't such a dick who hates everyone who isn't a wolf. But I guess prejudice is a part of life. We have to figure out how to deal with it without causing a war. We're trying to win a different war already. There's no way to win if we're divided. So, we have to let Gunnar's attitude go and focus on what's important.

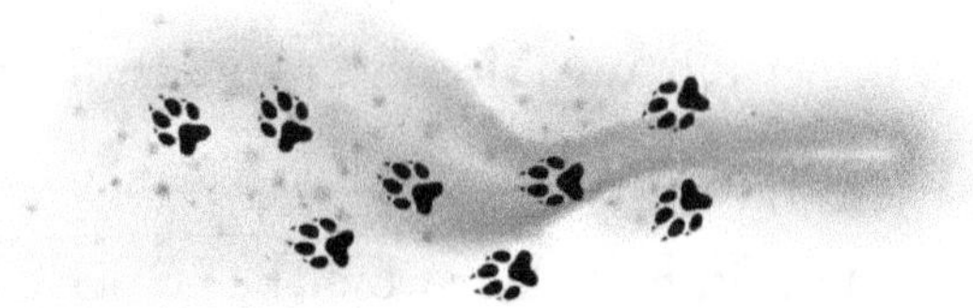

LUCA

Jack, Paul, and I finish our rounds just as people start to mutter about Red and the guys being back. From the sound of it, they didn't find anything good out there. Fuck, I should have gone with them. Maybe I could have helped find where Amber is hiding them.

"Hey, guys, it sounds like my girl is back. I need to see what they found. We're done, right?" I look from one to the other. We'd spent the day talking a little about Red and the threat from Amber. I refused to discuss my experience being taken. I know that they're just as curious as I am.

Both men nod and turn to follow me back to Gunnar's. "Do you think they found them?" Jack asks as we walk.

"I think if they did, we'd already know," Paul replies. I hate to admit it, but I agree with him. If Red had managed to rescue any more of the prisoners, there would be a much bigger crowd to fight through on our way to Gunnar's. That just proves the rumors we've been hearing.

I hope she's not too upset about it. I know that she beats herself up about failing, especially when she knows that Gunnar is depending on her. I hate the way he twists her up inside. The only thing she ever wanted was for him to love her and be proud of her. And somehow, he couldn't manage either one.

I never understood why he treated her so differently. But given that he's not her father, it makes sense now. As many times as she defended him when we were kids, I don't know how I never suspected. They look nothing alike, and their personalities could not be more different. The only thing they have in common is their shared love of the wolves and this territory.

"That's her, right?" Paul points to where James is practically holding Red up. I nod and push through the crowd, worried that she's hurt.

I have to get to her. "Excuse me," I say as I shove people out of the way. James passes Red to me easily, and I press my hands to her cheeks. "Are you okay?"

"Why does everyone keep asking me that? Do I look that bad?" She gives me a sad smile, and I press my lips to hers. I know that I've been pushing against the bond and completing it, but I need to feel her lips against mine.

When I pull back, I whisper against her lips, "You look perfect. I thought you were hurt, though, with the way James was keeping you on your feet."

She flicks her eyes to the man she used to call father. I nod and pull her into a hug. Gunnar still messes with her head, and I hate it. Suddenly, I want to fight him again. But I can't. Because I'm not about to challenge the territory leader. Even if I could win.

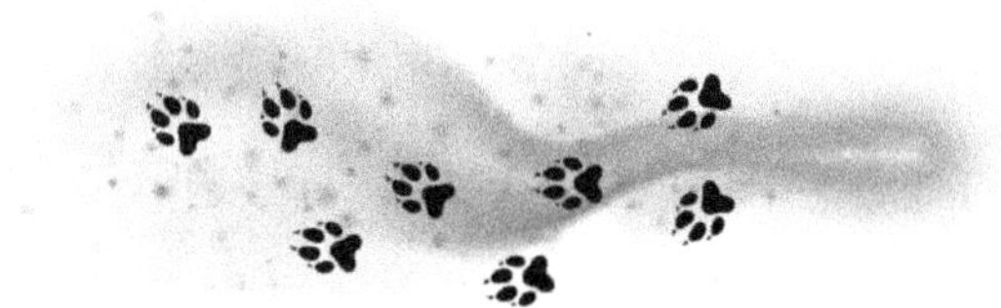

GARNET

I can't convince anyone to let me go searching again after our fruitless trip. So, I throw myself into training over the next few weeks. Ry insists that we all train together, because James and I both need to get stronger. I also need to get better at using my magic as a weapon and a defense system.

The only upside to getting knocked around by the men I love is that it's helping us learn to work together as a team. Orym, James, Ry, and I are pretty good at that already, but adding Luca in changes the dynamic a bit. It takes us a while to adjust.

Ry convinces Gunnar to let some of the stronger wolves train with us, so that we're not constantly splitting up our team to play both sides. Everyone knows that we have to pull our punches, because we don't want to hurt them, and they don't want to hurt us. We're basically playing the fight version of flag football and hoping that we have enough power to do it for real.

We regroup and discuss the plan for a moment before the other team is ready to start again. "Everyone knows the plan, right? We don't need to go over it again. Too much overthinking is going to throw us off. Good job working together. Just make sure you're watching Red's back when she starts casting spells," Ry instructs.

Magic still takes me too much focus, and I've almost been taken out twice this morning by the opposition. Luckily, one of my guys has stepped up every time and taken out the attacker. We break from our huddle and move into our positions to wait.

This time, Luca follows me. "What are you doing?" I ask. I know that Ry told him to stay with James today.

"Shh, don't tell on me. We're supposed to be hiding right now. But we're also supposed to make sure we protect you. That's what I'm doing." Luca pulls me into his arms and presses his lips to mine.

He's still not fully himself, but maybe that's what makes this so hot. He fists a hand in my hair, urging me to open my lips for him. When I do, his tongue strokes along mine in slow teasing motions. I groan into his mouth and he nearly goes feral. He nips at my bottom lip, then licks it to soothe. The whole kiss sends shockwaves of pleasure straight to my clit.

I want to call off the training and drag him back to the bedroom, but I can't. I hear something behind us, and have to fight myself to break the kiss. One look at Luca, and I'm certain he's as worked up as I am. But he looks smug too, like he just proved something to himself. I'm not sure if it has to do with kissing me, or luring the other team to us to attack.

"Was this your plan?" I ask, in awe of his apparent ability to multi-task.

Luca grins at me sheepishly. "I wanted to kiss you. This way just helps us prepare for dealing with the cult, too."

I can't be mad at him. His plan makes sense. Letting the others think that we're distracted by passion—which I totally was—is an amazing tactic. Especially if Luca was aware the whole time. It doesn't quite seem fair that he'd be able to focus on our surroundings while I got lost in kissing him. I guess it's good that he did, though.

The first arrow hits the tree above my head. We're using rubber tipped arrows and foam knives so no one actually gets hurt even if they get hit. After a couple of weeks doing these exercises, we all have bruises, but no one has really been injured. It occurs to me that Amber hasn't attacked either. I wonder if she has someone spying for her.

It wouldn't be hard to slip someone in the camp. In fact, if she turned one of the people she captured, that we rescued, then we'd be the ones responsible for the spy. Fuck. Why didn't I think of that sooner? Of course, she has someone watching us. And that's why she only attacks when she knows that we're not prepared.

I need to discuss this with all of my mates before we take it to Gunnar. I wonder who the spy could be. It's the only thing that makes sense. And it explains how Amber is always two steps ahead of us. I can't let that bitch win this. There's too much at stake.

It doesn't matter that she's my aunt, and part of me wants to love her. I have to destroy her. She's crazy, and has no regard for human life. Luca notices the change in my posture as my thoughts distract me.

"What's wrong, Red?" His eyes search my face as if the answer is written there.

"I need to talk to everyone, as soon as possible. I think I've figured out how she's beating us," I admit quietly.

"Okay. Then we need to call this training off today." Since this isn't a real fight, we have white scraps of cloth we can wave if someone needs a break or were to actually get injured. Luca steps away from the tree and waves his cloth frantically. "Hey, guys, Red needs to talk to us. It's important. We have to stop for today."

I don't tell him that I could have gotten Orym, James, and Ry's attention without him calling out. I hate reminding him about the bond and its benefits. Hopefully soon, he'll decide that he's ready for it, and he'll be one of the voices in my head too. I wonder if that makes me sound crazy. I'm not sure that I care. I love these men, and I've adjusted to having each of them connected to me in a way that no one else is.

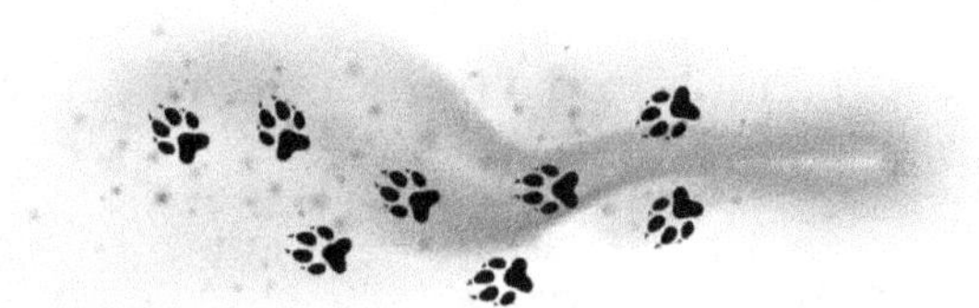

RYLAND

For a second, when Luca waves his flag, I think that Red's been hit. Then he says that she needs to talk to us, and I realize that she's either had a vision, or she's figured something out. I'm not sure which is better, honestly.

I step out of my hiding spot and wave my white flag as well. I don't know if the other team saw Luca's, and I need this to stop immediately. If Red needs to talk to us, and it's urgent enough to stop training, then that's what's going to happen.

"Hey! Everyone front and center. We're done for the day. Stand down. Training is complete for today. Thanks," I call to everyone. The members of the opposition slowly move toward me and line up. They're suspicious that this is a trick, and I don't blame them. It would be funny to take them out right now, but that's not what I'm doing here.

"Is everything okay, Ryland?" one of them asks. I think it's Luca's friend Jack. Luca answers before I can.

"Yeah, Paul, everything is okay. Red needs to talk to us and it can't wait. We'll fill you in as soon as we can." I guess I was wrong about which guy this was. Oh, well.

"Call us if you need anything," another man says to Luca. I'm not even going to try to figure out who this one is.

"Thanks, Jack. We will. You guys are awesome for helping us," Luca tells the man, pulling him in for a hug. See, I knew Jack was here somewhere. I just didn't know which one he was.

That's not important right now. Red needs us. We all wave as the other team heads back toward the main camp. I love having one of the outermost cabins. We have way more privacy than most of the others. As soon as everyone else disappears into the trees, I walk over to Red.

"What's going on?" I ask as Orym, James, and Luca crowd around us. "Did you have a vision?"

She shakes her head. "No, but I just realized why Amber is so far ahead of us on everything. Someone in the wolf camp is helping her. And it's someone who has access to information, so they're close to Gunnar or us." I stare at her in disbelief. How would Amber manage that?

"Think about it," Luca says. "Amber only attacks when we're not ready for her. She hides the hostages when we search for them. It's the only thing that makes sense. But who?"

"Someone she kidnapped and we rescued," Orym offers.

"Or someone who escaped," I say, looking at Luca. It would explain why he's been so distant and hard to read.

"You think it's me?" Luca's jaw drops and his eyes go wide. "Oh, shit. What if it is me, and I don't even know it?"

"It's not you," Red insists, taking Luca's hand. "It's not him." She addresses the second statement to me.

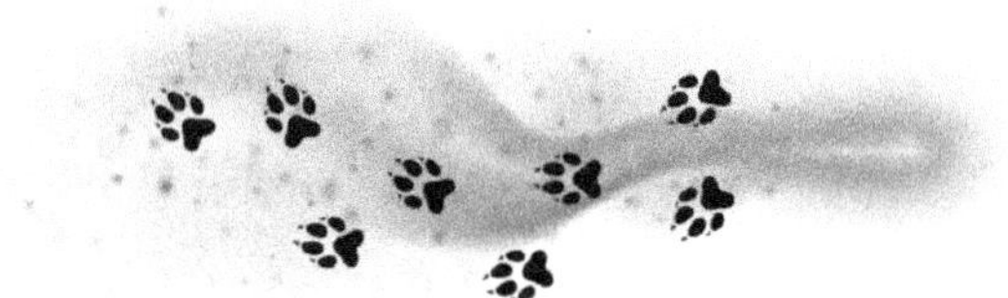

ORYM

Garnet insists that Luca isn't the spy. I agree with her, but I also understand why Ryland is suspicious of him. The timing of everything is just too convenient. If Luca isn't the spy, then someone is trying very hard to frame him for it.

"Who else could it be? I've known every move we were going to make. I'm close to all of you. I know what powers

Red has and what she's working on. It's the only thing that makes sense." Luca sounds paranoid, but who can blame him? During his time with Amber, we have very little information about what actually happened to him.

He doesn't like to talk about it, and claims that he doesn't remember a lot of what happened. It's definitely something to look into. "There has to be a way to tell for sure," I say, stepping forward and threading my fingers through Garnet's. She needs us to be strong right now.

"Don't tell me. Wait until I'm far enough away to talk about it. That's the only way to know for sure. If the four of you discuss it, and somehow Amber knows, then it's not me. If she doesn't find out, then it could be me." Luca races back to the cabin before we can stop him.

"Devil's advocate here, but what if it is him, and he's just hiding in the woods somewhere to listen to us and make it appear that it's not him?" James finally speaks up. I had begun to wonder if he had an opinion at all.

"You think he ran off to hide?" Garnet asks. Her voice is quiet, with a tremble that only happens when she's about to cry.

"I think that if it is him, he doesn't know it. I was just posing a potential scenario that we should be cautious of. I do agree that a spy makes the most sense. And if it's not Luca, it's someone who wants us to think it is," James offers. At least I'm not the only one thinking that a frame up is possible.

"It's not Luca. I'm sure of it. I don't know who it is, but I know it's not him," Garnet insists. Tears stream down her cheeks, and I reach up to wipe them away.

"If it helps, I believe you. I don't think it's him either, but it does look like it could be. I understand why Ryland is suspicious, and I understand why Luca is worried." I want to make all of this worry go away, but I don't know how.

"This whole situation is impossible. Because James is right. If it is Luca, he could be hiding and listening to us right now. If it's not, then someone is trying awfully hard to make us think it is Luca. There's no real way to know until it's too late." Ryland's words dance through my head, giving me an idea.

"What if we set a trap?" I suggest.

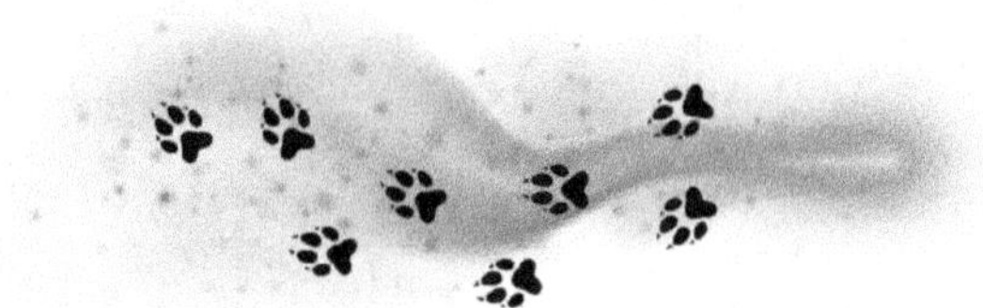

GARNET

We can use the bond to communicate. Then the four of us are the only ones who know what's been said. Orym's voice is sweet inside my head.

So, we don't talk about anything. We just use the bond? I ask. It could actually work. Since I'm not bonded with Luca yet, there's no way he could spy on our conversations. I don't want to think about him betraying us. I'm certain that he's not the one who's been telling Amber what we're planning. I just don't know how to prove it.

Yes, and we actually talk about different scenarios in front of other people to see which one Amber finds out about. Ry's voice is gruff, but he sounds excited.

Exactly. Orym agrees, and I can feel a tiny spark of hope light up in my heart. I knew there had to be a way to figure this out.

With our plan in place, we head back to the cabin. When we get there, Luca is inside, watching a movie. *See? He did come back here.* I feel a little smug knowing that I'm right about Luca and his motives.

He jumps when we burst through the door. "That didn't take long," he says as we all settle in around him.

"We figured out a way to test you and find out who the real spy is at the same time," Ry tells him. I'm surprised that they're going to give him that much info.

"That's great. What is it?" Luca makes a face. "On second thought, don't tell me."

"Don't worry, we won't." Ry grins. It's unnerving how hot he is when he's cocky. And that's almost all the time. I wish that I could bond with Luca, but I understand now why he's so hesitant. I think he's been suspicious of himself for a while.

For the rest of the day, we relax and watch movies. It's almost like we're normal people again. I can almost believe that we don't have a war to fight, and that we're not responsible for fighting against my crazy aunt who's on a quest for power. Almost.

Over the next few days, we work out the details of our plan to find the spy. Orym and Ry come up with different scenarios to share with random people. James and I work on the blocking spell to protect Luca. I believe that he's suspicious of himself because he still feels like Amber is in his head. And I understand that. But I don't think she has that kind of power over him.

I think he's just hearing echoes of things she said and did to him, and it's freaking him out. We don't hear from our Fae friend, and I begin to wonder if he really wants to help. Having Fae on our side could prove useful, but if we can't find a way to contact them, there's no reason to worry about it.

I should be thankful that they aren't working with Amber. If they were, she might be unstoppable. As it is, we're struggling to figure out how to defeat her.

"I understand that, but they're working on a spell. I can't just interrupt because you want an update," Ry says into the phone. I'm sure he's talking to Gunnar, and I'm amused that he's actually lying to the old man. It's not like Ry to pull punches or hide the truth.

When he hangs up, I raise an eyebrow at him. "What was that all about?"

"Gunnar wants to know when we'll be ready to move on Amber again. I keep pushing him off, since we're trying to find the person who's giving Amber our plans, but he's starting to ask too many questions. I might have to clue him in on the plan, if we can't get this sorted soon." Ry's annoyance is clear. We had already decided that keeping Gunnar in the dark was for the best.

"I trust you. If we have to tell him, we will. It's going to work out. You'll see." I'm confident that we will get through this together, even if James and I can't figure out this damned spell.

"How much longer do you think it'll be before you get the protection spell figured out?" Ry asks, looking at James, even though I'm sure he's talking to me.

"We're testing possibilities," James answers.

"That's a nice way to say that we're still stuck. Nothing is working so far," I explain. "But we're not giving up. We just have to try something different."

I'm annoyed that we've spent weeks trying to find a way to block Amber from having any contact with Luca. The lack of progress we're making is driving me crazy. It may not be possible to block her. Or maybe there's no connection, and that's why we can't figure it out.

Fuck, what if this is all just some huge conspiracy that's designed to make us think Luca isn't the spy while he really is? I take a deep breath and refocus myself. I can't start doubting him now. I know that Luca isn't the one who's giving Amber information. He can't be. I just have to trust that my men will find the responsible person and handle it.

"I think it's time for a break," James says. It's hilarious to me how in tune he is with my emotions. From the look he gives me, I know that he's aware of the weird path my thoughts just took. I've learned how to shield my thoughts, though, so I know he's not reading them.

"That's probably a good idea. I'm getting hungry anyway," I respond. Ry nods at us and we head back into the house. Orym was apparently working on lunch already.

"I made a fresh salad," he offers. Each of us grabs a bowl and we circle the table to eat as a family.

"Hey, I helped chop veggies," Luca claims. I laugh at the easy way they get along.

FIFTEEN
CHALLENGES

LUCA

Things are going pretty well for us, besides not being able to find Amber's captives. Everyone is on edge, especially

Gunnar. He wants results, and is pissed that he has very little leverage to force Red to cooperate. He's already threatened to kick us from the pack. Ryland is taking the threat seriously. He's already spoken with Kayden about helping us find another place to live.

I think he should just challenge Gunnar and take over, but Ryland claims that he doesn't want the responsibility. I would do it myself, but being unbonded would cause too much controversy when I finally do bond with Red. As much as I hate to admit it, Ryland has already proven himself capable of leading. I managed to get kidnapped and held prisoner by the woman who's out to destroy our race.

Leaving the forest is the only thing that makes sense. If Red would agree, we'd all be staying in the warehouse Kayden let them use when they were preparing to rescue me. It's out of the way and secure. I keep arguing with her about it, but she refuses to even consider it.

There has to be something we can do to find the missing people and rescue them. They should be home with their families, not slaving away for Amber or being used in her experiments. I'm still pissed at myself for not being able to find out more about those. If only I had pretended to be on her side, maybe I could have learned something useful.

"Stop beating yourself up over everything," James says, nudging my shoulder.

"What?" I have no idea how he knew what I was thinking about.

"Your poker face is horrible. Don't try to hide it. You were thinking about when you got kidnapped again." This man is so in tune with everyone, it's almost like he can read minds. I don't know how he does it.

"I have no idea how you do that, but stop it. It's not fair for you to know what we're all thinking when we have no idea what you're thinking." Turning it around on him isn't fair, but right now, I'm not worried about fair. I'm worried about deflecting.

"I can just tell." His answer gives nothing away. "For what it's worth, I agree that Ryland should just challenge Gunnar. It wasn't fair of him to yell at you about it, when he's not even really given it any consideration. He should at least be willing to have a conversation with all of us before he brushes away the suggestion." I like that James is on my side, even if I don't understand why.

He knows very little about wolf politics, and doesn't really seem interested. Of course, neither is Red, and she knows all about it. "I really wish that talking to him helped." I'm relieved that he changed the subject, and I don't want to mention it.

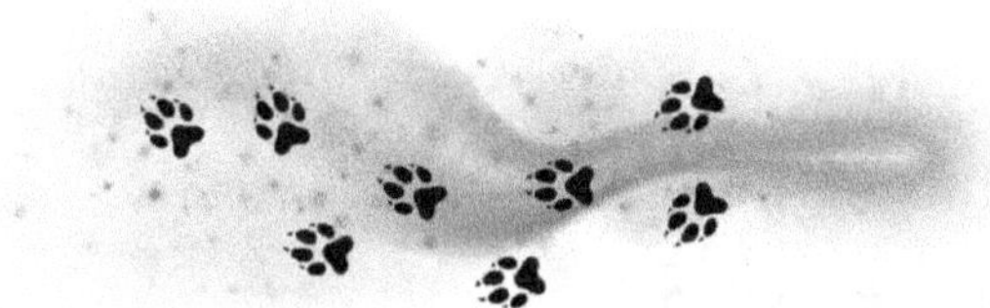

RYLAND

"For the last time, I'm not going to challenge Gunnar. If you think it's such a good idea, then you do it. I'm sick of having this conversation with each of you," I snarl. I just yelled at Luca

for suggesting it, then Orym comes up and tries to talk me into i
t.

I don't want Gunnar's job. Being the territory alpha sounds great, but there's so much to it that most people don't know about. I'd rather have that time to myself than to give it away to people who don't appreciate me at all.

"Fine. Maybe I will," Orym responds. My jaw drops. I can't tell if he's serious or not. That would definitely change the power dynamic here if he took over the territory. I'm not sure how I feel about it. I'd like to think that I would be happy for him and support him. But I know better. I'd be jealous and pissed that I didn't do it.

Fuck. These assholes are going to make me challenge Gunnar. I don't know if I can survive that. For one thing, he doesn't fight fair. A challenge is supposed to be no weapons, one-on-one, and respectful. There is no way Gunnar would do any of those things.

But I guess that's why they want me to challenge him. I don't know if I can do it. "Look, Orym. Can we just talk about this later? After everyone has calmed down, maybe? I just don't want any of us to do something we're going to regret." Is that a chicken shit answer to the suggestion? Yes.

Am I ashamed of it? Also, yes. But I think it's what I have to do to protect my family.

"Okay. But you know we're not going to wait forever. If you won't challenge him, one of us will." There are only three wolves in our pack, plus a witch and a human. Literally the only ones who could challenge are me, Luca, or Orym. I understand why Luca wants it to be me. Hell, I understand why Orym wants it to be me. I'm just not sure that *I* want it to be me.

"I'll think about it, okay? Just back off," I concede. It seems to be enough to get him moving. Today is his day for patrols with Gunnar's crew. Somehow, I managed to work out a schedule where the three of us take turns. It makes training and preparing easier, because we're only ever down one guy. But it stinks, because they always come up with the stupidest ideas when it's my day to be away.

I don't even know how Red feels about the idea that I could challenge Gunnar. She grew up thinking he was her father, after all. I'm sure that won't be something she'll be happy about. But if I'm really going to think about it, maybe I should talk to her and see what she thinks. If it would upset or hurt her, I won't do it.

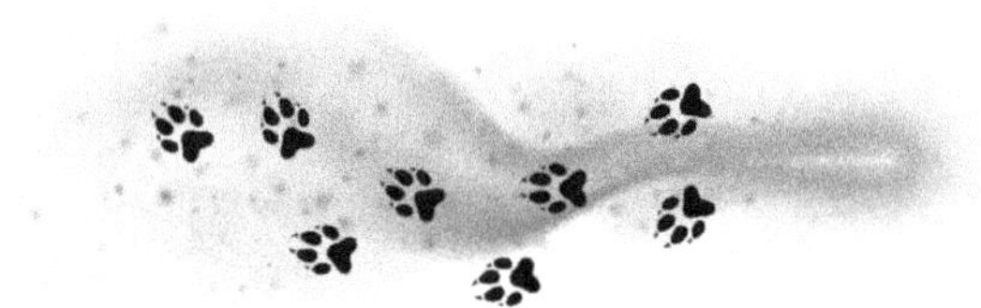

GARNET

They don't think I know, but the guys have been hounding Ry about challenging Gunnar for a while now. They think that Ry should issue the challenge and take over control of the territory. Honestly, I think he should too. But I understand why he won't.

At least, I think I do. For one thing, it's a big responsibility. For another, I'm sure he's conflicted about it because of me. My big growly wolf has been extremely gentle and understanding where I'm concerned lately. It's sweet and strange at the same time. I'm not used to him being so nice.

So, when he walks into the clearing where I'm working on the protection spell, I decide that this is the time to bring it up. "Hey, there," I say casually.

"Can we talk?" Suddenly, he's my growly, serious alpha. As much as I want to let him say whatever it is and see where it goes, I'm not willing to let go enough to do it.

"About you challenging Gunnar?" The look of surprise on his face is priceless.

"How did you know?"

"The guys aren't as quiet as they think. I know they've been after you about it for a while. Why don't you want to do it?" I'm truly curious to know if I have him figured out or not.

"Why do you think?" I hate when he answers my questions with questions, but in this instance, I think he needs to hear my thoughts.

"I think you probably have more than one reason. But possibly, the fact that Gunnar raised me and is the only father I've ever known—no matter how shitty—might prevent you from jumping at the chance," I suggest.

"And what would you say if that was the reason that I haven't done it yet?" Typical Ry, avoid and deflect to get more information instead of just answering the damned question.

"I would say that you need to figure out why you want it or why you don't. Then you can go from there." Two can play at the vague, non-answer game. I feel like we're playing a game of chess, and I can't tell who's winning.

"I deserve that answer. Okay. Full confession. I would love to challenge Gunnar. But I won't, for two reasons." He pauses and locks eyes with me. "Number one, he doesn't fight fair. There is no way he will accept a challenge and follow the rules of it. Number two, he raised you. I won't do something that will upset you."

"What if it wouldn't upset me? Then how would you feel about it?" I'm pushing without answering his unspoken question. It may not be fair, but I want to know what he really wants, not what the others want him to do. "Like, if the whole thing was up to you...what would you do?"

"If I knew that you and the guys were behind me on it, I would challenge him. I might not win, because we all know how he cheats. But I would stand up for everyone he's ever mistreated and do my best to make it right." By the time he's done talking, tears are rolling down my cheeks.

"Ry, that is the most beautiful thing I've ever heard." I press my lips to his. "Let me make this easier for you. If you want to challenge Gunnar, the four of us will stand behind you. If you don't, then I will make them drop it. This is your call."

He sighs, then pulls me into his arms and kisses me hard. There's a chance that he could be killed if he fights against Gunnar. I've watched it happen a few times over the years. The difference is that I think Ry could take him in a fair fight. I need to think about what I can do to help make it a fair battle if it comes to that.

"Do you really think this is a good idea?" he asks when he pulls back.

"I don't know. There are so many ways this could play out. But we're your pack, and we will stand by you, no matter what you decide."

"Thank you. I want to do it, but I'm worried that this isn't the right time. With the missing wolves, vamps, and now humans, and the ongoing war with Amber—you don't think that me issuing a challenge will mess all that up?" Ry furrows his brow and stares into my eyes.

"I think that you will know when the time is right. And it's not going to be easy, because we still have a spy in the territory, too. So, if you do challenge him, there could be an attack while you're fighting. If that happens, we will deal with it. Don't let a fear of 'what if' keep you from doing what you feel is right to protect your people."

"You're my people. I will always protect you," he says, pressing a kiss to my temple.

"Can I ask you something?" I look up at him again, and he nods. "Do you want to lead the territory? Or do you think you should because it's the 'right thing' to do?"

"Honestly? I'm not really sure. When I was younger, I watched the guys who challenged Gunnar. I thought to myself, someday, that will be me. Except I planned to win. Now that I have you, I'm not sure anymore." His vulnerable answer touches me.

"I appreciate you being honest. I don't want you to do this, unless you're sure. Because if you win, you're stuck leading these people. If that's not what you want to be doing, you shouldn't challenge." I don't want to talk him out of it, but I do want him to be sure that it's what *he* wants.

Ry wraps his arms around me and hugs me tightly. "Thank you for this. Knowing that you'll support me no matter what means everything."

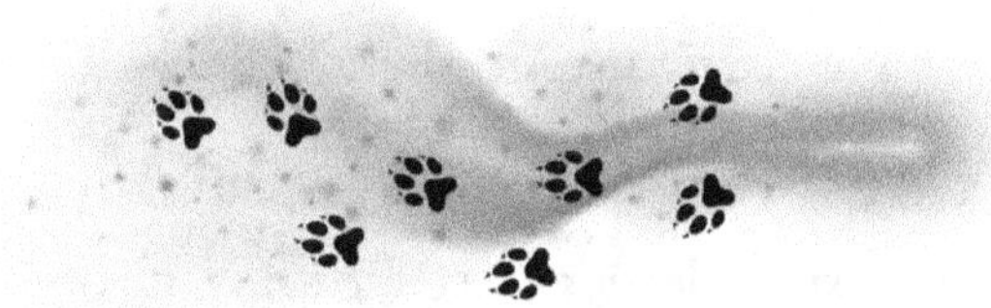

ORYM

Everyone settles in for dinner, just as I set the casserole on the table. Ryland made a big deal out of all of us being here tonight, so I think he has something important to discuss. Maybe there's a lead on the prisoners, or he's learned something about the spy.

"This looks and smells amazing, Orym, thank you for cooking tonight," Ryland says. Now I'm really suspicious. He's been nicer to me since we both bonded with Garnet, but he's still not usually this nice.

"What is it that you need to talk to us about?" I ask. The look I give him is enough to make him uncomfortable. I'm not the only one who knows that he's not usually this nice.

"I guess we'll get right to it, then." He pauses and looks at Garnet. When she nods, he continues. "I'm going to challenge Gunnar for territory leader. I need to know if you're all behind me on this."

My jaw drops. I never thought he'd agree. I'm not sure how I feel about this, but I know it's something he's always wanted. One of the reasons we stopped hanging out as kids was his obsession with taking over for Gunnar and destroying any possible competition he might have. I wonder if he remembers that.

I know this is the right thing to do, but I'm a little disappointed that Ryland made the decision to challenge. I was hoping I would get the chance.

"That's great news!" Luca exclaims. Of course, he's all in for Ryland to challenge Gunnar. I'm kind of surprised that Luca isn't the one challenging the old man. I mean, I could do it. But that would mean that one of us would be taking away Ryland's dream. No matter how fucked up he got about it as a kid, I won't do that to him.

Even James seems to be on board for it. "Hey, man, congrats! You know we're all behind you."

"Do you think it's a bad idea, Orym?" Garnet asks. She leans forward and locks eyes with me.

I shake my head. "No, I think he should do it. I just wonder if Amber will use this against us, since we're in the middle of a conflict with her." I know that it's a valid concern, and I'm surprised that no one else has voiced it.

"Ry and I talked about that. We'll have to be ready for that possibility. But he didn't make this decision lightly. I know that he's spoken with each of you individually, and I encouraged him as well. What he needs right now is to know that his family supports his decision and will do what we can to keep the challenge honest." Garnet looks at each of us as she speaks. All the wolves know that Gunnar does not fight fair, and will cheat to win.

James doesn't look shocked by her words, so someone must have filled him in as well.

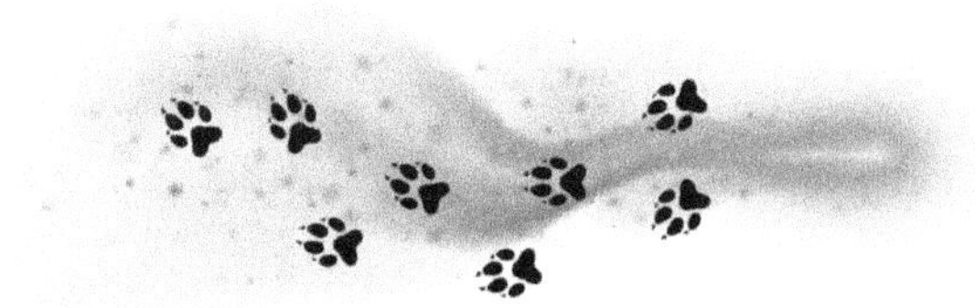

JAMES

Ryland's announcement is huge. Challenging the territory leader is a big decision. Even though I encouraged him to do it, I didn't think that he would. If he wins, he'll get a seat on the council. I wonder if that would get me removed from my seat on the council. Amusingly, I find that I really don't care about that.

We'll have to replace Amber anyway, since she's the witch representative and, well, she started a fucking war. I can't help smiling as I consider the council completely restructuring again. Vik will be pissed at having to be around new people.

"So, when will you issue the challenge?" I ask.

"Tomorrow morning. I'd like for all of you to accompany me," Ryland answers. The fact that he wants all of us there makes me feel like a valued part of the family.

"Are you afraid of a negative reaction from other packs?" I pause and look at each of them carefully. "I just mean, since your pack has a human and a witch in it, and all the others are wolves." I didn't mean it the way it sounded, but I can tell that they all understand.

"Red grew up here. No one looks at her differently. And you're one of her fated mates. They can't really object to that. It would be different if you or Red were the ones challenging Gunnar," Luca explains.

Orym agrees. "Yeah. They could argue against Gunnar accepting a challenge from either of you. But from Ryland, he has to accept or step down and transfer his power. That would be like what happened with Levi, when Gunnar took over from him. They fought, but Levi abdicated his position before Gunnar could kill him."

I wasn't aware of that particular practice, but I know that challenging the alpha usually means a fight to the death. I look at Garnet. "Are you sure you're okay with this? If Ryland kills Gunnar, that won't hurt you?"

"I'm sure it won't be a comfortable feeling, but every memory I have of that old bastard is uncomfortable. He wasn't ever really a loving father. There are things no one else knows, that I will not talk about. I will say, though, that he never sexually abused me. That was the one line he wouldn't cross. Probably because I'm not actually a wolf." Her explanation pisses me off, and I want to rip the old man's head off.

"I'm not going into it planning to kill him. I want to make him bow to me. I want to rule over him the way he has us. To make him see how horrible he was to all of us, but to Red especially." Anger flares in Ryland's eyes, and I'm certain that he could kill Gunnar if it came down to that.

If Garnet is okay with it, I am too. The old man didn't torture me, but he hasn't ever been nice to me, either.

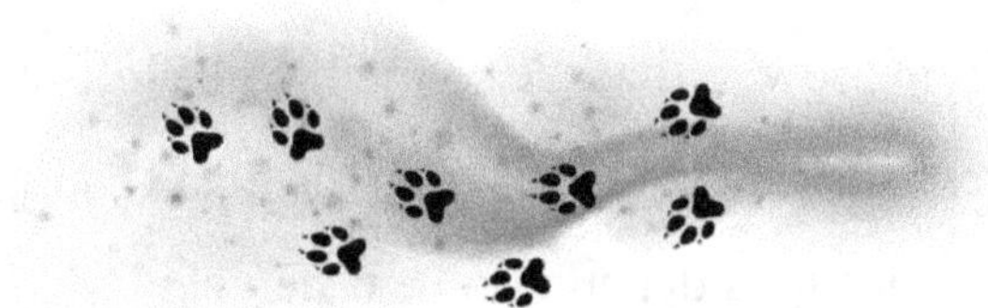

GARNET

The conversation at dinner was intense, but everyone agrees that Ry should challenge Gunnar. The old man is getting more and more over-the-top with his demands for control, and someone has to put him in his place. When we're standing in front of his cabin, I want to run away. I know that I can't. Just like I knew that I couldn't stand in Ry's way when he admitted that he wants to do this.

It doesn't matter if I'm feeling conflicted. This is what has to happen. Ry is going to issue the challenge and insist that the fight happens as soon as possible. It will give Gunnar less time to cheat. Once the challenge is issued, James is going to call Dec and let him know so that the council can be informed.

The rest of us are going to watch the man I thought was my father like our lives depend on it. If he does try to cheat, I'm going to use my magic to stop him. I won't interfere with the outcome of the fight, but I won't let him use unfair methods to win.

My heart races as we stand in front of the cabin and wait for Gunnar to come outside. Grammy answers the door when Luca knocks. "Gunnar, you need to come here," she calls over her shoulder as she walks outside. I jump when she stands next to me.

"You can't let him do anything illegal here, Red. You have to be ready to use your magic on him," she whispers.

"How did you know?" I can't stop myself from asking. Luca didn't say anything to her. Somehow, she just knew.

"I've been waiting for this day for years. I know that Ryland wants to lead, and I think he'll be good at it. But you know my son as well as anyone else does. He won't play fair." She says the words as if we're talking about the weather. There's no emotion in her tone or on her face.

I take a deep breath as Gunnar steps out of the cabin and stalks toward us. I know that he's heading straight for me, expecting to intimidate. Before he gets to me, though, Ry takes a step to his left and blocks Gunnar.

"Move, boy. I'm gonna take care of this problem once and for all," Gunnar growls. Is he really telling my mate that he's going to kill me? I can't stop the laugh that bubbles up in my chest.

Ry presses a hand to his chest, stopping him. "No, sir. I'm here to challenge you for the territory leader position. We can either fight it out today, right now; or you can submit and hand over control. Which will it be?" Ry's voice is calm, and even though I can't see his eyes, I know that they're filled with anger.

He won't take Gunnar's threat lightly. Of course, that was the point of it. Gunnar wants to intimidate me and force me to submit. I won't, because I'm not one of his wolves. It's amusing to me, because I never was his to break.

Luca and Orym step up on either side of me and take my hands. I feel James' hands on my hips. Each point of contact feels like I'm being anchored in place. They are both protecting me and Gunnar. We all know that I could easily kill him if I wanted to. I've never wanted to before. But his threat might just change my mind.

He growls at Ry, trying to intimidate him, too. Ry's shoulders tense, but he doesn't back down. He's been preparing for this moment his entire life. Or most of it, anyway. Watching the fear creep up on Gunnar's face is priceless. I wish I'd brought my phone so I could take a picture.

"You wanna fight me, boy?" the old man spits the words at my mate.

Ry wipes his face with his free hand before answering. "More than anything. And when I win, you're going to apologize. For real this time. You'll say the words and you'll mean them. Or I'll end you."

I barely hear the words. Ry speaks so quietly, as if they're meant only for Gunnar's ears. The taunt works, because instead of responding, Gunnar swings at him. Ry is fast and manages to duck. But Gunnar striking first means that the challenge is not only accepted, but it's already begun.

We watch as they circle each other, one stepping forward to throw a punch, the other dodging if they can. For a brief period of time, it looks like Gunnar is actually going to fight fair. Then

I see the glint of the knife that he pulls from his boot. I won't risk calling out, because I don't want to distract Ry.

Ry, he has a knife. Just pulled it from his boot. Be careful. I send the warning along our bond like a prayer. I'm ready to jerk the knife from his hand with my magic, but Ry's voice in my head stops me.

Don't do it. Give me a minute. I can end this quickly. Trust me, Red. He doesn't sound anxious or upset. His words are calm inside my head. I glance at the three men surrounding me, and for a second, I'm not sure who is holding who back. They're holding onto me as if I'm their lifeline.

"He's got this. We have to trust him," I whisper. I feel reassuring squeezes so I know that they've heard me and agree. I'm still ready to do whatever I have to in order to protect Ry, but I'm going to trust him first.

We watch in silence as Ry focuses his attention on Gunnar's right hand, where the metal of the knife glints in the sunlight. "Is this really how you want to go out, old man?" he asks quietly.

Gunnar growls and lunges at him, but Ry stops him by wrenching his wrist.

Sixteen
MY BEST FRIEND

RYLAND

The move makes the knife visible to everyone who's watching. I take that moment to raise my voice and speak to the crowd. "Is this the kind of leader you want? One who would bring a knife to a fist fight?"

I hear muttering but can't take my eyes off Gunnar. I'm barely able to hold him still, and if I get distracted, that knife is coming down on me hard. I sense people moving but have to trust that Red and the guys will protect me from an attack.

Grammy's hand closes over my arm, encouraging me to bring the knife down. I take a step back as I do. Two of Gunnar's larger enforcers grab him and hold him still while Grammy pries the knife from his hand. "This is not how a challenge should be conducted. As the elder of the territory, I advise you to relinquish control now." Grammy's words to her son are cold. I see something in her eyes, and I'm not sure if it's sadness or disappointment.

She's dealt with a lot of Gunnar's bullshit since he became the leader of the territory. It appears that she's tired of it now. I can't say that I blame her. Gunnar's eyes meet mine as his enforcers hold him still. "Let me go," he growls, barely containing his shift.

"We can't do that, sir. Our job is to make sure challenges are handled properly. That means no weapons. You've broken our laws by trying to attack your challenger with a weapon. The laws are very strict about the punishment for that," one of the enforcers explains as Gunnar struggles against their hold.

Well, at least I won't have to kill him now. I think. I don't really know what the law says about cheating and the punishment for that. I've seen Gunnar do things like this before and get by with it. I'm not sure what makes this time different.

"I'll never surrender the territory to you. It's mine. You can't have it. You're not man enough to take it from me." Logically, I know he's baiting me. But it works.

"Let him go but watch him. If he pulls out another weapon, grab him. I'm not scared to fight him. I will have to insist that he follow the rules, though," I instruct the men holding Gunnar.

They exchange a glance with each other, then pat Gunnar down and remove the other knives he had hidden. Once they're sure he's not hiding other weapons, they release him.

It only takes a second for him to punch me in the face. The blow catches me off guard, and he takes a few kidney shots while I'm dealing with the blood pouring from my nose. It's been broken before, so I'm not concerned.

Ry, you have to beat him. Please. Red's voice echoes in my head. She needs me to do this. So, I will do this.

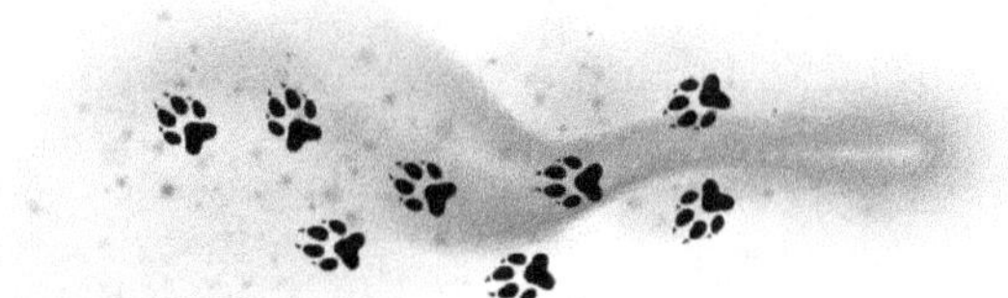

ORYM

"Come on, Ryland. Fight. Don't let him take you down." I don't realize that I've said the words out loud until I hear Garnet's voice in my head.

He's gonna be okay. He'll win this. He has to. I know that Gunnar traumatized her as a child. Hell, he traumatized her as an adult, too. And he's tried everything to drive us apart since we bonded with her. Nothing he did was an outright attack on the bond, because he wouldn't get away with that.

All I can think is that if he doesn't win, I'll finally get my chance to challenge Gunnar. But do I want it this way? Would losing Ryland be worth having my shot at territory alpha? I don't think I want it that badly. Ryland has to win. He needs to stay focused, and that means we have to keep quiet.

Gunnar's foot connects with Ryland's back, and my rival falls to his knees. Is this the end? I'm more scared than I want to admit. Just when I think it's over, Gunnar aims a kick to Ryland's head. At the very last possible moment, Ryland rolls out of the way and grabs Gunnar's leg, jerking it out from under him.

The old man hits the rocky ground hard, and his head bounces. Then he's still. Almost too still. I don't trust that he's been knocked out. He has to be faking it, right? The two enforcers step forward again as Ryland takes a few steps back. The look on his face is something between triumph and terror.

The two men confer over Gunnar, checking him over. One shakes his head and the other nods. I don't understand what's happening here. Is the old man alive? They turn to the crowd and the one who spoke before steps forward. "Gunnar Trion is dead. He has been defeated in challenge by Ryland Turner, who is the new territory leader. If you wish to challenge him, you must wait the traditional three days before you may do so."

A mixture of disappointment, pride, and relief washes over me. Ryland is our new alpha. Gunnar is dead. He'll never torture or manipulate our mate again.

The crowd cheers, and Garnet pulls us toward Ryland. We all throw our arms around him, and she kisses him hard on the lips. I don't know why I'm so surprised that he won. I knew that he could take Gunnar in a fair fight. I guess I just didn't think the old man was capable of fighting fair. Honestly, he wasn't, until he was forced.

"I'm so sorry, Red. I didn't want to kill him. I didn't think that move would," Ryland whispers in her ear.

"You did what you had to. This wasn't murder. You're protecting everyone from his tyranny," she answers. "You are a good man, and a good alpha. You'll be a great territory leader."

Her faith is contagious.

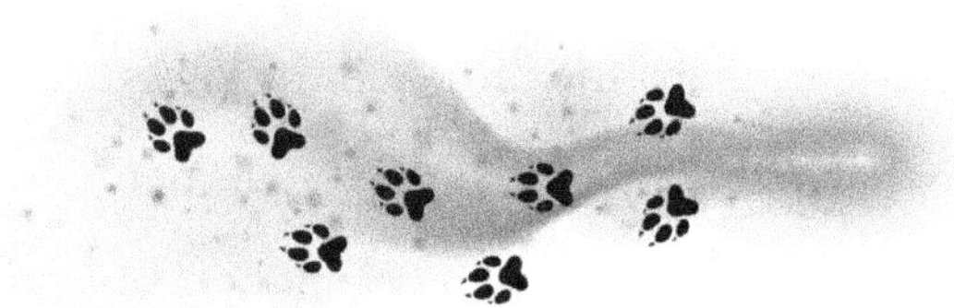

GARNET

Ry won. He defeated Gunnar, even though the man I'd grown up thinking was my father had tried to cheat. Ry still won. Now he's the territory leader and I don't have to worry about being kicked out anymore. Even more important, Gunnar will never be able to hurt me again. I can't believe how relieved I am that he's dead. I'd expected there to be some pain, but instead, it's like a weight has been lifted from my heart. I'm so proud of Ry.

Then it hits me. Grammy. The one person who loved me when I was growing up. The person who stood up to Gunnar and fought for me. This could destroy her. I pull from my mates' embrace and they part to let me go, as if they know what I'm thinking.

As soon as my eyes lock with Grammy's, the tears fall. I'm not crying for him. My tears are for the mother who just lost her son. No matter how awful he was, Gunnar was Grammy's child. I know that she loved him. Just like she loves me. I run to her, and we hug as the tears fall. "I'm so sorry."

"It's not your fault, child. I wish I could have protected you more. I'm sorry for all the things he did to make you miserable. And I'm glad it was one of your men who took care of him." Grammy's words make the tears fall faster. We hold each other and sob quietly for a while.

I don't notice when the crowd starts to disburse. I'm clinging to Grammy as if she's the only thing keeping me on this planet. I don't let go of Grammy until James pulls her away from me. Orym wraps his arms around me and leads me back to our cabin.

"It's okay, love. James will get her settled in and make sure she's okay. If he has to stay with her so she's not alone, he will. Don't worry. Ryland is taking care of some business, and Luca will be home shortly." His words hit the numbness that's settled across my chest.

The business Ry has to deal with is Gunnar's body. I know that Luca stayed behind to help him. Orym must have drawn the short straw if he has to babysit me. Of course, James would be the one to offer to take care of Grammy. I hope that she's okay. I can't imagine what she's feeling right now.

I don't want to go back to the cabin. It's early afternoon, and I don't want to waste the day. But I'm too numb to protest. It's probably better to go home and try to process everything that's happened today. Changes are coming faster than we can prepare for.

I can't help thinking about the future and wondering exactly what Ry has in mind for us. Will we stay in his tiny cabin? Or will he prefer to take Gunnar's much larger one? I can't imagine him wanting to put me back in a place that holds so many bad memories, but I also can't know what he's thinking unless he wants me to.

Orym settles me on the couch and turns on a movie to fill the silence. Then he goes to the kitchen and makes me some tea. When he comes back, I'm staring out the window.

"Are you okay?" he asks as he offers the cup. I take it from him and nod.

"I think so. It's just so surreal. I expected to feel more, you know?" I don't know how he can know when I'm not even sure what I mean myself.

"I do. You got justice, but it doesn't feel like justice. It feels strange and scary. You think you should feel bad when all you feel is relief, but at the same time, you feel kind of numb inside. Am I close?"

"That's exactly how I feel. I will never understand how you guys can express my emotions better than I can." I shake my head and chuckle sadly. "It's like I miss him, but not him. I miss the father I should have had."

Orym nods and wraps an arm around my shoulder, pulling me closer to him. I'm careful not to spill my tea, but I settle in with my head on his shoulder. I think he had the right idea with tea and a movie. I need the distraction.

My mind wanders as we sit there, waiting for the others to come back. How long will it be before Amber learns of what's happened here today? Will she attack when she finds out?

Ideally, it would be better if she didn't find out for a while. I don't know how to make that happen since we still have no leads on who the spy is. Guilt eats at me. I should be working on finding out who's betraying my family. Even if I'm not a wolf, this is my family. I need to fight to protect them.

Instead, I'm sitting here on the couch like a scared little bunny. I'm hiding from my fears, letting someone else take care of what needs done. I should have been the one to face Gunnar. It was my responsibility. I was the one he'd hurt, after all. But I let Ry do it because I was scared.

That's not fair. I let Ry face Gunnar because that was the right thing to do. I'm not a wolf. I can't interfere in pack rules and traditions. A wolf needs to lead these people. I have to remind myself that I've done nothing wrong here.

I can't keep beating myself up for my lack of emotion where Gunnar is concerned. That man was horrible to me for my entire life. I'm allowed to be glad he's gone and sad that he wasn't a better person. Orym leans over a little and presses a gentle kiss to my forehead.

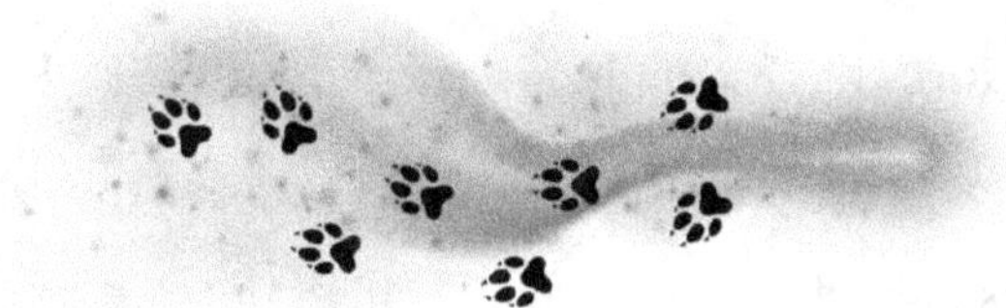

JAMES

I take Grammy inside her cabin and steer her to the overstuffed chair by the window. "I understand that grief hits everyone differently. Please let us know if there's anything we can do for you," I offer.

She nods and stares out the window where Ryland is helping to remove Gunnar's body. "You know he wasn't always an asshole. As a child, he was the exact opposite. In his early teens, he wanted to make a difference here. Then he met Emilia and had Vincent. She died a few years after he was born. Gunnar never was the same after that. I was barely able to convince him to let me tell people that Emilia had given birth before she passed."

"I'm sure that losing her was hard for him," I answer. I'm floored by her admission. And I feel sad for the children who were raised in this camp after Emilia's death. I'm certain they were all treated just as poorly as Garnet was.

"It was hard for everyone. But the rest of us didn't turn our backs on basic human kindness the way he did. In some ways, it would have been kinder if he'd died with her. As his mother, I know that is an awful thing to say." She turns and stares at me. "He didn't approve of letting you or Red stay here. 'This place is for wolves, not witches or humans.' That was his argument. But I threatened him. If he had chased either of you off, I would have gone to the council about how he treated the wolves."

"He was scared that you'd essentially remove him from power by turning him in to the council. That makes much more sense than anything we were told about his decision." I hate trying not to call the guy a dick. He's dead after all. That in and of itself deserves some respect.

"I know that I should have stepped in before. But I'd convinced myself that things were better if I didn't interfere. It was stupid. I deserve to be cast out for my lack of action." The old woman buries her face in her hands.

"I'll make you some tea." I head into the kitchen and start to brew some tea for her. I hate feeling like there's nothing I can do to help. I can't take her guilt or hurt away, though. All I can do is listen when she wants to talk and be supportive. I put together a tray with the tea and cups and carry it to the living room.

Grammy looks at me when I return. "Thank you. You are a kind man, and she definitely needs you." For some reason, her approval means a lot to me.

"I appreciate that. Would you like to talk more about Gunnar before tragedy changed him? I would love to learn more about the territory." It seems like a small thing to do, and her face lights up as she talks.

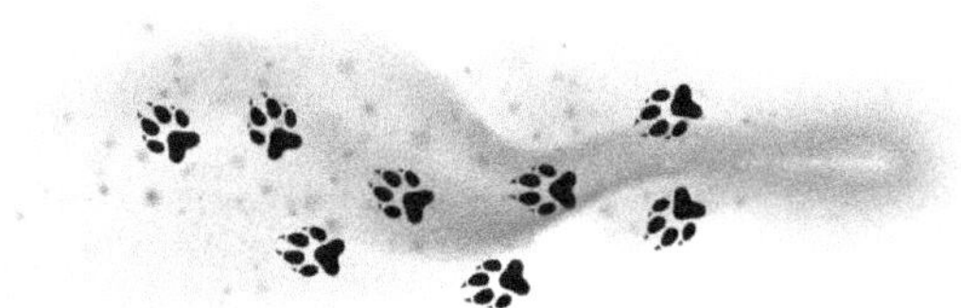

LUCA

"Where's Red? I thought she was going to wait for us," I ask Ryland. He's distracted and not really paying attention to me. "Ryland. Where is she?" I grab his arm and he growls at me in response.

I realize that he's not even looking at me, so he can't know who grabbed him. "Ryland. Look at me." I pull his attention away from the swarm of wolves who want to get in good with their new leader.

"Sorry, Luca. It's just so much to deal with." His apology is sad, but I understand that he actually means it.

"It's okay. Where's Red? I came back from moving Gunnar's body and she was gone." I'm already tired of asking this question repeatedly.

"Orym took her home. I didn't think to tell you." He winces for a second, then his face returns to its usual blank expression. He only drops that mask when he's with us.

"You guys discussed it along the bond, huh?" I'm a little jealous of that, but I understand not wanting to announce that he was taking her away from what had just happened. It could make Ryland look bad for killing Gunnar. Even if it was accidental. "Do you need me for anything?"

I need to go to her. I have to comfort her, even if she doesn't think she needs it. This is a big thing to deal with; even bigger than learning that Gunnar isn't her father.

Ryland stops for a moment and holds up a hand. "Give me just a moment, please." Everyone steps back and gives him room to walk past them. He nods his head for me to follow. "Go take care of her. Complete the bond. Send Orym back to help me. James will be occupied for a while. And I'll be busy here for weeks. Just let us know when it's safe to come home, okay?" He smiles at me as he speaks.

I have no idea how he knew it was the bond pulling me to go to Red, but I'm glad he did. I shift and race through the forest, dodging trees and wolves, to get to her. I've waited so long for this, that I'm scared. I know there's nothing to be scared of, but the idea of being the last one to bond with her is terrifying.

That's why I've been so hesitant. At least, that's the reason I gave myself. When I escaped from Amber, I wasn't sure I deserved her. Then I wasn't sure who I could trust, myself included. I'm not sure what changed or when, but I know this is the time for us to bond.

And joining an already established pack means that I'm starting over in a way. I always considered myself her number one, but Ryland took that spot when he bonded with her first. Can I be happy as her number four? I don't know, but she's worth it, so I'll try. Anything for her.

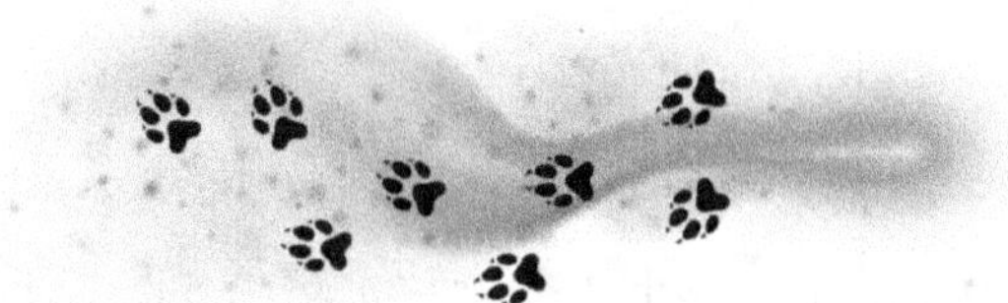

GARNET

I don't know how long Orym and I have been sitting on the couch when Luca practically bursts through the door. "Is everything okay?" Orym jumps to his feet and stands in front of me, ever my protector.

"Yeah, sorry for scaring you. Ryland needs your help, so he sent me to stay with Red," Luca pants out. I'm certain that he's just shifted from his wolf form. It must be something urgent if Ry sent him to get Orym. But why wouldn't he have said something along the bond? And what could he need Orym for that Luca couldn't handle?

The lack of argument from Orym tells me that he's just asked Ry about it, and gotten an amusing response. He's trying not to smile. These fuckers. If they don't stop hiding things from me, I'm going to scream. I wonder if Amber attacked after I left and that's what they need Orym for. I'll get it out of Luca after Orym leaves.

"Okay, I'll head that way. Take care of her," Orym says before he drags me to him and kisses me hard. "Have fun." That seems like an odd thing to say. Wait, no. There's no way. Orym races out the door and Luca looks at me sheepishly.

"I guess it's just us now," he says quietly. I can tell that he's up to something. He's got that mischievous glint in his eyes.

"Looks like it. So, what do you want to do?" It seems odd that he hasn't kissed my cheek or anything since he came in. I won't push him for affection, though.

"I thought maybe you could use a nap," he suggests. I'll never say no to snuggling, so I nod.

"That's probably a good idea. You are planning to snuggle me, right?"

"You couldn't stop me if you tried." His grin widens, and if I didn't know better, I'd say he's hinting at something else.

You can't push him, Garnet. I have to remind myself, because it's so hard not to reach out and grab him. He gently threads his fingers through mine and leads me to the bedroom. I follow, trying to figure out if I'm going crazy or not. It really seems like he's nervous, though I can't tell exactly why.

Luca releases my hand when we're standing next to the bed. When I start to climb in, he grabs my waist and turns me to face him. "What's wrong?" I ask, searching his face for answers.

"I'm not sure that I deserve you," he whispers. Before I can answer, he pulls me closer and crashes his mouth to mine. His tongue fights its way into my mouth and strokes along mine. Luca's hands are everywhere at once. I don't even realize that he's stripping me down, because of the assault from his mouth.

He finally pulls back and starts taking his clothes off. I hold a hand out to stop him, then I realize that I'm naked. How the fuck did he manage that? "Are you sure?" I have to hear him say it. I have to know that he wants this, even though his cock pointing straight at me should tell me everything.

"I'm sure. I should have done this sooner." His confession gives me butterflies, and suddenly I'm the one who's nervous.

Now that we're both naked, he lifts me onto the bed and climbs on top of me. "Are you sure?" He's turned my question back on me, and I understand why.

"Yes. I've wanted you for so long; loved you for so long." My whispered response is all he needs. Luca eases my legs apart, baring me to him. My nerves fall away with the appreciative look he gives me as he takes in my body.

He dips his head and buries his face in my mound. Luca's tongue laps at my slit, then circles my clit. I buck my hips, wanting more. As much as I want to savor and enjoy him, I want to race through this and complete our bond. I want to feel him inside me—his cock and his mind.

"Luca, please," I beg.

"Be a good girl, and I'll give you what you want. I just need another taste," he growls back. Goosebumps pepper my arms and legs at his breath on my pussy. If he doesn't hurry, I might finish without him. That would be unfortunate.

He licks at my clit again, easing two fingers inside of me. The pressure is perfect, and I fall over that edge into my release. "Oh, Luca."

His name on my lips pushes him to move. Luca kisses his way up my stomach and chest, nipping and sucking as he goes.

He only pauses for a moment to tease my nipples before taking my mouth again. The kiss is hard and demanding.

I raise my hips at him, trying to get his dick where I want it. He chuckles against my mouth, then thrusts into me, hard and fast. I come again, and he swallows my moans of pleasure. I rake my nails down his back, then grip his ass, encouraging him to move faster, harder. I need more.

I can tell he's getting close, because he breaks our kiss and starts to trail kisses down my neck to my shoulder. His cock thrusts into me, over and over, slamming harder, pulling almost completely out, just to slide back in again. I lose myself in the sensations.

I feel myself clenching against him as I come again, forcing him to come with me. The moment his release hits, he bites down on my shoulder, and I bite his. I probably don't need to bite him, since I'm not a wolf, but I left my mark on the other wolves, so it seems fair.

Fuck, that was amazing. I think, forgetting that Luca will hear me.

We know. It had to be pretty intense for you to scream through the bond like that. Luca and I exchange a glance. They heard us.

SEVENTEEN
HORRORS

ORYM

Knowing that Luca and Garnet finally completed the bond feels better than it should. It's like we're finally complete.

James' response to it amuses me. Ryland and I knew what was happening, and were able to prepare ourselves. James is taking care of Grammy and the poor guy had no idea. I guess one of us should have told him.

Sorry, guys. We weren't trying to project. But I guess that was just me, wasn't it? Garnet's voice in my head sounds sweet and embarrassed.

We kind of forgot to tell James what was going on. Ryland and I were prepared, he wasn't. Sorry, James. I offer the apology, hoping that he's not pissed.

No apology needed. It just caught me off guard. Grammy was quite amused by it though. Oh, no. That has to be embarrassing. Because I know that both Ryland and I were struggling with our reaction to Garnet projecting what Luca was doing to her. I can't imagine having an audience.

Wow, this is a lot to adjust to. Is it like this all the time? Luca asks.

We'll teach you how to block. But no, it's not like this all the time. At least, not since we learned how to control it. Ryland offers. I'm glad, because I'm not sure how to explain the process of blocking.

Since we no longer have to worry about Luca, I can focus on organizing the people who want to talk to Ryland. I don't know when I became his second-in-command, but I don't hate it. I'm good at calming people, and can provide muscle when needed. Somehow, I'd expected this duty to fall to Luca, given my history with Ryland.

Once I have a list of people and their concerns, I begin to make a schedule. "I'll let you all know when it's time for you to speak with Ryland. Everything will be organized in order of urgency. Our leader is also focused on rescuing the missing wolves, vamps, and humans who've been kidnapped by Amber. Please return to your duties now. Thank you."

"You're really good at that," Ryland says, walking up behind me.

"Thanks. You know, I expected you to choose someone else," I admit. He cocks an eyebrow at me.

"You think someone else could really be my second? Nah, man. It had to be you. You're the only one not scared to tell me off if I need it. And I need it a lot," he laughs.

"You're not wrong," I agree. "I'm working out a schedule for them to bring their concerns to you in an orderly fashion. It's going to be based on the most urgent issues first. Apparently, that's not the way Gunnar did it."

Ryland shakes his head. "That doesn't surprise me. The old man was all about what other people could do for him."

"That explains the way some of them came to me, offering favors and such."

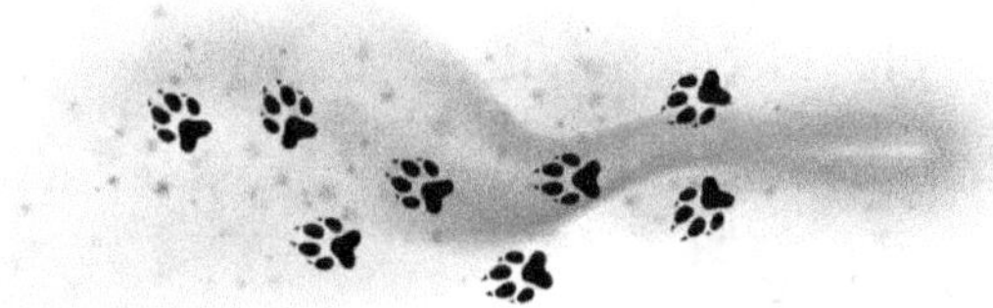

JAMES

Feeling Garnet's waves of pleasure as she and Luca finally complete the mate bond is extremely disconcerting. At least Grammy's amused by it.

"There's no reason to worry, boy. Once that bond is complete, the five of you will be a stronger unit. It's a natural process," she insists.

"I understand that, ma'am. I would just prefer not to discuss it, if you don't mind." I can't be talking about my sex life with the woman who raised Garnet. I just can't.

"Well, if you need to go, I'll be okay here. I'm not so grief-stricken that I'm a danger to anyone. I know that what happened is what was meant to be. I don't have to like it to accept it." Her melancholy tone goes against her words, but I trust that she means it. She won't hurt herself or go after Ryland for revenge.

"If you need anything, please let us know. I'm leaving my cell number on the fridge for you." After writing my number down and putting it on the fridge, I walk outside. I'm not even sure where Gunnar's base of operations was, so I don't know where to find Ryland. I could ask along the bond, but I've been blocking them since Garnet and Luca completed their bond.

I decide to stop one of the wolf shifters who are milling about. "Excuse me, can you tell me where Ryland is?"

The guy looks me up and down, and for a moment, I think he's going to snub me the way Gunnar did. "You're James, right? Red's other mate." I nod, and he continues. "Hey, man,

I'm sorry for the way everyone treated you. Gunnar was a dick, and made us miserable if we didn't do what he said. Ryland will be at the training center. The old man had an office there. I can show you."

Even though I know where the training center is, I let this man show me the way. I didn't expect an apology, much less for someone to admit that Gunnar had been the one to instruct them to treat me that way. We chat a little as we walk and I learn that his name is Timothy. He seems nice enough.

Timothy shows me to the office inside the training center, where Orym is standing guard at the door. "I've got it from here, thanks." He nods and leaves.

"I'm not sure how I feel about learning that Gunnar hated me enough to force his people to be rude to me," I admit after he's gone.

"If it makes you feel better, he never tried that with us. Ryland, Luca, and I would never have stood for that. And if Garnet actually had been his daughter, she would have been able to force him to recant that order. The only reason he got away with it is because we found out she isn't a wolf."

I know he's right, and hope that Ryland can change things for the better.

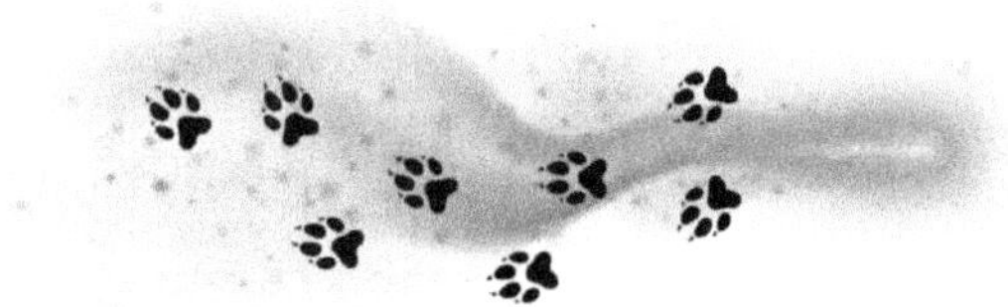

GARNET

Luca and I stay wrapped up together in bed, cuddling for a while. It's slightly embarrassing that I projected the whole thing to the other guys, but they're going to have to get used to it. We're all bonded now, so there's a chance of me doing that when my senses get overloaded. I can't help thinking about all the group fun we can have, if the guys are into it.

Luca kisses me softly. I know that he's exhausted. "Are you tired?" I ask, knowing that he'll argue that he's fine.

"I am. Everything has been so much lately. I've been so paranoid and felt like everyone was out to get me. I think the bond pushed those feelings away. I know now that I can trust you and the guys completely. I also know that I'm not the spy. Which means we have some work to do to discover who that is. But I'm wiped. Would you be offended if I slept for a while?"

I kiss his forehead and pull the blanket up to his shoulder. "Not at all. You've been through a lot recently and need to rest. I promise I won't go anywhere, except the shower and the living room. I'll be here when you wake up." Luca smiles at me as his eyes drift closed. Once his breathing is slow and regulated, I slide out of the bed, tucking him in more tightly. I'm glad he's resting.

I know he hasn't been sleeping well, because he's refused to sleep with us in here. So, one of the others usually sleeps in the living room with him. We don't want him to be alone. Now, he never will be. How did I not realize that his paranoia and pulling away were symptoms of the bond being incomplete? I feel stupid for not knowing that.

I take a long, hot shower. The water warms me and relaxes my tense muscles. I close my eyes for a minute, enjoying the heat. The room starts to spin, so I ease myself down onto the tiled floor and lean against the wall, where I can still feel the warmth.

It feels like my soul is ripped from my body as my vision tunnels into darkness. I try to call out for Luca, but I don't hear anything. When I open my eyes, Amber is standing in front of me. I look down, covering myself, but I'm fully dressed. She doesn't see me, and I wonder how that's possible.

Glancing around, I see that we're in a camp, not far from the first cabin she took us to. How did we miss this place when we were searching? I shake the thought away, focusing on memorizing where I am in relation to home. This is another vision, like I had at the cabin. I'm certain this one is happening right now, instead of in the past, like the last one.

She has the prisoners lined up on their knees. I have to give the wolves and vamps credit; they're faking bravery better than anyone I've ever seen. The humans cry and beg for their lives. I still don't know what Amber is doing with these people. What can she possibly want from them?

I watch, horrified, as she walks down the line. A man follows her with a tray of syringes. Amber stops at each person and jabs a syringe into their neck. The fluid contained in the needles is red, but milky. What is that?

I don't have time to wonder, as the victims start reacting to the liquid as soon as it's in them. The humans start to foam at the mouth and bleed from their eyes before falling over and spasming. A moment later, they're still, and I know they've died.

I step forward as if to stop her from continuing, but my hand passes right through her arm. I'm not really here. I can't do anything but watch as this happens.

Amber injects the vampires next. I expect the same reaction, but nothing happens. She waits, muttering to herself. I'm braced for the worst. First one, then another, and another start to shake. It's as if they're on a paint mixer, shaking faster and faster. Just when I think it can't get worse, the vamps explode, sending blood and gore flying through the air. I think it will hit me, but it passes right through, just like when I tried to touch Amber.

The wolves are last. What is this poison she's injecting them with? How did she come up with something that would kill humans and vampires? Is that what this is all about—testing her poison?

I watch in horror as she injects the wolves. I can see the pain on their faces as they fight against the liquid that's been injected into them. Some of them spasm like the humans did, and others shake like the vamps did. My heart breaks as I watch these wolves, people I grew up with, die. One by one, blood runs from their eyes and ears. One by one, parts of them explode. It's not quite as bad as the vamps, but it's close.

I close my eyes and scream again.

"Red! Come back to me. Please, Red. Don't leave me," Luca's voice breaks through, and I open my eyes. He's sitting in the shower with his arms wrapped around me. I'm disoriented and confused.

"What happened?" I ask, shaking my head a little. Everything is hazy and I'm not sure what's going on.

"You were just sitting here, but you were screaming as if something was tearing you apart. I called for the others, but they were already on their way. I thought I was losing you. I've never been so terrified in my life," Luca admits, holding me tighter.

"I'm okay now. I'll tell you about it when everyone is here. I just don't think I can go through it twice."

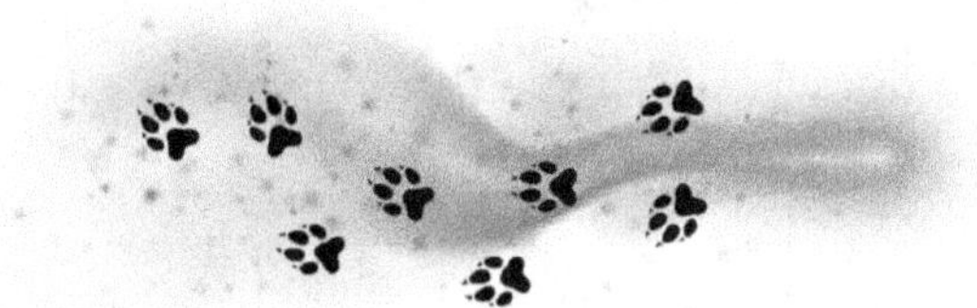

LUCA

Red's screams wake me and I'm instantly on the move. I wasn't asleep for very long, but I'm wide awake now. I call along the bond for the others only to find that they're already on the move. I burst into the bathroom, expecting blood and chaos. Instead, I find Red sitting in the shower, screaming as the water rushes over her body. I can tell from her eyes that she's not seeing anything in front of her. I drop down next to her, dragging her into my arms.

"Red! Come back to me. Please, Red. Don't leave me," I beg her as I press gentle kisses to her temples and forehead. The screaming stops as soon as I touch her. But it takes a few times of me begging for her to fight her way back to me. When she does, I can tell that she's confused, and maybe a little disoriented.

"What happened?" Red asks, shaking her head a little. She seems unsure of herself. Her eyes are wide and glossy.

"You were just sitting here, but you were screaming as if something was tearing you apart. I called for the others, but they were already on their way. I thought I was losing you. I've never been so terrified in my life," I admit, holding her tighter. I don't want to let her go.

"I'm okay now. I'll tell you about it when everyone is here. I just don't think I can go through it twice."

"That's fine. Let me help you up." I stand up, pulling her with me. She shivers, so I step closer to the water. I have no idea how long she's been in here, but the water is still warm. I have to give Ryland props for the tankless water heater. It was a brilliant idea.

After a while, Red turns to me. "I'm okay now." I understand her meaning, turning the water off and grabbing one of the huge, fluffy towels to wrap her in. I wrap another one around my waist before ushering her out of the shower. She starts to protest as I dry her off, but I give her a look and the protest stops.

I think she understands that this is as much for me as it is for her. As I dry her body, I'm checking for bruises or cuts. I need to know that she didn't fall down in the shower when the vision hit. There's no way that wasn't a vision. And I'm almost as terrified of what she saw as I was when I found her sitting there screaming.

I hate that she'll have to relive that fear and pain. But we'll take care of her. I hear the guys enter the cabin. *We're in the bathroom. Give me a minute and I'll bring her in the living room. She's gonna want a cup of tea.* Communicating is getting easier, especially when I don't hear them constantly.

I help Red dress, slip on my pants, and take her to the others.

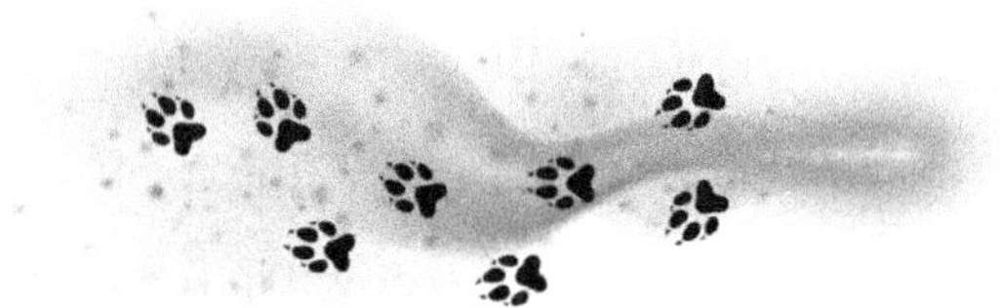

RYLAND

Luca's emergency call startles us into action. I've never seen James run so fast. Orym and I shifted, so we get home first, but James is right behind us. Luca asks us to give him a minute, so we wait. The moment Red and Luca come into the living room, we swarm them, speaking at the same time.

"Are you okay?" I ask.

"What happened?" Orym asks.

"Are you hurt?" James asks.

"I'm fine. Please, just sit down so I can tell you about it." Luca settles Red on the couch and sits next to her. I can tell he's not going to move from her side for anything. It's nice to see him back to his old self again.

Orym hands them each a cup of tea and we all settle around them. I'm dying to ask more questions, but I have to let her tell us in her own time.

"After we completed the bond, Luca was tired. I let him sleep. Don't give me that look, Ry. I promised him that I wouldn't go any further away than the living room. I just wanted a shower first." She pauses to glare at me.

I lower my head and she continues, "While I was in the shower, I felt dizzy, so I sat down. I didn't fall. I'm fine. But I saw things. It was horrible."

Luca wraps his arm around her. I thread my fingers through hers. Orym rests his hand on the back of her neck, and James holds her other hand. "You can tell us anything," I insist.

Red starts talking, and as she explains what she watched Amber do, tears stream down her face. I want to wipe them away and tell her that everything is going to be okay. I can't, though. What she tells us is horrific. Amber killing wolves, vamps, and humans with some kind of poison that's injected? It's barbaric.

"I don't think that's the worst of it." Red pauses again, making sure that we're all paying attention to her. I don't think I could look away if I wanted to. "She was upset when they died. Someone was taking notes and they were murmuring about the poison being too strong and not working right. I think she's doing something besides trying to kill. I just can't figure out what."

Well, that's terrifying. I'll never admit it, though. I'm the leader of this entire territory now. I'm responsible for those wolves who were killed today. "Can you describe exactly where this happened?"

After Red details the location, I step away to call some of my enforcers. I send them to find the bodies and return them home. I hope this isn't a trap or a huge mistake. I just feel like these victims deserve a proper burial, and their families deserve to know what happened to their loved ones.

"You're starting out as a great leader," Red whispers, wrapping her arms around my back.

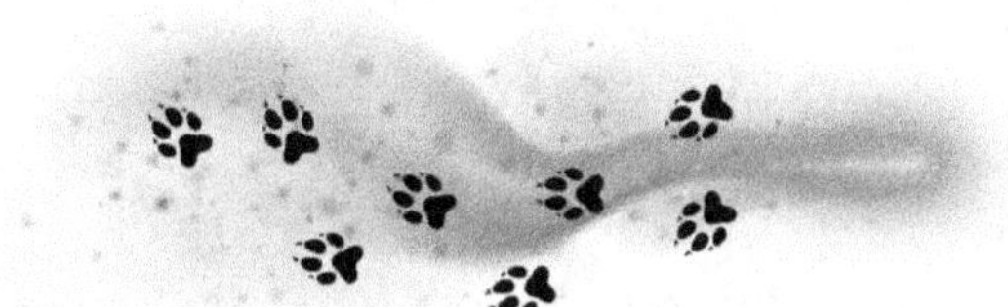

GARNET

After explaining the vision and where the victims are, I focus on my tea while Ry steps outside to make a call. He'll send his strongest wolves to retrieve the bodies. And he'll feel guilty for it, too. I set down my cup and follow him outside.

As soon as he hangs up the phone, I wrap my arms around him from behind. "You're starting out as a great leader," I whisper. He turns, and I barely keep my hold on him.

"Were you eavesdropping?" he accuses. I can tell that he's trying to tease me, even though his heart just isn't in it. Being the leader is already wearing on him.

"No, just checking on my mate who has to make tough decisions now. What can I do to help?" I ask, knowing that he won't tell me. His eyes go soft, and a tiny smile plays at the corners of his mouth.

"What did I do to convince the goddess that I deserve you?" He presses a kiss to my cheek and hugs me tightly. I can feel all of his worry and tension.

"I ask myself that question daily. I'm not sure any of you *actually* deserve me," I tease. From his expression, I can tell that he knows that I'm not serious.

"Oh, yeah?" he asks, moving his hands to my sides.

"Don't you dare," I threaten, knowing what he's planning. It's nice to see him finally relax, though. Even if I'm not going to like what's coming.

"Oh, I dare." His fingers gently dig into my sides as he tickles me. I squeal and try to get away, but he holds me still. Ry doesn't stop until I'm laughing so hard that I can't stand up. "Are you going to behave now?"

"I guess I don't have much choice, do I?" I toss back at him.

"Thank you. I needed that moment of silly to counteract the sad. I promise I will do my best to turn this territory around." His words hit me in the chest and my lungs close up for a second.

I gasp for breath and he looks concerned again. "I'm okay. I just wasn't expecting you to get all serious and mushy on me."

"You put your faith in me for this, and I won't let you down. We do have some logistics things to discuss. But that doesn't have to be tonight," he offers.

"I think tonight is the perfect time. It'll take everyone's minds off what happened today. Both Gunnar and the murders. We do have a lot to discuss, since Luca has finally joined us," I counter. I thread my fingers through his and pull him back inside.

Orym, James, and Luca look at us as we drop onto the couch. "What's wrong?" Luca asks.

"Nothing. We just have a lot to discuss, since you and I completed our bond, and Ry is the new territory leader. There's no better time to do it than now." I look at each of them, wondering how they're going to react to Ry asking where they want to live. I'm sure that's part of what has him worried.

"With all of us joined, we're probably going to need a bigger bedroom. And since I'm the leader now, this cabin might not be the best place for us." I'm not expecting that to be where he takes this conversation.

"You don't want to stay here?" I ask, my eyes wide.

"I don't think it's big enough for us, long term. We can stay here while we build something else. But I don't think this is the right cabin for our family. Especially if we want kids in the future," he replies.

Kids. Oh, shit. I hadn't even thought about having kids. Oh, wow. This conversation just got way more serious than I was ready for. I thought we'd argue about staying here or moving to Gunnar's place. I was prepared for that. I'm not prepared for talk of kids and building a bigger cabin.

"She's freaking out," Luca says.

"Why'd you have to bring up kids?" James asks, glaring.

"Just breathe, Garnet. We don't have to decide about kids right now. It's okay. That's it, deep breath in, hold for a second, and out." Orym squats in front of me on the couch. "Ryland didn't mean to spring this on you the way he did. None of us are worried about kids right now. He's just thinking that we could use some more space, that's all. Right, Ryland?"

"Yeah, that's all. I didn't mean to make it sound like I was pushing for anything. I just think we need a bigger cabin for the five of us, that's all. Maybe a second bathroom." The way he's fumbling, I know that he didn't mean to freak me out.

I feel bad for having a panic attack about this. It's kind of funny how I have a very emotional reaction to thinking about having kids, but when the man I'd thought was my father is killed, I have no reaction at all. I'm a horrible person. I might even be a monster.

"Do you have a spot picked out for the new cabin?" Luca asks. "I can give mine to someone who needs it." I'd forgotten that Luca's cabin was sitting empty right now. Orym had been living with his cousins before he moved in here.

"Building a new, bigger cabin is a good idea. But can we just not talk about kids for a while? I just completed the bond with all of you, and I don't think I'm ready for that kind of thing just yet. Is that okay?" I'm worried that they'll reject me if I tell them that I'm not sure I want kids. After everything I've been through, I just haven't had time to consider the possibility.

"Whatever you want is fine with me. I think we can all agree," James says confidently.

ROUNDING UP STRAYS

JAMES

PART OF ME WISHES Ryland had kept his mouth shut about why he wanted to build a bigger cabin. There's no reason for anyone to start pressuring her about having children. We don't even know if we're going to beat Amber. I can't even consider bringing children into this world with that kind of danger out there.

"No one is going to push you into anything." Orym echoes my sentiment. Luca nods his agreement and Ryland at least has the decency to look ashamed.

"Since we've agreed on a bigger cabin, where will it go? And are there enough guys here to help build it, or do I need to call my brother?" I ask, steering the conversation away from things Garnet obviously doesn't want to talk about.

"There's a large, cleared plot next to Grammy's cabin that we can use. If you can get Dec's help, that would be great. I would love it if he'd design the cabin and oversee the men building it." Ryland's excitement is clear.

"I'll give him a call later and discuss it." I already know that he'll agree to do it. What big brother could refuse his little brother? "He'll probably come out for a consultation. Dec likes to see the space and figure out what fits it best."

"That sounds fancy," Garnet laughs. I'm glad she's relaxing again.

Ryland's phone rings before we can discuss the cabin more, and he excuses himself to take the call. We can all feel his tension along the bond, and it worries me. This has to be the moment Amber chose to attack. It's perfect, really. Ryland has just taken control of the territory, and we're waiting to see how the wolves react to him being connected to a human and a witch.

Of course, most of the wolves acted hateful because Gunnar had forced them to. That doesn't mean that there aren't some who agree with his ideals. It's amusing to me, in a twisted sort of way, that Gunnar and Amber had a lot in common. Neither one cares much for anyone but themselves and their followers.

The grim look on his face when Ryland returns tells me that I was right. That call was an update on Amber. "What happened?" Garnet voices the question we're all thinking.

"They caught Amber."

"Why is that bad news?" Garnet asks.

Luca stares at Ryland. "Because it was too easy. There's no way they should have been able to catch her unless she wanted to be caught."

Ryland nods in agreement. "She's up to something. We have to figure out what. They caught some of her followers too. I think it's a set up. She may be here to kidnap more wolves, or to do some spying for herself."

"You know," Orym pauses. "I hate to say it, but this makes it look like Gunnar might have been her spy."

"What? No. He wouldn't have. Would he?" Garnet is shocked. Me? Not so much.

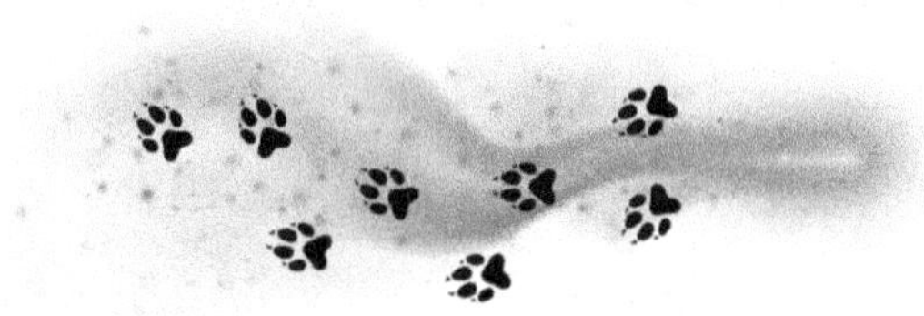

LUCA

The thought that Gunnar might have been Amber's spy is terrifying. Could he betray his people like that? Why would he allow her to kill the people he was supposed to protect? It doesn't make sense. But with the timing of everything, that is how it looks.

"We don't know that for sure. Since he's dead, we can't know. Because even if she tells us, there's no way to know if she's telling the truth." I hope the others will let Red focus on my thoughts. I don't need her upset because she feels responsible for not realizing that Gunnar could have been the spy.

"Even if he was, it doesn't matter now. Gunnar is dead. If he was her spy, she doesn't have one now. We can hand her over to the council for a trial and punishment." James pulls out his phone and walks outside. I'm sure he's going to call his brother.

"That is a good point. I agree it will be better to hand her over to them instead of trying to hold her ourselves. I told my guys to keep an eye on her until I get there. I figured you might want to try talking to her again," Ryland says to Red.

I don't want her anywhere near Amber, but I know that she can handle herself. I've seen her take down witches and wolves twice her size. That won't stop me from worrying, though. I don't need Amber getting inside Red's head and messing with her.

"I'm going with you," I insist. I won't let her face Amber alone. I'll fight Ryland if I have to. Luckily, he just nods.

"We're all going. Not all of us will talk to her, but we'll stay close," he responds. Good. I'm glad we're on the same page about protecting Red.

"You have to talk to her, don't you? Since you're the territory leader now," Red looks to Ryland expectantly.

"I do, but I'll growl at her before you go in. Then I can wait outside and listen through the wall."

I laugh. "That is a sneaky plan. But it could work. I'm staying with Red, though." Ryland stares at me for a minute, then shrugs and walks away. The rest of us follow, heading toward the training center. It's the only place where Amber could be locked up.

Ryland goes inside first, and I hear him growl at her. While I can't understand his words, I do hear her laughter. I want to race in there and rip her face off. Not just for what she did to me, but for what she put everyone here through.

I know that Red wants to know what Amber's plan is. She wants to understand what her aunt hopes to accomplish. Somehow, understanding is supposed to fix it. But it won't.

Knowing will only make it worse. Especially since she's killing all the prisoners she took. I guess it's lucky I escaped when I did.

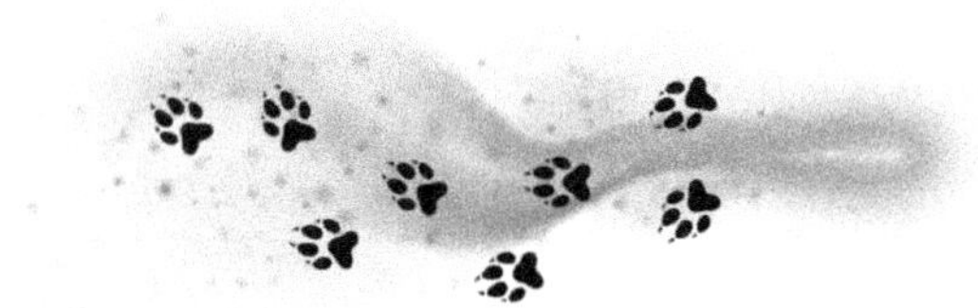

GARNET

Ry comes out and holds the door for me. Luca follows me inside, and we stop walking in front of Amber's cell. I know what

I'm going to have to do to stop her. I don't like it, and wish there was another way. But I know there isn't. She won't stop until someone stops her. And while I don't have proof, I'm certain that she's managed to get around the magic blocking cuffs I put on her.

We need a more permanent solution. I have to take her powers before she can take mine. I'll have to get James started on research as soon as we're done here. While he researches, I'll write the spell. We will do what we have to in order to protect our family. *I* will do what I have to, no matter how much I don't want to.

"Amber," I say as we stand in front of her.

"My darling niece, to what do I owe the pleasure of your company?" Her voice drips with false sweetness, and I want to gag.

"I want to know what you're planning. I know about the syringes, but I don't know what's inside of them. What are they for?" I don't expect her to answer me, at least, not honestly. If she does offer an explanation, it will be a lie. I'm sure of it.

"Now, why would I tell you that?" she cackles. I want to thrust my hand through the bars and punch her in the face.

"Because you don't want us to kill you," I offer.

"You can't kill me, dear. I know the law. You forget, I helped to write most of it. You are bound by law to hand me over to the council, and you know it." Her smug attitude is almost too much for me. I ball my hands into fists, squeezing tightly.

"Accidents happen," Luca offers with a dark chuckle. Amber's eyes go wide.

"I see you've reclaimed my lap dog. I hope you don't mind getting my seconds," she smirks. I know that she didn't sleep with him. She's just trying to mess with my head. That is the one thing Luca would have told me. I let her claims slide off me. I don't even react to her words.

"I suggest you talk, auntie, before I get impatient. I've been dying to play around with my electricity powers again," I threaten, stepping closer to the cage. She backs away from the bars, horror scrunching her features for a moment before she smooths them out again.

"I won't tell you what my plan is, or what was in the syringes. How do you even know about that?" She pauses, then continues, "It'll be so much more fun to see your face when my plan is complete."

"Don't worry about how I know. I know enough. I will find a way to stop you." It's an empty threat and we both know it. If I don't know what she's doing, how will I stop her?

I turn to Luca. "We should go now. She's not going to talk."

Ry is by my side in an instant when we walk out of the training center. "Are you okay?"

I nod. "She won't tell us anything, and that's frustrating, but it's what I expected."

Before he can say anything else, a car pulls up and three figures climb out. Vik, Dec, and Delilah walk toward us. I can't stop myself from running to my friend and practically jumping into her arms. "Delilah! I've missed you so much!"

"I missed you too, Garnet. We heard about Gunnar. Are you okay?" she asks quietly.

"I am. It's not an easy situation, but I watched the whole thing, and Ry didn't do anything wrong. Part of me is glad he's gone. Now he can't be cruel to anyone else," I admit.

She doesn't look convinced, but only nods. "If you need anything, just let us know."

"James was going to talk to Dec about designing a new cabin for us and overseeing the construction. I hope that's something we can work out." It's not the time or place to talk about this, but I can't stop myself.

Vik and Dec are speaking with Ry, and I think I should stay back. I'm not good at staying quiet, since Gunnar isn't here to punish me for it. Who am I kidding? I couldn't stay quiet when he was here to punish me for it. I can't count how many times I had to clean the training course, or run it in the dark, just because I'd pissed the old man off. And that was only after Grammy caught him beating me and made that stop.

None of that matters now. He's dead, and Ry is the new territory leader. I'm safer now than I've ever been. Mostly. We do still have Amber to deal with. But I don't have to worry about Ry punishing me for speaking up. Which is exactly why I'm keeping my mouth shut.

I'll do whatever I can to help him be successful. I know that part of that will involve making sure everyone respects him. Even our little family. If we don't agree, then we'll have to talk about it in private. Otherwise, the wolves may decide not to listen to him, and that will put everyone in more danger.

Delilah tells me about new updates to Midnight, the nightclub she owns and runs. I would love to go back there, but I can't do that until Amber is handled. "Are you guys here to take Amber to the council?" I should just let Ry handle it, but it can't hurt to ask, right?

"Vik is arranging transport. I think Dec wanted to make sure his little brother was actually okay. Meeting you has helped their relationship. James was hesitant to forgive Dec after he was turned. Your mate sees it as a flaw, but Dec is proud to be a vampire."

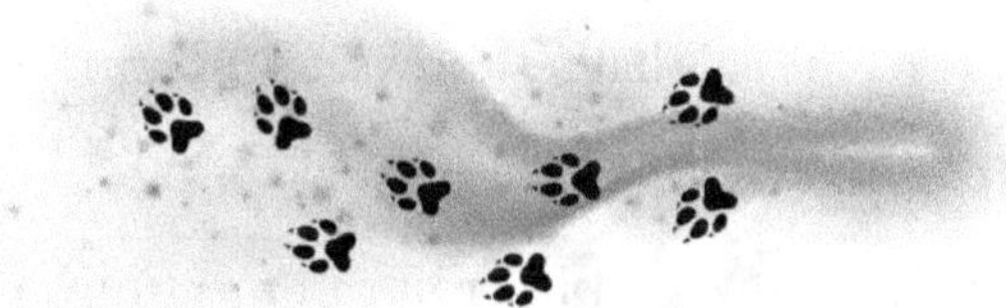

RYLAND

"The council will send a military group to bring her in. They'll be here in a couple of hours. Will you be ready to release her to them?" Vik asks. I still can't believe that this vamp is deferring to me.

"Absolutely. She's not giving us anything useful. There's no reason to keep her here any longer than it takes for them to get a cell ready for her," I respond. He shakes my hand.

"Is my brother around?" Dec asks.

"Yeah, just a sec." I reach out to James along the bond. *You have company. Where'd you go?*

Checking on Grammy. Tell Dec to come up here. I don't know if I should be relieved that he knows it's his brother or annoyed that I'm passing messages.

"He's at Grammy's cabin. You can meet him there." I gesture in the direction, and he nods before heading that way. I hadn't realized that they knew their way around our camp so well. I know they've all been here before, though, so it shouldn't surprise me.

"I'm sure you have responsibilities to attend to. Is there anything I can assist with?" Vik offers. I can't pass that up.

"I do have some thoughts about ways to expand our income and give the packs a better future. Could I get your advice on that?" I know it's not the right time to ask, but I can't help myself.

"Sure. Do you have plans drawn up, or a proposal?"

I wonder if he knows that the territory has been largely self-sufficient until now. I'm not going to continue the isolationist bullshit that Gunnar started. I want our packs to be integrated into society, not separate from it. "For some of it. Here, I'll show you," I offer. Vik follows me into my office.

I quickly locate the folder Orym helped me put together and hand it to him. I wait as he peruses the file. My hands start to sweat, and I wonder why I'm suddenly nervous about showing these plans to him. Part of my idea involves asking for his family to help us get this started. I won't take a hand out, but I do plan to ask for a loan.

If he doesn't approve of our plans, then there's no way they'll invest. The longer Vik takes to respond, the more I'm prepared to defend the idea and explain my reasoning.

When he finally meets my eyes, I can't tell what he's thinking. "This is a solid plan. I like the idea of your farms supplying fresh produce to the restaurants. And I think having some of your people get jobs in the city is also a good idea. We can definitely integrate them into security at Midnight, or one of our other holdings."

He likes the plan. I hold back a sigh. I can't believe he actually likes it. I'd been ready to fight for my people. "Thank you."

"How are you going to pay for it?"

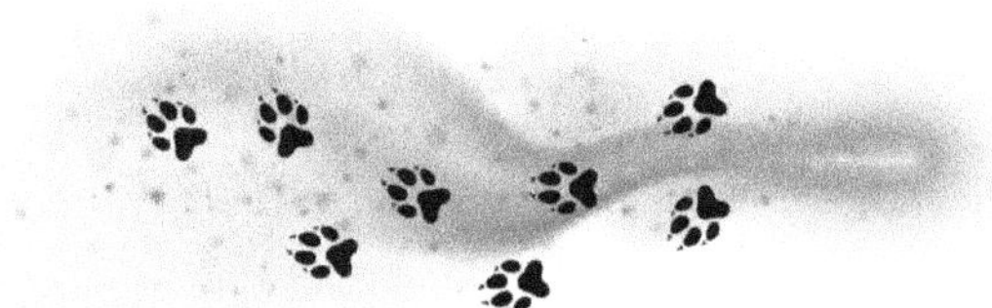

ORYM

As Ryland's second, it's my job to stay close. I know that he's talking to Vik about his business ideas. I hope that's going well, but I can't stick around to find out. I have to make sure that Amber is ready to move when the team from the council gets here.

And it's my job to interrogate her lackeys. I walk into the main room of the training center. Amber smirks at me, and I ignore her. I know it grates at her when people don't pay attention, so I make sure to pretend like she doesn't exist as much as I can.

It's too bad we're not keeping her here. I'm pretty sure I could emotionally torture the woman to death if they'd let me. I know I could physically do it. I want to. She's caused so much pain to my family. I hate this entire situation.

"I can help you," she calls. I stop walking, but don't turn. "I can give you the information you want." I know she's lying, and I will not walk over to her cage. Instead, I motion for one of the guards to bring another of the prisoners out.

I gesture to the chair that's anchored to the ground in the center of the room. She'll have a good view of the show from where her cage is. With any luck, this will hurt her as much as she's hurt us. I don't think she's capable of emotion, but it is a nice thing to hope for.

When the man is strapped to the chair, I finally glance at Amber. She's staring at the man with wide eyes. "What's your name?" I ask. He sputters a few times, but doesn't answer. I step closer and punch him in the face. "Your name," I say again.

When he refuses to answer again, I turn to the guard who strapped him in. "I'm gonna need a knife and some pruning shears." The prisoner's eyes go wider than Amber's did, and I know he's terrified.

I make eye contact with him and lean down. "Unless you want to lose a few body parts, I suggest you start talking."

He pales and stammers. "John. My name is John. Please don't kill me."

"Why would I kill you, John? I just want to have a conversation with you," I offer quietly. If he talks, I don't know that we'll let him go, but at least he'll get to keep his fingers and toes.

"Revenge. You want to hurt Amber, so you'll hurt me." This guy is smart. And from the look on her face, it might actually hurt her if I tortured him a bit.

"I don't want revenge. If I wanted that, I'd be punching her. What's the plan, John?" I don't expect him to tell me, but I need to give him a chance before he decides that death is preferable.

"I don't know the plan. She won't tell any of us."

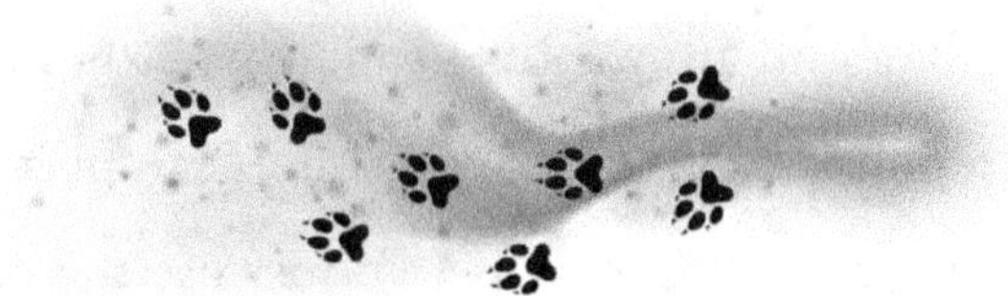

GARNET

Delilah and I have a nice visit before Vik comes to get her. Dec meets them at their car, and they leave right after the military group comes to get Amber. I hate letting her go, but I understand that we can't keep her. Not when we're not certain that the spy has been dealt with.

We say our goodbyes, and promise to get together soon. I'm not sure how we'll be able to do that until after this situation is done. I don't think for a second that capturing Amber this time will be the end of it. She'll find a way to escape and we'll have to fight her again. That is the only thing I'm certain of. I just wish I knew what her plan was.

Once they pull away, I turn to James. "I need your help making a power stripping potion. I don't want it to kill her, just take her magic. Otherwise, I'd just use the one she was planning for me."

"We can do that. I'll go make a list of ingredients and see if I can figure out what part of her spell was lethal," he offers. I kiss him hard, and he takes off.

Luca hasn't left my side all day, and I know he won't now. "I'm going to be working on writing a spell. It's gonna be super boring."

He smiles. "I'll watch. It'll be fine."

I kiss Orym and Ry before we head back to the cabin. They have prisoners to question, so it'll be a few hours before they head home. I don't mention the blood on Orym's shirt, even though I know it means he beat up one of the guys they caught. I wonder if he did it in front of Amber. If so, did she react at all? I try to push the thoughts away. I need to focus on writing this spell so we can strip her powers and keep her locked away.

"Do you think this is the end?" Luca asks as we get close to the cabin.

"I wish it was. But I expect her to escape again. I think she's playing with us. That's why I want this spell done. Then I can use it on her as soon as possible and put an end to this for good."

I thread my fingers through Luca's and we stop just outside the cabin. "I'm glad you're back."

"I've been back for a while," he replies.

I shake my head. "Not really. You were here, but you weren't really you. We know that was the incomplete bond, but it still worried us all. Now it feels like you're you again."

"I know exactly what you mean. I felt like myself as soon as the bond was complete. Before, I felt off. Now I know what's real and what's important." He presses his lips to mine. I pull him closer and dig my fingers into his hair. As much as I want to rip his clothes off and fuck him right here, I know we have work to do.

I let myself get lost in the kiss for a moment, and just before I pull away, I feel James pressing against my back. "This is nice, but we have to get this spell figured out." I hate pushing them away, but we can't get distracted now. We're too close to finishing this.

Both men groan, but release me. "And here I thought I was going to slide into the action," James teases. I know they're disappointed, but neither man is actually upset with me. There will be plenty of time for fun after we beat Amber.

"Don't try to guilt me. You two can wait until tonight, at least, can't you?" I ask, teasing back.

"You think you'll figure it out by then?" Luca's voice is hopeful.

"I don't know, but we have to take breaks sometime, right?" I offer with a smirk.

"You're killing me. Just show me how to help," Luca replies. I laugh as we head inside the cabin. James has the books spread across the living room floor and I can tell that he made good use of the little time he had here alone.

"This is the spell Amber was going to use on Garnet," James says, handing a book to Luca. "I'm making a list of ingredients and trying to research them in these books," he gestures, "to see what needs removed to make the spell usable."

"Why can't it be used the way it is now?" Luca asks James. I understand why he would want to kill Amber, but I just can't do it. Only if it's the last option. I have to know that I've tried everything else first.

"Because Garnet doesn't want to kill anyone unless she has to. So, if we can't fix this spell, we'll have to come up with another one. If everything else fails, Garnet will consider this one. Maybe," James explains. I'm glad he said the words out loud. I can't see myself killing Amber unless one of my mates was in danger.

"That's exactly it. I don't want to kill her. I just want to take her magic away and lock her up for her crimes. If someone else wants to execute her, that's on them." I shrug and pick up a book.

I try to focus on what I'm reading, but I can feel their eyes on me. I'm not sure if they're staring because of my decision to let someone else decide Amber's fate, or if there's something wrong. "What?"

I glance at them and see that they're still just staring at me. "Do you need something?" I ask again. I'm starting to get self-conscious here.

"We're just impressed that you're sticking to your convictions, that's all," James says.

Luca laughs. "I just like to look at you, really." I laugh at him. I can't even pretend to be mad at these two cuties.

Nineteen
One Last Fight

LUCA

Figuring out how to make the power removing spell non-lethal proves to be more difficult than I'd expected. By the time Ryland comes back with the news that Amber is now being held by the council, we've looked at several different ways for Red to cast the spell. None of them look promising. It's not like we have a way to test them, though.

I should be relieved that the council took Amber, but something about it bothers me. "Do any of you feel like this was too easy?"

"What do you mean, Luca?" Orym asks.

"How long did you guys search for me and try to find Amber while I was being held? Then suddenly out of nowhere, the guys watching the border just capture her and a bunch of her guys? That just seems really suspicious to me." I know I sound crazy, but I don't care. She has to be up to something.

"We can't trust her, that's for sure," Red agrees.

"All we can do is prepare to fight her if she escapes and comes back," Ryland offers. "Which is why I have the men in teams, securing the border as well as keeping an eye on the captives. I don't trust it either."

"Dec said that Vik wanted to send some vamps to help. Did you guys talk about that?" James turns to Ryland.

"Briefly. Once we know where to find the rest of her prisoners, they'll help us with the rescue mission. He sent a few of his best guys on a scouting mission using Eli's tech," Ryland explains. It's a good idea, but now I'm worried for their safety.

Amber's people are manipulative and cunning. We cannot underestimate them. Otherwise, she'll win. I wish I knew how to contact our Fae friend. I feel like he could help us with this, if he wanted to. I have a few questions for him about other things, too.

"I think the best option is for me to work on this spell. I trust you guys to protect me. There's always a chance that Amber can escape the council, but there was just as much chance of her escaping when she was here. It's just something we're going to have to deal with. If we spend all of our time discussing that option, though, we're not going to be ready when she does attack," Red insists.

I know she's right. I should focus on preparing for Amber's imminent escape and attack. But part of me is frozen with fear when it comes to her. I'm terrified of Amber. I've seen what she can do, and I don't want to witness it again. She's not bothered to kill or maim just to get what she wants. And what she wants is my mate's power. I have to do everything I can to protect Red from this woman.

"What if you can't figure out how to take her power without taking her life?"

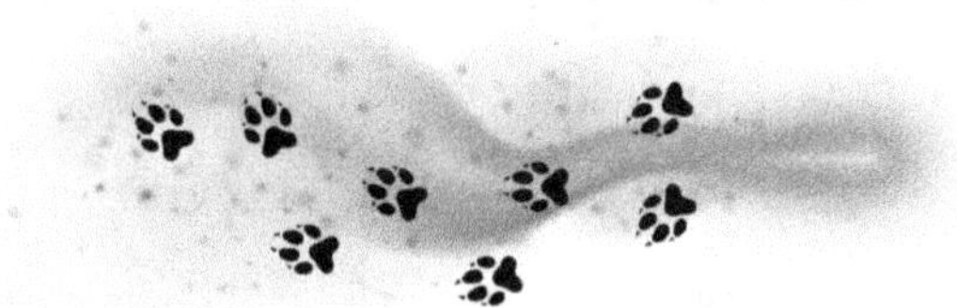

RYLAND

"Then I'll have to re-evaluate in the moment and make a deci-sion. We talked about this earlier, Luca. I don't want to kill her unless I have to," Red says with a sigh. I know she's frustrated, and part of that is Luca's insistence that Amber needs to be dealt with in a permanent way.

And while I understand, I don't agree. I think that Luca is on the right track. The only way to prevent Amber from remaining a problem is to kill her. I can't tell Red that, or even hint that I disagree with her decision to create a power stripping spell that won't kill.

I have to trust that she means what she says and will take care of Amber when it comes to that. Because it will come to that. Amber will no doubt escape the council and come after Red again. Somehow, getting captured and transferred to the council's custody was part of her plan. I just wish we understood the plan. Since we don't, there's no point in stressing over it.

"How much longer do you think it will take to get the spell right? I know it's not an exact science, but can you give a rough estimate?" Maybe I can refocus everyone before I get called away again. Being the territory leader is going to be more work than I realized. People have been texting and calling at all hours, and I've only been doing this for a day.

I'm glad that Orym is stepping up as my second, but we're going to need someone outside the family to be my third, or we'll never get to have any time together as a unit. We'll need that time to bond, especially if I ever hope to talk Red into having kids with us. It was a stupid mistake to let it slip that kids were the real reason I wanted to build a new cabin. I should have said anything but that.

I can't worry about the future right now. We all need to be concerned with Amber and her people. They have a lot of power, and like to fight dirty. It wouldn't surprise me to discover that Gunnar was the spy for her. They had a lot in common, after all.

"Ry?" Red says my name with a huff of frustration. This isn't the first time she's said it, and I'm caught not paying attention.

"Yes, sorry." I hope she isn't too angry. I have to stay focused and in the moment.

"I said, 'It might take me a day or two' in reference to how long I need to work on this spell. I don't really know. It could take months to get it right. I know we don't have that kind of time, though. I'll keep working and have it done as soon as I can." Annoyance is clear in her tone, but I can't tell if it's directed at my lack of attention or herself.

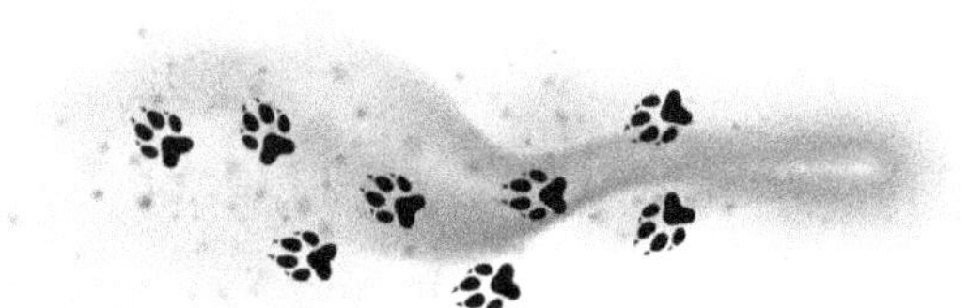

GARNET

Ry spaces out after asking me how long the spell will take to prepare. I say his name three times before he finally gives me a half-hearted apology. After I explain what I'd said before, he nods and walks away. I don't know if he's upset or just trying not to push me.

I'm frustrated and annoyed about not being able to figure out how to make this spell non-lethal. I've almost decided to give up and just use it the way she was going to. Part of me would love that, but the rest would feel guilty forever about it. I'm not her. I can't behave the way she would.

It's hard enough to wrap my head around the fact that my own aunt wanted to kill me just to take my magic. Could I do the same to her? I don't want her magic. I don't need it. I have more than she does already. I just need to stop her from hurting people.

"I really want to know what was in those syringes. It's driving me crazy." At this point, I'm more talking to myself than anyone else. I stare at the spell book in my hands. "What could it have been? She acted upset when the prisoners died, so it wasn't a poison."

"If it wasn't a poison, what else could it have been?" Luca asks. I jump, because I really was just talking it through, and didn't expect an answer.

"Oh, I have no idea. That's what I was brainstorming." I laugh at myself, and Luca joins in. James and Orym look at us funny, but they wouldn't get the joke. I don't know how many times over the years that Luca has caught me talking something through and done just what he did tonight.

"I wonder if she's trying to mutate them somehow," James says quietly.

"Wait, what?" My jaw drops. Why hadn't I thought of that? It makes perfect sense. It's been Amber the whole time.

"I just said," James starts to repeat himself, but I hold up a hand.

"I heard you. Sorry, it just all makes sense now. I know exactly what Amber is trying to do. If she succeeds, we'll all die. There will be no way to defend ourselves against the army she's trying to create."

They all stare at me. I know that they're waiting for me to explain it, but I can't yet. I have to wrap my head around how it all connects. My head is still spinning when Ry comes back in the room.

"We have to get ready. The scouts have found the camp where the rest of the prisoners are being held. We're moving in an hour," he says grimly.

"But Garnet was about to tell us something," Orym announces.

"It'll have to wait. I'm sorry. We have to move quickly, or they'll get away again." Ry's tone is serious and there's no room for argument. I'm a bit relieved, because it gives me time to consider what I need to say to explain the whole thing to them.

It sounds crazy in my head. Could Amber have been behind everything that happened a few months ago? Was she the one who kidnapped and brainwashed Dec? I don't know. If she's trying to make hybrids, that would explain why someone took Delilah's blood when we rescued Dec.

I've always heard that once you eliminate the impossible, what's left is the truth. So, it has to be, right? I don't have time right now to go through the whole thing and figure it out. We have to get ready to go to war.

I gather some supplies for healing spells, and write out the incantations I think will be useful. I don't want to take the books with me and risk losing them or worse, Amber taking them from me. I can't let her do that, or we'll be defenseless. I'm so new to magic and don't fully understand how it all works yet.

I wish my mother was here to teach me. I can't let those thoughts take over. I have to stay focused. Ry needs us to fight with him. We have to rescue these people. They've been through enough already. My heart breaks when I think about Amber experimenting on people.

"Ry, Vik and his family aren't coming to fight with us, right?" If I'm right about what Amber is doing, I have to make sure that Delilah isn't anywhere around. Fuck, what if that's why Amber wanted to get caught? She needs more blood. That has to be it. And I can't let that happen.

"No. They're locked up at Midnight. Dec won't even let any of them leave the building until Amber has been dealt with. He's afraid that Delilah will get kidnapped," Ry answers.

"That's a relief," I respond before turning back to gathering supplies. I'll take a couple of knives, although I plan to depend more on my magic. Ry doesn't press me asking questions then ignoring him, so I don't worry about it.

Luca keeps staring at me, and I think he may have figured out what I think is happening. We exchange a glance and continue getting ready. I try to meditate while the guys gather weapons. I'm starting to panic and need to calm down. I can't go off into the forest like this and face witches who've been practicing their magic longer than I've known I'm a witch.

James is the first one to interrupt my breathing exercise. He kisses me gently and pulls me to my feet. "We're ready."

Orym hugs me tightly and presses his lips to mine. I want to lose myself in him, but I can't. When he pulls away, Luca kisses me hard. Before I realize what's happening, I'm in Ry's arms and he's kissing me so softly, it's like a promise. I know that these men would give their lives to protect me. I'd do the same for them.

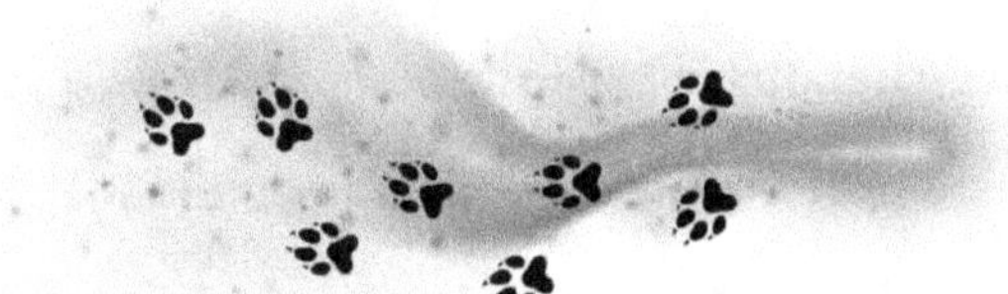

ORYM

I don't want Garnet to come with us, but I know she won't stay home. She wouldn't be safe here alone anyway. Amber is up to something. I just know it. Her capture and transfer to the council was a little too easy.

Somehow, she thinks Garnet will join her, which will make us join her. But we won't. If Garnet tried, we'd find a way to lock her up until she came to her senses. Our mate would never forgive herself if she became like Amber.

I know that's why she's against killing Amber. Ryland doesn't like the idea of letting Amber live, though, and I understand why. Even if Garnet can take her power, we have no way to keep her out of the forest. We all know that she'll never stop. There's no way we can let her go while she's still a threat. And she'll always be a threat.

Ryland was irritated after the council guards took Amber because the leaders who are left wouldn't agree with him. They refuse to sentence her to death without a trial. Our gamble with involving the council turned out to be a bad idea. We'd expected them to be on our side, to understand that we need to protect our family. I can't dwell on this right now. I have to be ready to fight. We need to rescue the remaining prisoners.

We follow Ryland into battle, an army at his back. In a way, it's amusing to me. A year ago, I would have fought against him instead of with him. I wouldn't have expected him to be trying to save people. We were both so self-centered that Garnet wouldn't give either of us the time of day. When I consider how badly we nearly fucked up getting with our fated mate because we were too busy fighting each other, it makes my heart sad.

James and Luca stay beside Garnet. I insist that she walk behind Ryland, and I protect her back. I think we'll always approach these kinds of situations like this, with her in the middle where we can protect her. I'm keeping an eye on James, too. It's not easy to allow a human to get involved in this battle. There are too many chances and ways that he can get hurt. If something happened to him, Garnet would never forgive us.

We move as a unit. Anyone watching would think that we had practiced this for months, years even. But it's just our natural need to protect our mate. *I want to try the vision thing.* She tells us in our heads. James scoops her up to carry her while she focuses. We know from past experience that she won't be able to see us or hear us while she's in the vision. It'll be up to us to keep her safe.

My heart swells with pride that she trusts us enough to put her life in our hands.

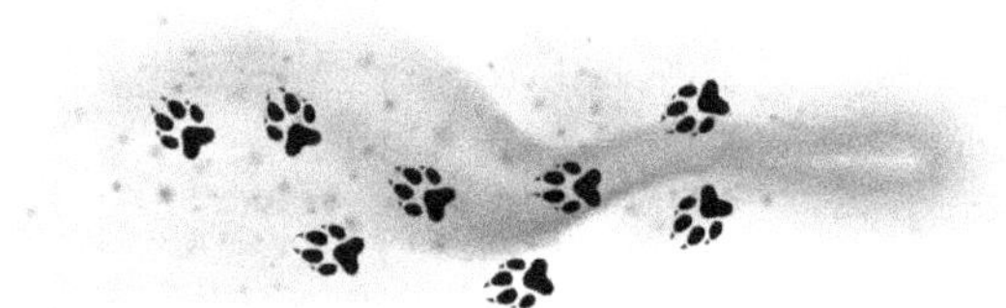

JAMES

When Garnet wants to use her power to see what we're up against, I don't argue. I pick her up and Orym shifts to my side. Our goal is to protect her, no matter what. I don't know if she'll be able to communicate with us what she sees, but I know she wants to do everything she can to help free these people.

I feel her relax into my embrace, and I know that she's managed to get into a vision. I just hope it's one of where we're headed, and happens in real time. Sometimes her magic is a little off because of the Fae blood. We've been working on solutions to that, but I'm not sure that we've figured it out yet.

The further we walk into the forest, the more my hair stands up. A chill runs down my spine, and that's all the warning I get that we're being ambushed. *Fuck.* Ryland's voice in my head has me dropping to my knees. I won't let them hit her. The thought repeats itself as magic blasts hit the ground all around us. I'm not sure how we manage to avoid them as we move toward the shelter of a grouping of trees.

The witches who ambushed us are trying to steer us in one direction, so of course, Orym guides us the opposite way. We don't want to let them trap us. But there are risks no matter which way we go. What if they anticipated Orym's move and purposefully guided us the wrong way? There's no way to know.

Magic hits my leg and I'm almost knocked off my feet. I adjust my hold on Garnet and keep moving. *James is hit.* I hear Luca's voice in my head.

I'm okay. We have to get to shelter. I know that I'm not as okay as I want them to think. But I'm not about to put Garnet at risk here. We can worry about my leg once we're in a safe place that we can defend.

Over here. We can hide in these bushes. Orym encourages us to move quickly. Luca takes Garnet from me so I can move easier. I wish he hadn't, because keeping her safe was the only thing preventing my mind from focusing on the pain in my leg.

Luca gets Garnet in the hiding spot, and Ryland follows after them. I'm close, but not close enough. Orym ducks back into the bushes, trying to keep the spot unseen by our enemies. I run the best I can, but the pain in my leg is getting worse. I look down and see marks moving up my leg where my pants have burned away.

As an EMT, I know what infection looks like, and this is it. But this is different. This is magical infection. This is something I don't know how to deal with. Sure, it hurts. It burns like my veins are on fire. But the pain as the magic digs its way through me is nearly unbearable.

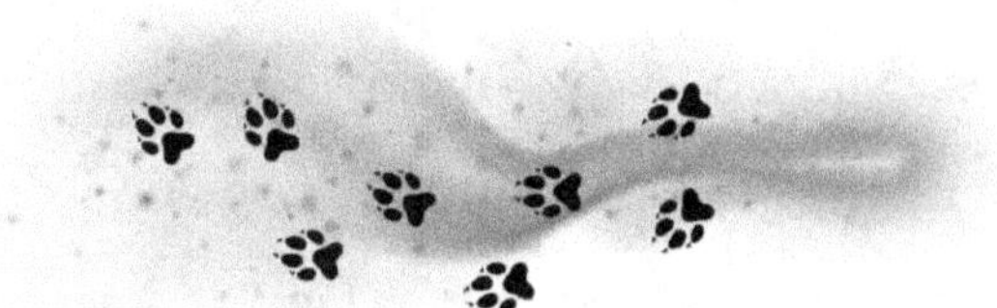

GARNET

The moment I go into the vision, I know it's a mistake. I see where Amber's people are hiding. They're just waiting for us to get close enough for them to ambush. I fight myself, trying to get back to the present. My loves are in danger and I need to get back to them.

Since I know that Amber's people can't hear me, I scream. I scream for Orym to get them to safety. I yell at Ry, telling him it's a trap. I raise my voice as loud as I can, until I'm nearly hoarse from yelling and screaming at my men. It does no good, of course.

Then I get flashes of the present in a different location. I see my mates being attacked while trying to protect me. I can't seem to force myself back into my body. I race through the forest until I'm in the midst of my family. James is hit by some sort of magic bomb. His pants are mostly burned away, and the magic is climbing his leg.

I need to heal him, but I don't even know what he was hit with. The wound is black, and the tendrils climbing his leg are a mixture of black, purple, and red. I have to get back to him before it's too late. He needs me to heal him.

I scream into the void once more. This is it. Amber has won. I can't get back to my body to heal James, and I can't stop what's happening. With any luck, they'll kill me quickly and I won't have to watch my mates suffer.

They've found shelter, which is a relief, but James is moving so slowly that he's not under cover yet. Why aren't they helping him? Fuck, they're too focused on protecting me. Please don't let James die because you wanted to protect me. I know they can't hear me, and even if they could, James would tell them that I'm more important. Most likely, he told them that he's okay, even though the pain is nearly unbearable. I can see it on his face.

What can I do? I drop to my knees and start to pray. The only person who can help us now is the Moon Goddess, and I have no idea if she will.

"You set me on this path for a reason. My faith is shaken, but not destroyed. Please don't let my love die because I did something stupid. I was only trying to help prevent a situation like this." I don't know how long I kneel there, begging her to help us.

When I look up, I see that James is lying on the ground, and Orym is leaning out of the shelter. I'm sure he's trying to decide if it's safe to go to James, but it breaks my heart. "Please. You have to help me. Just put my soul back in my body, and I'll do the rest. I have to save him."

Tears stream down my face. I repeat the words over and over. I don't think she's listening, though. A swirl of pink sparkles catches my attention as it works its way around my body. What is this? A moment later, I wake in Luca's arms.

"Let me go," I order. Luca's eyes go wide. I don't even recognize my voice. "I have to save him."

"Garnet, it's too late. He won't respond," Orym says gently.

I shake my head and shove Luca's arms off me. Ry stares at me for a second, then nods. At least he understands. One look from him, and Luca doesn't grab me again. Orym shakes his head, but moves so I can crawl out of the bush they've hidden me in.

I race over to James, dodging the blasts of magic that are being tossed at me. *Guys, get over here. Now.* I order through the bond. I throw up a shield to protect James from being hit with anything else. If only I'd been in my body when all this happened. I could have protected them all.

I can't waste time beating myself up about this. All I can do is move forward. Once Ry, Orym, and Luca are huddled next to me, surrounding James, I push the shield around us all. It creates a dome that will stop the magic blasts from hitting us. At least until I get tired. I have to work quickly.

"I need to heal him," I say out loud. I try to speak more, but a knot forms in my throat and I can't get the words out.

It's okay, Red. You can do this. Use the bond and let us know how to help. Luca's voice in my head is like a balm to my blistered soul. In my growing panic, I'd forgotten that we can communicate without words. I feel ridiculous, since I'd just done it a moment ago.

I need to make a poultice. The ingredients are in my bag, each marked with a capital H. James thought that would make it easier if I needed one of you to help me. Tears fall hard at that thought. It's like he knew that he would get hurt and I would have to rely on one of the others to get me through it.

Luca takes my bag and carefully grabs the ingredients. He hands me a small mortar and pestle to crush them with. I carefully measure out what I think I need, and start mixing. *We need to get out of here, Red.* Ry's voice breaks my concentration for a moment.

I know. But I have to get this done first. I can't lose him. If he insists on moving, I'll have to stay back with James. I wish there was a way to get out of here quickly, but I don't have that ability. We've tested every possible witch power, and that's not one I have.

EPILOGUE

RYLAND

I'M SHOCKED WHEN A portal opens next to us and a strange figure in a hooded cloak ushers us inside. Orym and I grab James and Luca scoops up Red. We rush through the portal.

Somehow, this seems better than waiting for Amber's people to kill us.

"Who are you?" I ask as soon as we're on the other side. The figure shakes their head and points to another portal. I can see home through it. "We need to go. Now." Orym and I run, carrying James through the second portal. A moment later, Luca carries Red through as well.

She's pissed. "Put me down. We have to save James." In the rush to get through the portal, she dropped the stuff she was mixing. I understand her anger, but we had to get away from Amber's cult.

"Red, we have more supplies here. Just hold on a minute. We'll take him inside and you can heal him there," I insist, trying to placate her. I can tell it's not working. "I'll get a couple of guys to bring Grammy down to help. Just breathe."

She growls at me and fights Luca harder. "Stop fighting me. I'm not the enemy here. Red, please." Luca tries to reason with her, but she won't stop flailing. Orym and I carry James into the cabin and settle him on the couch, with his injured leg unobstructed. Red will have to be able to get to it if she has any hopes of healing it.

With him settled in, I step away to make the call. I watch Orym approach Luca and Red through the window. I know she's freaking out because she's worried about James, but I wish she'd just calm down.

Grammy agrees to come help us, and I send two of my security to bring her. No one is allowed to go anywhere alone. It's my new rule, and so far, there haven't been any objections.

I check on James. He's not doing well at all. There are vine-like things spreading up his leg, and the wound itself is open and oozing. It's a weird combination of black, red, and purple, and almost looks like it's glowing. While I'm standing there, Luca opens the door, and Orym drops Red inside. She's still swinging and cursing at them.

I give her a stern look and she freezes. I understand her pain and fear, but she understands the silent command in my look. *Red, you won't do him any good by fighting against us. Let us help you. Grammy is on her way.*

She stares at me, tears filling her eyes. *I can't, Ry. I can't lose him. Please.* I understand without words what she's saying.

We've got you. Just tell us how to make the poultice. We can help. But you have to stop growling and hitting. I feel like an ass for scolding her, but it seems to help. She opens a book and hands it to Luca.

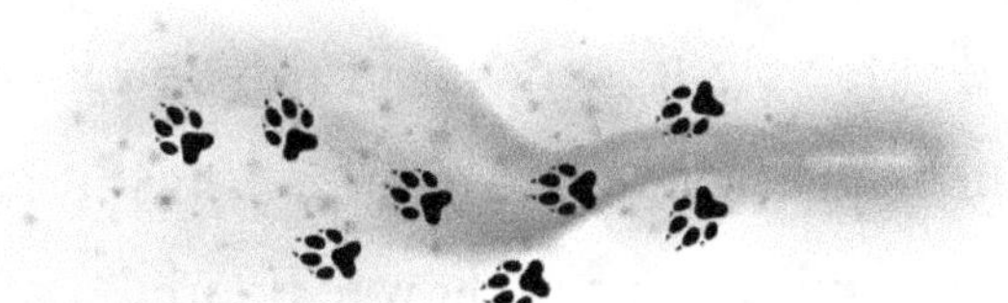

ORYM

Luca reads off a list of ingredients, then Ryland and I scramble to get them together. I feel the panic rolling off Garnet in waves. If she can't calm down, there's no hope of her getting this spell right. I've watched her train enough with James to know. He was constantly telling her that she had to clear her mind and focus.

Maybe I can help her with that. "Garnet, love, can we talk for a minute?"

"Okay," she says hesitantly. I know she doesn't want to leave James' side, but I need to get a little space between them so I can calm her emotions. She walks across the room and takes my hands.

"Good girl. Now, let's try one of those breathing exercises that James taught you. Can you help me with it?" I think if she's focused on teaching me how to breathe, that she'll relax more. It seems to work.

"It's easy. Deep breath in while counting to five, hold for two, breathe out while counting to five. Like this," she explains with her eyes locked on mine. After she does a couple of the deep breaths, I can tell she's feeling better. "Thank you. That helped. I just can't imagine losing him."

"You don't have to. We're going to save him. Show me how to make the poultice for his wound," I insist. She stays calmer and walks me through the steps. We make it together, mixing the ingredients and preparing it for James.

"All that's left is to apply it and repeat the incantation," she says, taking the bowl from me. This part will have to be her. Garnet is the only one here with magic. None of us can help her now. I send up a silent prayer for this to work as she spreads the mixture on James' wound.

The glow of it changes slightly, but it doesn't look like it's getting better. I have no idea how long it will take, or if it will work at all. "I guess we just have to wait now. Maybe Grammy will know more when she gets here," Garnet says quietly. She drops to her knees on the floor next to James and takes his hand.

Watching her beg him to fight breaks my heart. I want to drag him back to consciousness. Sadly, I don't know how to do that. But there are other things we should discuss. "Now that we've done what we can for James, can we talk about something?" I ask, looking from Garnet to Luca.

"What?" he asks in return.

"The figure who saved us. Who was that?"

Before either of them can answer, Ryland does. "That was the Fae guy that Red and Luca know. I'm sure of it. We took a portal through the Fae Realm to get back here. I don't know how he knew where we were or that we needed help, though."

"The Moon Goddess," Garnet whispers, gripping James' hand tighter.

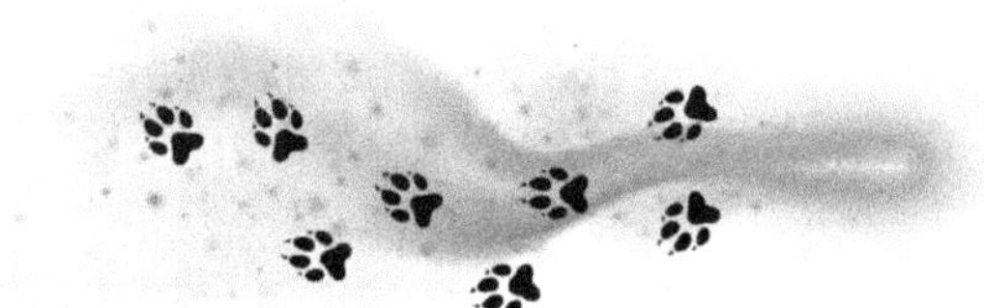

GARNET

"I prayed to her when I couldn't get back to you guys. I could see what was happening, but nothing worked to put me back in my body. I fell to my knees and prayed. Then I opened my eyes and I was in my body. It had to be her." I have no idea how or why the Moon Goddess would have a Fae man help us, but I'm relieved that she did.

I hate that James doesn't seem to be reacting to the healing potion I made for him. I thought it would work. I don't know what else we can do for him. At least he seems stable, for now. Maybe the herbs will take a while to get into his system. I have to stay hopeful. I can't lose him.

"What else can we do?" Luca asks. I don't have an answer for him. I'm as lost as he is. I feel the tears coming again, but I fight them as much as I can. I refuse to let myself break down.

"We'll just have to wait for Grammy and hope the medicine starts to work," Orym offers. I nod at him, then turn my attention back to James. I can't deal with the defeated looks in their eyes right now. That won't keep me strong.

I start talking to James along the bond. I don't care if the others are listening. *Please don't leave me. I love you. We all need you to stay with us. Please don't give up. Fight this. We're looking for a way to fix it.* I keep talking to him this way, barely noticing when Ry's phone rings.

"Fuck," his voice breaks through my begging.

"What happened?" I ask, even though I'm sure I know the answer. Amber has escaped. I'm certain of it. I still wait for him to confirm.

"Amber escaped somehow. They have no idea how she did it. She may have stolen some artifact and book when she left. I don't understand what's going on here," Ry fills us in.

"I do," I admit. I haven't taken any time to consider the epiphany I had earlier, but I know it's true. And they need to know if we're going to fight her.

"What is it?" Orym asks. Luca and I exchange a look. He nods for me to tell them. It doesn't surprise me that he figured it out, too, since he was there with me when it all started.

"Amber is making an army. Or trying to. The syringes...have something mixed with Delilah's blood in them. She wants to make hybrids," I explain. Ry's eyes go wide and Orym turns pale.

Luca nods. "That's what I suspected as well. And before you go all alpha male on us, we wanted to tell you, but all of this happened so fast." He directs his words to Ry, who just shakes his head. He's trying to process what we've told him.

I know it's true, but part of me wishes it wasn't. "How do we fight that?" Orym asks. "An army of hybrids would be nearly impossible to defeat."

"Nearly. But she has to get it right before it becomes an issue. And so far, she's only killed every test subject she's had. So, we do have a little time. Just not much. We have to find her and stop her. I hate to admit it, but I think the only way to stop her will be if I kill her." The words hurt me, because I don't want to be like her, but I recognize that this is the only way. There's nothing else we can do. I tried to find an alternative, and where did that get me?

I almost lost James. I still could. A knock at the door catches me off guard and I crouch defensively in front of James. I will protect him this time.

"It's okay, Red, it's just Grammy. Is it okay to let her in?" Ry asks, and I wonder why. Then I realize that I've been growling since the knock happened.

I relax a little. "Yeah, let her in. Maybe she can help."

He opens the door and Grammy comes in. "You guys can head back to patrols. Let the others know that Amber escaped. Stay alert, and let me know if you see anything." Ry dismisses his men, sending them back to protect the camp.

"Oh, child. Are you okay?" Grammy pulls me into a big hug before I can protest.

"I am, but he's not. I made a healing poultice, but it's not working. I don't know how to heal him." I hate admitting that I can't do something, and she knows it.

"Let's take a look, shall we?" She sets down her bag, and I wonder what's inside. Grammy is the pack medic, so she probably has a lot of medical supplies in there. She gets closer to the couch, and I feel myself growling again. "May I look at your mate's leg?" The question calms me, and I nod.

She carefully touches near the wound, but not the wound itself. Grammy mutters to herself as she looks at the tendrils climbing up his leg. "Has this gotten worse since you put the medicine on?"

"No, it's stayed the same," I answer. She nods and turns back to James. After a moment, she turns back to me.

"You've stalled it, but not stopped it. The tendrils of magic are moving very slowly right now. If they reach his heart, he'll die. We have to find a way to pull the magic out of him before that happens. Otherwise, there won't be a way to save him," she says sadly.

Tears burn my eyes, but I refuse to break down. We will save him. There's no other choice. "We have to save him, Grammy. There has to be a way. Please."

"There is another option, but it must be saved for a very last option."

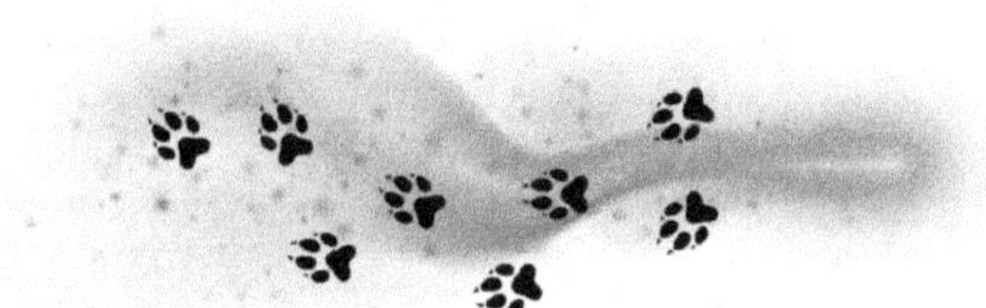

JAMES

The moment I fall to the ground, I know I'm dying. There's nothing I can do to stop it. I can't even tell Garnet goodbye. I'll never be able to tell her how much she changed my life for the better.

I hear her talking to me, begging me not to give up. I don't know how to fight this. I don't even know what hit me. I hate that I can't respond to her and make her feel better. The pain is so intense that it's hard to focus on her words.

I see a bright light in the distance. Something in me is drawn to it. I want to walk over and bask in its warmth. I take two steps, and a hand grabs my arm. "You don't want to do that, boy."

I jump at the contact, realizing that I'm standing now. Wasn't I just lying down? Weird. "What do you mean? Who are you?"

"If you go to the light, you'll die. Your soul will leave, and you'll never see her again. That's not what you want, is it?" He pauses and looks at me. I can't tell what he looks like, because he's glowing. It's strange, but not even close to the strangest thing that's happened to me today.

"No, I want to go back to her," I admit. "But this pain is unbearable. I can't take it."

"I know, boy, but you're going to have to tough it out. If you give up now, she'll never forgive you," he says.

"Who are you?" I ask again, staring at him. I still can't make out his features because of the glow. I wonder if he's doing it on purpose or if it's a trick of my mind, since I'm dying.

"I'm a friend, who's trying to help you. I just need you to hold on. Do not go toward that light. I'm going to try to stop the poison, but it's going to be hard with your body in a different realm. I need you to trust me. I can take your soul somewhere that the light cant reach."

My eyes go wide, and I don't know if I should trust him or not. He's trying to save my life, though. Or at least, that's what he tells me. At this point, what do I have to lose? I nod. I'll go with him if it'll save me. I'd do anything to have another moment with Garnet.

"What's your name, friend?" I ask as I follow him to a strange shimmering hole in midair.

"Trevan," he answers, holding out a hand. I take it, deciding that trusting him is the least dangerous thing I can do at this point. He did stop me from going into the light, so I think he's trying to help. I follow him through the opening.

Please don't let this be the last mistake I ever make. I don't know who I'm praying to, but hopefully someone is listening.

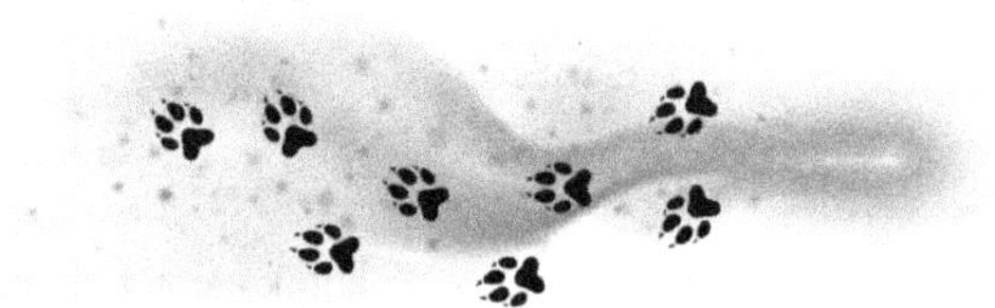

LUCA

I pace the floor as Grammy and Red brainstorm ways to stop the poison that's slowly killing James. I can feel her pain and fear along the bond. I know that Orym and Ryland can too. Her pain stabs me in the heart, but her fear rips me apart from the inside. I want to fix this for her. I know that she'll never be the same if James doesn't survive this.

"Please, Grammy, we have to do whatever it takes to save him," Red begs with tears streaming down her face. She wipes at them as she speaks.

"Let's try another herbal remedy. Maybe the two together will be enough," Grammy answers. She pulls a book from her bag and they huddle around it. I'm glad they have each other. The worst thing Gunnar did to Red was make her think that her grandmother didn't love her. If I could, I would bring him back to life and kill him myself.

All I want is to pull Red into my arms and hold her. If there was something I could do to fix this, I would. Guilt eats at me, and I wonder if they all felt this way when I was taken. I shake the thought away. They couldn't have, right? There's no way they would have learned how to work together so well if they felt like this inside. Maybe I'm wrong. I hope I'm wrong. I can't be the only one of us who cares so much about the others.

It's strange to realize that you're falling in love with multiple people when you've been in love with your best friend for as long as you can remember. At some point, we'll all have to sit down and talk about our relationships and what we want this to be. But first, we have to save James. I'm not ready to say goodbye to him yet.

I can't focus on that right now. I have to find a way to help them save James. I shake myself out of the funk I'm falling into. Then I walk over to where Grammy and Red are discussing the remedy they're studying.

"What can I do?" I offer. I'm not sure what response I expect, but it isn't being pulled into a hug by both women.

"You are so sweet, Luca," Grammy says.

"Thank you, love," Red adds.

"You're welcome. I care about him too. I want to help. Please. Can I gather supplies? Or do you want some tea? I need to do something," I admit.

"Tea would be a lovely place to start. Then we'll make a list of supplies we will need." Grammy has never had a problem telling me what to do, and I'm relieved for it right now.

I head to the kitchen and start heating a kettle of water. I take my time prepping the tray with the tea bags, sugar, honey, and Red's favorite mugs. When the water is ready, I take it all out to them.

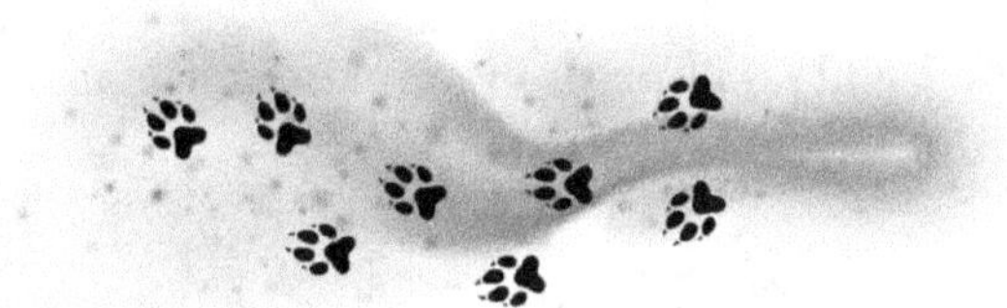

GARNET

Luca's offer to help touches me as much as his admission that he cares about James. I know Orym and Ry care too, they just don't really know how to help right now. I'm not sure what they could do, either. Ry brought Grammy to me, and that's enough. Orym hasn't left the room, so I know he's here if I need him. It's enough. It has to be.

Grammy and I look over the recipe in her book and make a list of ingredients and supplies for Luca to gather. I don't know if this is going to work. No, it has to work. I refuse to think for a second that the Moon Goddess would take James from me now.

Even if I'm feeling defeated, I can't give up. I have to make this work. I will save him, if by sheer determination alone. The list of supplies that we need is rather long, so we ask Luca and Orym to go together. Ry doesn't want anyone outside alone, so it makes sense. I don't need anyone else risking being caught by Amber.

We don't even know where she is now. It makes me feel a little better than we've figured out what she's doing, even if we don't know why.

While the guys are gathering ingredients, Grammy and I set up the kitchen to brew the recipe. She swears it's not magical, but I think she's stretching the truth a bit. I always liked to watch her in the kitchen. It was like magic then, and it still is now. The way she moves around the space as if she knows where everything is amazes me. She never once opens a door or drawer without finding what she was looking for.

Grammy must have some magic in her, even if she refuses to admit it. I know she has secrets; it seems like we all do, whether we know it or not. I want to ask her about it, but I know that she won't tell me. Maybe someday.

We have a pot on the stove with mineral water just starting to boil when Orym and Luca get back. The sort the ingredients out on the table and Grammy looks them over. "You're missing something," she tells them.

"What?" Luca asks. "I thought we got it all."

Orym looks over the list. "I'm pretty sure we did. What's missing?" He hands her the list and she looks over it.

"Damn, that's my fault. I didn't write it on there. I could have sworn that I did, though," she pauses and looks at me. "We need red honeysuckle. It only grows next to the waterfall."

Luca and Orym share a confused look. My eyes light up. "I know exactly where it is. It'll take me ten minutes, tops to get there, grab it, and get back. One of you can help Grammy while I'm gone, and the other can come with me."

After a quick game of rock, paper, scissors, Orym and I are on our way. We race through the woods to the waterfall. I climb up to the top and grab the flower easily. Then I climb down and hand it to him. "I need a second to catch my breath," I tell him, bending over and holding my knees.

He takes a step back so I have a little space and I instantly miss his warmth. Orym holds the flowers so gently, as if he's scared to crush them. "I hope this works. I like James; he's a good guy." Orym's words make me smile.

"I hope so too. I don't know what else we can do. Grammy says there's one other option, but she won't even tell me what it is until we try everything else. I just want him to be okay," I admit.

"We should get back," he responds. I nod, and we start to quickly walk back toward the cabin. He's still cradling the flowers in his arms like they're precious cargo. Everything these men do makes me love them even more than I did yesterday.

When we're stepping out of the woods into the clearing by the cabin, a bright light flashes. I close my eyes against it. When I open them, I'm not in the clearing anymore. "Where the fuck am I?" I ask out loud. "Orym?" I turn in a circle, looking for my mate. We were just together; where could he have disappeared to?

I look around, noticing that Orym is not here. Then I realize where I am. Fuck. How did this happen? I didn't step through a portal. I would have recognized it and avoided that. I hope that Orym at least got back to the cabin with the flowers. Grammy needs them to save James.

"Where are you? I know you're here. This isn't funny!" I call out, hoping that the person responsible for my current location is the man who helped Luca escape from Amber. I think he would try to help us. But I don't really know him, so I can't be sure. Fuck.

I don't get a response, and I'm fighting against the tightening sensation in my chest. I can't break down, not here, not now. I have to get back to save James. I can't lose him. As if summoned by my thoughts, James appears. "What? How?" I can't form logical sentences.

"I can't explain it, but this Fae saved me. I almost went into the light. He stopped me. I think he's a friend," James explains.

"Where is he?" I ask, turning around to look for this mysterious stranger who kept my mate from leaving me permanently. "Maybe he knows how to heal you."

James shakes his head. "I don't think he does. But he said I'd be safe here while you figure it out. Although, I don't know how you'll do that from here, if I'm there."

"Me neither," I say, tears filling my eyes. I fight against the sadness as it settles in my chest. How can I save James if I'm trapped in an alternate realm with his soul?

THE STORY CONTINUES...

In Wolf Moon, Hunters of the Forest, Book Three! Don't miss the epic conclusion to the series!

Pre-order your copy here: https://books2read.com/HoF3-WM

Being pulled through a portal into the Fae Realm is a bit disconcerting. Who am I kidding? It's scary as hell! I'm in a new world, with foreign customs and have no idea what I'm doing here.

I can feel my mates, but the connections are weak. A mysterious stranger, the man who brought me here, offers his help. Can I trust him? I have no idea, and no choice. I need to find a way home before it's too late. The Wolf Moon is approaching, and I'm running out of time.

Panic grips my heart when I find out that James is fatally injured for the second time since we've bonded. Will his brother do what's necessary—what I beg him for— to keep James with us? If he does, will James ever forgive me?

Once I make it back home, things are different. I must fix our mate bonds so we can work together. We're fighting for more than just our peace. I can't let Amber win this battle, or I'll lose my life along with my powers.

ACKNOWLEDGMENTS

I would like to thank:

My Alpha and Beta Teams who try hard to keep me on track;

My Editing Team who does their best to make sure my books make sense and have as few typos as possible;

My Cover Artist, Wynter Designs, who's responsible for the gorgeous images on the front of this book

and My ARC Team, who catch some of the things the rest of us miss.

ABOUT THE AUTHOR

M.P. Starkweather is a wife, mother, author, poet, casual online gamer, self-proclaimed fan-girl, and full-time nerd. She writes free-form poetry, paranormal romance, sci-fi romance, reverse harem romance, and is branching out into contemporary romance. In her free time, she enjoys writing, reading, Dungeons & Dragons, table top games with her husband and friends, and playing with her son. M.P. also enjoys tv, movies, and music across various genres.

To get the most up-to-date information about her latest releases and book signings, check out www.mpstarkweather

.com and join her newsletter, or follow her on your favorite social media site.

ALSO BY M.P. STARKWEATHER

Anthology – Contemporary RH

Blemished Beauty Anthology

Standalones - Contemporary RH OV

Cold Princes

Knot My Valentine

The Pack Next Door – Contemporary RH OV series

Princess or Knot

Fiancée or Knot

Queen or Knot

Christmas or Knot

Vampires at Midnight - Paranormal RH series

Blood Moon

Blood Lost

Blood War

A Vampires at Midnight and Hunters of the Forest Crossover Novella - Paranormal RH, free on all available platforms

Blood Wolf

Hunters of the Forest - Paranormal RH series

Wolf Bane

Wolf Caged

Wolf Moon

Forged by Magic - Sci-fi/Fantasy M/F series

Hidden

Betrayed

<u>Saved</u>

Daydreams and Sunsets - a collection of poetry

<u>Daydreams and Sunsets</u>